A WAR HERO RETURNS
BY
JOHNNY RAY

After serving eight years in the army, Suzan Mercer returns from Afghanistan to Florida as a female war hero–her works as a CIA operative, of course, would always be hidden.

She couldn't believe her mother had used a power of attorney while she was gone to sell the land her father had left her. After learning her mother also has early onset Alzheimer's and claims to have been taken advantage of by Matt Harris, the billionaire developer involved, Suzan uses her military and CIA training to plot her revenge and to reacquire her land.

Entering a world where high heels replace combat boots and deep red lipstick becomes more deadly than a colt 45, Suzan never anticipated the cost to reacquire her land would be losing her heart.

Matt also learns his money and power cannot acquire the one asset he has always lacked in his life as he ventures into untested skies without a golden parachute to save him. Also, would the ghost of his playboy image come back to haunt him?

While Suzan Mercer's father promised in his dying words the land he left her would bring her love, she never anticipated the events involved in the process. Now, could she balance her new love life with her hidden CIA commitment? Could she?

A WAR HERO RETURNS
BY
Johnny Ray
Copyright © 2013
SIR JOHN PUBLISHING

ALL RIGHTS ARE HEREBY RESERVED
BY JOHNNY RAY

Johnny Ray is an award winning novelist who won the Royal Palm literary award for best thriller and is quickly making a name for himself as the master of the romantic thriller. He loves social interaction with his readers and can be found on

Twitter **www.twitter.com/sirjohn_writer**

Facebook **www.facebook.com/authorjohnnyray**

He can also be reached by
 e-mailing at **sirjohnnyray@gmail.com**

Or you can just follow him on his blog at
 www.sirjohn.us
 for updates and future releases.

Johnny Ray's previous works include:

LITERARY AGENT–BEWARE
Published by Sir John Publishing in 2012

SCANDAL–THE DEATH OF A LEGACY
Published by Sir John Publishing in 2012

MODELS AND LOVERS
Published by Sir John Publishing in 2012

HER HONOR'S BODYGUARD
Published by Sir John Publishing in 2012

FOR LOVE AND VENGEANCE
Published by Sir John Publishing in 2012

THE SALSA CONNECTION
Published by Sir John Publishing in 2012

THE JOURNEY TO WHITESTONE
Published by Sir John Publishing in 2012

STALKING LOVE
Published by Sir John Publishing in 2013

Chapter 1

"I hate to disturb your Memorial Day cook-out, but my name is Suzan Mercer and I'm here to see Matt Harris." Suzan brushed her long, black hair to one side to allow her a better view. The freedom to allow her hair to fall free for a change and not having to be tied in a required military style ponytail felt strange.

The security guard, a tall slim man with a deep tan thanks to the Florida sun, glanced at his pad as he stood his ground at the gate guarding the Harris Estate in West Palm Beach. "I don't see your name on my list. I'm sorry, but I can't give you permission to enter."

"I didn't ask for permission." Suzan slammed the pedal to the floor of her red Mini Cooper, leaving him shouting at her as she squealed into a spot in front of the large entrance to the main house.

As she emerged from the car, the front gate guard ran toward her, with another uniformed guard rushing from the front of the house. "Listen, lady. You can't do this!"

"I just did."

Suzan watched him study her uniform. Her travel clothes were a present of the U. S. Army, her life for the last eight years. "Lady, I don't know who you are, but I'll ask you one more time to leave."

Suzan turned to look at the front door as the second guard joined them. "I heard he arrived here today."

The gate guard reached for her arm. "You need to leave."

Suzan grabbed his hand and located the joint and tendon she wanted. With a quick twist, the guy twice her size hit the ground with both knees. "DAMN!"

The second guard rushed closer to assist his colleague squirming on the ground, until Suzan kicked her right foot at his face–stopping inches in front of his nose. "You don't really want to do this, do you?" The shock of her shoe poised inches from his face paralyzed his movements for a second.

After regaining control, the guard's eyes glanced at his sidearm before shifting his attention back to the other guard who was groaning on his knees. "You know you can go to jail for this," he shouted.

"The only one going to jail is Matt Harris. I simply came by to see what he had to say in his defense."

Suzan watched the front door behind them open and three men walk out. "What's going on here?" A tall guy in a dark tailored suit stepped forward.

"I'm here to see Matt Harris."

The guy motioned for the guard to back away as he offered a smug smile. "What do you want with Matt Harris?"

"I want my land back."

"And which land are you referring to?"

"I'm referring to my land outside Ft. Myers and next to the Everglades."

"Are you talking about the Mercer property?"

"That would be correct. I'm Suzan Mercer, the real owner of the land. I recently arrived back in the states and heard he stole my land when I was gone."

"The Mercer property deal closed over a year ago."

"I only heard about the sale a few days ago. Now, do I get to see Matt Harris, or do you want me to go through you three as well?"

The guy laughed. "Do you think you can go through all five of us? I know the Army has women fighting now, but come on, give me a break."

Suzan noticed the guard on her right preparing to make a move on her. A quick kick to his knee dropped him. The guard on the ground slipped free, but a quick hand to the back of his head slammed it down on her upcoming knee. When he crumbled to the ground the remaining three men backed away.

Finally, a man stepped forward who she recognized from his photos. His rugged jaw and slim well built body, covered in a million dollar looking suit, completed the assumptions of what she had forged in her mind. His playboy reputation, which was reputed by some accounts due to his strong work ethics, confronted her. He offered the fantastic good looks of a professional model, mixed with the masculine sexy allure of the kind of man she wanted to meet one day. His charismatic appeal startled her as she stumbled in maintaining her focus on her mission.

He placed his right hand in a pocket of his trousers as he started to speak, leisurely indicating he remained in control and was not one to be rushed. "I'm Matt Harris, and I remember this purchase. You must be the daughter away in the Army. Mrs. Mercer, I think her first name was Ann, sold the property by use of a power of attorney you signed for her. It's amazing she never told you about the sale."

"I never approved the sale. I want the land back."

The last guy in the group, a younger dark haired man with a French accent stepped forward. "I'm Dan Panella, Mr. Harris' attorney, and I can tell you the sale was legally completed, as Matt said, over a year ago."

"If I need to, I'll hire my own attorney, and then we'll see what the courts have to say. I came today to see what I was dealing with and that's all. I take it you've no intentions in selling the land back to me."

"I'm a businessman and this is what I do. I develop property."

"This property needs to stay exactly as it has been for centuries. There's no more land like mine anywhere on earth."

Suzan watched Matt laugh. "If I remember, this is all swamp land."

"Have you ever been to it?"

"I've seen photos of the property, but no, I've never visited the site. I will after it's under development, but not before." Matt stepped forward. "I paid a lot of cash for this land. You should have enough to buy whatever you want somewhere else."

"Somewhere else is not what I want. My father willed this land to me. Why would my mother even think about selling my property to you?"

"That point, you'll need to ask her. I made an offer, and she accepted it." As the other men stayed out of her striking range, Matt acted fearless but intrigued as he waited for an answer.

Suzan didn't know why her mother had sold the property, but she planned to see her next. Thinking about it, she now wished she had visited her mother first, but she had made her mind up on the way back to the States to make this her first stop. "I don't have the details yet, but I promise you I will soon."

While concentrating hard on what she wanted to accomplish, she studied the man she'd hated since the first time she heard his name. However, he looked much different than she had assumed. He looked to be around forty, about ten years older than her. With his hair cut short and professional and his posture perfect, he carried himself with an audacity, a sense of power she'd seldom witnessed before. His eyes offered the unexpected surprise. They radiated in a bright emerald color, which seemed to penetrate her inner thoughts.

Perhaps the training she received in retaining details, a skill which protected her for the last eight years, alerted her to the way the men now appeared to be stalling. While she felt sure the police would arrive soon, she had accomplished what she had intended to do by facing her opponent. There would be another day.

"I think you might like what I've planned for the property. I assure you, many people love our work. " Matt stepped forward as the others backed behind him.

"I don't want to hear it, and I'm sure you know this isn't over." Suzan offered a sarcastic smile as she prepared to leave. She would find answers first and return later. Still, the color of his eyes dominated her attention. With his smooth yet radiating complexion and his hair a dark dirty blond, his features looked so different than what she had imagined. She needed to cool down. After she swiftly walked to her car and cranked the motor, she squealed the tires as she gunned the engine, leaving black marks on his front driveway.

Suzan glanced at him one more time in the rear view mirror as she raced down the driveway. He retained an air of arrogance, appearing much slimmer and well built than the others who stood behind him. He continued to remind her in many respects of the type of guy she hoped to meet when she returned to the States. Her sexual needs haven't been met for a long time, and her biological ticker often gave her hell, like now. Why did he have to look so damn hot? She hit the top of the steering wheel with her hand as she fought off a moment of fantasy that she knew would return later that night. She had given it her all in Afghanistan and hoped to avoid problems like this; especially on her first day back. How could a guy be such a monster and be so damn hot looking at the same time?

As she reached the gate, she glanced one last time in her rear view mirror. Matt still stood in front of the group, watching her leave. Yes, she must have made an impression on him. Maybe not, as she remembered the research on him.

Yes, she had seen his name on the internet where he befriended many top celebrities, which also increased his name recognition and her distain for him. He had never married and lived the life of a playboy who made his money developing properties all over the world.

Breaking into his place was much easier than she had assumed. She had prepared for many contingencies, but didn't need to do any more than drive right in. He needed much better protection. She could imagine the lecture Matt gave to his security detail after she left, and she felt sure he would be much better prepared the next time. Yes, she would return as soon as she confronted her mother.

Chapter 2

Matt glanced at his two guards as Suzan roared away. "I think this is a little ridiculous, don't you? Why do I need you? You can't even keep one little girl out of here!"

Phil Ector, the man on Matt's side who hadn't spoken yet, pointed toward the exiting car. "She was a hell of a fireball, and this could escalate into a problem. I don't think it would have been good for us to have her assaulted on your grounds."

Matt slapped Phil on the shoulder. "Well old buddy, public relations is what your job is. How do you suggest we handle her?"

"Don't worry, I'll start working on it now. She looked very determined, and shall I say, mad as hell." Phil ran his hand through his silver hair as his mouth tightened.

Matt glanced at the guards nursing their injuries. "It appears they teach the woman to fight in the Army much better than I had realized. She definitely knew how to handle herself." Matt turned toward the door. "See if you can make sure these guards say nothing about this. Make sure their injuries are looked at by a doctor before you fire them, and hire me some real guards."

The three men walked back inside the house, where the large foyer stretched three floors high. The display of art work decorating the walls made Matt proud of what he had accomplished. His fortress in the heart of where some of the wealthiest people in the world lived had been an excellent investment. To build his empire he needed funds and lots of investors, since he found many investment opportunities on a daily basis. In fact, in this market, banks begged him to take properties off their hands, while often providing additional funds to the deals to make improvements. The parties he threw here attracted the right people he needed for his future plans.

Matt turned toward Dan as they walked through one room after another to the back of the house. "You told me all was in order when we closed this deal."

"Don't worry. The sale was completely legal. Her mother had a power of attorney we verified, and we obtained a title binder to protect us." Dan carried a small attaché with him, a trademark he appeared to be stuck with for life. Dan's dark black hair, a gift of his French-born parents, grew almost down to his shoulders, but he combed it straight back and tied in a small ponytail. Matt always wondered how Dan managed to act as the peacekeeper in the group.

"It appears Suzan was never told about the sale. Shouldn't we have contacted her?"

"We attempted to do so. She was off in Afghanistan fighting a war. I think it would be good to do some more research on her now since she has surfaced."

"Good, I can tell you and Phil need to compare some notes. I'm curious to see what you find out. This Suzan is much different than any woman I think I've ever met. Did you see how she handled the guards outside?"

Dan rushed ahead to open the door exiting to the pool. "You know, it was hard to see beyond the military uniform, but I think she might be a beautiful woman under all of the fury we saw."

Matt turned to grin at Dan. "Fury is a good word, but I think passionate is a better choice. And you know, you might be right."

"Whatever, she definitely isn't my type." Dan walked fast to stay next to Matt.

Matt retrieved a set of sunglasses and adjusted them as he surveyed the pool area. The Olympic size water garden attracted many guests who lounged around the edges. With the waterfalls creating a slight cooling mist for those soaking up a little too much sun, the afternoon party looked successful. "I think I might enjoy some sun today. I assume we've accomplished all we can for a while."

Matt watched Phil analyze the crowd as he pointed to some of the guests for Matt. "I think it would be good to take some photos of you mingling with the people here today." He waived toward Big John Townsley, one of his main associates he had attending.

"Yes, it's good to see him enjoying himself. With some good photos of us circulating, it will make it hard for him to say no to us when we need some more funds." Matt allowed his eyes to search for Chelsea, Big John's daughter.

Dan stepped forward and whispered. "In case they're needed, I prepared several agreements for Big John to sign. Let me know which one you want to hit him with."

"Patience, my boy. We have lots of time to close this one. For right now, I want you to double check on this Mercer case."

"Like I said, I don't foresee any problem." Dan looked flustered at being doubted in his legal ability to handle Matt's affairs. "However, I'll check more into it."

"Good." Matt continued to study his guests, as he was glad to see that none of them had noticed the confrontation in front of his estate. Suzan had really made an impression on him as his interest in learning more about her grew. But for now, where was Chelsea? If only Big John knew how little Matt actually liked his daughter. Matt knew Big John hoped the two would unite, but Matt knew such a union would never happen.

Dan motioned toward the inside of the house. "I think Ronald and Tony are waiting for you in your office to discuss a few details. They're planning to fly back to New York soon."

"Yes, they have some details we need to discuss, however I want them to stay until after the party tonight. I purchased some special Cuban cigars I want to share with everyone."

Dan grinned at the mention of a good old boy's time they would enjoy later. "I'll let the pilot know to expect a late night flight."

"I also want Gail to stay behind with me. I might need her to arrange a few meetings." He always needed Gail, his secretary, to handle some changes to his calendar.

"When do you think you'll return to New York?" Dan asked.

"In a day or two. The timing depends on how long Big John wants to stay. I think he might like a fishing trip." Matt glanced at Big John one more time before turning to go inside, as he realized how much Big John loved the pool side women–women Matt had hired for the occasion. Although he appeared to be enjoying the view, Matt knew him as a happily married man in many respects and harmless. Suddenly, Matt noticed Chelsea walking around the side of the pool. She stood at close to six feet tall, with long legs and inflated breasts. The bikini she wore revealed a sex bomb shell that could excite any guy. Well any guy but him. Women like her were so easy to obtain, and nothing like the fireball he had seen earlier on his front steps.

Still, Big John acted as if they made the perfect couple, and it wouldn't hurt to keep him happy. He also knew Phil loved the chance to have them photographed together. "I think I need to make the meeting with everyone quick and change, what do you think?"

Dan laughed. "I don't think she's going anywhere."

"True, but still . . . let's start the meeting. The sunshine feels great today."

Walking through the house Matt saw Gail marching straight for him. "I've been looking for you."

"Yes, we had a little distraction earlier." Matt offered an amused laugh.

"I heard. The girl who crashed in here earlier may have broken the guards kneecap."

Dan stepped forward. "An injury doesn't sound good. I think I need to see what I can do to stop any lawsuits from developing."

Matt checked his Rolex for the time. "I think we need to find out more about Suzan, especially before she decides to come after me again."

"I'll work on finding some answers now. I think you can handle the meeting with Ronald and Tony without me."

Matt turned back to Gail. "Do you have any more good news for me?"

"Not really. I'll let the men give you the latest."

"Okay, I look forward to seeing what Ronald Sirani, our new man on the team, has for us." Matt winked as he entered his office and walked to the side conference room he designed specifically for these kinds of meetings.

Tony Korth, his Operations VP, walked over to him in a hurry. "I heard about the fight out front earlier."

"Wow, word of this incident spread fast."

Matt turned to face Gail who raised her hands to indicate it wasn't her.

"I've invested a lot of time and efforts in this project to have it go south now." Tony's face expressed his concerns.

"Excuse the south expression, but you understand, right?"

"Dan tells me we've nothing to worry about."

"I'm just checking. Shall I keep pushing forward on obtaining the building permits on this swamp land, or shall I wait to see how it develops on the contract?"

"No, I think we're safe. I'm looking forward to developing this property. I want to know what we can do, and what you suggest is the best use for it. Keep working on the project development. I think this will become one of our best investments to date."

"It'll also be one of our most expensive projects. I hope you have the money lined up for it."

"Not to worry, I think we have all in order, don't we Ronald?"

Ronald remained seated as he studied papers in front of him. Finally, he turned to face Matt. "The more I study this project, the more costly it appears to be. However, I also think we can sell these for a fantastic profit. It's going to be a challenge to raise this kind of money in the environment we're in now."

Matt accepted some papers from Ronald. "I think you know we've already spent millions on this project, and it'll all be lost if we decide to abandon this."

"Yes, but if we spend more on it, we'll have much more of a loss."

"So, what are you suggesting?"

"I'm looking at the risk versus rewards now. I need some time to do some more research on the numbers, and then it'll all come down to an educated guess by everyone here. We all need to have our act together on this one."

"I fully agree. When we all return to New York next week, we need to obtain enough answers to decide what we need to do next." Matt glanced around the room as he remembered his decision to sell an interest in his company to his best friends in the company. This proved to be one sure fire way to obtain everyone's commitment to working hard and smart. Success required the efforts of all of them to pull projects like this off.

Ronald shifted the papers. "I can be ready in a week. Do you think the rest of the team can be?"

Matt looked at the ceiling for a minute, contemplating the hell he would have to endure if this challenge to his purchase escalated out of hand. He also reflected on the woman who had confronted him, completely unafraid of taking him on. He needed to defuse the tension in his team. "I think so. I want to have a good time tonight and enjoy some Cuban cigars by the pool. We'll have an informal meeting as we smoke them. I think a good smoke will be fantastic for us. Don't worry, we'll pull this together. I know we should think about the new events presented to us today. We need to make damn sure we don't have problems with the purchase of the land."

Gail walked in and stepped forward. "I have everything set for you and the guys tonight. Yes, the cigars arrived." She laughed as she waved her hands at pretended smoke around her. Gail's long reddish hair and slim but curvy figure gave her the look of a professional model, something Matt needed as they often appeared in public together.

"Thanks, now I need to go for a swim." Matt wondered if Chelsea would still be waiting for him. What he had to do for the sake of the company.

Chapter 3

Suzan made great time crossing alligator alley on the way home in her new Mini Cooper. Home, a funny word to her, considering her mother had sold her place, her legacy her dad wanted her to keep forever. What was her mother thinking?

Suzan double checked her mother's new address when she pulled into the parking lot. Her mother had never mentioned that she wanted to live in a condo before. Something didn't appear right. She wondered how Matt had strong armed her into this. Her mother always loved the small garden behind their house which always remained so peaceful, so relaxing to her. She had envisioned for years the time she could come home and enjoy her piece of heaven.

Suzan studied the guard setting at a desk in front of the stainless steel elevators. "Can I help you?"

"I'm Suzan Mercer. I own a condo here with my mother."

The older guard glanced at a pad before offering a warm pleasant smile. "I think this is the first time I've seen you. Do you have some identification on you, or do you want me to call your mother, Ann Mercer, to verify who you are?"

Suzan pulled out a military card "I think this'll do."

"Thanks. It's good to see you here. Let me know if I can ever do anything for you."

So, this was what the sale of her home, her land, had purchased. She entered the elevator and breathed deeply, knowing she had missed her Mom, but furious at her for now. How could she?

Suzan knocked on the door and waited for which seemed to take forever as she envisioned the last time she had seen her mother. Memories of her father's funeral still haunted her. At the age of forty five he died much too early. She wanted more time with him. The cancer had claimed her father's life two months after they discovered the tumor, barely giving her enough time to return home from Afghanistan.

The door creaked open with her mother standing on the other side reading a paper before glancing at her. Her mother's face fixed in a deathly stare. "Can I help you?"

"Mom, it's me Suzan." She didn't expect much from her mom, but at least more than this.

"Oh, how are you?" A strange smile curled out of one side of her mother's mouth. "I didn't know you would be coming to see me."

"I sent you a message, didn't you receive it?" Suzan glanced passed her mother to see the inside of the condo.

"I don't know, yes, well maybe I did. Come on in." Her mother moved to one side and allowed Suzan to enter. She offered no hug to her daughter.

The time Suzan spent planning this moment appeared to be in vain. The last time she saw her mother they had departed with words. Suzan's father meant the world to her, and somehow her mother had allowed him to die. She should've noticed signs of his cancer earlier. He could've received treatments.

With a forced attempt, Suzan stopped as she passed by her and offered a small hug, but she received nothing in return. Her mother did feel much slimmer than she remembered. She would love to think her mother properly exercised to stay trim, but she assumed she wasn't eating well. A closer look revealed hair needing brushing and a face devoid of makeup, much unlike her mother's attention to her looks before . But . . . this was home for her, and perhaps a day of no anticipation of going anywhere or receiving friends.

"I have tea if you want. You know, tea is good for you." Her mother drifted toward a kitchen which looked fantastic in design, but needed cleaning badly. Dishes lined the sink, and boxes of Chinese carry outs from The Panda covered the counter.

"Yes, I think tea sounds good." Suzan continued to study the kitchen equipped with a marble table top of an incredible rose blended color and stainless steel appliances. She could imagine having some people over and entertaining them here. While she loved to cook and had dreamed of such for a long time, this wasn't home, not the super sized kitchen she grew up in.

As her mother turned a burner on to heat some water, Suzan glanced at the littered dining room next to the kitchen. The dining table contained various forms of trash on top of it which gave the impression of being there for a long time. Had her mother grown this lazy? Her dad would die to see such a wreck. The odor made her wish she hadn't come to see her mother, but she had business she needed to take care of.

"Suzan, how long will you be staying with us?"

Us? Was she living with someone else? "I'm back for good now. You said us, are you living with someone else now?"

Her mother stopped concentrating on the water kettle and glanced sideways. "Oh, I'm sorry. I'm so used to speaking for your father and me."

"Mom, dad died almost three and a half years ago."

"I know, but I still miss him." Small tears formed in both

eyes.

Finding it hard to hold back her the tears, Suzan wiped her own eyes. "I still cannot believe he's gone. He always acted so proud of me serving in the Army. I wish he could see what we accomplished in Afghanistan. I did manage to see Uncle Todd, who still lives in India. He looks so much like Dad."

"I can still imagine him having dark black hair like your father, like you."

"Yes, he does." His dark hair reminded Suzan of her own hair and brown complexion, a fact which played a vital role in her work with a joint mission conducted between the Army and the CIA in Afghanistan. Posing as an Afghanistan woman, she could go completely unnoticed when she became the eyes on the street while performing recon missions for the task force. The training she went through made her tough, both physically and mentally.

"Okay, how do you like the condo? I know it's not much, but I think it's everything we'll ever need."

Suzan had planned to wait before she ventured into the reasons for the sale with her mom, but since she initiated the discussion Suzan decided to obtain some answers. "I'm sure the place looked nice at one time, but it's not home. You sent me a letter saying the home place was sold and you had moved in here. I don't understand."

"The old home place needed lots of work, which I couldn't take care of. We also owed a lot of back taxes I hadn't paid."

"Mom, I sent you plenty of money to pay someone to take care of my home, and I'm sure dad left you plenty of insurance money."

"I tried to reach you. All I ever received were letters saying you were unavailable."

Suzan tightened her jaw, remembering her missions. While she knew by working for the CIA she had been segregated from the world for long periods of time, important messages would come through eventually. Her mother should have tried harder. "I think you know what the land means to me. Dad willed the land to me, not to you. We discussed this at the probation hearing, and we agreed all of his others assets would go to you. You signed a release to your homestead rights."

"What was I to do? Where was I to live?"

"You know you could have lived in the house as long as you wanted. I would never kick you out. After all, the house was plenty large enough for a big family, and with room to build many other houses if we needed to. In fact, I wanted to build a new home on the land one day, especially if I decided to marry."

"With the money they paid us, you can buy whatever you want. I haven't touched it, except for the taxes which had to be paid on the profit from the sale."

Suzan breathed a little easier as she received one answer she liked. She would need the money to buy her land back from Matt Harris. She glanced around at the condo. "How did you afford this?"

"This was a bonus for selling the land. Matt Harris knew I needed somewhere to live. He is such a nice guy. I know he stays busy with his empire, but I think he likes me."

"Do what?"

"Don't act so excited. You know he seduced me into going to visit him in New York."

Suzan couldn't believe what she heard. "Are you saying Matt Harris seduced you into giving away my land, my home?"

Her mother reverted to a defensive pose with her arms

crossed and her back arched. "You don't think I have the looks anymore to attract a man, is that it?"

Suzan forced her mind to clear and erase the images of her mother with Matt Harris as she focused on her mother's face. Doing a quick math calculation she estimated her mother to be around forty eight, since her mom was eighteen when she was born. However, today her mother looked much older.

Her training on gathering information kicked in as she decided to find answers in what happened. Funny, the questioning made her feel like she was now treating her mom as an asset to be used in a mission. Still she pushed on. "I'm sure you have a story to tell, and I definitely want to hear it."

Suzan watched her mother smile. "Okay, I'm not sure I can tell you everything, but I think you're old enough to let me tell you a few things."

"Good." Suzan hunted for the tea bags. Her mother acted amused and lifted a plastic sack from a corner. With all of the storage space available, why did she operate out of sacks? "Why don't you take time to keep this clean, mom?"

"I'm the only one here. I'll work on cleaning it one day."

Suzan walked to the refrigerator and opened it. The smell overtook her as she studied the leftover food packed inside. She glanced at her mom again. Something wasn't right. "If I'm going to live here for now, this has to be cleaned."

"Do whatever you want. I need to stay busy with my work."

"Your work?"

"Yes, I still paint."

Memories of her mother painting returned. She never painted anything good, but she spent endless hours at it. "Do you have a studio set up here in the condo?"

"Oh yes, come and I'll show you."

Suzan followed her mother, who shuffled along a back hallway to the master bedroom. When the door opened, reality set in. Her mother must have lost it. Paint drippings covered the floor, and half-finished paintings hung on the wall. The room looked completely ruined, and thus needing to be gutted and refurbished. The smell of paint fumes caused her to fight the urge to vomit.

Rather than being ashamed for what she had caused, her mother looked proud of her room. "I spend a lot of time in here."

"Isn't this the master bedroom?"

"Yes, it's the largest room, and I knew I would need the space."

As if in a daze, her mother walked around the room admiring the paintings on the wall. After glancing at a few completed paintings, Suzan acknowledged they at least looked better than she remembered. "I can't believe this."

It dawned on Suzan that if she wanted her land back she might have to give back the condo also, and remodeling this room would cost a bundle. She turned to study her Mother again and watched her stare into space. Her mind appeared to be a thousand miles away. What was going on with her?

Suzan backed away from the room, hoping to avoid the fresh paint. "How many bedrooms do you have here?"

Her mother didn't answer.

"Mom." Suzan reached over to shake her.

"Sorry, I was thinking about my husband. Do you think he'll like what I'm painting? He always encourages me so."

Present tense, her mother talked in present tense. Her father died over three years ago. "Mom, are you okay?"

"I'm fine, don't worry about me. I sometimes feel like he never left me."

Suzan wasn't convinced. "Mom, have you ever sold anything, ever?"

"Oh yes, I found this one nice guy who comes by on occasions and takes my work to sell in his gallery. I can't believe how much he receives for them. I must have someone who likes my paintings."

"Okay let me see the other bedrooms." Suzan had images of moving into a rental unit somewhere else until this mess could be taken care of. Why was all of this happening to her? Why now?

Opening a door Suzan saw a bedroom reflecting the same housekeeping skills as the kitchen. The bed unmade, clothes skewed around the room and a smell of body odor. This was not good. *What has happened to my mother*?

Suzan moved to the next bedroom and held her breath, as the door opened to a room much in contrast to the others. The bedroom looked professionally decorated and ready to be photographed for a magazine. The glossy rosewood headboard contained intricate carvings and extended over six feet high. Although the matching table lights on both sides of the bed looked almost gaudy, they stayed in harmony with the rest of the room. A makeup table was even set between two matching drawers. Perhaps a little too much girly girl for her, but after leaving the Army, this might be exactly what she needed.

"I can't believe this. This is beautiful!"

"I try to make sure this room stays in perfect shape. I know my daughter will love it when she sees it."

The shock set in. Suzan didn't know too much about Alzheimer's disease, but she knew enough to recognize that she needed to force her mother to see a doctor. How long had she been like this?

"Matt insisted on this room when he located this place

for me. You'll have to meet him one day. I don't think I've ever been seduced by a man like him before."

"Mom!"

"I think my late husband would want me to move on."

"Isn't he a little too young for you?"

"Yes, he's younger than me, but I think I can still turn a young stud's head when I want to."

Suzan studied her mother. It would take some time to obtain the truth. Either Matt strong armed her mother or seduced her in the state she had lapsed. Either way, she had a score to settle. She needed to find out more about this Alzheimer's disease for sure. Matt may be powerful and rich, but so were many tribal leaders in Afghanistan before she took them out. And this was war, much like the one in Afghanistan.

Suzan remembered their first meeting. Yes, he looked arrogant and as if the world belonged to him, but he didn't come across as abusive. Although impressed with his control, she had only begun to exert pressure on him. His eyes offered the unexpected. She had never seen a man with such bright green eyes before. The curiosity in wanting to know his background increased as she reflected on their unique appeal.

She remembered her training in the CIA which taught her to focus on remembering details. They used her to do the unexpected. No one would ever expect an operative to be an Afghanistan woman walking the streets. Her training would serve her well, now when she needed the skills the most.

Funny, this charge directly into Matt's estate had gained her so much useful information. She needed to make a plan and find a lawyer for many reasons now. She wanted answers to the best way to handle her mom and to the validity of the contract. She also wanted to know what happened between her mom and Matt. Could her mother really have traded her home, her land, and her dreams for a mere romp in the bed with Matt?

Chapter 4

Matt enjoyed his swim, but his mind continued to wander back to the woman who had crashed into his estate earlier. He had seen woman in movies like her, but never knew such creatures really existed. He toweled himself dry and tossed the towel back to the attendant standing by the side of the pool. She stepped behind him and helped him slip on a pool side robe. The Florida weather felt fantastic, and perhaps he should have planned a large party tonight. However, he knew he had to leave soon for New York, where he had several problems that he needed to address. Worldwide projects grew daily as the real estate market deteriorated everywhere, which was good for him since it brought him more and more investment opportunities that were too damn good to ignore.

Matt walked to the far corner of the estate size pool and an area he had loved designing–a tiki bar for enjoying his one big vice, Cuban cigars. He located his favorite seat and settled in, knowing his friends would show soon, hopefully with some answers. Although this was a night to relax, business always remained on his mind. Casual meetings like this always helped to relieve some of the stress and bind his team together. The gathering allowed them time to express themselves in an out of the box time atmosphere. Matt needed this tonight.

Phil Ector, the oldest member of his inner management, and someone Matt completely trusted with his image, soon walked around the pool. Phil had worked in public relations all of his life. The large HP symbol, short for Harris Properties, on the top of their signature buildings built a trademark of excellence which translated into great prices they cashed in on. This icon required constant monitoring and feeding to the press to maintain its prestigious role for the company.

"Matt, I'm glad I caught you here early. I received some news about Suzan I think you might be interested in."

Matt motioned for him to take a seat at the tiki bar. "I thought you would jump at this."

"Suzan returned from Afghanistan a few days ago. She's considered a very big war hero. She single handedly saved most of a small detail which came under fire. The reports vary, but she's credited with killing about a half dozen attackers. Two of them in hand to hand combat."

"That doesn't surprise me at all, since I saw her in action today."

"A large part of her time is unaccounted for. Those activities are classified, and I can't find anyone who can shed more light on them."

"So, she does have a bit of mystery surrounding her. Is she out of the service now, or is this a leave of absence?"

"I think she's completing her last tour and will be officially discharged any day. You'll have to ask her about her future. The only thing for sure is she wants her land back."

"It does appear she has reasons for wanting to hold on to the land, but from what I can tell, this was unusable swamp land. Am I missing something here?"

"The land was given to her by her father, who, by the way, was born in India. Her mother signed a waiver of homestead rights which we have copies of."

"Hum, her heritage would explain the black hair and those large expressive eyes."

"I should've known you would've noticed her. She was a

nice looking girl if you could take the GI Joe out of her."

"So Phil, the question is . . . can you contain this problem, or could this become a major blemish on our name?"

"Just let me say that I'm working on the situation. We might have to do some renegotiating on the contract to make her happy."

"Like what?"

"I don't know, but I'll see if I can find out what she wants. I think we need to handle her as quietly and quickly as we can. We have lobbyists at work in Tallahassee, Florida. We still need approval to take on such a project. Some people can be very sensitive when you decide to develop anything close to the Everglades."

"I think we have one of the best plans for the area Florida could ever hope for. The desires of the conservationist will be more than taken care of. In fact, I think we'll enhance what they want." Matt turned to face the ocean and inhale the salty air.

"Oh, I agree, but one hot-headed woman could give the wrong impression, and at the wrong time. Big John has lots of influence with the Florida legislature here, and we're lucky to have him here as a guest this week." Phil shifted closer to Matt. "It also doesn't hurt that his daughter, Chelsea really has a thing for you either."

"Chelsea is interested in anyone she can have fun with. You would think Big John would find some way to control her. I don't think Chelsea has any interest other than partying and spending money. She's a very beautiful woman, but with what they've spent on plastic, she should be."

"Be careful, my friend, and don't forget you need to come back to Florida in a week to attend the annual fundraiser he throws. I told him you would donate tickets to a private party aboard the company yacht, which would sail to Miami and back later that night, as one of the items for the attendees to bid on. ”

"Oh, I'll be careful. A beautiful woman that sexy can make most men happy for a lifetime, but I'm thinking there has to be more in a woman to build a life. As far as the trip goes, I think we need to take Lady Luck out more, so a party on-board will be great. I'm sure Chelsea will have her hooks out for the trip. ”

Phil laughed. "Now, if you want me to arrange a date with Suzan, I think you'll soon find that excitement can only last so long, and you'll find the charm of Chelsea much more to your liking."

"Now, Phil, what kind of date would you recommend? Maybe paintball?"

"Paintball may be fun for you, but I think fun games like this would bore Suzan to death."

"I agree, but still, let me know when you find out more about her. We need to take care of this situation."

Matt glanced at the house to see the rest of his friends, his team, coming to join him. The only one missing would be his secretary, Gail. He didn't blame her. This was a guy's night. He glanced at the box of smokes and the bottle of cognac they would dip into. Ronald, Dan and Tony dressed casual, much different than the normal stiff neck image they maintained in the New York office. All had an interest in the company, but he still retained the major part of the stock himself. Their stock ownership had transformed all of them into wealthy businessmen. But their dedication to him is what made him what he is, and he would never forget their efforts. They were a team. Yes, he needed the company of a woman like any man, but finding one to keep his interest appeared to be out of the cards.

Chapter 5

"I never thought I would be faced with something like this." Suzan studied the papers in front of her as she watched the psychologist waiting on her to make a decision. "My mother's only forty eight. I thought Alzheimer's hit people like in their seventies."

"Generally, memory loss happens over time, and usually much later, however, I've seen many cases of people suffering from an early onset of Alzheimer's disease. We'll have to do many tests to see the extent of your mother's condition. It should take us about a week to fully evaluate her and recommend the best course of action for her. I promise you that she'll be in good hands." Dr. Laranzo maintained perfect manners, as she would expect from someone in his position. She only hoped she could manage her growing concerns for her mother and her anger directed at Matt.

Suzan wanted what was best for her mother, but she also knew one reason she had her here was to prove her incompetent later if she needed to in order to get her land back. Her actions made her feel cold and heartless, but confused. She lost her father while she was away, and always assumed she had time to reconnect with her mother. She thought wrong. She had to think smart now. "I don't know."

"These are just tests. We won't start her on any medication until they are completed and we talk again."

Suzan glanced at her mother, who remained quiet and inattentive. As important as this was to her, she thought that her mother would be more active in this decision. She would need to make decisions for her. "Okay. It'll be good to see how the tests come back. I'm at home now, and I'll do what I can to take care of her."

"We've come a long way with the medications in the last few years, and perhaps we can restore most of her ability to focus. We'll see."

"I purchased a new cell phone. I want you to call me with any questions or concerns you might have." Suzan handed him a piece of paper with the number on it.

"I will. You might want to talk to an attorney about having her placed under your care, along with a power of attorney to take care of her affairs also."

The words "power of attorney" made her tense. That's what caused her problems now. If she had just not signed those papers years ago. "I do need to talk to an attorney. I returned home, like you know, only a few days ago, and I don't know any attorneys here."

"I can recommend some names if you want me to."

"Yes, recommendations would be great. I need to talk to one. As I mentioned earlier, my mother sold some property of mine when I was away. I never wanted my land sold, and I was looking forward to returning to my place to build a house for myself. My dreams may be gone now. I'm wondering if I need to have Mom declared . . ." Suzan glanced at her mother and wondered if she should use the word.

Dr. Loranzo smiled. "I understand. We'll talk much more in a week, when I can give you the results."

"I tried to talk to my mother about the real estate sale many times, but I've only become frustrated. She mentioned several times that Matt had *seduced* her into signing the papers. However, I never obtained much in the way of details. This guy, Matt, is much younger than her. I wouldn't put it pass him to capitalize on her state of mind."

"Have you talked to him about this?"

Well, she went to see him, but got nowhere. About the only thing she accomplished was making a scene–not very professional. She wasn't thinking clear. The point she wanted them to understand is that she wanted her land back and intended to fight for it. "I went to see him, but he's so insulated behind his fortress I think it'll be impossible to approach him to have a normal conversation."

"Don't be so sure. Everyone can be approached. You need to find a way to do so on his level."

"Like sure, that's never going to happen."

"I guess it all depends on if you want to discover the truth or not. Sometimes finding the truth requires one to do some onsite research. Have you tried to set up a meeting with him?"

"No, I know it'll be impossible to talk to him without all of his attorneys around him." Suzan said.

"I think you need to learn how business is conducted in his world."

"Such as?"

"I'm sure he has a social world he operates in. That's where the real deals are cut, and the way to break into the front door. I think you'll find out he spends much more time socializing than he does at his office in New York."

"How do you know so much about this?"

"I've been to many parties Matt Harris attended."

"So, you know him?"

"I've shaken his hand before, and I've invested some money in one of his projects. I even lived in one of his properties once when I lived in Miami."

Suzan realized this might be the way to obtain some answers. Memories of her work in Afghanistan surfaced.

She needed answers. "Okay, I need some help in finding the truth. How do I get started?"

With the details planned to perfection, Suzan clutched her invitation to the charity ball hosted by the yacht club in West Palm Beach, as her rented limo pulled in front of the entrance. Her Armani suit felt strange, and it was not nearly as comfortable as the Army fatigues she had worn for the last eight years. While she had never been a girly girl before, she thought she could get used to this. Well, maybe not. Much like her missions inside Afghanistan, she had a purpose for entering enemy territory. While she felt like the chances of reclaiming her land were impossible, she wanted answers and for someone to pay for what they did. She also wanted to discover the truth to her mother's story. Was she seduced? Was she . . . ? Although she didn't want to think about her mother with Matt, she needed to know if he sexually took advantage of her mother. If so, retaliation would definitely be in order. Not a good trait, but one she couldn't control. She had to clear her mind. She needed answers.

As the limo door opened, she paused to give the other guests arriving time to watch her make her grand entrance. She moved to the door and slid out slowly, allowing her dress to reveal her legs. The drama felt strange, but well rehearsed. Her hair had endured four hours in a stylist chair. Four hours! She usually had her hair pulled into a pony tail in two minutes. The makeup felt so unnatural on her face, making her have images of a clown. This might be harder than she thought to accomplish, but she moved forward. She had no backup plan.

As she stood, a man turned in her direction, but she didn't see the large crowd she had hoped for. Perhaps she would have more attention when she walked inside. If not, this money spent would be wasted. She walked toward the entrance as this one man approached her. "How are you?"

Suzan didn't recognize him. In fact, she assumed she wouldn't recognize anyone here unless they happened to be a movie star. Yeah, she imagined that would happen. She watched him analyzing her. Something looked familiar about him, but she couldn't place where.

"Hello, I'm Phil Ector." He extended an arm to help her walk through the front door. "They're having problems with welcoming everyone, and they asked me to help out."

"I see. You must have a large crowd here tonight."

"Oh yes, we've an incredible turnout tonight. Have we met before?"

"I'm not sure." She decided to hand him her invitation.

He glanced at it for a brief moment and stopped walking. "I didn't know you would be here."

"I received the invitation a few days ago. I hope it's okay."

"I'm sure the invitation will be fine. I'm not connected officially to the charity. They solicited my help a few minutes ago. I work for Matt Harris."

Now, she remembered seeing him at Matt's estate. He stood beside Matt on the front steps of his mansion a week ago. She didn't know his name then, and had never heard him say a word earlier. What did he do for Matt? Her body shifted into a defensive mode. "I think I saw you earlier."

"Yes, I don't think we had time to be introduced."

Suzan blinked before she glanced deep into his eyes. "Is Matt Harris here tonight?"

"I hope you're not planning on repeating what I saw earlier."

"I'm not here to cause problems. I didn't know he would

be here." She lied, but knew if she didn't, he might be able to have her barred from the gala and thus lose her chance to talk to him.

"In any case, since you're here, I'd love to talk to you for a few minutes. I hope to find out more about your complaints and see what I can do to resolve any misunderstanding."

Perhaps he had information she could use. She didn't trust him, but she hoped she could use him. He might make a good asset if she approached him properly. "I think it would be good to talk to you, but I don't think there's a misunderstanding. Matt purchased my land without my consent or authorization, and I'll get it back. There's also the matter of him seducing my mother."

"Seducing your mother?"

"That's what she's telling me."

A large woman walked in their direction ending the discussion for now. "Phil, thank you so much for helping out. Who is this beautiful lady you found?"

As Phil turned to introduce her, she decided to take the initiative and reached for the arm of the lady wearing an expensive evening dress, but looked more accustomed to a Florida beach robe. "Hi, my name is Suzan Mercer." She handed the lady her invitation.

The woman studied her for a minute before biting her lip. "Hi, I'm Gloria Zeman. I was hoping you could make the gala, I know my invitation arrived at the last minute. How is your mother?"

"She's fine for now. They'll let me know in a week what they think."

Phil made a point of over exaggerating the questioning look on his face until Gloria detected the look and turned toward him. "Suzan's mother is being evaluated for the extent of her Alzheimer condition, and Suzan contacted the Florida Alzheimer Foundation where I work. After the generous contribution she gifted to the Foundation, I knew we could count on her to attend this gala as well."

"I see. How long has your mother had a problem with Alzheimer's?"

"That I'm not sure. I've been in Afghanistan for most of the last eight years. and my dad died almost four years ago. They don't allow me a lot of contact in the Army."

"I'm sorry to hear about your father. I never met your mother, but I heard good things about her from Matt."

Gloria glanced back and forth at the two. "I'm sorry. I didn't know you knew each other?"

Again Suzan assumed the initiative. "No, we just met, but we realized we . . . know the same person." That felt difficult in explaining.

"I see. Well, come on in, since most of the guests are already here. I want to introduce you to some people."

Phil lingered for a minute. "I'm sure I'll see you later, Suzan."

Yes, he could count on seeing her again. She smiled at him and walked toward a hallway. The inside walls were constructed of a shiny wood she thought may be cherry. She studied artifacts of ancient boat parts decorating a corner, as they walked around into another major room where she saw a large gathering of people. Several stopped talking as she walked over to join them.

Gloria introduced her to one person after another, as if she should know who they were. She had no clue. She knew most of them had to be in their seventies or older. The older men intrigued her in one respect. Their eyes always focused on her breasts. Maybe it was the fact she never wore such a dress before which allowed men, any man, to see her cleavage. The push up bra they talked her into at the dress shop felt uncomfortable, but it was necessary to make the dress look proper. She couldn't wait to get out of the torture trap, but for now she had to endure it. She knew Matt was here somewhere, and she wanted him to know she had arrived.

The Florida Alzheimer's Foundation banner hung above the stage area where a band was setting up. While music would be good, she hoped she didn't have to dance with anyone. A waiter walked by with some champagne. Hum, a quick drink sounded like a good idea as she accepted a glass. Now where was Matt?

She wanted answers. Did Matt really seduce her mother? It would be a few more days before the psychologist would let her know his thoughts on this, but this gala she had heard about was too good to pass up, especially when she heard Matt Harris would be attending. She couldn't understand his angle in this. Perhaps attending charities was his way of boasting and mixing with the old money people here.

Suzan tried to maneuver through the crowds. If she never found Matt here, the five thousand she donated to the fund would be wasted money. Well, not totally useless, as she assumed the funds they raised might help her mother in some way. Concerns of the money flooded her mind. She had learned her mother had deposited the proceeds from the sale into a separate account. She studied the account a few days ago, and the only deduction had been for income taxes and back property taxes. Since they had deposited the money in a trust account, the accountant had filed a separate income tax return. After all of the deductions she had almost three million. Not bad, but she wanted her land back. She had saved most of her earnings working in the Army. She could live on those funds for a long time. While the Army paid her some, the CIA paid much better.

After working her way around one corner that offered a fantastic view of the harbor where many members moored their boats, she stopped to take in the view. The boats looked incredible. Some of the members here must be extremely wealthy. This presented a life she knew nothing about, and one that she didn't care too much about. But, again, the view mesmerized her as she rested against the rail gazing at them for a long time.

Suddenly, Phil approached her with an extra glass of champagne. "They have some fantastic yachts docked here."

"Yes, I saw some of them already." Glancing at Phil, he acted as a trusted father, much like the one she lost. While his mannerism reflected a calm and caring gentleman, she still she didn't trust him. Anything associated with Matt she didn't care for.

"Matt has a lot of friends and guests here."

"And you don't want me to make a scene."

"Yes . . . that would be nice. However, I don't think we're going to have a problem tonight, are we?"

"Phil, what do you do for Mr. Harris?"

"I work for his company as the vice president of public affairs."

"I see. So it makes sense you would want to know my intentions."

"It would appear so."

"I've tried to contact Matt many times, and I've never gotten anywhere. I keep getting referred to a Dan Panella, who I don't know."

"Dan is the company's vice president of legal affairs."

"I assumed he was an attorney of some kind. He always managed to block me from seeing Matt."

"Okay, tell me what it is you want us to do?"

"Return my land to me, void out the contract."

"I don't think that'll be possible. The company has already invested a large amount of funds into this project."

"I don't think that's my problem. Now . . . if you'll excuse me."

"I could have you escorted from here."

"You can try, but I don't think you have the manpower." Suzan stopped in front of him and watched him freeze.

He smiled and tapped their glasses together. "I can wish for the best I guess. I hope you enjoy the evening."

As he left, her instincts alerted her to watch her back. She had no back up, and she had walked totally off the reservation without any help from her friends in the CIA. This was all her baby. While she decided to keep walking around and hoped to have luck in finding Matt, she knew Phil had intentions of keeping them apart.

An hour later, the foundation started an auction. The items for bid sounded attractive for someone with money and who could afford to spend it on such unnecessary items as spa treatments, over priced wine, hideous jewelry, etc.

Nothing interested her until she saw the next item for bid. She listened intensely as the auctioneer pointed to a large screen behind him. "Ladies and gentleman, we've one last item tonight, and the one I think everyone has been waiting on. Matt Harris, I know you're here somewhere."

A rumble built in the crowd as word circulated. She saw one hand after another pointing to her far left. A man stood and waved around him. Yes, he looked arrogant. His black tux looked custom fitted, and he looked like he was born wearing the outfit. She missed him somehow in her hunt, and she felt sure Phil had kept them apart.

Suzan watched him retake his seat as she studied those around him. He had a blonde-haired girl with a hairdo that made her look more like a large Barbie than a real person. This didn't surprise her at all. She felt surprise he didn't sport one on both arms, as she reflected on how she had heard about him being a real playboy. This confirmed her research. She didn't recognize the others at the table. However, she did notice the airhead blonde reach over and give an older man a hug.

After the clapping, the auctioneer continued as he pointed to the screen. "I think everyone here has heard of the Lucky Lady, the international lady of the sea owned by Matt Harris. This yacht has been on many documented shows, but now for those so lucky, Matt will be offering a moonlight cruise tonight following the gala. The yacht will sail to Miami and back. There'll be a total of twelve who will obtain the chance of a lifetime."

A large lump stuck in her throat. She had no idea how much such a yacht ride would cost, but it had to be expensive. How much would they go for? She leaned forward and concentrated on every movement, every sound. Would they take a check? She assumed they would.

"For those unable to stay up all night, I'm sure Matt will allow you to use one of his staterooms. However, I would imagine he'll keep champagne flowing for most of the night. For those who have never seen his boat before, allow me to give you a private tour." He motioned for the camera operator to start a presentation on the screen behind him.

For the next fifteen minutes she watched a narrator go over the finer points of the boat. Every detail met with applause or sighs from the crowd. They loved the ship, as she imagined they would. She assumed many of the attendees were members of the yacht club. The jewelry worn by most women indicated the economy hadn't put a dent in their lifestyle.

Finally, the lights grew brighter as the presentation ended. Suzan turned to find Matt with the Barbie doll still stuck to his side. She wondered who she was, but she assumed another notch in his bed post for the night. Suzan hoped she would have a chance to talk to her, and let her know what she was getting herself into. She was either his hired woman for the night or his next victim.

"I'm not sure where we should start this bidding. Who wants to give me a starting point?"

One hand shot in the air with a bid of one thousand. The price escalated to two, then three where it settled with small increases for a several minutes. She knew once the auctioneer set the price ten people would be picked from the crowd, which may not include her. Since this was her one chance to see him, and the perfect place to put him on the spot, she lifted her arm high and caught his attention as the auctioneer who pointed to her. "And your bid?"

"Five thousand."

A small mummer circulated as she looked over her shoulder and directly into the eyes of Matt, who appeared to recognize her. The events shifted into slow motions as the auctioneer waited for a minute to glance around. "Okay we have a good bid now of five thousand. Who'll give me six?"

Rather than ending the bidding like she hoped, she excited the crowd instead. She heard a seven then an eight. This was for a few hours on a boat! This was insane. But losing her land was more insane. She raised her hand again as the auctioneer begged for nine thousand.

The auctioneer smiled at her and waited.

Suzan closed her eyes and shouted as she questioned her own sanity. "Ten thousand!" She felt sure people in the yacht club would know who she was now. She glanced over her shoulder again at Matt. He sipped on a glass of champagne, but stopped long enough to salute her with his glass.

The auctioneer raised his hand high upon receiving the bid. "Okay I think we have a winner, and someone who has set the price. I have nine more tickets available."

The tickets sold in seconds. Wow, it must be nice to have money like this, but down deep this was crazy. She never intended to do this. She snapped out of her daze long enough to see many eyes on her. Yes, she was a complete mystery to them. She saw the whispers.

Then, she saw Phil walk toward the front of the room to talk to the auctioneer, who handed him the microphone. "For those who purchased a ticket on the boat tonight, you didn't know it, but you own a special ticket and bonus you never expected." He pointed at Suzan. "I would like to present to you a true war hero."

An eerie hush fell over the room as chairs turned around to face her. She knew what he was doing. Turning the tables on her and using her to add to the image of Matt Harris wasn't why she came, or spent this kind of money. She needed time to think about what she should say or do.

Phil stepped forward. "This is Suzan Mercer, back from Afghanistan a week ago and already taking a part in our great country. In a raid on our troops during one of their missions, she's credited with taking out a number of the attackers personally–two of them in hand to hand combat."

The applause thundered in the great hallway of the gala. First one person after another stood, until everyone attending had scrambled to their feet. Minutes later, the clapping still rattled the ceiling. Suddenly it dawned on her. They wanted some kind of speech. Nope, not from her! Publicity is not why she came. Too bad, she could've used the speech to expose Matt. Phil must have known she wouldn't be able to react in time to make her point.

She climbed to her feet and smiled, but she avoided the microphone and stared at Phil. He smiled and waved at the people around him. "It's our honor to have you back in America and we do salute you." Another round of applause followed with many waving or saluting her. The attention did make her feel good, but angry at Phil. His ploy wouldn't work, since she intended to expose Matt before the night ended.

The auctioneer accepted the microphone. "Thank you again, and for those going on the trip you still have about an hour until the yacht leaves. We've lots of wine left, and we hope you all enjoy it. And . . . we want some great photos of the trip for our members at the yacht club. I wish I was going."

As the auction ended, one person after another pushed toward her. The chances of seeing Matt alone now appeared to be impossible. She loved the Army and had no intention of making a scene causing it any kind of embarrassment. Too many asked questions she couldn't answer. She had no experience in this, and she assumed this would only be the beginning. She needed to walk away from them and find a place to breathe.

Several people in front of her looked over her head at something catching their attention. She turned to see what caused the interruption. Surprise, oh what a surprise! Matt stood behind her, moving several people to one side. His voice resonated strong and powerful as he dominated the center of attention. "I know everyone has good wishes for Suzan, but she's the one we need to honor on the cruise tonight. I hope you'll excuse us."

Valiant, but she didn't need rescuing. Listening to the

crowd asking for her, perhaps she did. She smiled and accepted his hand as he led her away from the small mob pressing in on her. The gap they escaped through closed as soon as they left. A few hands reaching in her direction quickly faded as they rushed to a side exit. Rescued–she didn't need to be rescued! However, the warmth and control in his hand did feel good–strange, but good.

Chapter 6

After leaving the grand hall, where the charity gala for Alzheimer research still hosted many people, Suzan continued to allow Matt to pull her behind him. The back hallway soon opened to a balcony facing a large channel with hundreds of boats parked along the banks. On the other side of her, the yacht club had their own private moorings. The size of these massive yachts rivaled many of the boats she remembered riding in at times when she trained for operations in the Army and the CIA.

After realizing they had lost the crowd, she turned to face Matt. Two body guards flanked him. As they stood firmly beside him, they reflected a nervous tension. She remembered one of them from his mansion. She forced herself to remember her mission.

Matt smiled, but said nothing, appearing to wait on her to finish her say.

Suzan stepped closer to Matt. "We have a lot to talk about."

"It would appear so. I don't think I've ever met anyone like you. I didn't know the Army had a special force composed of women."

"They don't. I'm simply a woman who knows how to handle herself in a man's world."

"I can tell you do and a little cocky also."

"I don't tend to mince words, and this is a little out of my normal world." She pointed to the gala dispersing behind her.

"I don't know, I think you handled yourself well tonight, and you established a fantastic impression on many people. Later, you'll have to tell me more about this war hero thing."

"Nothing really to tell–I simply do what's expected of

me."

"I get this impression you would love to kick my butt, and I'm still lost as to why?"

"You robbed me of my land, and I want it back."

"I think I paid a more than fair price for the land, and that you received a nice profit on it."

"Profit? I'm not interested in profit! My father left the land to me to keep forever. Which is what I planned to do."

"Your mother operated on your behalf while you were being a war hero. She appeared to be happy with the deal we worked out, and she did have a power of attorney that you signed when you left."

Suzan couldn't resist. "Yes, she did, but I think there's much more to the story than you're telling. She told me you seduced her into signing the papers."

"I did what?"

"I think you heard me, and that you know what I'm talking about."

A million dollar smile crossed his face as his alpha ego kicked in. Yes, she knew the look. As a part of the military police in Afghanistan, she had more experience with his type than he would ever know. "Is this what your mother told you? She said . . . I seduced her."

"Yes. You had to do something, or she wouldn't have sold my land to you."

"If you'll allow me to do so, I'll be glad to arrange a meeting with you and your mother to clear this up."

"I'm sure you would, but seeing how my mother's under a doctor's care and in a clinic for evaluation now, I don't think she'll be in any meetings."

"Why, what happened to her?"

"Let's say she's the reason I had an interest in this gala."

"Oh, I see, I'm so sorry to hear it. I really think she's a

nice lady."

Several people who were spilling out from the gala scattered as they left the main hall. "This has been a night to remember for sure."

"I promise you we'll discuss this in more detail and soon, but for tonight, I owe you and nine other people a cruise. I know this is asking a lot, but I'd appreciate it very much if we can enjoy the night."

"I bet you would."

His eyes focused on her, with their bright-green, mysterious color haunting her. "Perhaps we might have a few minutes to continue the conversation on board."

She recognized a weakness in him, and maybe a way to find out more information. "Yes, I think tonight we can see how the evening goes, but simply on the promise that you'll see me later, where we can talk about the land being returned to me."

"I'll be glad to talk to you later, but I assure you I don't think I'll be selling the land back to you."

Confident was one thing, arrogance was another, and at times, the two were hard to distinguish. She needed to study him tonight and find his weaknesses. This recon mission would take a long time. "Okay which one is yours?" She pointed to the moors on the far side.

He smiled as his eyes radiated a smug confidence. He offered his left hand to her, and upon receiving her left hand, he pulled it under his right arm to escort her along the edge of the balcony. While his life as a gentleman remained in doubt, she knew he lived in a different world from her. Her steps in the high heels remained uncomfortable, and she couldn't imagine running in them or hiking in them for long. In fact, the shoes felt as bad as the push up bra. What a stupid game some women played, and it was one she had no intention of playing for long.

Her mind drifted back to Afghanistan where the CIA recruited her to become the eyes on the street. No one would expect the CIA to use a woman to walk along the street with her head covered and her posture reflecting a poor Afghanistan woman to provide recon. Since her father was born in India, she retained the dark olive looking skin and expressive eyes of the local women. They never knew she worked for the CIA, or suspected the intelligence she obtained. Yes, it was very dangerous, but to her worth the risk.

A warm but salty breeze swept across the balcony as they reached a corner and faced the docks. Without a cloud in the sky, the stars sparkled above, reflecting the perfect weather for the late night cruise. She now wished she had watched the video closer on his yacht so she could spot it.

He leaned over toward her. "I also want to thank you for raising the price at the auction. I'll assure you the money raised will be benefiting the research in Alzheimer." His voice carried a tender caring tone, contrasting to the images she had so ingrained about him.

"I hope so. This is something I knew nothing about until a week ago." She imagined the hours of research ahead of her, and the decisions she would have to face soon.

"I think you'll enjoy the others on the cruise. I know most of them, and I'll introduce you to them. I'll be busy for a large part of the cruise and I hope you understand."

"Not a problem. I think I'll be fine, but I do want to ask you some more questions." His eyes darted in her direction. "This will not be a negotiation on the land, but I do have questions about you and my mom."

"I understand. This is something we need to discuss, since I want to hear what your mother told you. We'll have some time later on the boat."

After passing one large yacht they turned toward a different dock, where a large white yacht glowed from lights showcasing the monster. After seeing it stand several decks high and with a large circular object on top, she had to blink her eyes. This wasn't a yacht, but a super yacht. Just how wealthy was Matt, anyway? "You've got to be kidding me. This . . . is your yacht?"

"I'll take that as a compliment. I look forward to showing you around."

A deck hand stepped forward. "Mr. Harris, we have all ready onboard."

Matt motioned toward Suzan. "This is a special guest of mine. Please make sure she's well taken care of. I need to wait here for a minute for some other guests."

"It'll be my pleasure." He offered his arm to help her walk the ramp to the boat. The heels made climbing the ramp awkward with the slick bottoms and the moist footing. She wished she could step out of them, knowing her boots would feel so much better. She had to force herself into her role and keep her anger under control if she has any chance in finding answers.

After nearing the top of the ramp, a captain or perhaps officer greeted her. "I see you're the first guest on board."

The staff member turned sideways to them. "Mr. Harris said she was a special guest of his and to take care of her."

Realizing they didn't know her name, she offered a smile. "My name is Suzan Mercer."

"Well, Ms. Mercer, I'm Captain Manfield, please allow me to show you around as the other guests arrive. I think I know the perfect place for you on top. We should have a great view of the coastline tonight."

"Thanks." She turned to glance back at Matt as more

guests had arrived and one blonde-haired woman offered him a large hug. She knew he would be busy tonight. While he had a charm with a certain look and he had money, the preying on women didn't settle well with Suzan.

She accepted the captain's arm and walked the stairs to the top level. Every detail reflected the skills of the boat builder. The exquisite lighting, brass fittings, and walls lined with expensive exotic woods all added to the show of wealth. This ship would take a long time to explore.

Finally on the top floor, a large parlor with a dark red carpet created an impression she would never forget. The windows on the sides allowed a view of the harbor and the night lights along this prestigious shoreline. A chef with a small feast of intricate pastries and other delicacies covered a large table in front of him. He wore a standard tall white hat and smiled at her as she entered the room. He also pointed to a small side table where many champagne glasses had been filled in preparation of the guests arrival.

She turned to the captain. "This is a great room, I love it."

"I'm glad to hear you like the place I call home. Please help yourself, and feel free to walk outside and enjoy the air. It's going to be a fantastic night." He bowed and turned toward the stairways. She knew he had many guests to take care of. At the table she studied the various items on the table and assumed some of the toppings were caviar. At least she would be getting something for the extraordinary amount of money she had spent. Yes, fifteen thousand dollars and counting, and she still had no answers.

She felt relieved to be alone for a minute, which allowed her some time to plan her next move as she reflected on Matt's promise of giving her time to discuss the situation. She could already tell Matt knew how to be a smooth talker.

Being prepared for this, she decided to pass on the champagne, since she needed to be able to think. It would be better if she saw him drink a lot tonight.

Suzan walked out onto the upper patio as a warm breeze blew pass her. The dress, something else she hadn't worn in years, fluttered slightly. The Army didn't allow much time to be a girly girl. She smiled, admitting it did feel different preparing for such an event. She wouldn't do this again, probably, but it did feel good in a funny way. She enjoyed the men staring at her as a woman rather than a soldier for a change.

When she heard someone behind her, she turned and watched several couples, who had also purchased tickets from the auction, walk over to her. Rounding out the group included a number of older women dressed in expensive party dresses and tons of jewelry.

A short introduction followed by questions about her military experience followed. She didn't want to be known as a war hero. She wanted to be herself, the girl who lived on a piece of land where no one bothered her–somewhere were all remained so peaceful and quiet that she could live out her life in peace. She had to stay focused.

Since this group might know more about Matt, she decided to ask some questions. The older lady on her right appeared talkative, and was perhaps the best one to start with. "I don't know Matt too well, how do you know him?"

The lady's smile faded as she stared at Suzan. "I think everyone knows his reputation as a guy who can get deals done. He has worked miracles no one else could ever attempt. Once he has his mind set on something, it's usually considered a done deal."

"I see. Determination can be a good thing, or a bad thing, I think."

"What do you mean?"

"I guess it depends on if he's helping or stepping on someone." Suzan thought she phrased this perfectly.

"You know, I think I like you. Not many women these days say what's on their mind. I'm sure it's a balancing act. Have you ever had dealings with Matt before?"

"Let me say, I've only been back in the states for a short time, but I've learned a lot. I'm sure Matt and I will have some conversations in the near future." She wanted to say more, but decided to bide her time. She wanted to talk to Matt tonight, and told herself she had to keep her mind on her missions of gaining some more information about what happened.

"All I can say is . . . be careful. He's very good at what he does."

"Oh, I'm sure he is."

A roar of laughter overrode their conversation as another group of people entered the inside galley. A quick glance confirmed Matt in the center of the group. The Barbie he had with him earlier stayed by his side, having a great time acting the part of an airhead.

Suzan leaned over to the older women she hoped would be a friend on this trip. "Who is the girl with Matt?"

"Ahhh, it's amusing you don't know, but of course, you've been gone for a long time. Her name is Chelsea Townsley. Her father, known as Big John, is the guy next to the food table. He's one of the money connections Matt uses a lot to finance his deals. Big John is also immensely involved in the charity circuit, which is why Matt is here."

"I see. I didn't know the connection and thought Matt might have a decent heart, but I should've known."

"Chelsea is set to inherit the entire fortune one day. This will be fun to follow, as she's known to have one thing on her mind–men, and more specifically, partying with men!"

"So, are they a regular couple or what?"

"Who knows for sure? She loves to hold onto Matt, and with Big John toting many of Matt's loans, he definitely will not want to upset her father. To me, I think it's all a big show, but who am I to say."

Although this woman pretended to be modest, Suzan knew better, especially after having spent ten thousand dollars for a short nighttime cruise. How much she could trust her, she didn't know. In fact, she hadn't asked her name. "By the way, my name is Suzan Mercer."

"Yes, I heard during the auction. I'm Denise Harris."

The last name registered. "Are you related to Matt?"

"Oh yes, for better or worse, he's my nephew. Matt's parents died a long time ago in a plane crash. They left him with a small empire, which he has extended much more than they would've ever dreamed. However, his career is the only life he has. He works all of the time and he has never had time for a family, or even any kind of hobby, except developing his next project."

"I know many men like him."

"Really!"

"Well. kind of, I guess. I know military men who pursue their career and nothing outside that world."

"It sounds like this might've been your world also."

Bingo, Denise assumed correctly. Being a part of the military police, she had concentrated on her career and nothing else. To survive she had to stay focused. For a woman, this represented the toughest job available, and she loved the action. "I had no choice but to apply myself. My kind of job left me with few options."

"There are always options, my dear. I've discovered everyone exercises the ones they really want."

"I'm not so sure. Once you commit you cannot turn back."

"Hum, perhaps you're just like Matt. That sounds like him talking." The crowd inside laughed louder, and the others outside glanced at each other, knowing they should join them.

Suzan stayed at the back of the crowd which was returning inside. She wanted to observe Matt in action, and she needed a moment to digest the observations given to her by his aunt. With around twenty-five people inside, the room still had space for all to mingle comfortably as the hostess delivered champagne to everyone in anticipation of a toast.

She appeared to be the last one to be served. Matt raised his glass as everyone turned their attention to him. "Here's to a fantastic gala, a night to relax and enjoy the company of great friends." A round of clinking glasses together, followed where people acted authentic but left Suzan in the sidelines. These weren't trusted friends she knew. She recognized no one here, and she hardly considered Matt a friend.

Denise walked over to her and touched her glass with Suzan's. "Drink up, honey. This should be one hell of a party before the night is over."

Suzan smiled. She had no reason to hate this woman. She wasn't as taken in by Matt as everyone else, and she thought that she might be able to find answers from her she couldn't from anyone else. "Okay, to the night." She extended her glass in a friendly toast.

Matt had several people around him listening to his every word. Some of the staff stayed close to him as if to anticipate his every need or desire. However, he also acted attentive to those around him, and wanted to make sure they were extended the same treatment from the crew that he received.

Suddenly, he lowered his glass and glanced in her direction as he stopped talking and paying attention to those around him. She would love to know what went on inside his head. His eyes had the chilling quality of turning colors from a bright green to a haunting allure of mixed colors. His complexion looked almost perfect, and as if he had been pampered all of his life, while his mannerism resembled much of what she envisioned a movie star or celebrity would offer. The charisma he generated seemed to come naturally, as he laughed with those around him.

If he thought, however, she was going to be one of his groupie-type friends, he would be mistaken. She came to find out more about him, obtain answers, and nothing more. She tried to imagine him forcing himself on her mother, or perhaps her mother coming under his trance. Manipulated entered her mind as a good word selection. Realizing she might not ever know details of what happened, she would, however, attempt to learn the truth.

As he studied her, she realized she had returned the favor much more than she had intended. The group around Matt shifted their eyes in her direction. The wait for the next move built a tension which cast an eerie hush over the crowd. Suzan knew she offered an unknown presence in the room.

Soon, the only one laughing or moving around in the crowd was his girlfriend, if that is what she was. She looked like she was either born to money or a call girl. If Chelsea had already become drunk, this would be an interesting trip later. Matt turned to Chelsea as he accepted the help of the captain behind him who stepped forward to talk to Chelsea, freeing him to turn back in her direction.

Would he come to her, or did he expect her to follow the others and fall victim to his snare? She decided to set her own trap, as she sipped her champagne and waited. She knew to go slowly, and that she wasn't the most beautiful woman he had seen by far. Perhaps she would see things in a different light later if she drank the champagne as the others, but she knew he was smarter than that. She would pace herself.

Since she had seen enough for now, she turned and slowly walked to the outside patio to allow the cool air to clear her head. What was she doing here? After walking to the edge she glanced at the city lights. A slight movement in the yachts position indicated that the ship had detached from the pier as she heard a slight purring of the motors. Yes, this would be a good place to relax.

She studied the location of all the exits, and where all of the crew came and entered from. The bodyguards, two of them, stood like statues, but observant as they should be. She had noticed the weapons they carried. Although intimidating for many people, she had to bring back many a soldier who had too much to drink, or had cracked for one reason or the other. These were the kind of men she had been trained to handle.

The boats glided through the harbor as she studied the lights around her. A life of luxury never impressed her before, but she did, like many people always wonder how people with this kind of wealth lived. Tonight she would see for herself.

She suddenly felt the presence of someone behind her. She didn't have to guess. She turned to see the same intense stare she had come to expect from Matt, assuming that he had used this often to get what he wanted.

He walked beside her and glanced around. "I can agree

the view is much better out here." He glanced above him and studied the stars.

"This is an intriguing life you live." She matched his stare above.

"It's the only life I know."

"So I've heard." He raised his eye brows to reflect the question she presented. "I talked to your aunt for a few minutes earlier. She had some fascinating observations about you."

"I can only imagine."

"I think you know why I came here tonight."

"I think I have a good idea. What is it about this swamp land I purchased that has you so enraged? I think I paid you a fair price for it."

"To you my place might be swamp land, but to me it's my piece of heaven. There will never be another place like it. I've heard how you like to develop land, and I'm not going to let that happen."

"Do you have any notion at all what my plans are?"

"It doesn't matter. I'll get the land back."

Matt acted amused, as if this represented a game to him. To her, this wasn't. He sipped on the champagne as he untied his bowtie and unbuttoned the top buttons to his shirt. "You don't mind if I make myself comfortable, do you?"

"Help yourself. It's your yacht and your party." Suzan waved at the party in full swing inside. She noticed a bodyguard occupying the entrance to the galley inside, perhaps for a reason, as she remembered Matt promising her some private time together. She studied his well-toned body under his shirt. While not a rugged body, he stayed in shape. She quickly imagined the personal trainers that he must be using.

"I've invested a lot of time and money in this project."

She interrupted, as she knew this would come up. "Not my problem."

"Okay, tell me one thing. What makes you think you can talk me into selling this land back to you?"

"I didn't say sell me. I think the sale will be voided."

"Oh really, and why do you think that will happen?"

"My mother said you seduced her."

"I know she's your mother and all, but do you really think I would seduce your mother to make a deal?"

"I think you might be the guy who would do whatever he had to do to make a deal."

"Since you don't know me, how can you judge me?"

"You've accumulated a lot of wealth. I don't think they give away yachts like this."

"I've been very fortunate in my life to become a little successful here and there."

"Listen, my mother knows how important this land is to me, and I don't think she would have sold it without some kind of undue influence from you."

"I do remember your mother, and I found her very remarkable. I even went out of my way to make sure she was taken care of. I gave her the condo she lives in as a bonus for doing business with us. My people helped her to furnish it and–"

"Like I said, you sweet talked her, or according to Mom, you seduced her into selling my land!"

"I'm sorry you see it that way. I'll be glad to sit down with your mother and you and go back over the deal."

"As you may have heard, my mother's in a clinic right now and being evaluated for early onset Alzheimer's."

"No I haven't heard about this." A look of apprehension crossed his face. "If there's anything I can do to help."

"Yes, sell my land back to me."

Matt grinned but remained defiant. "You said sell."

She felt her temper rising. She breathed in deep. "I'll have to talk to an attorney to see what has to be done."

"In the interim, I was thinking of your mother. I hope it works out. I know many advances are being discovered, which is the main reason behind raising the money here."

Suzan couldn't resist. "I'm sure the money raised from this charity will help, but I know you use this gala for business purposes also. I'm not totally stupid."

"Unfortunately, everything in my life involves my business. I've no personal life, even if I wanted one." She watched him stare into the heavens. For a brief moment an opening inside him emerged, a slight crack in the armor of the man who had everything.

She lifted her eyes to study the stars above them. By now the yacht had slipped out into the open water and the lights from the shore diminished enough for them to twinkle overhead. The heavens above reminded her of times when she was younger and had studied them from what used to be her land. In the edge of the Everglades no lights from nearby cities interfered as the stars shined much more brilliant than other places she had visited for the last eight years.

Looking back toward Matt, she realized he had stepped closer to her. She stood her ground, but noticed the guard had moved closer to where they stood. "I think you have guests you need to take care of. I'm sure we'll talk again after I talk to an attorney."

Matt glanced at the party inside. "Can we at least call a truce tonight? I promise you some information on this project you might find fascinating."

"Don't worry. I promised myself that I wouldn't make a scene tonight." Suzan glanced at him one more time, trying to avoid his eyes. "I think you have a girlfriend who might be getting a little jealous of you spending so much time with me."

"Girlfriend?"

"I think her name's Chelsea."

"We spend some time together. Her father is a good business associate of mine and causes our paths to cross often."

"I think I've already seen differently. Enjoy yourself. I think I'll enjoy this for a moment." She allowed her eyes to display her interest, as she studied the stars again.

He glanced above her for a moment. "I guess I can't blame you." He nodded at one of the guards to keep an eye on her and walked back inside, where as expected, Chelsea locked on him immediately. Perhaps Suzan did need some more of the champagne. She stepped inside and moved to the bar on the right, where several glasses filled with champagne shimmered in the lights of the large room. The overhead had thousands of small white lights, making her think of Christmas time and the parties she had attended so many years ago.

A small group of musicians played a slow inviting tune she had heard before, but one she couldn't remember the name of. The men on board looked old enough to be her father or grandfather, but she had no need for a man. She hadn't in years. Funny, with men everywhere around her in the Army, she had become dull to their virile and masculinity as she watched what the war could do to them. As part of the military police, she had seen it all.

She laughed inside for a minute. She assumed some guys thought she might be a lesbian, but that definitely wasn't the case. She had no time for men. Perhaps this is why the CIA had recruited her. She had no real ties, except for her mother, and that relationship had always remained a sore point. She blamed her mother for her father's untimely death. Now, she realized she might have made a large mistake. Her mother needed her now, and she would do what she could to help her. While the future appeared to be one big blur, she needed to think. She needed someone to give her advice–but whom?

Again she recognized the presence of Matt behind her, as she turned and studied the glances of others around her. Suzan knew they had questions about who she was, and she could only imagine the gossip in this group. Chelsea had a glass of champagne in one hand, and holding onto the captain with the other, as he attempted to dance with her. Her drunken movements looked pathetic in a way, with her low cut dress revealing lots of cleavage, and at times her nipples. It was funny how her dad never glanced at her, but stayed busy talking to other older couples in the room.

"I thought you might like a dance." Matt presented an impressive frame.

"Thanks, but I don't dance."

"Is that a can't, or a won't"

"Does it matter?" She had never danced in her entire life. The thought of such tempted her, but lessons, lots of lessons would be needed. The dress made her feel feminine and kind of girly girl, but hell no, not tonight.

"I promise I don't bite."

"That's still debatable. I'm sure you can talk your girlfriend into dancing with you." Suzan pointed to Chelsea staggering in his direction.

"Perhaps, I can talk you into a dance later." He looked bothered. "Please excuse me for a minute."

"Not a problem." She watched him walk over to her and wrap an arm around her to steady her. Suzan studied the looks of amusement on the faces of the guests as Matt helped her walk toward a side door. Although not sure where they were going, she knew they would be gone for a while. Still, this might be a good time to explore the yacht. She felt sure she had a lot more to see.

Suzan glanced at Phil, who was sipping on a glass of champagne, and strolled over to him. "I never did get a chance to explore the ship."

The muscles in his face lightened, offering a hint of surprise. "This would give us a chance to talk. It would be my honor to show you around." He offered her his arm.

For the next hour they toured the ships interior, including the captain's quarters, various galleys, staterooms, and even the engine room. The yacht had a permanent crew of six, and on special occasions the number could double that, she was told. The ship could accommodate about twelve guests comfortably, and had a range long enough to reach Europe easily.

She would love to know how much such a yacht would cost but never asked. Matt Harris had built an empire and amassed a fortune, but she wondered how much of his wealth came at the expense of others, people like her who lost their land to him. As they toured the state rooms, she ventured away from him for a minute as he received a phone call on his cell. A commotion, a giggling sound of a drunken woman echoed down a hallway. She could guess who that might be, but still intrigued, she sneaked along the hallway. Then she saw Matt hauling Chelsea along beside him. She stopped and watched him open a door and help Chelsea fall flat back into the bed.

She felt like a voyeur in a way, but she wondered just how much Matt would take advantage of this situation. Chelsea looked beautiful, big tits, long legs and not to forget the long, blonde hair. Images of him seducing her mother focused in her mind. She could see him taking advantage of her–just like he did to her mother.

Instead, she watched him reach for a blanket and cover her. After offering a light kiss on her forehead, he stood and turned out the lights. She pushed back into the hallway, attempting to hide. She didn't want to be seen watching him. She edged backward until she located another hallway and rushed to the last place she saw Phil. Luckily, he had remained on the phone and smiled at her as she pushed in closer to him.

Phil finished the call as Matt rounded the corner, where his eyes expressed a shock in seeing them.

Phil placed the phone back in his pocket and turned toward Matt. "Hi, I was showing Suzan the Lady."

Matt glanced around. "I hope you like her. Have you seen it all?"

"I think a good bit of it. The yacht is very impressive. He was showing me the state rooms on this level."

"Yes, on longer cruises this is where my guests spend the night." He paused for a moment. "Perhaps you would like to see the master stateroom. I don't show this to many people."

"I don't know, is this your way of seducing me to see your bedroom?"

Phil raised his hands, "I think I'll leave her in your hands, Matt."

Matt laughed. "I can tell you have the wrong impression of me."

"Do I?"

"The invitation is still open." He moved to one side and used his hand to flow in the direction of the hallway.

She decided to venture forward, as he guided her along to a small den. At one end she watched him walk in front of a full length mirrored wall and enter a code into a small hidden keypad that immediately opened a hidden door. The other side amazed her as she walked into a large sitting area, which looked both cozy and comfortable, but opulent. The sumptuous furnishings surpassed anything else on the ship. Magnificent artwork highlighted the room as she attempted to memorize the pieces.

"This is out of this world1" She walked along the walls and admired one piece after another. "You must have hired a fantastic decorator to put this all together for you."

"I'll take your words as a complement, Especially since most of these items I've purchased on my own. Well, some of them are gifts."

Suzan ventured further until she saw the actual bedroom. The super-sized king bed looked like it would accommodate royalty. The gorgeous attention to detail of every item in the room overwhelmed her senses. The training she received from the CIA helped, but still failed her in recording it all. For a long time she allowed her eyes to take in the abundance of wealth. Finally, she allowed her mind to clear, as she turned to find Matt waiting on her, but rather than appearing smug, she watched him tenderly studying her.

"Yes, this is incredible." What could she say? Yes, this was the most fabulous room she could have ever imagined. However, she didn't want to appear to be like some high school kid, or worse, a dumb blonde like he had for a girlfriend. Which made her wonder one thing: why didn't he bring Chelsea in here?

"I'm glad you like it. The private quarters are a good place to escape from the crowds on board and relax."

"I think this isn't the bachelor pad I would have imagined, knowing your reputation. I'm sure you have turned the heads of many girls in here."

"The truth is that I've allowed very few *girls* in here. In fact, you might be the first to ever see it."

"Come on and save it. You don't think I buy such a line, do you?"

"I guess not." He smiled before turning to lower the lights. "Perhaps we should rejoin my guests. I did promise everyone a good time tonight. I also think you'll enjoy something I've planned for everyone."

"What?"

"You'll see."

As he walked along the hallway, he reached back and found her hand and pulled her along. Holding hands with him felt so strange. She didn't need his help. Still, she enjoyed his attention.

The stairways to the top level extended wide enough for him to stand beside her and offer her his arm again. "We're far enough out to sea now so this will be, I hope, very entertaining for everyone."

So far, she had received much more attention from Matt than she thought she would. Not in answers or assurance she would get her land back, but she saw another side to him she didn't anticipate. She could imagine most men taking advantage of a woman drunk out of her mind, but he had acted like a perfect gentleman. And with Chelsea's father on the deck above not concerned in the least, it appears he had learned to trust Matt as well. Strange but intriguing–Suzan knew there had to be much more to the story.

After several hours of drinking champagne, the guests acted much as she had assumed. Their laughter reflected the good time they enjoyed, as many drifted to the outside patio. The weather had cooled and many had added small blankets or towels around their shoulders.

Matt accepted two more glasses of champagne and offered one to Suzan. "I want to thank everyone again and hope you might enjoy something special we've planned tonight. I know some of you might be a little cool, but I think you'll enjoy this." He stopped and pointed to one of the crew members who turned and walked away.

As Matt turned to face her, she focused on his face, the chiseled chin and the bright white teeth as she looked for any flaw. Not on his face, but on his hand she noticed one, a scar slightly above the pinky. There may be a story behind the scar. Oh to live such a sheltered life. The poor baby boy must have hurt himself somehow.

Suddenly she came in contact with his eyes again. He raised his hand so she could receive a better look. "I thought I might like scuba diving until this."

"What happened?"

"A small shark wanted to know what I tasted like."

She laughed, not meaning to, but couldn't control the emotional outburst. "Imagine that–a shark attacking a shark."

"Be nice."

"Don't worry, I'm just teasing you."

As he started to counter her comments, the first boom registered above them. Survival mode kicked in. Were they under attack? She scanned her perimeters. Her heart raced as she saw the burst of fireworks above. This wasn't funny. He should have prepared her for this. The last time she came under fire, fifteen men lost their lives.

"Oh shit, I'm sorry." He moved closer to her and pulled her beside him. She didn't need his comfort, but still the blast had shocked her, making her tremble. As she forced to hide how much the blast had affected her, memories of the attack replayed in her mind. She closed her eyes as she hoped she could end her nightmare. She had taken the life of several people. She would have to live with the memories, even if others wanted to call her a hero. To her, she saw no honor in ending a life.

She breathed easier as the display of lights cascaded above them. He stayed close to her with his arm wrapped around her waist. The warmth felt good while his smell drifted to her–nice, very nice. Nevertheless, she forced her mind back to why she came; even if he played unfair.

Fifteen minutes later the fireworks show ended, and the guests offered a round of applause. A small group of musicians stepped outside and played a sweet romantic tune as the lead singer sang in Italian. Although she couldn't understand the words, his voice resonated so strong and sexy. Matt pulled her to him again as he presented a frame. She stepped forward not knowing what to expect. He would learn soon enough she knew nothing about dancing. He stepped one step to the right and one step to the left. The movements appeared simple enough.

"I thought you said you couldn't dance?"

"I'm not sure I would call this dancing."

"As strange as it sounds this is all there is to dancing."

Well maybe so. It would be a page in her life to remember. "You know this changes nothing. I'm still going to see an attorney next week."

"I would assume nothing less."

Chapter 7

Mr. Dolbert sat at the head of the conference table in his law office, as he scribbled notes on a small pad. "This contract, as you can imagine, was written by one of the top lawyers in New York. They don't make many mistakes."

"Oh, I'm sure they're good at what they do." Suzan anticipated this. What she wanted was a way to fight this. She had read every piece of documentation she found at her mother's place. While the doctor at the clinic didn't allow her much contact with her mother, she knew he soon would. The opinion so far on her state of mind looked bleak.

"The amount of money they offered you appears to be generous. Are you sure you want to try to have this annulled?"

"I'm not interested in the money. My father made me promise on his death bed to keep this land and protect it, and I intend to honor his memory by doing exactly as he asked. In fact, my last tour was to make money to pay off the back taxcs." Yes, she also earned money working for the CIA, but she couldn't mention that connection to anyone.

"As you know, the company you'll be fighting is very large, and has the resources to see this to the end. This battle will be costly."

"I understand, but luckily for me, they provided the funds to fight them with."

"If you spend all of your money fighting this, how do you plan to pay back the money they paid you for the land?"

"That's for you to decide. I hope we can receive damages to cover the cost."

"Okay, if you insist. This is a preliminary assessment, but

here are some points we can consider. The power of attorney you signed for your mother can be contested. It wasn't a specific power of attorney. It could result in a judgment against your mother, and this will also have to be defended."

"I think I understand."

"And the other point is your mother's mental state. If she's ruled incompetent, it opens a whole new can of worms."

"I hate to think of this, but it might explain why she signed the papers. I'm sure she had to know I would never sign papers to sell the land."

"This might take some time, but proving this will be questioned by other experts. And to add to the problem, the case will be presented as to competence at the time she signed the papers, not her current state."

"Yes, and I have one more question?"

"Which is?"

"My mother said he seduced her."

"So, you're thinking undue influence or something else?"

"I would like to know what happened. I know for some reason he purchased her a condo as a bonus."

"Such a gift can be used to support our case."

"So, how do we get started?"

"We need to obtain statements from your mother's doctors, and then file our lawsuit, where we ask for more information from Harris Properties, which we as lawyers call discovery."

"In other words, this could be a long process."

"Yes, I'm afraid so, and I'm sure Harris Properties will take as long as they can, hoping that we give up. As a large corporation, they have time on their side."

"Okay, explain an injunction to me. Can't we make them stop all development on the property until our case is heard in a court of law?"

"I see you've been doing your homework, and yes we can push for this."

"Good. Let me know what you need from me, and I can always hope for the best."

###

Gail Pace, Matt's secretary, walked into his office and handed him an envelope. "I think you'll want to see this."

"What is it?"

"Dan dropped it by a few minutes ago and said he would come back after making a few phone calls." When Matt's attorney, Dan Panella, became involved with something it usually meant problems, but these kinds of problems are why he had him working for Harris Properties. Lawsuits were a part of the territory, especially in the development business.

While another law suit was never welcomed, the name of the plaintiff on this one caught his attention. Wow, that was fast, but she made it clear when they talked she would talk to a lawyer. "I expected Suzan to file suit, but I don't think she has any idea what she's up against. Who is her attorney?"

Gail flipped to the back page and pointed. "I've never heard of him, but I think he must be a local attorney in Florida. That may be what Dan's checking on now."

"I need to study this. Have Dan join me as soon as he can."

Gail left as Matt smiled. Suzan had kept her promise, but he knew she had little chance of winning. Amused, he read through the papers until he stopped when he saw the list of requested material. They wanted all documentation on contact with Mrs. Mercer. Apparently, Suzan never believed he hadn't seduced her mother. This was absolutely ridiculous.

Dan soon walked into his office. "I assume you've been studying the lawsuit."

"Yes, I've started reading through it. What do you think?"

"I don't think it's anything we can't handle over time. The one uncertainty is the Alzheimer's angle. This might be a problem, and it could subject us to not only compensatory damages but additional damages designed to make an example out of us, that is if they are able to show that we either knew or should have known we were dealing with a person with diminished capacity. Since Ann Mercer apparently wasn't receiving treatment at that time and hadn't even been diagnosed, it's going to be very difficult for them to prove their case. However, we're in the position of trying to prove a negative. That's always a challenge. So, what I'm saying is it's going to be hard for either us or them to prove the case, and it will more than likely be decided by the jury. And since this is Florida, with many older citizens sympathetic to this, we might have problems."

"That doesn't sound good."

"I think we have a larger problem. This could delay the project or worse, bring attention to it and have the permits permanently denied by the state of Florida."

"In other words, we need to do some kind of renegotiation."

"I think we need to invite her and her attorney here and work this out without going to trial. We have too much at stake to chance it."

"What about these requests for information?'

"I can stall on it for now. What makes Suzan think you seduced her mother?"

"I'm not sure, but I think her mother may have more

problems than we know. I wanted to be nice to her, and I knew she had no one to look out for her. Her daughter is her only living relative, and we never could reach her."

"I did some checking on Suzan and her service record. She could soon receive the Silver Star for her actions in Afghanistan. It's never good to go against such a hero and expect much. I'm sure Phil will have his hands full on this one."

"Yes, Phil met her and knows what we're working against."

"I'll see what I can do and leave it up to you to consider how to arrange a meeting with Suzan. I hope you can use that silver tongue of yours to work a miracle."

"Find me all of the information you can on her, and I'll have to see if we can arrange a meeting of some kind."

Dan left his office as Matt contemplated his next move. Suzan acted differently, and more so than any woman he had ever met before–much unlike Chelsea. This was the first time any woman had met him head on and treated him as such. Most women idolized him and threw themselves at him. She definitely didn't.

Her dark hair and expressive eyes gave her heritage background a slight mystery. He felt sure this would also be in the report he would have soon. Another point he couldn't understand was the importance of the land to her. He knew the price he paid was more than adequate, perhaps too much.

Tomorrow was Saturday, and a day he looked forward to, as most of the staff would be gone. This would allow him time to study details on his other projects without many interruptions. The cruise a few weeks ago on his yacht made him smile. Although he spent most of the time working and building relationships, especially with Big John, he did manage to enjoy himself. The few moments of dancing with Suzan replayed in his mind. She represented a challenge. Remarkably, he had a hard time getting her out of his mind.

He clicked on the intercom button and waited for Gail to answer. He needed to lay on the charm if he had a chance in talking Suzan into coming to New York. "Gail, see if you can get Suzan on the line for me."

Chapter 8

Suzan worked hard cleaning the condo. She hired someone to repair the damages her mother had created, but based on what her new psychiatrist told her, she left the master bedroom as a special place for her mother to use for her painting. Her mother walked about the condo almost as if in daze. The new medication would take some time to regulate, but the doctor told her it would help eventually.

Suzan felt bad about leaving her mom alone, but knew this might be the best way to cut though all of the legal hassles and receive any chance in having the land returned to her. They must have concerns, or they wouldn't want to have this meeting.

Suzan had located a sitter for her mother for the next few days, since she wasn't sure how long she would be in New York. She had never been to New York, and the thought of a mini-vacation sounded good to her. She had so much life to catch up on.

Suzan led her mother to the kitchen. "I went shopping for you, and the refrigerator is full of food that's easy for you to prepare. The woman staying with you also will help you. That's why she's here."

"I don't know why you're insisting on this. I've lived by myself for a long time."

"Yes, I saw how you were living, but it'll be okay, Mom. The medication they have you on will help."

"It makes me sick and gives me headaches."

"Do you have a headache now?"

"No, I'm fine."

Suzan realized her mother was comprehending her conversation much better than she had earlier. Maybe the medicine was starting to work. "I'm going to be gone for a few days."

"Now where are you going?"

Suzan stopped and stared at her mother. She realized the long battle ahead as she leaned over and hugged her. "Oh Mom, I wish I had known this earlier so we could've gotten you help."

Her mother nodded and glanced around the condo. "This is a nice place, isn't it?"

"Yes, Mom this is a good place." Suzan would have loved to be back in the house she grew up in, but perhaps this was a better place for her. She at least had neighbors close by. "Mom, I'm going to New York in a few hours. A friend will be staying with you, okay?"

"Okay. I went to New York about a year ago."

Her Mom went to New York? "When did you go there?"

"I went to see the guy who purchased this condo for me."

"You went to New York to see Matt?"

"Yes, he's one good looking guy."

Suzan needed to focus as her mother talked. "Mom, tell me about your trip?"

"He sent his private jet to fly me from Florida, and then he booked me in a great hotel room in York. Yes, he showed me the time of my life."

Hoping her mind would clear enough to obtain some answers, Suzan pushed on. "You knew I didn't want to sell the land. Why did you sign the papers?"

A look of fear crept across her mother's face as her body started to tremble. "You're not mad at me, are you?"

Suzan tighten her jaw, she had pushed too much too fast. "Mom, please concentrate for a moment. I need you to tell me something."

Her mother's voice became hysterical. "I'm so sorry. He told me I was doing the right thing. He seduced me into signing the papers."

"Mom, listen to me, you've said this several times. You need to tell me what you mean."

Her mother straightened her back and raised her head. "I can't talk about this with my daughter!"

"Mom. Please!"

Tears formed in her mother's eyes. "I miss my husband. He was such a lovely man."

The comments hit Suzan hard. She missed her father much more than she ever admitted. While she had blamed her mother for his death, she knew now her condition may have been why she didn't help him more. Her mother needed her and she would have to help her. She didn't want to lose her also. They had a lot of catching up to do.

After a wild stare into nowhere registered on her mother's pale face, Suzan hoped that she might obtain some answers, but she would have to take it slower next time. She remembered the words of the doctor who insisted she needed to keep her mother calm. "Mom, it's going to be okay. I'm going to reacquire my land and I'll take care of you." While her mother couldn't give her the answers she wanted, she knew Matt could. What happened in New York when her mother went to see Matt?

Soon the sitter knocked on the door and Suzan went over the list she had prepared for her. She smiled, knowing the sitter had worked with other elderly patients in the past. After checking her watch, she knew her ride to the airport would arrive soon. "Mom, I need to leave in a few minutes. Call me if you need anything."

"Go on and have a good time."

Shortly afterward, the driver picked her up and whisked her off to the airport. She tried to hide her excitement, but flying on a private jet to New York sent visions of a lifestyle she knew might happen only once in a life time. The driver soon pulled to the side of the jet, a small lean Lear, sparkling white with the HP icon on the side for Harris Properties.

One tall male attendant hustled to the car to retrieve her luggage. "Hello, Ms. Mercer, we're glad you'll be flying with us today."

"Thanks."

Suzan climbed the stairs and saw two men at the top. She assumed the first one to be the pilot who politely smiled and welcomed her aboard. The other man, more of a professional businessman, reached out his hand to her. "Hi, I'm your official welcoming party from Harris Properties. I'm Tony Korth, the vice president in charge of operations."

"Thanks, I'm Suzan." She wondered what his job involved, but assumed Matt sent him to soften her up for later. Suzan studied Tony as she followed him into the cabin which accommodated six people. The seats looked large and comfortable with four facing each other and two more behind them. Tony appeared to have a sexy Italian heritage and in excellent shape, almost like a body builder. The suit that fit him perfectly had to be tailored. He wore expensive looking gold jewelry that was wrapped around his wrist and his fingers.

"I came earlier today to visit the land in question. It looks much different up close."

"If I knew you wanted to see it at eye level I would've been glad to give you a tour of what I'm sure you plan to destroy."

"Well, I hope to add to its beauty rather than destroy it. I've made plans to fly over it before we leave. I thought you might like this."

"I've seen it from the air before."

"I'm sure you have, but I would like to ask you some

questions, if that's okay."

She didn't want to help him in any way, but seeing the land from the air again would be nice. "I would like to see the land again from the air, but as you probably know, I plan on having the land returned to me."

"I've heard. I was also told not to argue with you. I'm simply an employee doing what I'm told to do. You need to buckle up since we'll be airborne in a minute. However, if you need something to drink we have a full bar available."

It might not be lady-like, but a beer right now sounded good. "What do you have?"

The flight attendant stepped forward. "You name it and I can make it for you." He opened a cabinet which was filled with miniatures of everything she could imagine but beer.

Since it might be a long flight and to control her temper while talking to Tony, she glanced over the selection. Johnny Walker Red captured her attention as she pointed to the bottle. "Over ice would be great."

Tony looked happy as he turned to the attendant. "I think I'll have the same."

Suzan nodded in appreciation, and felt glad to not be drinking alone. "So tell me, Tony, what do you do for Matt?"

"Let me say my job is to take Matt's dreams and ideas for a piece of property and make them come true. All construction operations are under me. After it's completed another member of the team takes over."

An instant dislike of his work and what damage he must have caused to the environment stabbed her deep inside her soul. She forced herself to remain calm. "And you enjoy what you do to the earth?"

"How much do you know about Harris Properties?"

"I know they're one of the largest developers in the

world."

"Have you ever seen any of our properties?"

She glanced upward as she envisioned photos of their properties she had seen in some magazines, and of course on the internet where she did most of her research. "I've seen some photos, but I've never been on site with any of them."

"I thought so. We have a reputation for being very environmentally friendly." He motioned toward the attendant. "Tell the captain to also make a pass over the Ft. Myers property by the golden triangle before we leave. I think it would good for Ms. Mercer to see it from the air."

"Yes, sir." He walked to the front to relay the message to the captain.

"If you think you can change my mind, you have another thing coming."

"My job isn't to change your mind, but to give you some food for thought. How is the drink?" She hadn't tasted it yet, but decided to be a polite guest and reached over to tap her glass with his before taking a sip. It burned as it went down– perfect.

Shortly, the jet roared down the runway and banked hard to the right. "We'll stay low for a while so we can see the land better. I'm sure you'll recognize everything better than me. I'm sorry, but the Lear moves fast and we'll be over it very quickly."

Suzan glanced out of the window and remembered the scenery from taking off from this airport many times in the past. Soon they flew high enough to see the vast Everglades, consisting of miles and miles of nothing man made. As they circled and neared the edge of the swamp she pointed to her land. She studied a few clumps of land, or small islands, and one small road wandering along a ridge. She couldn't see her old home place from the air, but she knew where it was.

"I know it doesn't look like much from here, but it's serene and pristine land which is still private, and not part of the national park."

"I drove around some of it this morning. This project will be a challenge."

"What do you plan to do with it?"

"Honestly, I've many plans on the drawing board. Matt wanted me to wait until he meets with you to show you. I think you'll be impressed."

"I doubt it." She leaned closer to the window to study, to force her mind to memorize every detail. Nothing much had changed since the last time she saw it. That is, until now.

The jet banked and headed west. "We'll soon be over one of our developments. We had a project where we built three buildings on land many people thought would be impossible."

This must be a new project since she couldn't remember anything with the Harris Properties logo on it.

In minutes she watched Tony point to their right. "Those three tall building are ours."

The three buildings that he pointed to were on separate islands and had a small road extending to each. Each one sported boats anchored on every side. "We built those three islands out of the swamp around them, and we dug it deep enough for the boats to make it out to the gulf. We sold these units to families who love the gulf and also enjoy exploring the area."

"Yes, with this number of boats the Everglades will never have a chance to survive."

"These boats are too large to explore the everglades. Something you should know is that the people who buy these condos have a love for the swamp, perhaps as much as you do. I think you would love to see the bylaws they have to agree to."

A slight relief flowed over her, but questions remained. Yes, she would love to see those bylaws. "Is this what you have in store for my property?"

"I'm sure Matt will explain everything to you."

She knew she wouldn't squeeze any answers from Tony, but at least now she had an image of what they had planned for her. She wasn't buying it.

Chapter 9

A limo picked them up at the airport and delivered them to the center of Manhattan, where Tony helped her out of her door. "I think you'll like the home office here. I'll see to it your luggage is taken to your room. Is there anything personal you need to take with you?"

"No, I have everything I need with me for today." She studied the area and the sign indicating Fifth Avenue.

A man approached them she recognized. "Hello, Phil. I assumed I'd see you today."

"Yes, how are you? Matt is in a meeting, but he wanted me to personally make sure you're well taken care of."

Tony yelled over the city traffic at Phil, "She's all yours now. I'll be back later."

Phil nodded and offered his arm. "I think you'll enjoy New York while you're here. Have you ever been to New York before?"

"No, this is the first time, and I hope I have some time to explore it while I'm here."

"Matt has arranged for you to have a good time, but if there's anything you want to see I'm sure we can work it out." They walked through the main door and toward a private elevator with a guard standing by the entrance who smiled as they stepped in.

As the elevator raced upward, Suzan glanced at the floor counter indicating that the top floor was eighty two floors up. Her ears popped as they slowed upon arriving. She tapped her ears to relieve the pressure.

"Getting used to your ears popping is something you learn to live with in New York. We own this building, and the executive offices for Harris Properties are on this floor."

Stepping from the elevator, she walked into a world of wealth and power she thought only Hollywood could conjure up. The highly polished floors reflected expensive chandeliers above them, while intricate artwork adorned the walls. He walked next to her and held her arm. "It only gets better," he said proudly.

Walking through a glass door on one side they passed several elaborate offices which surpassed any sense of reality as she tried to hide her shock and awesome misbelieve in how anyone could work in such an office. Approaching the corner of the building, she sensed Matt's office. She breathed in deeply as they entered.

His office stretched perhaps forty feet by forty feet, with a spectacular conference room on one side. Matt had a phone to his ear, but offered a smile. Phil helped her to a chair in front of Matt. "I'm sure he'll only be a minute. It's good to see you again."

"Yes, and thanks for escorting me to his office."

As he studied her, she allowed her eyes to scan the room. Holy crap, this looked absolutely beautiful. This guy must be living in such a sea of wealth beyond what she could comprehend. She imagined kings or dictators in foreign lands living like this. Should she try to be unimpressed? What could she say?

The conversation soon ended as he replaced the phone. "I'm so glad you decided to come see me."

"Let's say you made me an offer I couldn't refuse."

He smiled at the reference to the Godfather movie. "I think you still have an image of me as an evil conspirator. I hope this trip gives me the chance to change that."

"I assume you received the papers on the lawsuit."

"Yes, my vice-president of legal affairs, Dan Panella,

mentioned it to me. I think you met him already. However, I think it would be good to visit him soon. You might be interested in seeing his department."

"Well, you did ask for this meeting."

"Yes, I did. I wanted to find out more about you and why you wanted the land back."

Suzan read an interest in his knowing her side of the story that she didn't expect. She realized her legal assault on him might not, but that she might be able to reach her goals with a little sugar rather than vinegar. Since she assumed he might be playing a game, she decided to play along. "This land has a value to me I think you might not be able to comprehend."

A small insult registered on his face. He shifted his eyes away from her and reached for a notepad. "Well, I guess we'll never know if you don't try, will we?"

He had a point. "This land was given to me by my father, and on his death bed." She hoped this short explanation would make her interest simple enough. The other reasons she would disclose soon enough.

"So, it's a sentimental reason rather than a financial one."

"As I'm sure you know . . . I knew nothing of this sale until arriving back in the States."

"The sale closed over a year ago. I assumed your mother had contacted you and you had given your approval. Direct contact with you was impossible. Trust me on this point. I know we tried."

The last year she had worked for a joint force with the CIA. This she could never divulge, but knew they kept any information from going to her. It would have been dangerous to do so. Flashbacks of her time on the streets posing as an Afghanistan woman filled her with mixed emotions. The danger excited her and the thoughts of accomplishment swelled in her chest, even if only a handful of people knew what she had accomplished.

"Are you okay?" Matt leaned forward and examined her.

"Yes, I had some . . . flashbacks from my time in the service." She adjusted her seat and forced herself to focus on the task at hand. "Perhaps, you should've tried harder."

"We did have the power of attorney you signed for your mother."

"Oh yes, and I've many questions about this. You know my mother has some mental conditions now, and she is being treated for them. She also says you seduced her."

"I can assure you I never *seduced* your mother. It's scandalous to me why she thinks so."

"I'm sure you would hate for it to be known. I understand my attorney asked for more information on what happened between you and my mother."

"Being a legal question, I'm sure the legal department will handle the lawsuit. I know you have no reason to trust me, so all I can offer at this point is my word."

Matt played with a pen for a minute before focusing his eyes on her again, their bright-green color had intensified since the last time she had studied them. Still, she sensed an openness to him she couldn't understand fully, almost as if this was new to him and he was testing his ability to understand her. "Trust is something I've learned comes from experience. In the Army I knew who to trust, but trust came from knowing them. I don't know you, and I can only base what I do on what I've read."

"That makes sense to me, and this is really the one reason I wanted you to come here. I think I can convince you we're not the enemy if you'll give me a chance. First, I want to give you a quick tour of the office here, and then I want to introduce you to others who have done business with us.

You can feel free to ask any questions you wish."

"This is all good to know, but I'm here with one intention. I want my land back."

"I'll make a deal with you. Allow me to show you my operation and I'll agree to listen to all arguments you have. I'll keep an open mind if you agree to do the same."

He offered her a challenge, one she knew he planned to win, but one she would take. "And if I accept and I win, you'll return the land to me?"

"I own this company, well at least most of the stock, and the decision will be mine. Remember, you need to be very convincing, since I don't give in easily. I'm being honest."

She realized by playing along she might receive more access to information she needed. In particular, she might find out what happened between him and her mother. She might also be able to spot any weakness in his defense. Being introduced to others who conducted business with him might prove to be fruitful, but she expected them to be handpicked. "Okay, for now I'm willing to play along. As long as you know I intend to have my land after all of this."

"Fair enough. The tour will start now if you're ready."

Suzan smiled and tossed her hair sideways. "About as ready as I'll ever be."

Matt stood and walked next to her. While passing by Gail's office, he stopped for a minute. "I'm going to be giving a personal tour. I think you can handle everything on your own."

"Yes, but do remember we have the Group from Italy meeting with you in about two hours."

"I understand. Two hours will give me plenty of time to show her around and enjoy some lunch."

Gail smiled as they turned and left. For the next hour they stopped by and said hello to his inner circle of Dan

Panella, his chief attorney or legal vice-president as he referred to him. She soon learned he had a small army of attorneys on the floor below working for him. With their vast holdings, she learned how they handled all contracts on development, financial arrangements, government filing, zoning issues, and, of course, lawsuits. Her lone attorney back in Ft. Myers would have his hands full. As if to add to the display, she heard how they had many law firms on retainer to do most of their grunt work.

Next, she visited Tony Korth, who she had been with earlier. His army consisted of construction engineers and architects two floors below them. Although still well appointed, they presented a different look, as they had papers and drawings everywhere. This had to be the heartbeat of the operation. Instead of seeing Italian tailored suits, she saw jeans and rolled up sleeves.

Suzan visited Ronald Sirani's office next, who was the vice-president of finance. She remembered seeing him once, but she had never talked to him before. His job of keeping the money flowing and accounted for included the accounting department below them. The only comment she remembered being passed to Matt concerned Big John and his daughter, which she tried to overhear but couldn't fully. She had met Big John on the cruise. His drunken daughter suddenly made her smile, as she realized Matt had a doozy of a girlfriend. Well, he at least acted like a gentleman in putting her to bed. Of course, the night on the cruise might be a onetime thing. She could imagine him taking advantage of the situation at other times.

Phil Ector was the last major office she entered before seeing the lower floors. His walls included, as she would expect, photos of many celebrities and governmental officials from all over the world. His mannerisms remained as smooth as silk. After talking to Phil, she recognized the click between the men. She assumed all of them remained single. They all acted like dominating alpha males in their own right. Somehow, Matt had enticed them into joining him at Harris Properties.

An hour later, they returned to the top floor and entered the executive dining room, where she studied the continental setting with deep blue colored tablecloths matching the coordinated colors of the furnishings. Several waiters or staff floated around five large tables. As she reached one table that Matt directed her to, he pulled out a chair.

She studied the exquisite two plate setting until a chef walked over to greet them. "We can offer you much of what you might like. Is there anything in particular you like?"

Suzan saw no menu and realized with a private chef there was no need for one. Still she hesitated until Matt spoke. "I try to stay healthy and love fish. Perhaps, you would like what I'm having."

"Fish sounds good."

They enjoyed a meal she knew she would never experience again. That realization quickly helped to develop a defensive stance she forced upon herself. She wouldn't let him get to her. She tried to act unimpressed and as if this was nothing special.

"Well, how did you like lunch?

Her manners overrode her resistance as she turned to him. "I think this is one of the best meals I've had in a long time."

His smile looked genuine as he turned to the chef. "Thank you for a great meal."

The chef bowed and turned to leave. "It must be great to have your own personal chef."

"Yes, and this makes meetings much easier to contain.

I've had so many go sideways because of uncontrolled circumstances. It also makes sense to save time. Many restaurants in New York will take half of the day in serving you."

Although she saw a laidback attitude today, she assumed many days turned out much different. It would be fascinating to see him in action later today when he met with his Italian group.

Almost as if he could read her mind he tossed his napkin on the table. "I have a meeting today which cannot be avoided. I'm so sorry. However, I know many women love to shop, and I've made arrangements for you this afternoon to see the best in the latest designs. I hope you allow me to, at least make a good impression on you. As I mentioned to you, I want you to meet some other people I've done business with, and as such I want you to attend a cocktail party later tonight. I'll assure you I'll leave you in very good hands. I'll pick you up around seven, and I hope you have a great day."

"I don't think you need to buy me anything. One could consider it a bribe, you know?"

Matt reached for her hand and raised it to his lips. "If I decide to bribe you, I promise I'll be much more direct." His eyes turned to a bright green, a crystal clear color displaying feelings of trust she had experienced few times in her life. She refocused as he raised her hand to kiss it again. Instead of feeling like his action was staged, she allowed her guard to lower. No one had ever kissed her hand before. She had never allowed a guy this close to her, especially to lock in eye contact with her. Her CIA training kicked in as she examined the size of his iris. He appeared to be telling the truth and interested in what he saw.

The silence extended to an awkward stage, she had to say

something. "I . . . do know you have a meeting today, and I do want to see New York. So, I'll go shopping, but I will be ready in time to see some of your clients tonight. I hope you know that I'll be asking questions."

"I fully expect that you would."

She had money now, and she didn't intend for him to buy her anything. However, the time alone would give her an opportunity to regroup and be prepared for the party tonight.

100

Chapter 10

The afternoon became one hell of a day to remember. She always suspected the super rich did things differently, now she knew. Shopping was not in a shop. The best of the stores come to you. Her escort directed her five floors below, where Matt owned his own personal condo. He occupied the entire floor. The room she entered naturally looked out of this world. Something was up. She felt smart enough to know he didn't do this for many people.

A personal concierge arrived moments after she adjusted into her room. She directed Suzan to a private room, where her and her assistants obtained measurements and asked many questions about what she liked. Visions of Julia Roberts in the movie Pretty Woman invaded her thoughts. They made objecting to the treatment impossible. Okay, so he had the money, why not see what this felt like. She would write him a check for whatever she purchased later.

As she studied many of the dresses they presented her with, which came presented on a model no less, she tried to hide her emotions. When she hadn't chosen a dress, the lady in charge, a Ms. Edgeworth, yelled at the woman ushering in the models, "You're going to have to hurry. We only have so much time before she has to start getting ready."

Glancing at her watch, she estimated she had three hours. Nevertheless, the shopping ended, with several dresses fitted on her with a seamstress making minor adjustments. "I didn't say I was buying anything."

"Matt has an account with us so don't worry, it's all taken care of."

Still she wanted to know. "How much are these dresses

anyway?"

The woman started to evade the question but saw Suzan would cause problems if not told. "It varies. The one you're wearing cost twelve thousand."

Twelve thousand for a dress! Sorry, too much. "I . . . don't think I need this dress at such a price."

"Like I said, it's all taken care of."

"I'll talk to Matt about this later."

Ms. Edgeworth pouted, but continued to direct those around her. "Please bring out all of the models one last time, and let us show them our appreciation."

The models returned and wore the best of what she saw. As she studied the dresses, she caught Ms. Edgeworth studying her. "I still didn't say I wanted any of these."

"I know, but now we have to work fast. Based on the one I think you like best and knowing where you're going tonight, I think I know what you might like. If you don't, I'm sure the stylist will accommodate you."

Suzan had submitted herself to this torture once a few weeks ago. Doesn't she have any say so in this? But then again, she enjoyed the girly girl feel. After eight years in Afghanistan, perhaps she did owe herself as she gave in.

As Matt checked over the meeting room to ensure all was in order, Phil examined a list and pointed to the name tags. "I know some of these names are hard to pronounce. Which one do I need to help you with?"

"I think I know them well enough, and we have a translator available for any problems that might arise. I think most, if not all the people in the group speak good English." Matt remembered meeting several of them.

"Yes, but don't be surprised if they speak in Italian amongst themselves. I know you're excited about this project in Milano."

Matt glanced at his watch and hoped the meeting would start on time. He didn't want to be late for the party tonight.

Phil noticed him watching the time. "This meeting should go smooth and might not last long at all. They feel like they need to have a meeting to settle last minute details, but we all know it's a done deal. It's later tonight and the next few days which are very important to us. Suzan is sitting on a powder keg, and she doesn't even know it."

"I think I have the situation under control. She'll meet some good friends of mine tonight who'll give us raving reviews." He quickly hid some private thoughts. "I think she'll be impressed with our other projects, and it would be good for me to visit these sites anyway." While most women he knew never confronted him, his name and position meant apparently nothing to Suzan. She had a goal and made no excuses for it. He knew she would never succeed, but admired her efforts.

"I've hired several photographers to take photos of you having a good time together. This will go a long way in preventing any fall-out if this does go to court."

"You don't think that'll happen, do you?"

"My job is to be prepared for any contingencies. Suzan is a fascinating woman. I don't think any of us have ever met anyone like her."

"That I'll agree with." Matt remembered her crashing into his place the first time he saw her. His bodyguards still talked about her, as he remembered how the one with a broken knee cap would be able to return in about a month. Although not nearly as effective as before, he felt obligated to keep him on the payroll and somewhat responsible for his injuries.

The transformation into the lady he had met at the gala

shocked him. She had a rough edge to her, but appeared to be honest, and so damn unpretentious. The fake fronts put on by so many others attempting to impress him forced him to laugh inside so many times earlier.

"I have already checked to make sure Chelsea was out of town tonight. I know you would hate for her to show up." Chelsea thought they had a relationship, yes, but Matt knew the farce existed for public relations and nothing else. Her father, Big John, never paid any attention to the press. He loved his daughter, but he had to be embarrassed by her frolics. They acted so different in every aspect of their life.

Tonight would be relaxing, and it felt good to be thinking of something other than pure business. He discovered himself wanting to know more about her. "Do you have a file on Suzan I can study again before tonight?"

Phil lifted an eyebrow. "Do I detect an interest more than business?"

Matt grinned. "Let's say some interest, but more curiosity than anything."

"In this city, I think she'll find herself totally lost. I hope you remember who she is, which for now is the plaintiff in a major lawsuit against us."

"I understand." Yes he did, but he still looked forward to the night and seeing her.

Suzan accepted a glass of champagne as she scanned the room, hoping to find anyone she recognized, as if she would. Although this was New York, these people all had a look of wealth, and perhaps well known celebrities might be in the mix. While she knew Matt planned to introduce her to many of them, she had already noticed the side glances from many of the women, apparently intrigued by who Matt had on his arm tonight.

A tall slim couple walked over as Matt stopped in the center of the room. Matt introduced them and about two dozen other people within a few minutes. Since remembering names would be impossible, she wasn't even going to try. She walked to one side, hoping she could maintain her balance on yet another set of high heels. A man with a sadistic mind must have designed them.

Matt leaned closer. "I know it'll be impossible to remember everyone's name tonight so don't worry about it, and if you see anyone you have questions about, let me know, okay?"

"Are all of these people owners in this building?"

"Yes, almost all of them. They enjoy an event like this about once a month to make use of this club room. Many of them are executives from Wall Street, but some are from old money."

"I can see where you could fit right in here. Tell me one thing. If you're so successful here, why do you want my land in Florida?"

"I'm glad you ask, and I'll show exactly what's on my mind in a few days."

"A few days, just how long are you planning on keeping me in New York on your chain?"

"I assure you there's no chain. The pilot who brought you here can take you home any time you want. However, I do have some developments I want you to see. Then, I think you'll be more receptive to what's on my mind."

A short bald man joined them and winked at Matt. "Is this someone interested in moving in here?"

"No, this is . . . this is Suzan. She's visiting me from Florida and allowing me to show her around New York."

Suzan wondered how he planned to introduce her. She was definitely not a girlfriend, not a mistress. She was the girl suing him. Yes, she could make remarkable conversation here if she wanted to. "It's nice meeting you. Are you one of the owners here?"

"Oh yes, and I love our place. Matt's one of the best developers in the world, and I would never consider living anywhere else."

Okay, so he had some friends, but she would expect such. These people could afford the best, and if they made a mistake they could afford to take the loss. Their comments changed nothing about how Matt had taken her land without her consent. Still, she glanced around the cozy yet friendly room.

An hour and several brief conversations later, Matt moved closer to her. The scent of his cologne smelled nice, and since she didn't know anyone else it made her feel good to have him beside her. She eventually felt out of place after a while and hoped this would be over soon. She was so thankful when he finally announced, "I think it's time for us to move on, I've several places I want to take you to tonight, if you're interested."

"Yes, I think I've had all of this I want tonight, and I could use some fresh air."

"In such a case I know the perfect place and something I haven't seen in a very long time."

###

True to his word, his limo soon reached the edge of Central Park. With his two bodyguards close by, he ushered her to a horse and carriage. While she had heard of this before many times, it surprised her that he would be interested in such. The fresh air cleared her head as she worked on fighting off the champagne consumed earlier. "These are good looking horses."

"Yes, they generally take good care of them, and if not,

I'm sure they'll receive lots of complaints. I haven't taken a ride on one of these in a long time. The thoughts of getting some fresh air made me think of this. I hope you don't mind."

"Do you do things on impulse often?"

"Next to never. However, lately I've been thinking I need to." He offered his hand to help her climb aboard.

Suzan watched the guards move to the back of the carriage, hoping for a place to hang on. She could see them running along behind for miles. She had heard how large the park was. While a six mile run in both directions would test most men, it generally offered a warm up exercise for her. She had to stay in shape as she had no clue what her future plans entailed. She had pushed options aside for days, knowing the CIA would contact her soon, especially since she had been successful on her last mission.

The back seat relaxed her as she rested next to Matt. The presence of a man next to her felt weird–yet exciting. Okay, she had to admit she loved his manly presence. As the air whipped around them with a clean smell coming from the park, she could detect the odors of the city. The cologne Matt wore also did a great job to cloak the night in this strange enchantment.

Matt leaned forward to talk to the driver. "I'm not sure where you're scheduled to go, but I would love to see a few things and show my guest."

"Mr. Harris, you name the place and I'll take you. This is an honor for me."

Wow, even the carriage drivers in New York know Matt, or at least his reputation.

Matt glanced around. "I hope we can keep this a little quiet and lose the main crowds, but I'd love for her to see the Wollman Rink, the Pond, of course, and perhaps the

Carousel." He turned toward Suzan. I think you would also enjoy seeing the Dakota, you know where the former Beatle, John Lennon, lived."

"Those are some of the most common places. Mr. Harris, with your permission, I think I know a few extra places to add to your night."

"In such a case, I'll let you take care of the driving. You don't happen to have any good champagne in here do you?"

"No sir, but I can have some delivered to me in about five minutes."

"That will be great."

Suzan glanced at him and couldn't picture him as an alcoholic, but he seemed to love champagne. The carriage moved forward as she glanced upward at the tall building on her left. Living here would definitely take some adjusting. She knew most people in New York didn't live like this, and she had heard how expensive living here was.

With Matt lowering his defenses, she decided this would be a good time to ask questions and find out more about him. "If I lived here, I think I would enjoy such a ride often. So . . . tell me what is it you like to do when you don't steal land to develop?"

"Be nice now." His smile indicated he enjoyed the teasing, but that he knew she intended to accomplish her goal and never waiver in her efforts.

"I don't think anyone has asked me to be nice in a long time."

"Oh yes, for the last eight years I understand you've had a very different life. Tell me, and I'm very curious, how is life for a woman serving in the Army?"

"I'm not sure it was so much different for me as it was for the men. We all had a job to do."

"I'm sure many people do their time and come home, but

I understand you did two tours in Afghanistan."

"I wanted to build up some funds to take care of my property when I returned, and I think we both know what happened while I was gone."

"Oh, I think I might see more why the land had become so important to you. Why didn't your mother know all of this?"

He was getting personal, something she was supposed to be doing. While playing along might obtain his trust, she studied her words carefully before she decided to answer. "My mother and I haven't been on the best of terms for a long time. I think she allowed my father to die. She should have been there for him. Cancer can be treated. He didn't have to stay at home and die without giving it a fight." She tried to control the anger in her voice, but knew she failed. She didn't need to make another mistake.

"I can see that you've faced some issues since you've returned. They must've kept you in the dark when you served in the Army."

"We had little contact with the outside world. As you could imagine, we had to stay focused."

"I've watched you in action. Since your martial art skills are impressive, I surely don't want to make you mad."

"Oh you have, but I do know how to control it, and also when to release it as needed." It was time to shift gears. She decided to ask him questions. "Okay, enough about me. I want to know more about you. What does a guy who has it all and can do anything he wants to do–do?"

"You're seeing a rare side of me. I work, and then I work some more. There's nothing I do that's not work related. Phil makes sure every part of my life is used for public relations."

"Even tonight?"

"I hope this will be an exception, but Phil works like me and appears to never sleep."

"Don't you get tired of working all of the time?"

"This is my life and I know nothing else." He laughed softly.

"That's such a shame and makes me feel sorry for you."

"I appreciate your concern, but I enjoy my life."

She couldn't help teasing him. "You know they say ignorance is bliss."

"So, are you telling me I have no idea on how to have a good time?" He shifted in her direction and focused his eyes on her face. His skin looked flawless, and she knew money did offer certain advantages in maintaining the perfect look. In his case she could see such being very important.

"Okay, tell me what you do for fun. Something not involving business, the use of your fortune, or people you have on strings."

She watched him pause as he searched for words. "Let me see, I went skiing in Vail last year."

She stopped him. "That doesn't count."

"Why?"

"I suspect it was all for publicity. Even without guessing, I would say you have a project or property interest in Colorado."

"Yes, but skiing was fun. Perhaps we should try it together one day." His smile failed to hide a layer of seduction, as he pointed to some of the buildings along the park. "I have an interest in a few of these, and I haven't been inside for over ten years."

"I'm sure you must've been asked this before, but maybe the question needs to be asked again: when is enough–enough?"

"Unless you've been in my position before it would be

hard to understand. It has never been about what I have, it's all about what I can accomplish."

"So, there can never be enough, even if it means totally missing out on life itself. By the way, what about your girlfriend? How does she like you taking girls on moonlight strolls around Central Park?"

"I don't have a girlfriend, and I've never been married. I assume you must be referring to Chelsea."

"When I see a girl hanging all over a guy, it's kind of like the saying where there's smoke, there is usually fire there somewhere."

Matt raised his arm and for the first time placed it around her shoulders. "I have many occasions when I need someone to accompany me to an event, an opening, a dinner. I'm sure you know what I mean."

"So, she's kind of a girlfriend of convenience for you."

"I never looked at the relationship like that, but it works out nicely. She enjoys the spotlight, and I can avoid any entanglements."

"Are you suggesting you two have never . . . ." Yes, she let the question drag on purpose, as she studied his reaction which he handled coolly.

"I'm sure there are some questions you understand I'll claim the fifth on, and I'm sure you would do the same."

The carriage stopped on the side of the street as a cab pulled beside them. The two bodyguards sprang into action, only to see the cab driver walk around and hand the carriage driver a small box. The biggest bodyguard handed the cab driver some money as he glanced over at Matt.

The carriage driver smiled. "Here, I think this is what you wanted."

"Oh yes, champagne. Thanks!"

The driver, a lanky man with a slight Russian accent,

grinned and waited for them to open the bottle. "I hope you like it, I asked for the best he could find on a moment's notice!"

"You did fantastic. I think it's time to drive through the park some. With my bodyguards along, I think we'll be safe enough."

"Yes, sir. You know, the limo following us will make us a target."

"We'll only go through once, but I want her to see the Pond, and with my men on foot we will be well protected."

The driver turned to yell at the horse, which trotted on.

The pop of the champagne added the perfect festive mood to the ride. If he planned to seduce her to make her forget her mission, he was doing a great job. She had to focus on her mission. And her mission was to find out more about him, something he had hidden very well so far. Perhaps the champagne would help.

"From what I can tell, you like champagne and it must be your preferred drink."

"I don't drink much, but when I do I think it is to celebrate. How about you?"

"I rarely drink much either. For the last eight years drinking anything was hard because of where I was stationed, but I do have a question. Exactly what are we celebrating?"

The question seemed to catch Matt off guard. "I think any time I can leave work and relax a minute would be time to celebrate, and I do love this park, where I played often when I was younger."

Matt poured the champagne and prepared to toast as Suzan moved first to raise her glass slightly higher than his."I know you're trying to persuade me into your way of thinking and all, but for tonight I think we might enjoy a few moments together.”

Matt pulled her closer to him. “I think I can agree to a time out and a little relaxation. Are you cold?”

“No, I’m fine. I’m still curious why you’re spending time with me. I can’t see you doing this with everyone you conduct business with.”

Matt laughed as he turned toward her. “That would be an understatement. I have such an effective team around me, I rarely see many people other than them. You could almost say I live in a very tight cocoon.”

“Okay, I buy what you’re saying, well maybe a little. That is, if you’ll tell me what you would really like to do with your time.”

Matt didn’t appear to hesitate with one answer. “Go somewhere no one recognizes me, and I can see what it’s like to relax and do nothing.”

“Relaxing cannot be too hard. I’m sure with your money you could arrange fantastic trips.”

“Perhaps, but it would be forced and still not natural. I think one reason I’m curious about you is because you’re so different from other woman I know.”

“I’m not sure if I should take your comments as a compliment or as an insult.”

Matt smiled and lifted his glass. “It was meant as neither, but simply an observation. In the business world I do see many strong business women, but not so secure in their self as I see you.” Matt reached for her hand and gave it a small squeeze. The connection felt nice, but the fact he continued to hold her hand intrigued her. He might be holding her hand, but he managed to massage her heart in the process.

Suzan studied the lights from the post and in the trees. This mystical location could be a fantastic place for a *couple in love* to explore, but with Matt this seemed so out of place.

Still, she didn't pull her hand away from him. He acted like a gentleman much more than she had anticipated, and so far he had made no moves out of character.

"We'll be next to the Pond in a few minutes. I haven't seen it at night in a very long time. I think you'll enjoy this."

After one turn she saw what he meant. The lights and the serene feeling hid the fact she was in New York City. While the traffic was almost nonexistent, she knew this was from the reputation the park had at night. The danger didn't appear to bother Matt, but of course he had two bodyguards with him that she assumed to be well armed.

Matt yelled at the drive, "Stop here for a minute, I think I'd love to walk around for a minute."

"Are you sure about that, sir? It's best to keep moving."

"Yes, we have the limo behind us." Suzan watched the carriage come to a stop and Matt move to one side to exit. He extended his hand to help her. Although it was still hard to get accustomed to, she accepted his hand anyway. A pleasant surprise greeted her as she looked above and saw an almost full moon. Again, she thought how this was the wrong time and the wrong guy. Life had a way of taunting her and definitely had a sense of humor.

Matt squeezed her hand and pulled her beside him. "I remember sailing boats here when I was a small boy."

"Since this place is minutes from your office and where you live, why don't you come here more often?"

"You've asked a good question and one I've no answer for." He tightened his grip on her hand. "I know you've recently left the service. What are your plans for the future?"

"As you know, my immediate plans are to reacquire my land and then to enjoy living on it."

He stepped forward and pointed to a bird gliding across the lake. "The first part of your goal sounds ambitious, but the second part doesn't. Life has to be more than simply living on a piece of land."

"I'm sure raising a family and searching for new opportunities will present themselves in due time, and I now also have my mother to think about."

As they walked along the side of the pond a blur caught her attention as two men ran toward them. "Don't move and you won't get hurt, you hear?"

The other man, a tall black guy with a rough beard, brandished a knife. "Yeah, like man, just give us your money and jewelry and you rich folks can go on about your fucking business."

Suzan glanced at the bodyguards running in their direction, but they were too far away to respond quickly enough to the glistening edge of a knife extending toward her. Her reflexes moved faster than the mugger, as she grabbed the back of his wrist and twisted, while her knee slammed into his crotch. He yelled, but he didn't drop the knife. She kneed him again as the knife fell. Before he could recover, she shoved his head down as she thrust her knee into his face, sending blood spurting.

The second guy jabbed at her as she contained his arm with one hand and shoved the palm of her other hand into his face, breaking his nose. She started to hammer the base of her palm into his nose again, but knew she could kill him by shoving a broken bone into his brain. She breathed hard and stopped, letting him fall to the ground.

The two bodyguards arrived and jumped on the two men, holding them face forward. They yelled like children, more than thugs on the street. "Damn man, don't kill us!"

The first bodyguard yelled at Matt. "What do you want us to do with them?"

"I know we should call the police, but we don't need the

damn publicity. Make sure they don't have any more weapons on them and get rid of them."

"Yes, sir."

Matt turned to Suzan. "Wow, I've never seen anyone handle themselves like you do before. I wish you had let me take care of them."

"This is what I was trained to do."

"I always thought that it was the man's job to protect his lady, and not the other way around."

Suzan glanced at her dress with blood splattered on it. "I think I might have ruined a good dress of yours." Suzan noticed Matt sweating. Yes, he had lived a sheltered life and while one of the most powerful men in the world, he still must have his moments. She knew he had never been in a fight or perhaps ever witness one before. However, he did look like he could handle himself. Perhaps she did move too fast.

Matt straightened his back. "I think we do need to let you change clothes, and afterwards I have a special place I want us to eat tonight. I hope you'll allow me to keep this out of the news."

"I've no reason to tell anyone." In fact, she needed to make sure no one knew about this. The CIA had told her to keep a low profile.

After returning to his building, Matt escorted Suzan to his private elevator connected to the executive level. The dress might be ruined, but he loved seeing her in it and would see what could be done. "Are you sure you're oaky? I can have someone look at your hand."

"I'm fine, it's not my blood."

Visions flooded his mind, almost like he was with a secret operative of a special task force, or maybe even a super spy. His heart beat faster than he wanted to admit. He knew he had to do more research on her. Her skills weren't normal. They were too advanced. He had studied martial arts, and he knew when he was in the presence of a master, even if it was a beautiful woman.

She smiled at him. "I hope I can find something to wear tonight. Where are we going?"

"I think you had a good day shopping today and you will find something you might like."

She offered him a coy smile. "I need to talk to you about the shopping also. That isn't exactly what I meant by my wanting to go shopping. I want to see some places here."

"We'll see what we can work out. Tonight, I want you to celebrate, let me say for not being robbed, and go to one of my favorite places. I think you'll like Per Se."

Per Se? What was this, a foreign word she didn't know, or the name of a place? She didn't want to appear ignorant, so she only smiled back at him. "So, how should I dress?"

"Since this is perhaps the best place to eat in New York, I think we should make you look fantastic, and by the way, I haven't seen what you selected today except for what you're wearing now. I think it would be fun to see what you like."

"So, you want a modeling show tonight?"

"No, I don't think we have time for you to model for me, but I would love to glance at your collection."

"My collection!"

"Have you never heard of Per Se?"

From the look on her face, he knew the answer. "I know you'll like the restaurant. It was inspired by the French Laundry in California." Watching another stare he accepted the fact she had been out of touch for a long time. The excitement of showing her the world as a new playground flashed in his mind. It could be fun.

One of the staff greeted them as they walked to her room. Matt stopped at her door, as he waited to be invited inside. With a small smile she acknowledged him with a nod to enter. He saw no evidence of her adjusting to her room. As she walked over to her closet to show what she had available, her mouth open wide when she opened the door. "Oh my God!" She stepped forward. "I didn't say I planned to buy everything."

"They're very good to me, and they worked hard on this I'm sure." Matt reached over to touch the fabric of one dress.

"These will have to be returned. I plan on paying for what I buy. I'm not totally broke, you know."

"These dresses are all altered to fit your body. Since they cannot be returned, perhaps you can accept these as a small gift from me for problems I've caused you. Please." He stepped forward as she studied one dress. Many of the women in his past would have jumped at an opportunity to receive dresses like these. He glanced at another dress. While he liked functionality more than the dramatic, the night did call for a little flare. Fortunately, he saw one that would work. Now, if he could only suggest it to her and have her pick it. He had already learned that she didn't like to be manipulated, and this would be a challenge–a challenge he would openly enjoy.

"I don't know. I think you're trying to bribe me again." A smile revealed her attempt to hide her pleasure in seeing the dresses. Good!

"If all it takes is a few dresses to bribe you, I think I underestimated you."

"If I were a girly girl this would be impressive, but I'm sure we both know better."

Matt appreciated the wit and demeanor of Suzan:

perfectly balanced enough to hold his interest and not too much to irritate him. "Well tonight, the perfect dress might be a girly girl type."

To his pleasure she pointed to the one black dress with a remarkable accent of taste, but containing a large display of sequins. His mind drifted to future photos of her on the front page. Word would circulate. Phil would make sure of the coverage.

###

Suzan held Matt's arm. The high heels would never do. With her expectations soaring on what *Per Se* looked like, she braced herself, but it wasn't nearly enough. The beautiful blue door and copper colored tile set a style she wasn't prepared for. She anticipated the marble and furnishings, but knew this place represented a true one-of-a-kind, as the staff welcomed Matt as if he was an old friend.

Without ordering, a bottle of champagne arrived at the table as Matt held her chair for her. A waiter lowered his head in a small bow at Suzan as Matt introduced her. It felt like she was floating outside her body. This kind of treatment had never happened to her before. She glanced at the table and counted eight forks—yes eight! This was going to be one hell of a night. "I take it you come here often."

"Yes, but not often enough." He paused to glance around. "They do have the best chefs in New York and I think you'll agree soon."

"What do they have on the menu here?"

"I don't know. I've never seen a menu. Our chef will be here in a minute, and he will love to hear what you like. His talent is discovering what you like and exceeding your expectations."

"Really!"

"Oh yes, really." Matt raised his glass of champagne

toward her.

He might not think of himself as an alcoholic, but he definitely liked champagne. She studied him and his smile. The more she became accustomed to his face the better he looked. Even his eyes, which looked somewhat haunting earlier, now had a peaceful tender resolution in them. She forced herself to focus. "In such a case, I think he might like a challenge."

Matt laughed. "Yes, I think so." The chef walked over and welcomed them as they finished the first glass. "This is a new friend of mine, and I think she might be your toughest challenge yet, what do you think?"

"A challenge is always welcome. What is it you have for me today?"

Suzan reflected about it for a minute. It would be intriguing what a top chef could do with a favorite meat of hers. "This maybe too much to ask, but I'm from Florida and . . ."

Matt smiled. "I think you'll find he prepares the best seafood in the world."

"I wasn't thinking seafood, but something a little higher on the food chain." A smug look crossed the chef's mind as if he welcomed a new challenge. "I was thinking alligator. Back home in Florida it is considered a challenge, and it would be nice to see what you can do with it here. "

As if a deep pleasure erupted under his professional demeanor, the chef replied, "I think I can make you happy, but please allow a few extra minutes tonight."

Matt raised his glass. "You're full of surprises, but I like that."

Suzan hoped so, since she saw one other surprise he might not enjoy later. When she had ridden in the back of the carriage with him, and he had placed his arm around her shoulder, apparently he had pulled her a little too close. A red reminder of her lipstick highlighted his collar. Should she tell him?

The chef prepared the alligator with a special dark red wine sauce, highlighted by a mixture of spices she had never tasted before. The meal lasted for a long time, while a bottle of great wine lowered another layer of her resistance. Matt had a sense of humor she didn't expect.

As he walked beside her to the waiting limo outside, a flash suddenly startled her. What was that? Then she saw another and another as the limo driver and several bodyguards rushed in closer to them, shielding them as best they could.

Matt hurried her in the door and jumped in beside her. "Damn, I didn't think they wouldn't catch us out tonight."

Suzan giggled as the wine blurred her ability to think. Why were photographers taking photos of them? She couldn't imagine her photo in papers or magazines. Then, her mind cleared. Not good! The CIA had told her to keep a low profile. She felt glad when the limo quickly sped ahead, while Matt glared out the window. "I'm so sorry for being caught off guard."

"Don't worry about it. I think it was kind of fun." She couldn't believe she heard a giggle.

He returned the laugh. "Perhaps you're right, and I take life a little too serious at times." He pulled her closer to him and snuggled. It felt comfortable and not the least bit intimidating. Well, maybe a little odd, but nice.

###

Matt slipped his hand around Suzan's waist as they walked into his place. The champagne and wine had reduced her fighting and free-wheeling spirit to a point that he felt like he could see a different side of her. She had a cute smile, not polished and refined like many women he knew, but one much more honest. Her laugh intrigued him the most. The spontaneous outbursts felt so refreshing compared to the fake attempts he had to endure for so long. He steadied her several times as her ankles quivered on her heels.

A housekeeper hurried over to him as he turned a corner. He raised a hand to his lips to whisper. "I need a little help." She walked ahead of him and opened the door to Suzan's room. He allowed her to fall sideways onto the bed.

Suzan scrambled to get back on her feet, but never left the bed. "I'm fine . . . really."

Matt leaned over and kissed her forehead. "I had a great time, and it was much different than I can ever remember. Get some rest and I'll see you in the morning."

She closed her eyes for a minute. "You know, I had a good time also." Matt reflected on how important it was to have a witness to record his actions tonight. He remembered a few times earlier when he had been threatened by women hoping to cash in on being with him.

"I've a special surprise for you tomorrow. Goodnight."

Chapter 11

Suzan woke late with a nagging headache. With the soft luxurious comforter snuggled around her, she enjoyed the warmth of the bed. She stretched and forced her eyes open. What time was it? She studied the table on one side of the bed. There was no way that it could be ten o'clock.

After tossing the comforter to one side, she swung her legs off the other side of the bed. The night dress she had slipped into later in the night looked elegant and as if it was produced from pure silk. While she had always slept in warm flannel types to stay warm, the girly girl type clothing was quickly growing on her. She knew this was temporary since she would eventually be returning to Florida.

Suzan stumbled toward the bathroom, which was larger than one she had to share with ten other women in the Army. She could establish a whole living quarters in this room alone. The marble tops were polished brightly enough to reflect the array of lights above. While she had her choice of a bathtub, a small whirlpool, or a large walk in shower, she dropped the delicate night dress and opted for the shower.

While the hot flood pouring from the shower head felt fantastic, she forced the water colder and colder to refresh her. Memories of the night before made her smile. Wow! If only the members of the military police squad she worked with in Afghanistan could see her now. She thought she had thrown the chef a curve in asking for alligator, but he had rose to the occasion and produced a meal she would remember forever.

After stepping from the shower, she toweled dry and reached for a fluffy white robe. While her hair had been so expertly styled the day before, today Matt would have to see her as she really looked. Nevertheless, she reached for a brush and hairdryer and went to work on the long black strands.

A woman waited for her when she walked out of the bathroom. "How are you, Ms. Mercer?"

"I'm fine, thank you."

"Mr. Harris has just returned from some early morning meetings. He wanted to know if you wanted to join him for breakfast."

"Yes, but it will take a few minutes for me to get ready."

"Good, I'll send in someone to help you." To help me? When did she need someone to help her dress?

Before she could object, the lady walked out and another woman soon entered. "I hope you slept well last night. I know you have a busy day and we'll see what we can do to make it a good one for you." She opened a makeup case and pointed to a dresser.

Okay, why not? She might not ever receive this kind of attention again. "I'm not used to all of this fuss over me."

"I understand Matt is taking you to Chicago as soon as you finish breakfast."

"Chicago?"

"I may have opened my mouth when I shouldn't have. In any case, I need to help you get ready."

Suzan soon walked into the dining room where Matt was waiting for her. He wore a deep blue suit, white shirt, and a tie with a fantastic swirl of various blues. He lowered his coffee cup and stood as she entered. "After last night I thought you might enjoy sleeping late."

"I don't think I've ever slept so late in a long time. You should've awakened me earlier, and what is this about going to Chicago?"

"Occasionally I need to make rounds of some of my properties, and I thought this would give us a good chance to get to know each other better."

Suzan glanced at Matt sideways with the intention to find out more about him, but not divulge more about herself. "Tell me, why do you want to know more about me?"

"Curiosity, for one thing. I've heard that you might be receiving the Silver Star for your work in Afghanistan."

"I doubt I will. The Silver Star is seldom given out, and what I did was blown all out of proportion." The real reason she knew it would be impossible is because the award would give her too much publicity. She hadn't dismissed the possibility of returning to the CIA for additional assignments. The last time she talked to them they had left the door open.

"I have to make these trips, and I think having you along would be fantastic. You have a way of bringing out a different side to me. For example, last night was totally unlike what I usually do."

"You mean eating at a restaurant I think you must go to often?"

"No, I was referring to the ride through the park last night. Your martial art skills are impressive, to say the least."

"I was perhaps a little hard on them, but from what I understand, the park isn't a safe place after dark."

"Like I said, you have a way of bringing out a part of me no one else has in a long time. Although many people think I live an exciting life, they have no clue how my life really is."

Sensing a chance to work on her mission, Suzan decided to press forward. "You know, I heard a saying once that was something like, in order to find out more about someone, you first also have to share. Do you think you can be open and honest? It is a two way street."

She watched him sip his coffee and stare at her above the rim. His eyes clear green color concentrated on her. She knew he had years of practice in not giving away his thoughts; however, she had the best training the CIA offered on reading people. His charm surfaced from an inner strength she forced herself to face. Sexual advances by men annoyed her. Her work in the military police taught her many things like what men wanted–which was often just pure raw sex on the spot. This felt different. Although she still considered him a predator, he remained a predator with a brain.

Suzan explored the luxurious interior of the Gulfstream 4, and while the Lear looked fantastic inside, she wasn't prepared for the size and extravagant life Matt lived in. The two pilots glanced at her and said hello as they adjusted instrumentation in the cockpit. The interior cabin, divided into two sections with four seats in each, allowed all passengers room to stretch and enjoy the flight. The interior color of a deep blue theme expressed the appearance of royalty. She would have loved to have seen the back of the plane, but tried her best to stay composed and keep from acting like a kid in a candy store with Matt staring at her.

However, she felt compelled to say something. "This is much nicer than the other jet I flew on."

"I thought you might like this one. We have four in the fleet, and they all have a purpose."

"Four!"

"I've a lot of employees who need to be in one place or another, and commercial flights take forever. They are also never available when we need to fly. Working all day in a stressful environment leaves little time to be stuck in an airport. Additionally, we actually conduct many board meetings in the plane here."

As Matt answered his cell phone, Suzan glanced around. On today's flight she saw the same two bodyguards Matt often had with him and Gail, his secretary. As if for the first time, Suzan studied Gail, who seemed to always press a phone to her ear. She had beautiful features, including long dark hair with a strong red overtone. Her face looked flawless, but her makeup looked too heavy. Suzan guessed earlier Gail might be in her early thirties, but on closer examination she thought Gail might be closer to forty. She dressed like an executive by wearing a professional business suit and high heels.

As Matt turned to one side and intensified his conversation, Suzan used the time to analyze him closer. His deep dark suit had all of the trademarks of being tailored to fit his body like a glove. Standing slightly less than six feet tall, Matt stayed in good shape, with a narrow waist and firm body. She remembered never loving the big bulky guys she saw serving in the Army. The gyms in Afghanistan set up to keep the men in shape always smelled bad. In contrast, Matt's cologne smelled intoxicating.

As she heard the phone conversation coming to an end, she concentrated on Matt's eyes, as she slowly noticed the object of his stare. The dress line she wore had slipped enough to reveal part of her legs. The stare caught her off guard, making her feel uncomfortable. In the years of working as a military police, she had become accustomed to wearing a uniform designed to keep her from appearing as a female in any way.

Did he find her sexy? You've got to be kidding! While she currently dressed the part of business woman, underneath she remained Suzan, a tough military policewoman. Making a change in real life would never happen, but then again, this was real life.

The waitress walked forward. "What can I get you to drink?"

"Anything but champagne." Suzan glanced at Matt, who offered a quirky smile.

"I agree. Champagne should be reserved for celebrating. I think I'll have a purple passion."

"A purple passion?" Suzan asked.

He slipped the phone into his pocket as he ended the call. "Yes, I think you'll like my favorite drink. It's grape juice, bananas, honey and ice all blended, and very healthy."

"It does sound good. Are you telling me you're a health nut?"

"I think we should all try to stay in our best shape." His smile brightened as he leaned closer to her. "You appear to be in excellent shape."

"I guess I can thank Uncle Sam for pushing me, but I had little choice if I wanted to handle my job."

"So, tell me more about what you did in Afghanistan?"

"I worked with the military police." She knew he knew that much already. The various CIA contacts she had worked with had trained her how to hide her other missions. She enjoyed the excitement, but she knew that her CIA adventures would always be a part of her life she could never tell anyone. She still hadn't decided if she wanted to work with them again in the future, but they had left the decision up to her.

Matt waited patiently for additional information, but he finally must have decided she would offer none. "It appears they trained you well. I hope you don't consider this a male chauvinist statement, but I've never seen a woman handle herself like you."

"It does come in handy at times." She decided to shift the

attention back to him. "Tell me what you do to stay in shape."

"My meals are carefully planned most of the time by a personal chef you met, and my personal trainers force me to work out every day."

"A regimen must be nice, but what do you do for fun?"

"I work."

"Boring!"

"I will at times agree with you, but I do have a large company requiring my attention every day." He stretched backward in the seat and darted his eyes to one side. "What would you think I should do?"

Suzan sat back for a minute in a mocking pose. "Have you ever competed against someone without all of your corporate muscle behind you?"

"Many people assume I use the corporation, but I think you'll learn it's the other way around, I'm the muscle behind the corporation."

"I'm not sold, and what I'm talking about is something like tennis, or basketball of a one on one matchup."

"Are you offering me a challenge?" Matt lowered his stare to focus on her.

"Perhaps, do you think you can handle it?"

"You mean against you?"

"You pick the sport, and the contest has to be me against you."

"I think I detect a prize for winning is at stake." Matt rubbed his chin. "I don't think I've ever accepted such a challenge."

"I thought so."

"Wait a minute, a challenge does sound intriguing. I'll think about your offer, but I can assure you it will not be hand to hand combat." His stare intensified as he scanned her body.

She watched the hostess walk forward with the purple passions. "I'm not going anywhere. Let me know when you get your nerve up."

Matt closed the door to the racket ball room. He never dreamed when he designed the facility he would actually play in it one day. He studied the outfit Suzan wore, revealing the woman he had anticipated all along, with long legs, a slim firm stomach, and breasts the perfect size, not to mention her tight butt. The confines of the enclosed room had been a perfect response to her challenge. He had played racket ball before, but only a few times.

Suzan opened the can of balls and placed the tin in the corner of the room. "Are you sure you're ready for this?" Her voice echoed around the room.

An hour later sweat poured from his body as he chased after another ball. His concentration was destroyed by Suzan's rush to get into position. The shorts raised high on her legs, revealing perfectly toned muscles, and the way she leaned over, pulling the shorts tight against her butt was a perky delicacy he couldn't avoid or resist much longer. After rushing to cover an overhead smash they collided in the center and wrapped arms around each other as they fell to the floor. Neither saw the point of impact behind them. Was the ball in or out? It was only the game point.

Neither called the shot as they sat beside each other, his arm wrapped around her side. The sweat merged their two bodies together as they caught their breath. Her body felt as firm as he had expected. It had been a long time since he had wanted a woman, and her youthful figure presented him with new questions. Should he continue to hold her, should he apologize for such an intimate situation? Or . . . should he take advantage of the timing and press forward?

Several minutes later his breathing returned to normal. "Did you see where the ball landed?"

"Honestly–no!"

"Shall we replay the ball, or call the match a draw?"

"I don't think we ever agreed to what we're playing for, did we?"

As Matt analyzed the outcomes he knew what she wanted, but he wasn't about to give her land back to her. And if he won, he knew she would never agree to what he had on his mind. "I know you want to know what I want for my prize. I do, however, know what you want."

"I've never hid my agenda, and I won't stop until I get my land back."

"In one respect we're very much alike."

"And?"

"I think this is what intrigues me so much about you." Until now, he didn't know. It has always been his determination which brought him success. Suzan had never wavered on her intentions and, in fact, stayed directly in his face demanding it.

"I know you want something from me, or you wouldn't be spending time with me. And your intentions confuse me. Do you think I'll call off the lawsuit if you buy me expensive dinners or fly me around in your jet?"

"I don't really think so–no." He squeezed her body as a rush of excitement flowed through him. He didn't know how long she would allow him such liberties. "The lawsuit is something my legal team will handle. Getting to know you is what I want to do on my own."

Matt glanced at her lips, as he analyzed her mouth's luscious and plump attraction to a place he shouldn't visit. But it was her expressive eyes which always captured his attention. while he wondered about her heritage, he knew some of her background. How did she become so lucky in such a great set of genes? He knew Indian women always had these dynamic eyes, but this was the first time he had ever been so close to such.

The moment lingered into minutes, as he noticed she was analyzing him just as much as he studied her. He knew he needed to stand, but he hesitated with his arm still clinging to her side. With her not pulling away, he felt like she remained receptive to his attention.

He watched Suzan glance around the room. "It looks like you discovered a way to get me all alone without me fighting you, but I'll say this; you played much harder than I would've guessed."

"Why is that?"

"We have a word in the Army for suits."

"I'm sure *a suit* is what you might think of me."

"Well . . . I was being nice. Another word we often use is *candy ass*. Maybe that definition might fit better."

"Well, I can tell you know how to give compliments, and I'll say you're much different than most women I know."

"In which way?"

"You've already shown several times you're very capable in handling yourself, you're determined to get what you want, which is much like me . . . but you're much more beautiful than I can say, knowing your background. I just can't imagine a beautiful woman in the Army I guess."

He watched Suzan blush for a minute. "I hardly consider myself beautiful, but thanks for the compliment. I know you're trying to, shall I say, *butter me up,* but you're going to have to try harder." She pouted her lips in a teasing manner he hadn't seen before.

"How you perceive the compliment is, of course, up to

you, but it was my honest opinion. I think calling it a draw today would be good. I know something else we need to take advantage of here, which I think you'll like. How about a massage?"

"Are you offering me a massage? For some reason I knew you wanted to get your hands on me."

"I already told you once I thought you were a beautiful girl, and while I might be tempted to give a massage to you myself, I think a professional masseuse would be better. So, what do you say?"

He watched her eyes flirt with him, as she contemplated her answer. "I think relaxing might be good, but I don't think I've ever received a professional massage before."

Matt leaned over to kiss her cheek. She complied, but hesitantly, as he fought the urge to engage in a much more passionate kiss. Her seductive mouth and luscious lips held an attraction he had considered exploring for a long time. However, he would be patient–time was on his side.

###

Suzan wrapped the towel around her, with her inner apprehension mounting. This may be the way the rich enjoyed life, but still, the thoughts of having someone else touch her sent quivers through her body. She never asked if it was a male or female masseuse, or perhaps she should say *masseur*.

Suzan stepped from the changing room to see Matt lying on his stomach. His back was exposed, but a towel covered his butt. An oriental woman stood behind him with another one, almost like a sister, was waiting behind another table beside him.

Matt opened his eyes to glance at her. "I think you'll enjoy this."

"You know I've had many guys trying to get me naked

before, but this is the first time this has been tried." She forced herself to stay calm, as she breathed in deeply. Yes under the towel she had nothing on. She felt more vulnerable than she had ever felt before in her life.

She heard him laugh. "If you want to go to a private room, it's up to you, but I thought you might want to talk some more."

Since he acted so casual about being half naked, and she didn't want to appear embarrassed and give him the upper hand later, she walked over to the table. "Conversation might be good, and especially with the woman in here to protect me from you, if you, you know, lose control or anything."

She heard a deep low laugh. "I think I can control myself."

"Okay, a few minutes ago I heard you say I was beautiful and I assumed sexy."

"I never used the word sexy. However . . . since you mentioned it."

"So, you've noticed." Suzan helped herself onto the table and watched the oriental woman cover her with a sheet and adjust it so she remained decent but exposed enough for the masseuse to go to work on her.

"Yes, I noticed. Not only are your natural features outstanding, you stay in very good shape. You must maintain a good workout regimen."

"Thanks." She decided to finally accept his compliment as the fingers stretched her back muscles. She had no clue how good the massage would feel, or how much tension she had built up over the last few weeks. Wow, it felt fantastic! Suzan turned her head to face Matt, who smiled back at her. "You said you worked all of the time."

"I do. This is like a small vacation for me, but you'll see I still have a lot of duties to complete before the day is over. This place is large and many people will want to greet us since we're here, and of course, I'll hear about all of the extra needs they have."

"Still doesn't sound like a lot of work to me."

"As soon as we finish here we need to fly on to Denver. I think you'll really like one of our newest luxury condos. It recently opened, and I'm also anxious to see the final product."

"Okay, what's so different about it?"

"We've blended the condos into the side of a ski slope so it's very aesthetic, but beautiful at the same time. We're marketing this one to what I call our green conscious buyers."

"We'll see, I guess, since you're dragging me with you."

She heard him laugh again. "I don't think I have you hand tied and gagged, do I?"

Maybe she over did it on the teasing. He did act nice to her. The massage had an immediate effect on her as the fingers continued to melt into her back. "Okay, I'm sorry. You've been kind to me."

"Hum, I sense a degree of accomplishment in your words."

"Okay, but don't read too much into them. A massage isn't playing fair, you know?" She glanced over as she forced her eyes open. The masseuse worked on his legs, squeezing them and rubbing his muscles. He had nice, very nice and powerful legs. Although not a muscle builder as so many guys she saw in Afghanistan who had nothing better to do besides working out day after day, he looked so damn well toned.

"I don't know. I try to make people around me happy. It's important to me to make sure they're well taken care of." She watched him stare into her face, studying her as she lay limp and partially exposed.

"From the people around you I can tell you have a good working relationship with them. But . . . I do have a question?"

"And?"

"What about your girlfriend? How does she like you sharing an intimate massage with a, like you said, a beautiful girl?"

"I have several women I know and spend time with, but I assume you're referring to Chelsea again."

"I assumed she's your girlfriend, but it's nice to know you have *many women* in your life."

"First, Chelsea's not my girlfriend, but a woman I spend some time with. Her father's one of my largest business associates."

"I don't want to dig too deep into your personal life, but I still find it fascinating. So, you have a girl in every port?"

"I have many functions I must attend and it's awkward to go on my own."

"I've heard call girls are good for this."

"Well, I could see the headlines on using call girls. My reputation's extremely important to me and the company. It's what projects this company's image and I'll always defend it."

"You sound a little conceited, but in a way also like it's a responsibility you take seriously."

"Precisely, and that's why Phil is with us. His job is to make sure our image stays where it's supposed to be."

"Phil seems much like you, very dedicated."

"Yes, he is, and he's one of the best in the public relation industry. I'm lucky to have him working for me."

The masseuse indicated Suzan needed to turn over. She

felt the apprehension as she anticipated the turn. She didn't want to expose too much, especially with Matt studying her so intensely. "You're enjoying this, aren't you?"

"I always enjoy life." He shifted to his back as the oriental woman kept him covered.

Expecting the same treatment, Suzan shifted to lie on her back. The massage felt so good she remained quiet, allowing the tension in her body to melt away. When she felt the gentle fingers giving her a facial, she drifted into a trance, almost asleep but aware of the presence of Matt beside her.

Slowly coming back to reality she noticed the woman gone and Matt staring at her. "Wow, how long have I been sleeping?"

"Not long, I thought you might be tired. However, we do need to hurry a little."

Suzan anticipated the problems of standing with the towel. "I guess we do need to shower and dress."

"Yes we do." He stood and wrapped his towel around his waist. His well toned chest had little if almost no hair on it. He walked over to her and leaned over to give her a kiss on the forehead. "I can tell you're a little shy, but it's okay. I'm not one to step over the boundaries until you're ready."

A challenge? He offered her a challenge like she was a little girl. He turned to walk toward one of the showers. His manly smell still floated around her. He was single, she was single. She might not ever obtain this chance again. So, why not as she allowed the words to ring in her head–go for it. She dropped her towel and followed him to the shower.

Chapter 12

Suzan enjoyed the tour and the attention she had received from Matt. His reputation flourished more than she had realized, as fans constantly pursued them as they examined the building and all of the facilities in Chicago. She never remembered having her photo taken every few minutes before. Matt frequently reminded her to make sure she always had a smile on her face.

It felt good to be on the way back to the airport in the limo. She told herself she could get used to this, but she knew this was only for a short time and she had to keep reminding herself of her mission.

Her cell phone rang. After she glanced at the caller id and saw nothing identified, she knew to answer it carefully. "Hello."

"Suzan, I'm glad I could reach you. Can you talk?"

"Not completely."

"Understood, just listen. You're being given the Silver Star for your actions in Afghanistan. We've decided to not block it, and we now think we can capitalize on the situation. However, we do need to talk. Someone will contact you before the ceremony with some instructions. Congratulations, you deserve the recognition. I'm sure the pentagon will contact you in a few minutes to let you know. Do not say anything about your involvement with the company. I'm sure you know this. We'll see you tomorrow."

Another call came in as the first one closed. "Hello."

"Suzan Mercer?"

"Yes."

"I'm so glad we could find you. I'm General Fullbright. It gives me great pride in informing you that you're to receive the Silver Star."

"Sir, like wow! What an honor. I had no idea, sir."

"I know this is short notice, but we need you to come to Washington as fast as you can make it here and we can arrange transportation. Where are you now?"

"Sir, I'm in Chicago and on my way to Denver right now. Sir, can you give me a minute?"

"Sure."

Suzan clicked on the mute button. "Matt, you're not going to believe this. I'm receiving the Silver Star tomorrow in Washington. I won't be able to go on to Denver with you."

"Not a problem. We can reroute to Washington if you wish."

"Matt, I can't ask you to fly me to Washington."

"I insist, especially if you need an escort for this event. Of course, unless you have someone else you want to ask?"

"Besides some of my military friends, I've no one else here except my mother. I wish she could see me receive it."

"Done. I'll send Phil to Florida to get her."

"You know, you're a much nicer guy than I imagined."

"Well, I'm glad to see I'm making progress." As Matt retrieved his cell phone and called his pilot to make changes, Suzan studied him again. With them intimately involved now, it would be hard to stay focused on her mission. Maybe she needed to re-evaluate her life and her goals for the future.

Suzan switched back to her call. "Sir, I have transportation, and I can be in Washington shortly."

"Very good."

###

The briefing room looked standard, but she knew the one way mirrors hid someone who wanted to see and hear her statements. Matt had been patient while they had been separated. She knew he would be in good hands as they questioned and briefed her on her new role.

Two men entered the room, dark suits and polished CIA officers for sure. "Hello, Suzan. I'm agent Kenneth Groan and this is agent Derek Waldrop. First off, I want to personally thank you for your contribution to your country. I know this isn't often acknowledged because of the nature of our work. It's good when you can receive something as prestigious as a Silver Star."

"I heard this would be bad for me. I was told earlier when the prospect came up to ignore it."

"At first this was our thinking, but the award has been reevaluated, especially in light of the guy you're spending time with."

"You mean Matt Harris."

"Yes, he has put a special spot-light on you."

"Does this mean I have no future with the CIA?"

"No, what it means is you now bring a different set of assets to the table."

"I see."

"When you left the Army, your main mission for us was over, but your future was never decided. Have you had any time to think about what you want?"

"Not really. I don't know how much you know about what's going on with me or not. Well, you might. I came home to find my land sold without my knowledge, and I'm trying to get it back now."

"Yes, it was an unfortunate set of events. It's also intriguing how you're going about it."

"I'm using what I know and what I've been taught. I've

no idea if I'll be successful in having the land returned to me or not."

"When will you know?"

"Who knows?"

"I see. If you want to work for us, I think we can leave the door open for you, but remember, you're off the reservation for now and on your own."

"I don't think anyone knows I worked for you, other than those who needed to know. I only have one person I'm locked into negotiations with, and I don't think he'll ever know about my work for the CIA."

"I'm sure you know how important it is that he never knows. Matt Harris is a man with enormous resources, and he might find out more than he needs to know."

"You said a few minutes ago you've reconsidered my role. Do you want to expand on your comment?"

She watched him hesitate for several seconds. "Let me just say that with the spotlight on you we might be able to use this notoriety to sneak you into places we might not be able to place other people."

"I assume you want me to use Matt as an asset."

"Is using him a problem?"

"I'll . . . have to think about the situation. I don't know him well, and I'm entering something I've never experienced before."

"We can understand. As long as you know how important your work for us is and how to keep our connection private, we'll check back with you later. I think it was good to have this conversation with you."

"And . . . if I want to contact you later?"

"You've been given a new code name. Call it in and we'll find you."

"Which name?"

"We assumed you might like this–bright star." The men glanced at each other. "Again, thank you for all of your efforts, they've saved a lot of men's lives and helped us more than I can really tell you."

"Thank you, and I'm sure this is off the record."

"Yes, but look at it this way, you're receiving the Silver Star today, and I know that the seven men you saved in the attack will always be thankful."

"Just doing my job."

"And that's why we think you'll be a good agent for us. Congratulations again." The men turned and walked out the door as another guy in street clothes walked in. She needed to go back to the real world.

Soon she saw Matt at the hotel they had checked in to. He had a large smile and dressed impeccable as usual. "The presentation is all set, and I've obtained a special invitation for you to join me."

"Fantastic. I'm happy for you." Matt walked over and hugged her, stopping for a second to study her face before he leaned over and kissed her lightly on the lips. After earlier, she knew she couldn't stop Matt from kissing her now, but she still felt uneasy with him. She searched for a reason, but she knew it would be a long time for her to truly accept him.

"Thanks. This has been given to only a few women ever, and they're making a big deal out of it."

"I heard about the situation which resulted in you receiving this award. The attack must have been terrifying."

"I think terrifying is a good word, but at the time I had no time to think."

"I'm sure the rest of America is proud of you, and for what it's worth, I am also."

"Thanks, we need to hurry. They're going to fit me into a

new military suit for the presentation. They want me to look perfect. You can go with me, or I can let you know later when I'm ready."

"I can go with you."

As they walked out of the Hotel and toward a waiting limo, the flash of cameras started. "How do these people know where you are all of the time?"

"It's how they make their living, and they have their own network of photographers."

She watched him slide in behind her as they rushed into the limo. She accepted his hand and rested close to him. With his presence becoming so familiar, his smell so recognizable, she knew she was losing all resistance to him, as well as her objective reasoning. "I don't know if I could live with cameras focusing on me all of the time."

"It takes some getting used to, but it's possible." He squeezed her hand again. "I'll try to keep it more private in the future if it bothers you."

"Thanks, I would appreciate it since I'm not used to it."

"Well today I think you'll have to, as I know you'll have a ton of photographers taking your photo today."

She squeezed his hand back. "Thank you for being with me. It does mean a lot to have someone with me."

"It's my pleasure, and I'm so sorry about your mother's decision not to come."

"We don't need to go there right now. She still says you seduced her."

"I promise I didn't."

"I'm starting to trust you, but you have to realize I still have reservations and suspicions."

Matt said nothing as he looked out the window. What was the truth, and would she ever know?

###

The presentation went as scheduled, but it was much more draining than she had realized. Phil had flown in for the presentation also. Matt was correct when he said Phil knew how to handle the media. She really appreciated Phil's help. She also appreciated Matt's promise to help her stay out of the media later. A private dinner in their suite felt perfect, and this time she appreciated the champagne.

She also enjoyed the company of Phil and Matt's secretary, Gail, who had joined them for the celebration. They would be spending the night also, and flying with them to New York before she went with Matt on to Denver. She knew they had many items they needed to discuss concerning the running of Harris Properties. However, she loved the way they concentrated on her moment in time. Yes, oh damn yes, she had just received the Silver Star!

Phil stood first and offered his hand to Gail. "I think Matt and Suzan may want some time to relax. It has been a big day for them."

Suzan walked over to Phil. "Thank you for handling the press today, and for prepping me with what to say and do. This is a first for me."

"You did great, and we'll make sure all of the media covers the story properly. This will make you famous for a long time. You should possibly look for a public relations firm to handle you."

"What do you mean?"

"I'm sure any number of people will want to interview you. You can almost pick the talk show you want to go on."

"What if publicity isn't what I want?"

"In the same respect they can help you avoid the media. Either way, you're on many people's radar for now."

"I didn't think about this." This could be a problem, and one she needed to talk to the CIA about. She needed advice, but like they said, she was off the reservation now and on her own. Still, she hoped that they would give her some advice.

Phil kissed her hand. "I know this is a lot to think about. Let me know if I can help you."

Gail walked in front of Phil, but suddenly stopped and turned to Matt. "Let me know of any other changes you need to make to your schedule. This is so unlike you to take off for so long, but don't worry, you have a great team to cover for you."

"I know I do, and tell everyone at the office tomorrow that I'll be back in a few days."

Matt walked them to the door before rejoining Suzan at the table. "You have had a long day. Are you tired?"

"I think I'm wired."

"I see. It's too bad we didn't plan to have the massage today, rather than yesterday." He reached over for the champagne and poured two more glasses. "Maybe one more glass will help."

"You've been a big help, and I appreciate the way you personally flew me here. I know you must have a lot of demands on your time."

"I always work hard, and for once it feels good to take a break from everything. I hope you'll like Denver tomorrow." He reached out his glass and tapped her glass, creating a distinctive ring. "We do need to get to bed soon. It'll be a long day tomorrow."

"I think you're right." She yawned. When he mentioned bed, a thought suddenly occurred to her. Did he mean going to bed together or separately? Yes, she enjoyed the time in the shower with him, and she knew she had teased him. She touched him intimately and allowed him to also, but she had stopped short of allowing him to penetrate her. The effort took more will power than she thought she had. She knew she didn't have enough to stop him again. Although acting interested in her, he'd also displayed how understanding and patient he could be.

Matt finished his glass and walked behind her to help her out of her chair. "I really enjoyed the day and spending time with you."

"Matt, you don't need to keep saying nice things to me. I know you want to go to bed with me tonight." She turned to wrap her arms around his neck. "I've thought about us all day, and I would be lying if I said I don't want you."

"I want you to be sure. It's not like me too act like this, but yes, I've wanted you ever since yesterday. You really surprised me by joining me in the shower."

With his stare intensifying on her, she leaned over and grazed his lips with her own. With a firm and powerful response he pressed toward her with a returned kiss. His hand slid to the back of her head and pulled her firmly into him. His tongue flittered against her lips, looking for a way inside. She hesitated, but finally yielded. How could she not?

"Unless you're one of those guys who wants to make it with a woman in uniform, I think I need to make myself more comfortable."

Suzan watched a smile widen as Matt's pearly white teeth enhanced his rugged masculine chin. "We have two bedrooms in this suite. I really didn't know if you if you wanted me tonight or not. You can use the one on the right, and I'll be waiting for you in the other one down the hallway."

Suzan giggled like a small girl, but the laughter felt good. "I think you knew." She slipped her hand toward his manhood. The slightest touch made his tool respond as it grew instantly. She remembered how his manhood looked so large in the shower. She remembered how velvety smooth it felt encasing such a rigid upright tool. Wow, she had to force herself back to the here and now. She would hurry.

"I at least hoped." He pulled her closer and placed both hands to the back of her head and ran them through her hair to massage her scalp before pulling her closer to him. As he kissed her passionately, he slid his tongue into her mouth. His tongue blossomed as it explored every part of her mouth and played with her own. Her resulting moans matched his, as she left all walls of resistance far behind her.

After what seemed a life time, he parted, but he returned to plant one last sweet kiss on her lips. When she concentrated on her hand firmly feeling him through his pants, she hoped she didn't hurt him, since she knew she had squeezed hard. She wanted him. It had been a long time, and she knew this would be one night she would remember forever; she wanted the sex to be perfect. "I want you right now, right here, but I think a few minutes to prepare myself would be great." She couldn't believe she opened her mouth giving away her hidden thoughts, but she did want a minute. Damn yes, but only a minute.

"I understand, and I'll be waiting for you. It will give me a minute also." He kissed her cheek and squeezed her tightly before he let her stand on her own. He turned and left her as she reached for a wall to steady herself. What was she doing? This wasn't the Suzan she knew. Whatever, she wanted him. Tomorrow she would still be able to work on her mission, wouldn't she?

Suzan staggered to her room and closed the door where she stripped as fast as she could while examining herself in the mirror. She didn't think of herself as a sex goddess, but she considered herself relatively slim and curvy. She assumed her long black hair would appear sexy to a man, and more specifically, she hoped Matt liked the way she looked. Her eyes looked too large, she thought, and they always required attention with makeup. But enough concentrating on her looks, she needed something sexy to put on to present him with.

Suzan hunted in her luggage, but she saw nothing new or sexy enough except the one she wore the previous night. It would have to do. After refreshing herself in the bathroom, she slipped it on and walked toward Matt's room.

With his door open she walked in and saw him sitting in the bed with his back against the headrest, a large soft designed cushion that was perfect for reading, like he was doing until she entered. He immediately tossed it to the side table.

She stopped and waited for him to speak first. Instead, his grin simply indicated that he approved of her choice. As he tossed the comforter to one side and offered room for her beside him, she blinked once and stepped forward. There was no turning back as she studied his naked chest, and as anticipated, he had removed everything else beneath the covers. She lifted the nightshirt over her head and slid in beside him.

Matt reached around her and turned off the overhead lights, but allowed the soft glow of several nightlights to add a romantic feel to the spacious room. Although the super king size bed allowed them both room to spread out, they clung to each other in the center of the bed.

"Matt, you feel so warm." She snuggled closer to him and rubbed his chest.

"I hope so. You've kept my engine running for a long time." Matt kissed her forehead as he pulled her closer to him. His skin melted into her own as she adjusted and snuggled into a perfect alignment with him. Her breasts squeezed closer to him as he shifted his weight to face her.

His hand slipped lower until it rested firmly on her butt, where memories of him holding her in the shower returned. She wanted him then, but she had stopped him. This would be much better. She knew she was ready for him as her mouth dried and her liquids began to flow, making penetration easy for him. She remembered how large he had grown in the shower, but lost all resistance as she reached and enclosed her hand around him. It immediately began to throb.

As he snuggled closer she wanted to tell him how she felt. The words I love you surfaced, but no, not now. She forced herself to control words she couldn't retract later. The sex is what he wanted, but sex is what she wanted as well.

His mouth covered her and stopped her from whispering any words–good. She didn't need to be prepared for sex, she wanted him now. She pulled his large joy stick toward her. He understood.

Suzan's cell phone woke her early the next morning. Matt never moved as she whispered. "Hello."

"Hello, Suzan, this is mom. I hope you're not too mad at me for not coming yesterday. After you becoming so upset at me for signing the contract with Matt, I thought it was best if I didn't go."

"Mom, give me a minute." Suzan walked lightly to the bathroom and closed the door. "You should have come."

"I wanted to be there for you, but I didn't want to interfere with you and Matt."

"Mom, Matt has turned out to be different than what I've

anticipated."

"I see. He's using his magic of seducing you."

"Mom." Suzan studied her mother's voice and word choices as she expressed herself clearer than she had at any time before. "I know I asked you before to explain what you meant when you say he seduced you."

"Let me ask you this. Is he offering you champagne all of the time. Is he buying you flowers, offering you massages?"

Suzan held her breath. Are gifts like this what he did for her Mother also? How did she know about the flowers and the massage? Was she correct? Did she have sex with Matt? "Mother, listen I need to know what happened between you and Matt."

"I told you, but you didn't want to listen. By the way, congratulations on the Silver Star."

"Mom, listen to me. I need to know." She didn't want to wake Matt, but her voice rose sharper and louder as she shook with a new sense of humiliation.

Her mother started to weep on the phone. "I'm sorry. I didn't mean to upset you. I love my baby."

Suzan started to yell at her again but stopped. Her mother had relapsed into a state she had seen many times lately. "Please don't cry."

Instead she heard louder whimpering. She forced herself to stay cool. She hated when anyone acted like this. The Army had trained her to be tough. This was so unacceptable. While how to handle her mother had eluded her, she needed to talk to her doctor again and soon. She glanced at the bathroom door. Was Matt still asleep?

"Mom, don't worry. I'm coming home. I believe you." Matt had given her a massage, not personally, but he had arranged one for her. And . . . he had poured a lot of champagne. But what about flowers–what flowers?

Suzan sneaked back into the bedroom and to the closet. She had too many clothes to take them all. She opened a suitcase and packed several she liked and the new Army uniform. With Matt sleeping soundly, she dressed as fast as she could. She needed to get out of Matt's suite before he woke up.

Her mother's words stung her. She mentioned what Matt had done to her. She still didn't know if they had sex or not, but she wondered. Oh God, how could they? Could it be Matt had a notch on his bed post for a mother and daughter? She couldn't stand thinking about the weird triangle anymore. She rushed out the door.

Crossing the suite she ran into Gail. "Oh, I didn't know you would be up so soon."

"Matt wanted his reading material ready for him when he woke. He also wanted to make sure you received these flowers this morning."

Flowers, now she knew for sure he had his system perfected. "They are pretty." She lied–she hated them.

"What are you doing with your suitcase?"

"What does it look like I'm doing? I'm leaving before Matt wakes."

"I'm sure Matt will want to know why?"

"Tell him he has another notch on his post. That should do. He can add it right next to my mother's."

"I think you have Matt all wrong."

"I don't!" Suzan shoved passed her, and rushed out the door without giving her a chance to say anything else. She needed to hurry, knowing that Gail would be giving Matt the news in a few minutes. She hoped the front door man could find her a taxi fast.

In seconds, she jumped inside a waiting taxi. Now what? She needed to hurry to the airport. She needed to fly back to

Florida and talk more with her mother.

Chapter 13

Matt pounded his fist together, his run to the bottom of the stairs in his bath robe resulted in him being embarrassed but accomplishing nothing else. He hoped no one with a camera saw him. He glanced over at Gail. "Tell me again what she said."

"She acted upset, and she said you would be happy with a mother and daughter notch on your bed post."

"I can't believe this. For some reason she thinks her mother and I had an affair. As you know, we never had sex."

"I hate to say this, but from a woman's point of view, some women like to take their time and build a relationship. If you moved fast with her, she would normally think you move fast with all women. And she might also think you did have sex with her mother."

"Of course I can see your point, but it's not true."

"I'm not sure she'll ever listen to you again or not. It all depends on her mother. I'm sure she's going to see her again now."

He glanced at the table full of food. "I'm not hungry. Let's pack and fly back to New York. I have many projects to do that I've left undone over the last few days."

"I'm sorry. I think I understand you a little. She acted different from other woman I know you spend time with."

"I'm sure you're referring to Chelsea."

"She was the first one to come to mind. Chelsea has left you several messages lately, and I'm sure it will only be a matter of time until she hears about you jetting around with Suzan."

"This is something I should've ended a long time ago,

but I need to talk to her father first and prepare him."

"You're a brave soul."

"I think Big John is more interested in our current project, and he would prefer me to concentrate on it. I really don't want to fight with Suzan in court. I want to work this out. If only she had given me a chance to show her what I had planned for the land she owned."

"She seemed determined to leave this morning, but shocked at the flowers."

"We had a great time yesterday and last night. I don't understand."

"Perhaps a little remorse in moving too fast."

"So, your advice would be?"

"Get your house in order with Chelsea and go after Suzan, or prepare to fight her and defend your company."

"I see. Try to reach her for me, since she doesn't answer my phone calls. I want to at least try to talk to her."

"Okay, but you might want to give her a little time to think about things and maybe talk to her mother to clear this up."

"You might be right, and I do need to handle things with Chelsea. I'm sure she'll hear about us being together soon. Let me call her and see what she's doing this afternoon."

"This afternoon?"

"Yes, I want to get this over with. Also, see if we can arrange a short board meeting tomorrow morning. We need to decide what to do with her lawsuit if Suzan cannot be convinced otherwise to drop it."

"I'll take care of setting up the meeting. I can tell you're starting to like Suzan. She might have been good for you."

###

Matt stretched out his hand to Big John as he entered his office. "I'm glad you could see me on such short notice."

"Not a problem at all. I saw you on the news last night."

"I can guess what you saw or heard. I thought I had a problem contained, but now I don't know."

"I've talked to Dan Panella in your legal department a few times the last few days, and he keeps me up to date on Suzan's lawsuit. The chances of her winning are next to none, but the chances of her delaying the project and costing us millions are very high."

"I've spent a lot of time with her the last few days and really like her. I still cannot understand why she wants the piece of swamp land back. I hoped to find out when she apparently got mad at me and left yesterday."

"Yes, Chelsea asked me about this yesterday." He raised an eyebrow to add emphasize to his comment.

"I'm sure she would, and I don't know what to do about this also. I need your advice."

"Matt, I know what you're going to say. Let me just say that Chelsea is my only daughter and I love her dearly. It's going to take a special man to satisfy her and spoil her like her mother and I have. And I know what kind of drain she can be on someone. I'm sure you know how to handle the situation. Don't worry about having to explain things to me. Trust me, I know."

"Thanks, I think we understand each other."

"Now, back to the problem at hand–what are you going to do about Suzan?"

"She's another problem. She can be difficult, and she's definitely not one to be intimidated into anything. She's so unlike any woman we had to work with before."

"It sounds like you've taken a liking to Suzan."

"Yes, and perhaps more than I want to admit."

"Well, it does sound like you have the incentive to work this out. Let me know if I can do anything to help. When are you seeing Chelsea again?"

"I plan to shortly, but I still don't know exactly what to say to her."

"I'll see to it that her mother takes her shopping for a few days. It usually always helps. They have fashion week coming up in Milan next week."

"Thanks. I really appreciate your help and understanding."

Big John grinned and pulled out a cigar. "Now, we can concentrate on the business at hand."

###

"Hello, Chelsea. How are you?" Matt walked through her large apartment overlooking Central park.

She pouted. "I've been fine, but I wonder how you've been doing. I've been seeing you in the paper with the . . . military girl."

"Yes, I'm sure the press is having a field day with our time together."

"How much longer are you going to be showing her around? You know, you can only extract so much hype out of someone like her."

"The truth is she owned a piece of land I purchased for Harris Properties that your father and I want to develop. If it's not handled properly, we could be facing some major losses on the project."

"You know I never get involved in business dealings. They're too boring for me. I would rather have fun. Perhaps, I could talk you into going skiing with me soon. You sure didn't mind taking off work for Suzan." Chelsea pointed to the front page of a magazine with both of them on the cover.

"I would say being with Suzan was all work, but I actually enjoyed getting away from work for a while."

"Oh, I can see what you mean. You have to be careful, or

you might lose me to other hunks wanting me. You know I can't be held on a chain forever."

"Chelsea, you know I never stopped you from seeing anyone, at any time."

"I don't have you mesmerized, do I?"

"We've had our moments, and I think you're a . . . shall I say, an out-of-the-ordinary girl for me."

"Girl?" Chelsea pointed to the photo of Matt and Suzan again. "When did taking a woman for a ride in Central Park at night in a carriage become normal operating procedure for Harris Properties?"

"The carriage ride was a spontaneous moment."

"It's too bad you didn't allow yourself to have more *spontaneous* moments with me, it could've been fun." Chelsea leaned forward allowing Matt to see her entire naked breasts under her pink cashmere sweater.

Matt turned his head and didn't feel like arguing, but knew he had to handle this discretely and keep Big John happy at the same time. He knew Chelsea would get over him in no time. With her millions in support from her dad, she would always be on every guy in New York's hit list; but, hopefully not on his anymore.

"You like this military girl, don't you?"

"I enjoy her company, but for your information, she's back in Florida, and she is still planning on going forward with the lawsuit against us."

"Well, maybe there's hope for me after all." Chelsea dropped the loose fitting sweater off of one shoulder. Her skin radiated as usual, but Matt fought back any attempt to give in.

"I wanted to stop by a minute. I heard from Big John that you plan to go to Milan in a few days."

"Yes, it will be a fantastic trip. You should go with me."

"I don't think the fashion world's what I'm interested in. I hope you have a good time."

"Will I see you when I return?" As she put every effort into becoming a sex goddess, Matt fought back an awkward grin.

"I think this might give us a good time to readjust our lives. What do you think?"

"I think you're a jackass, but who am I to say. We'll talk about this more when I return. I'm sure you'll have the military girl out of your head by the time I return." Chelsea didn't say goodbye but turned and left, stomping the floor as she walked.

Chapter 14

Mr. Dolbert read the papers as Suzan waited for him to respond. "Harris Properties is countersuing you for damages. However they make it clear if you drop the suit they will also. It will cost a lot in legal fees to defend these charges. They're asking for a lot of information and bringing up many legal questions. It appears they have an army of lawyers working for them. Properly defending yourself is going to be very expensive. I hate to tell you this." He paused. "And I'm afraid it gets worse. Because its undisputed that you signed a power of attorney before you went to Afghanistan, giving your mother the legal right to dispose of your property, they're claiming this is a frivolous lawsuit."

"A frivolous . . . What does that mean?"

"There's a Florida statute that allows a party to a lawsuit to recover all their attorney's fees from the other side, if they convince the judge that the claim against them had no basis in fact or in law. They're demanding that you dismiss your lawsuit immediately, or they'll go after you to reimburse them for all their legal costs when the suits over if they win. I won't lie to you Suzan, there's a risk here. You're trying to set aside a transaction Harris Properties entered into more than a year ago relying on what appears on its face to be a valid power of attorney. Plus, there's some evidence they actually did try to contact you while you were deployed, but were unable to get through. You could lose this case, Suzan, and end up spending all the proceeds of the sale to pay your own legal fees, their legal fees, and possibly additional damages to Harris Properties for any losses they suffered due to the delays on their project."

Suzan reflected on the time she had spent with Matt. Could he be so damn cold? She knew she walked out on him and had refused to talk to him. She still couldn't believe she had slept with him and made love all night. "So, tell me what you think I should do?"

"You need to think about how you're going to fund this litigation. Since you're trying to get the contract rescinded, that means if you win you get your land back and Harris Properties gets the full purchase price returned to them. So you need to keep those funds segregated, rather than using them to pay legal expenses. At this point, however, you don't have the full proceeds of the sale intact, because your mother already used a portion of those funds to pay back taxes on the property itself, and to pay your income taxes from the sale."

"I would get the income taxes back, wouldn't I?"

"Yes, but receiving a refund would take some time. Have you spent any of the monies you received?"

"Well, I've spent a little of it."

"The best advice I can offer you now is to try to reach some kind of compromise. Perhaps they would resell a portion of the land to you, although that's a long shot and really depends on what their development plans are. It makes more sense to make a settlement with them where you drop the lawsuit in exchange for their payment of the expenses you've incurred to date, such as my fees and other costs in attempting to recover the land."

"How much do you think we can ask for?"

"I think we need to toss a reply in their court and see what kind of response we can receive. The fact we have in our favor is the project we're delaying, which I'm sure is costing them money."

"I'm also concerned about what they have planned for the land. This is a very clean pristine area few men have ever seen. I know my father would hate to see it drained and developed into some kind of giant commercial district."

"I can ask for additional information in our letter. I wish I had better news for you. If you decide to proceed with the lawsuit, the condition of your mother when she signed the papers will be scrutinized extensively in the court. They'll hire experts, and she'll have to subject to medical and psychological examinations prior to the trial to determine her mental competence at the time the sales contract was executed. You'll have to ask yourself if that's what you want also."

Suzan could envision one of Matt's attorneys questioning her mother on the stand with reporters and anyone else who was interested in the courtroom. The fact of her mother's alleged affair with Matt would become public knowledge. She still couldn't believe the two made love. Of course, Matt still denied having sex with her, and the only proof would be her mother's statement, and with her attempting to show her mother incompetent, she knew her attorney would be hard pressed to prove it.

"You don't have to decide today. I know this is a lot for you think about."

"Yes, and it's not what I had hoped to hear. I need to talk to Mom and ask her psychologist to help me determine the truth. I don't want to embarrass her in front of the whole world. She needs me now also."

"I can understand."

"How long do we have to respond?"

"We have twenty days to file a formal answer to the counterclaim, and thirty days to respond to their discovery requests. I'm confident we can get an extension if I tell the attorneys that you are interested in discussing settlement options. They know that if the case moves forward their project could be put on hold for six months, a year, maybe even longer. That gives us some leverage, since the longer this matter is tied up in court; the more costly the project is for them. Knowing we have cards to play, it should force them to make a good offer back to us."

"You talked to my mother while I was gone. What do you think of her story?"

"Honestly, I think she was caught up the excitement of the moment and perhaps taken advantage of by not using an attorney. In defense of Harris Properties, they did nothing wrong in enticing her to accept the offer."

Suzan leaned forward. "The terms aren't exactly what I meant. I want to know if Matt Harris had sex with my mother and seduced her into signing the papers."

"Is that what you think really happened? Matt's a wealthy man, and although your parcel of land was certainly a good investment for his business, I doubt if he would have sex with any woman simply to make a deal. Think about it. And remember, becoming sexually involved with the other party in a real estate transaction may raise questions about his business ethics, but that in and of itself isn't enough to void a sale. Your undue influence argument depends on the mental capacity of your mother, and equally important, whether Matt had reason to suspect he was dealing with an individual who wasn't legally competent to sign a contract. Becoming sexually involved with another party to obtain a business deal would have the potential to backfire if those sorts of tactics became public knowledge."

Suzan bit her lip before she continued. "It didn't stop him from seducing me to his bed."

Suzan watched his mouth open. "You didn't!"

"I thought Matt was different after I spent some time with him. I found him attractive. What can I say? I obviously wasn't using my best judgment."

"Oh my. This does complicate things."

"I'm sure it does for you, I hope you understand having sex with Matt has made my life unbearable. I received the Silver Star and you would think have the world leaning over to help me. It appears I'm the one being screwed royally right now."

"I hate to say it, but working things out with Matt outside a lawsuit would be the best way to handle this. Perhaps if we set up a meeting between the two of you."

"Thanks, but no thanks!"

"Well, the decision as to how you want to proceed is totally up to you. Let me know what you want me to do."

"I will. I'm not blaming you. I know Matt has a large, as you said . . . army of attorneys, I saw some of them. He has a whole floor of them. I need to talk to my mother first before I'll let you know what to do."

Chapter 15

Matt led the way through one of the most exclusive clubs in New York City, and maybe even the entire country, as he anticipated the cigar smoking camaraderie he would enjoy with the rest of the top management team at Harris Properties. He remembered when this place had some great dining and was known as the Top of the Sixes, but thanks to those who know better and wanted to end life's simple pleasure of lighting up an excellent handmade work of art, this place had been converted to the Grand Havana, which occupied about 17,000 square feet on the thirty ninth floor of the building located at 666 Fifth Avenue. With the membership extended to a choice few who love smoking the best, it had become one of Matt's favorite places to escape to. Luckily, all of his top management loved cigars as much as he did. The one left out of the crowd was Gail, his secretary.

Matt knew the elite of New York could often be seen here, as well as some of the top celebrities of the city. But with several smaller rooms offering a kind of club inside a club, he knew they would have all of the privacy they needed. As they all settled into large lounge chairs in their favorite room, several beautiful hostesses joined the men and asked what they could bring.

As usual, a central table included the basics, a bowl for brandy, a number of exquisite ash trays, cigar snipers, and what Matt had asked for, a never ending bottle of champagne, something he had become accustomed to having available with all of his meetings. Some of the guys would make a toast occasionally, and Matt considered champagne the drink of choice at these gatherings.

Matt remained standing until they all located a place to become comfortable. He reached for a special box he had ordered and watched the beaming smiles coming from his men. Tony Korth, his vice president in charge of operations, had a love for cigars resulting from his Cuban background. His ability to control the actual field operation during construction made him a great leader. People looked up to him because of his strong determination to build the best properties on the market. Matt provided him with a chance to prove himself one time after another. It had always been a great match up. He was also the first one reaching for a cigar.

Dan Panella represented the kind of lawyer Matt felt comfortable with. His job was to avoid conflict, and as such, he had been well known as the peacemaker in the group. Not a soft easy pushover type, but one who forced it on others. He insisted on it, and often mediated cases without going to court. It was never out of weakness, but by giving the other side little options but to negotiate behind closed doors.

Phil also shared the ability to bring peace to a group, but in a much more subtle way. Being such a perfect match for his passion for public relations, Phil could easily work for any company he wanted to. The stock options Matt had given him made Phil happy to stay exactly where he worked. Phil was such a guy that he insisted on everyone else being taken care of before he settled in.

Everyone smiled, knowing one more guy would be making an entrance in a minute. Ronald Sirani, the vice president of finance, didn't fit the mold of an accountant or financial guru, who often had the image of the dullest person in the company. Instead, he often led the team into taking adventures they never imagined they would. He also made the others wonder how anyone had the time to take on what he did. Whatever kept him so hyped all of the time worked great in his ability to keep the finances under control. As if on cue, they heard him working his way through the club and talking loudly to others at the door, while of course, flirting with the stunning beauties who worked as hostess at Grand Havana.

With Ronald rushing in to join them, Matt laughed. "I'm glad you could make it."

Everyone quickly lit their cigars at the same time and inhaled deeply. With plumes of smoke curling across the room, Matt motioned to one of the hostesses to start handing everyone a glass of champagne. "Okay, guys, it has been a long time since we've been here, so what are we celebrating?"

As if on cue they all raised their glasses and shouted in unison, "Harris Properties!"

All glasses thrust forward in a salute and rather than being sipped, the whole contents in everyone's glass disappeared in one gulp. Matt laughed as he looked around. This one custom had been repeated every time they had met here. He had always promised them anything they wanted after the first glass.

Small talk erupted between individuals until they all returned to their seats except for Matt. "I think we have much to celebrate. All of the projects are moving forward as we expected, and our profits are going to be better than we estimated on many of them." He eyed his cigar. "Damn, these are good cigars, aren't they?"

The men offered sharp yells and whistles, knowing they all would be receiving fantastic bonuses. Matt enjoyed the men he had recruited as much as, if not more so, than his other accomplishments. They all had the ability to run a major corporation, but they worked for him instead. If he lost everything but managed to hold on to these men, he would have it all back again.

"Since we have the team together for once, who wants to go first and give us an update?" Matt decided to have a seat.

Dan rose to his feet first. "I know my job is to protect our ass, and I'm happy to report although we have many suits and legal challenges, we have them all under control. I thought we might be having a problem with our Everglades project, but from what I've learned, the attorney who handles the Mercer account has no money to confront us, and I think he has persuaded Suzan Mercer that it will be a long fight. I hope to be able to announce a settlement soon, and we can get back to our task of having the project approved by the state."

As he returned to his seat, Phil stood. "Since you mentioned Suzan, I guess I should follow up on it. She has helped us tremendously and she doesn't know it. By being seen with Matt in Washington, his image has been improved substantially. Many of our buyers are older and very patriotic. I spent a little time with Suzan, and she's a very unusual woman. I don't think she realizes she has the upper hand in these negotiations. It would've cost us a fortune in public relation costs to fight her lawsuit, plus the delay in starting the project. I wish her well and hope all can be finalized in a good manner."

Ronald soon followed with the next piece of information. "As many of you know, a major piece of the financing for the project is coming from Big John. He told me how Matt and Big John's daughter have decided to . . . as he put it, cool it for now. After avoiding what could've been a major heart attack, I learned Matt had talked to him already and he's still on board with us. I know Matt has spent some time with Suzan, and I hoped it wouldn't send Chelsea off on a rage. I feel sorry for her, but I know she'll survive. Matt, what do you think? Is Chelsea my type?" He raised his eye brows in a test of wits before laughing at the possibility and enduring the laughs of the others. "For all of the rest of our projects, we're in fantastic shape. With the market as it is now, many investors are looking for investment opportunities, and we should have no shortage of money anytime in the future."

As expected, Tony waited until last to report in. His passion for building, and his desire to make a statement for Harris Properties as environmental friendly and green, meant he wanted to concentrate on his part, and leave the rest to other members of the team. He was the *get it done guy,* and one Matt trusted entirely. "As everyone knows, we're finishing many projects now, and we only have the final details to complete. I'm so excited about the Everglades project. I know many people think we'll ruin the area, but I think my plans will enhance the land. We have taken every situation into consideration. This should make a statement for us much more than we have in the past. People with strong environmental views will pay the prices we'll charge to make it so. The bylaws for the project should protect the Everglades area forever. We're not in the national park, but this land is next to it. If we don't protect this sensitive area, someone else will ruin it. Phil, I know I can count on you to put our best face forward. I'm looking forward to working on it." He turned to Matt. "I also wish Suzan had given you the chance to show her what we had planned."

As if the ball was being passed back to him, Matt accepted his position. "I can see the only concerns for everyone is the Everglades project. It's important to me also. Yes, I wish I had been able to convince Suzan we had the interest of the best use and preservation of the property at heart, but I, how shall I say it guys, struck out on this one."

Phil raised his cigar. "I'm not so sure about your conclusion. It may be she has given you more of a challenge than you want to take on."

"A challenge?"

"We all know we can all have almost any woman we want. Listen, I'm not blowing smoke here. It's not too often we have someone reject us or give us a run for our money. I think sometimes we forget what it's like to have to pursue and compete for a woman." Phil's words hit home as many in the crowd considered his argument. All eyes drifted toward Matt.

"Okay guys, I understand. Yes, I felt an attraction toward Suzan. I think everyone here likes her to some extent. She's totally different than what we're used to and I think she is a very beautiful woman." Matt studied his words. He wasn't sure how many times in his life he had referred to a woman as beautiful and really meant it. With his circle of friends he felt comfortable in continuing. "Okay what does everyone have on their mind that I'm missing? I know all of the conversation today has been on Suzan."

A smile flashed among his friends.

With no comments, he continued with a large grin. "Yes, I liked her to, but she did leave me without saying goodbye."

Phil blew a large smoke plume. "I know it's hard to go chasing after someone who rejected you, but the consequences might be harder to live with if you don't try."

"So, everyone thinks I should go to Florida and see her?"

Dan answered for the group. "I think everyone will

breathe better once this is concluded. You have the ability to finish this. Once she sees the facts, I think she'll call off the suit."

"I'm hearing two different objectives here. Yes, I would love to have this settled like everyone, but I'm not sure I want to settle down with one woman and get married now. Getting dropped isn't easy for me."

Dan continued. "I think you've always put the business ahead of everything. You have the ability to bring this to an end quickly."

Matt cleared his throat. "I might be able to. For some reason I want to know why she wants to hold on to the land. I want to know why she's feeling so hurt about us buying the land. I know it's not the price."

Phil slapped Dan on the shoulder. "In both cases, it will take you going to Florida to see her."

"I'll consider your advice and let you know. For now, let's see what the cognac does to these cigars." Matt leaned over and dipped the tip of his cigar in the expensive cognac and watched his friends join him. They knew him too well, and he had to admit, they have always looked out for his best interest.

Chapter 16

Suzan held her mother's arm as they entered the psychiatrist's small office. She wanted her mother to look nice and used the morning to help her fix her hair before encouraging her to use makeup. Her mother possessed beautiful features she wish she had, and had an elegant look and poise much different than the one she had learned in the Army. With her appearance so much better than the first time she saw her, Suzan felt proud of her mother in the way she presented herself. She also realized that this would be the kind of woman Matt would like much more than herself.

Dr. Reynolds soon joined them. "I'm glad to see you two this afternoon. I'll have to say you both look great today." He eased his large body into a chair behind his oversized desk covering most of the room. Besides the two chairs occupied by Suzan and her mother, he had one small couch and wall to wall book cases filled with books.

"Thanks." It felt good to see her mother looking good for a change. Her mother's memory had faded in and out all morning, but remained better than normal. Suzan wanted to know what other medication they had available, and how to know when her mother operated in the good part of her mind and when she faded. She had to know.

"I take it you're doing much better on your new medication. Are you feeling any kind of side effects this time?"

"Such as?" Her mother spoke clearly today.

"I'm looking for anything out of the normal for you. Do you have any headaches or pains?"

"Not really." Her mother looked annoyed, but she

continued to engage the doctor.

"How about your appetite and the way your body feels?"

"I'm fine really. It sounds like you're questioning me like my daughter. I feel great, and I'm just tired of all of the questions."

"I see. So maybe this medication is good for you. The dosage might need to be regulated occasionally, and knowing how the medication affects you is the reason for all of the questions."

Suzan decided to ask the doctor a few questions. "As you know, I might need you to testify for me in the case of my suit against Harris Properties. Mother signed the contract a long time ago, and it may be hard to give a good accounting of my Mom's mental ability when she signed the papers."

"I understand and I'll soon be able to offer you a better assessment. Your mother's making great improvements."

"I understand, but I don't have a lot of time. This suit is expensive, and I don't know if I can keep it going."

"I'm sure you know these kinds of cases can take a long time, and the process of evaluating your mom will take a long time also."

Suzan hung her head. What was she going to do? She tightened her muscles throughout her body as she looked straight at her mom. "We need to talk. I need you to think as hard as you can for me."

Suzan watched her mother's face stare inattentively at her. "What do you want from me?"

"I think you know I wanted to hold on to this land. I want to know why you signed the papers with Matt and why you didn't contact me."

A tear grew in her mother's eyes. "The land was a sore point for me. I couldn't keep paying the bills, and it reminded me too much of your father and how he died. He didn't want to leave the land to me, but to you. Yes, I agreed to a settlement to allow the land to pass to you. I thought it would be good to start over fresh when you left for the Army. Now, I think I screwed up. I really didn't mean to." Her mother lowered her head as Suzan glanced at the doctor.

Suzan felt a new compassion for her mother. "It will be okay, and we'll work it out."

Her mother whimpered as Suzan leaned over and offered her a hug. "Mom, I know this is hard on you, but I have one more question. I need to know what you meant by Matt seducing you?"

"I've never had anyone treat me like he did. He's so good looking. I'm sure you know what I mean. Oh my God. I wanted to do right. He sent me flowers when he first heard I might be willing to come to New York to see him. Your Father never purchased me flowers."

"I understand. Matt can be very generous."

"When we met in his office, and he stared at me with his eyes I felt totally helpless. I've never been seduced by a man like him before."

"Mom, when you say seduced what else did he do to scducc you?"

"After we signed the papers, he took me to a nice restaurant to eat."

"I understand. He wanted to celebrate the transaction. They have a lot of nice restaurants in New York City."

"You know, I hoped it would just be the two of us, but he invited several others from his office to join us. I think he might be a little shy."

Matt . . . shy. Suzan didn't think so. "Mom, I need to know what happen between you and Matt after the diner."

"What do you mean? You don't think I went to bed with him, do you?"

Suzan bit her lip–hard. "Mom, I'm sorry I have a hard time understanding you ever since I came home."

"You really don't know me, do you?"

"I guess not, but if you'll let me, I want to know you better."

Suzan reached over and hugged her mother close for a long time. Finally she heard the doctor clear his throat. "Mom, I need to ask the doctor a few things before we leave concerning your medication."

"Okay, I need to find my coat."

"Good, I'll be outside in a minute."

The doctor looked like he was going to burst with the breakthrough. "I would say this medication is working great, but you have to keep her monitored."

"I guess this isn't too good for my case, is it?"

"I'm no lawyer, but she still didn't have a perfect mind when she signed, and I can attest to that. She also sold the property without your permission, but legally I don't know if that matters since she did have your power of attorney. I'm not sure how she'll act if they put her on the stand."

"You don't think they'll put her on the stand, do you?"

"Like I said, I'm no lawyer. I'll continue to work with her and hopefully she'll keep improving. However, with her condition you never know when it might turn worse."

Thinking about Matt, Suzan glanced at the ceiling. She had been wrong about him. Could she admit it to him? She doubted it. What would she do now? She had no clue. The night they had spent together had played in her mind constantly, now it would have a whole new meaning as a bitter sweet moment frozen forever in her memory. She couldn't go back in time, and if she could, she doubted she would change anything.

Chapter 17

Suzan had not slept for the last two nights. Visions of missions in Afghanistan were waking her one moment, and dreams of making love to Matt were taunting her the next minute. She forced herself to look objectively at her situation, to assess her options, to make her plans for her future. Her land was gone, but her mother was improving, and perhaps even able to live on her own with some help from time to time.

While the dusty road to the old home place reminded her of times she had lived in the family house, it now simply cluttered her thoughts. Her dad loved this place. She loved this place. But it was her mother who always wanted a city life. She laughed, as she considered the words of her father who had promised her this land would bring her love one day. Heartbreak was more like it.

She glanced at her watch. She had plenty of time before she knew the contact from the CIA would show, which was good, since she needed this time to think. Once she committed this time, she might not ever be able to turn back the clock. Very few times when someone leaves the reservation, as they call it, do they ever allow them back in. However, she knew she had presented them with a special situation.

She had proved she could accomplish her missions. She had always been successful. This was, in fact, the only life she knew. And now she would be doing her country a bigger service. No one would know her sacrifices but her, but she had no one she wanted to impress, much different than Matt, who she knew wanted to astonish everyone.

She knew she would be questioned extensively. They had picked this site, not her. Why, she couldn't guess, other than the privacy it offered. Trying to anticipate the questions they would ask, she concentrated on those concerning Matt Harris. They told her to keep a low profile, but since they were the ones clearing the Silver Star award, she would love to know their reasoning behind this decisions.

The old home place looked as if it had been abandoned for a long time, creating a sad feeling inside of her. She could see the house being pushed over by a bulldozer, making way for Harris Properties grand building scheme. She had to force her mind to forget the future events, to move on. She had wanted to go inside, but now remained idly waiting for the contact to show.

She heard an air boat approaching from the back. One last ride would be fantastic, and perhaps the perfect way to say good bye to the place. She also realized this might be her contact's method of arriving unnoticed. She walked toward the back yard which stretched into the swamp.

She heard the motor being cut as she turned the corner. Two men jumped on the dry land as she approached them. Wearing black jumper suits and black baseball hats they left little to be recognized, especially with the dark glasses.

"Suzan, how are you?"

"I'm fine. I didn't expect you to come by boat."

"We kind of thought you might like to see this area one more time. Would you like to go for a ride?"

"Absolutely!"

The boat ride ventured around a winding river she knew by heart as she pointed to the direction she wanted to go. A half hour later they pulled into a small pool and turned off the engine.

"I think this place will do well." A man behind her

tossed her a beer. "Compliments of my boss."

"As hot as it is today, that's very thoughtful of him. I don't guess there's any way of you telling me who he is." With his head turned sideways, she knew the answer. "Let's just say he wanted to buy you a beer for a long time for a job well done."

Suzan opened the beer and gulped. "Well, at least tell him thank you for me."

"You contacted us. We were hoping you would. Are you sure you want to dedicate your life to this? Your role will be different from here on out. I'm sure you know what I mean."

"I can understand how it would be. I never asked questions before and have nothing else to live for."

"We watched you with Matt Harris intently, as you might imagine."

"I sure you did." She wondered how much they really knew. Did they know they were lovers?

"Your record speaks for itself. The question we have concerns Matt. Are you sure it's over between you two? He'll bring a major spotlight on you, which will change things."

"I don't think we have a life to look forward to. We only knew each other a few weeks."

"It's still a consideration. We would like you to think about your decision a little more."

Suzan rose from her seat. "I've already thought about it, and I see no reason in putting this off. Let me know what your decision is and when I can start."

Chapter 18

Matt leaned forward to retrieve some fresh fruit from the center of the breakfast table in his condo. With his favorite morning papers positioned to his side, he hoped to find good news for a change. He massaged a small pain above his eyes.

Gail walked in and glanced at him rubbing his forehead. "I see you still have a headache. I think you've had one for several days now."

"Yes, I haven't slept well in several nights."

"Everything appears to be going good at the company now. Are you stressed about anything I can help you with?"

"I need to go to Florida and talk to Suzan, and I'm not looking forward to the confrontation."

"Really?"

"Well, I guess yes and no. I have pressure to take care of the problem by everyone here. They want to get on with business, but Suzan thinks I had an affair with her mother, which I never did."

"And you were starting to have feelings for Suzan." Gail stopped to wink.

"Maybe, but definitely something. I still have no idea why she wants to hold on to the land so bad. I wanted her to see what we had planned for her land and I guess I wanted her approval."

"Approval, when have you ever wanted approval from someone so much?"

"I guess the day I saw someone with as much passion as me." Funny, he may have answered his own questions. Perhaps her passion is what he liked about her. She went after what she wanted and never hesitated or flinched, even with the odds she faced. He couldn't imagine taking on a company as large as Harris Properties on his own.

"I can tell you'll always have this haunting you if you don't handle it now. You know Florida isn't that far of a trip, right?"

"I know, but I'm not sure how I'll react when I see her. As I said, the board is after me to finish this and they know we have the upper hand now. I don't know if that's what I want totally. I also don't think she'll listen to me. I think I made her mad when she left here."

"Being rejected is a bad feeling, I know. I wish I could make it easier for you, but I never had much of a chance to talk to Suzan."

Matt realized Gail might have a point. Perhaps Suzan would open to another woman and explain thing to her. It might be worth a shot. "See if you can arrange a meeting with her. We can leave as soon as you do. Perhaps she'll talk to you. I'm not sure how we can work it, but I know you'll try for me."

"You know I will. I don't like seeing you so miserable."

"It shows that bad, huh?"

"Worse! Enjoy your breakfast and I'll see if I can get in touch with her."

Matt played with his food as he considered what might be waiting for him. He needed to take care of business for the company, but he needed to make Suzan happy. His stomach felt tight and his head light. He knew he had one shot at this before the attorneys would insist on handling everything.

He watched Gail, who was not a bad looking woman at all, walk out of the room. She always looked out for him, true to her giver type personality. However, her job was to take care of his personal needs. She always had the ability to take care of situations for him before he knew he needed her. He had heard of many men falling for their secretary, but she was much more than a mere secretary. She acted as a true executive in many ways and handled many of his day to day chores. In fact, if he disappeared, she could run the company almost as effective as he could. She didn't have the charisma he had, but she had the knowledge and skills needed. She was the person behind the scene most of the time, the one who did the real work but never received the recognition. They both knew her role, and he tried to find other ways to make her happy. She might be the most highly paid secretary in the country.

With Gail gone, Matt turned his attention back to Suzan. The memories of her face, the short snappy replies replayed often. The problem he had with women all of his life is their inability to interact with him. He knew he intimidated most woman, but not Suzan. She teased at times, and insulted at others. She knew what she wanted and expressed her passion on every corner. If he ever wanted to be in a relationship, it had to be with someone he considered a life partner. While not an equal in many respects of his business life, she was in the one area he valued most. He knew Gail spoke correctly in one assessment. He needed to know what it was about her that dominated his interest. Why was she the one girl he couldn't forget?

Chapter 19

Suzan had talked to Gail for a long time the day before. Gail had expressed a concern she needed to hear from someone. Suzan could tell why Matt used her. Gail had a caring attitude much stronger than she had seen from anyone before, as she listened to her and encouraged her to talk. How much of the conversation made it back to Matt, she knew she would never know. Part of the conversation she did want him to know, and as far as others, well . . . she hoped Gail would respect her privacy.

Nonetheless, Gail had talked her into seeing Matt one more time. Suzan thought she might as well, since her lawsuit was a lost cause and this might give her some closure. In the back of her mind she wondered if she did show him the land he might think different. It remained a long shot, but it was all she had left. She assumed Matt had never seen the property up close and personal. And today, well . . . she planned to make sure he ventured deep inside the swamp. She had rented an airboat and planned to take Matt for the ride of his life.

With the airboat secured behind her old home place, she waited and enjoyed the sounds of the swamp. The alligators had roamed this place forever, and the Florida panther could be seen from time to time. With the panther on the endangered list, she had always hoped it would be impossible to do much development. However, with the money, power and influence of Matt and his company, she knew he might. She forced herself to not think about their future.

Her thoughts returned to her father's dying word

concerning the land, and how it would bring her love one day. What love? She had no one, and she now had decided to dedicate her life to the work of the CIA. What they had in store for her, she didn't know for sure, but she knew it would be a life of sorts, just the same.

She heard the sound of a helicopter approaching from the east. The loud noise of the engines indicated it was flying low and fast, and exactly the kind of noise which scared the animals in the swamp. She could imagine the fright they had coming when the real construction started.

Suzan waited as the corporate helicopter circled overhead once, while looking for a place to land. The front yard provided the only place large enough. The wind from the blades battered the grass as it descended, as she remained still and quiet until Matt exited the copter. Being in plain sight, she knew he saw her when they passed over the house.

As she waited patiently on him to approach her, she watched his two bodyguards and Gail follow behind him. She should've known he would bring others with him. Still, this might be good and help her to hold her tongue. She did owe him an apology, and swallowing her pride wouldn't be easy.

"I see you like to make an entrance." She offered a smile to see if he would return the same.

"It's the easiest way to travel here. I'm so glad you agreed to see me, and I'm sorry if I upset you the last time we were together."

"First, let me say I owe you an apology."

"Really?"

"Yes, I thought my mother had an affair with you and–" Suzan stopped as she glanced over his shoulder at Gail approaching close enough to hear her. "I'll tell you more later."

Matt's face tightened. "I understand, but I promise I never intended to hurt you, and I never had sex with your mother."

"I know that now." She felt the relief flow through her, as she made it past what she assumed to be the impossible.

"I never had the chance to tell you I wanted to come here with you. I hoped you could see my other projects first, but still the same, I hope you'll like what I plan to do with this land."

"I'll listen to you, but first, buster, you're going on a trip with me." She glanced at his clothing, the first time he didn't wear a suit. He wore lose jeans and a camp type shirt, a combination she assumed he had purchased especially for this trip. "You know you're going to get wet, right?"

"I've been warned. Gail and the pilot will stay here, but I hope you have room for the security."

"We have room, but I don't think we need them here." She laughed. "That's unless they're good at wrestling alligators."

The two guards glanced at each other before they surveyed the swamp.

Matt walked closer to her, as his presence invaded her space. His smell penetrated her nostrils as she remembered the intoxicating moments they had spent together. His eyes locked in on her own with the same intensity she remembered the first time he ventured so near. He lingered, not saying a word, as he moved closer and wrapped an arm around her. "I missed you."

Wow, she didn't expect this, but loved it. She lingered and wanted to give him a hug, but she wanted to make sure he really felt this way. She knew she should say something, anything for being perceived as a weak, infatuated high school kid. But . . . she waited for him.

"Okay, you have me here. I'm looking forward to your tour, and I guess I can say, I'm in your hands for now."

She allowed the walls of resistance around her to fall. "Yes, this is my world and I think you'll soon see why I wanted to hold on to this land." She leaned forward and offered a cheek which he kissed. She knew he wanted lips, but she wanted to wait until later when they were alone. "Come on aboard and we'll get started."

For the next two hours she navigated one part of a stream to another and pointed out the beauty of the world she knew. She hoped to see a panther, but knew the chances were next to zero. They lived here, and she needed to point it out. The boat slid sideways time after time as she rounded corners, and she watched him smile as if a teenager enjoying a ride, his mannerism revealed the sheltered life he had lived. She felt glad to give him something to remember as the water soaked him over and over on each turn.

When they soon returned to the house, she hoped he would start to understand how fragile this area was. Damn, she wanted him to know how special the swamp was. She hoped now he would understand why her dad wanted her to retain this land to find love. She stopped in deep thought, as she wondered about her father's words. Could it be this is the love he talked about? She glanced at Matt again. Could he be the one?

Matt glanced at the house. "Is this where you lived?"

"Yes, it's not the same as Fifth Avenue, but it's where I spent my life until I joined the Army. Would you like to see inside?"

"Sure."

As they walked to the back door she had already managed to open with an old key they had hidden, she wondered what he thought about someone who lived in the swamps. "I promise you my home looked much better when my father was alive. The last four years haven't been good for the place."

"I can understand your feelings, and I know it hurts to see it in this condition."

"More than you'll ever understand."

As soon as they entered the back door, Matt reached for her hand and stopped her from walking forward. She turned to face him as he wrapped the other arm around her, pulling her close to him. "I've missed you, and I'm so glad you agreed to see me."

She couldn't deny she missed him also. The night they had together felt like a long time ago, but it was still fresh enough to ignite her need for his manly presence. She had lost so much sleep thinking about him, and now he was back with her again, but for how long? What was the purpose of them pretending? He had his life and she had her own–only her life was so uncertain.

Matt leaned forward and went straight for her lips, his intentions clearly displayed. As a man who always seemed to get what he wanted, he acted like he knew what he desired, which made her feel more confident in herself and the belief he might really have feelings for her. He parted almost as quick. "I'm sorry. I wanted to kiss you again ever since the last time. I hope you'll forgive me."

She decided the best way to answer him was to lean forward and kiss back. With her mouth open and ready for his tongue, she felt all walls of resistance destroyed. She wanted him again, but not here, somewhere more romantic, and with time to enjoy every detail of their time together.

After a long kiss, she parted slightly from him, but remained close enough to hear him breath. "I'll admit it, I missed you to, but . . . we're so different."

"Yes, but no. The part we're alike we can build on, and the part where we're different will make life fun and exciting. What do you think?"

Did he think they could build a relationship? Really? "It'll take some time, and I'm not sure."

He raised a hand to almost beg for a moment. "I've wanted to show you something for as long as I've known you. If you'll give me the chance to make a proposal to you on what I've planned for this property, I think you'll like it, and perhaps maybe me and my life in the process. Will you keep an open mind and allow me to show you something?"

Part of her agreed instantly, but part of her still worried he might be trying to pull a fast one. Still, he looked genuinely interested in telling his story and as if he wanted to impress her. So, why not let him? "Okay, you win."

"Good. We have a meeting room at a place I developed back in Fort Myers. I know you'll like it. I hope so at least."

###

Suzan, dressed in her jeans and a faded blue pull over, ignored the looks of those in the lobby as she held on to the arm of Matt Harris. In spite of dressing in casual clothes, he carried the million dollar smile and charisma which had made him famous. Today, however, he shunned the attention of those around him and directed it at her. Yes, she loved his way of focusing on her. Still hesitated in letting him know exactly how she felt about him, she wanted to know his true feelings first. Would he go there? Was there more to this meeting than convincing her he was a great developer? She already knew he had developed some great properties.

She held on to his arm and felt the well toned muscle underneath. The staff at the complex rushed ahead of them as the two guards and Gail followed them. She knew getting accustomed to such a following would take some time.

The group turned into a large impressive meeting room, with dark walnut looking walls covered with beautiful paintings. The lighting shimmered from many large lamps across the wooden topped conference table. Matt pulled a chair out for her at the head of the table, giving her the best place before he leaned over and kissed her cheek and settled into the chair next to her. "This is the room we used to sell these units, but rather than showing you the presentation we used to sell these, I want you to see the one we're working on for what I have planned for the land you sold me. Please keep an open mind until you see the entire presentation. Afterwards, I'll make you a very special offer."

"Oh really?"

Gail waved as the two guards turned to the door and pulled it behind them as they left. "I'm not the normal salesman we use, so you'll have to bear with me. I'm sure Matt will add to this."

Suzan watched the presentation, but she had her mind on Matt. He knew what he wanted, and she knew only a man like him could ever make her happy. With the memories of them making love replaying in her mind, she fought back to concentrate on the video presentation. He reached over and placed an arm around her as she felt her soul melting.

Matt had researched the project much more than she could believe. He had plans to preserve the area with limited intrusions. The properties would be marketed to environmentalists who were committed to maintaining the unique character of the land. Yes, the bylaws were extensive. The houses to be built on the available land were to be placed in harmony with the area, and a large gate would restrict the entrance to members only. The houses would be built on reinforced stilts, and designed to allow the wildlife to flourish around them. A special accommodation for the Florida panther would help to make sure they would survive. He had added so much more to the project than she would have believed.

"Okay, this is impressive. I've always known you do great work, but I do have one question for you."

"Okay."

"You already have my land and there's nothing I can do to get it back, so why are you showing me all of this?"

Matt turned to Gail and winked. "I think I can take it from here."

Gail returned the smile and glanced at Suzan. "Let me know if he gets out of hand." After a quick returned wink, she left.

As Matt pulled her closer to him she laid her head on his shoulder, melting into his presence, as she studied the lights still left lowered to a subtle glow. Did he plan for this romantic mood, or did the gods of love look out for them?

"I'm glad to see the land will be put to good use. You win."

Matt used his hand to turn her face toward him, as his eyes cast their spell in the low light. If he wanted her again, she felt willing. He didn't need to work so hard at it. She knew this might be the last time she saw him, since a man like him had so many opportunities, not to mention many more empires to build.

She instigated the first move and leaned toward his lips, but hesitated inches from them. "I know I might not respect myself tomorrow, but I'm thinking about it, I don't have a lot planned for tomorrow."

"I'm glad you mentioned the future. I'm still treading on land I've never developed before. I hope you like the analogy. I . . . don't want to lose you. You hurt me when you left last time."

"I'm sorry about leaving without saying goodbye, but I made a bad assumption." Suzan opened her eyes. "What do you mean I hurt you? Are you saying you have feelings for me?"

"I think you know I do. As you probably know from the little time we spent together, my whole life is involved with my properties."

"Yes, I know."

"I would love for you to come to New York and spend some time with me."

"New York. Is it that hard to find a woman in the big apple?"

"To find a woman isn't hard at all. To find one I care about–impossible."

"I remember your condo in New York. It looked large and nice, but still cold and stiff. I hope you don't mind me saying such. What would I be? Maybe your girl when you need me to take care of you?"

"No, nothing like that."

Suzan pulled from him and lowered her head, but maintained a steady stare into his eyes, matching him with her quest for what was going on. "So, tell me what you're proposing?" Okay, she thought hard about her choice of the word *propose,* and now wished she had selected another.

"What I'm *proposing* is that you come to live with me."

"And how will you introduce me, perhaps as your *live in*?"

"You know, you might have a career in being a negotiator."

"Yeah."

"This will not be easy for me. I've never had to ask anyone for anything in my life, but I'm asking you to come live with me."

"I understand your invitation. The question is: what are you offering me in exchange?"

"I've never married anyone before, and perhaps I'm too old of a dog to learn new trick, but I'm willing to explore the possibilities."

"You're talking marriage, and you've never told me that you loved me."

"I thought you understood."

"I see we have some things to work on here."

Matt laughed. "I know we do, and I think that will be what is so remarkable about this relationship. I always thought a marriage should be between equals."

"So, you consider me an equal. In which way am I an equal?"

"I think in the ability to stand toe-to-toe with me. To express passion for what you want and not back down until you get it."

"But you did win on the land deal."

"Maybe, but, that is, if you'll join me and help develop it . . . ."

"Me?"

"Why not? You know the land better than anyone. If I can win you over to this project, perhaps I can win you over to me."

Suzan considered his comments. "You've been trying to show me this project since day one. Why?"

"I think when we return to New York you'll be interested in seeing something I have for you." Matt leaned over and kissed her forehead, his scent intoxicating her soul.

"So, you think I'll go with you and you not tell me first?"

"I hoped to wait and share this with you, but if you insist. Your mother's a good painter."

"My mother? I've seen her work."

"Well you may have seen some of them–but not all."

"Why do you think so, Matt?"

"Because I own most of her collection at my place in New York."

"So, you're the one who purchases her work."

"Yes, I'm afraid so."

"But what does this have to do with me?" She asked as her interest grew.

"One of the first pieces I purchased from her was a portrait of you."

"Of me?" A sense of intrigue flowed over her as her mind wondered to her mother. What did she paint?

"Yes, it's one of my favorite paintings. I've gazed at it for a long time, and I've always wondered what the beautiful woman in the painting was thinking. I never anticipated the woman would be so passionate about life. I guess I can admit you're like a fantasy come true for me."

"Wow. This I never expected. Tell me about this partnership."

"I will when we arrive in New York. You can let me know what you decide there. I know this is a lot to think about."

Suzan started to resist, but thoughts of her commitment to the CIA rained on her spirits. What was she going to tell them? Was it too late to make a change in plans? "Thank you, but I do need some time." She watched him move closer and kiss her lips tenderly at first, only to rush into a heated passion moments later. She wanted him but felt scared of what she might have to tell him.

His hand slipped toward her breasts. He breathed hard and pulled her closer with his other hand. Stopping for a second he looked at the top of the table. "I had a thought, but no, this is crazy. I can find us a room if you're interested?"

"You know I loved making love to you the first time. I'm sure it will be good again." She kissed him again, exploring his mouth and rubbing his chest. "I don't want to be hurt, and I don't want to hurt you."

"If you can trust me for a little longer, I'm sure we'll both have what we want. I need to tell everyone outside we'll be spending the night. And with your permission, I want to tell them to make plans for us to go to New York."

Suzan opened her mouth to speak, but he cut her off. "Remember I do things in a dramatic way, so please don't rob me of this moment, this one time I ask someone for something as important as what I plan to ask you." With his eye begging with her, she couldn't turn away such a request. She offered him another kiss, as she wanted him right now and hoped he would hurry. She felt powerless in turning him down now. Oh hell! How would the CIA take the news when she told them she was getting married?

Chapter 20

After arriving in New York the next morning, Suzan didn't know who had more pent up needs the night before. Matt wanted her all night, and who was she to complain. Now, she had to face the music. She had given her word to the CIA. Her contact would meet her in a few minutes, which were only a few hours from the time she assumed Matt would propose to her. What was she to do?

After she had asked for a few minutes to get some fresh air, she had watched the staff look at her with large question marks all over their faces. Were they as afraid as Matt must be that she would run again? The small café a block away held the answers. Hopefully something could be worked out.

She ordered a bagel and coffee and moved to the back booth, placing her back to the crowd ordering at the counter. In seconds she felt someone seating behind her. She started to turn and heard a muffled voice. "Stay where you are."

"Okay."

"I know you have concerns. We've been following you, and you've made life difficult for us, but you may have opened some interesting doors for both of us." While not what she expected to hear, it was intriguing enough for her to hear more as she waited for more details. "We have many operatives who live normal lives, and their spouses never know of their service to the country. Harris can provide a cover we couldn't obtain if we had planned it our self. You can have the best of all worlds if you want. The country needs you."

"I wasn't expecting this. You know I love my country."

"We know, and we also assume you'll do what is best.

We'll be in touch soon, and allow me to be the first to congratulate you and Matt."

"Congratulate me for what?"

Suzan never heard another word. A minute later she looked over her seat to see the back of a man leaving the shop. She had her answer. Could she really pull this off? Yes, she knew it would be wrong to lie to Matt, but the interest of the country was involved. Perhaps a dual life would be the best of all worlds. She would trust their judgment for now. What did they know she didn't?

###

Matt had planned a large party at his condo. Many people circulated which exhibited an air of sophistication she was getting used to fast, as everyone wanted to meet her. Matt openly introduced her as his girlfriend. Well, a girlfriend was a start, a beginning.

Bottles of champagne popped as hostesses attended to the needs of the guests. She knew she couldn't remember all of the names. This part of being with Matt would be hard to accomplish, but she would try her best. The attention made her feel like a princess, much different than her life in the service.

A piano player stopped playing, directing everyone to end their conversation. The raised hands of Matt also insured the ensuing stillness. He raised a glass of champagne in his hand and turned in a large circle to point to his friend and members of his team. They were all here.

"I think I have everyone's attention now, so I need to say a few words. I know I have a reputation of making fast decision, and luckily most have worked out well. Tonight I have another one I wanted to share with my best friends and those who know me best. I know we all want to make the land deal next to the Everglades work."

Matt glanced at Dan. "I think I need to do a little renegotiation on the deal we made on the land we purchased from Suzan."

Dan looked puzzled as he crossed his arms and twisted his jaw. Apparently he had no idea what Matt was talking about.

Suzan watched him hunt for her.

"Okay, Suzan, will you come here for one minute please?" He waited for her to work her way around several people. "From the first moment I saw you I've been mesmerized by you. And for the first time in my life I feel helpless, since there is one item in my life I've never accomplished and hope you'll help me."

"Well maybe." Suzan stepped closer.

Matt turned around slower as the whispers passed among his friends. He reached for his vest pocket and retrieved a small box as the *ahhhs* echoed around the room.

Suzan raised her hands to her mouth. He wasn't going to, not here, was he?

He stepped forward and went on one knee as his friends displayed an array of shocks and smiles. "Suzan."

"Yes."

"I have an offer for you."

Suzan leaned over closer to him. "Do you have collateral?"

Matt lowered his head. He soon raised his bright green eyes with a small tear building in the corners. "I hope this will do." He opened the box and displayed one of the largest diamonds she had ever seen.

"I don't know, have you had it appraised?"

"Let's say that you have my word on it."

"Well, in such a case, I think we're good. Now about this offer."

"Yes, I've worked on some great mergers in my life, but this is the first one I've really taken personal. Suzan, will you marry me?"

Suzan considered being coy one more time, but how could she with tears in his eyes. "Matt, I would love to." She rushed into his arms feeling like a Cinderella princess who finally received her deepest wish. The land had led her to love after all, just like her father told her it would.

Could this be actually happening to her? Only time would tell.

Chapter 21

TWO MONTHS LATER

"Chelsea's pregnant! How could you? Is it that damn hard to keep it in your pants?" Suzan grabbed a vase next to the window of the condo overlooking Central Park and prepared to throw. Slowly, she forced herself to breathe as she watched Matt raise his arms to protect his face.

"What makes you think I'm the father?" Matt's brilliant green eyes flashed defiance as he glared back at her.

Yes, she wanted to hit him, to kick his face in, but decided to pat the vase in her hand several times before she replaced it on the tabletop. "Chelsea called me to tell me you were the father and told me how she was planning to come back to you."

"Come back to me! I think we both know she didn't leave me–I left her! We discussed my past several times. I stopped seeing her long before we met, and you know that." Matt arched his back as his eyes, an attraction she never could resist before, forged a deeper hold on her heart. Could she believe him? No, not yet.

"She didn't say how long she was along. I'm sure that'll come out soon enough."

"You know a simple blood test will provide the answer." Matt's face flushed while he intensified his stare.

"I can't take this. How long will it take to determine who the father is?"

"I don't know, but believe me I'll have an answer as fast as possible. I'll also call Chelsea in a few minutes to see what she's trying to pull." Matt pointed to a phone. "You're more than welcome to listen in."

At least he wasn't trying to hide, and it would be nice to hear what Chelsea had to say for herself. Thoughts of the wedding flashed in her mind, which was only a month away. It was better now than later that this came into the open. How could Matt embarrass her like this?

Gail walked into the corner of the dining room of Matt's Manhattan condo. She acted skittish but insistent as she stared at the uneaten breakfast. "Big John is on the phone and demanding to talk to you."

Suzan knew exactly why Big John called. Word of this had surely reached him by now. Chelsea was his daughter. This would be one hell of a conversation.

Matt motioned to Gail. "I want Suzan to hear this, that is, if she'll have a seat and just listen for a minute."

"I'm all ears."

"Okay, have it directed to the speaker phone." They both moved to opposite sides of the table.

"Matt. This is John. I'm sure you've heard by now about Chelsea."

"Yes a few minutes ago. I promise. It wasn't me."

"I've always known you as an honest man. I need you to tell me the truth on this and I will believe you."

"I haven't seen Chelsea for a while now. I think you know that. How far along is she?"

"I don't know yet. She's so damn emotional now I can't get answers out of her. However, if it's determined that you're the father, I expect you to do the right thing."

"You know I'm getting married to Suzan in a month."

"I know. Life's a bitch, isn't it?"

"See if you can get some answers for me. I know you want them as well." Matt maintained eye contact with Suzan as he talked. Why couldn't she believe him? Part of her wanted to, but . . .

"Chelsea is my only daughter, and you know I'll have to support her. I know you want to call Chelsea, but let me talk to her first and try to get to the truth. I'll let you know what I find out."

Suzan felt sorry for Big John. He had to be catching hell from his daughter if she was telling the truth. Her head hurt as she recalled the Chelsea's words. Nothing had ever hurt her like this before.

"Thanks." Matt reached over and ended the call before smiling at Suzan. "Does that sound like I'm hiding anything?"

"It still doesn't prove who the father is. I heard the pain in Chelsea's voice. She sounded like she was telling the truth." Suzan rubbed her eyes and her temple trying to erase her pounding headache.

Matt rose and walked around the table.

"Stop! Don't come near me."

"What do you want me to do, Suzan?"

"Give me some space. I need to check on my mother anyway, and this might be the perfect time to get away for a little while."

"You know the wedding is only a month off."

"Yes, but we'll have to get this out of the way first." Suzan needed time to think. She had rushed too fast into this engagement, and with all of the parties Matt had thrown for her, she had no time to think. She wanted space, especially in light of the news from Chelsea, his old girlfriend.

Suzan watched Matt relax for a minute. "Suzan, I want you to be happy. I don't want to lose you, and I will not. However, it might be good for you to spend some time with your mother, and I still hope she comes to our wedding. It will give me a little time to talk to Big John and see if he can talk Chelsea into a DNA test. I promise I haven't been with her in a long time, and the times we were together in the past I know I was protected."

"I hope you're right, but I heard the pain in Chelsea's voice. She sounded sincere. She wants you back and you know it." With so many thoughts swirling around in her head, Suzan forced herself to think. She knew she needed to take care of a few things she had lined up, and like it or not, before she left. She also needed to contact the CIA and let them know what was going on. She still couldn't believe she had to hide this commitment from Matt.

She had fallen so hard for Matt and perhaps this was why this hurt as bad as it did. She needed to trust him, but how could she? She knew he had the money to hide almost anything. She still didn't know that much about him as a person. Perhaps she was rushing this too fast. She did need the time.

Matt tried to approach her, but she backed away. He lowered his voice and continued talking in a smooth steady voice. "I know you're upset, but I do want to marry you. The wedding we planned is only weeks away."

"I'm sorry, but I don't think I can do this. How long do you think it will take to obtain the DNA results?"

"I can promise you that I'll have them as fast as I can talk Chelsea into cooperating."

"And if she doesn't cooperate?"

Matt's face flushed as his green eyes radiated with passion and a look she hadn't seen before–pain. "I don't know. I hope to have her father, Big John on my side, and I would think he would want to know the truth also."

Suzan's stomach churned. She felt sick and hoped she could hold her breakfast down. The future prospects of this haunting her forever scared her. She needed time to think. Damn you, Chelsea!

"What do you want me to tell everyone? I can have Phil cover for us if you'll give me some time."

"You can do what you want, but I'll not give you an answer until I know for sure Chelsea isn't pregnant with your baby. I want to go back to Florida to see my Mom, and I surely don't want to read the papers with my name in them as the *other woman*. I hate having photographers after me, and reporters asking questions. I need time, Matt."

"I understand. As long as you remember that I love you." He stepped forward again. She felt too dizzy to resist. His charm and mannerism is why she fell in love with him in the first place. No, she had to leave. While she knew she would miss him, she needed to escape, she had to. Matt finally hugged her tight. "I can have the corporate jet fly you. I don't want you to remember bad experiences and have them associated with our wedding. I plan on handling this and keeping the date for our wedding. All will work out. You'll see."

She leaned into his arms. "I hope you're right. If not, I'll come back after you for ruining my life. I'm sure you know that." His lean, well toned body reassured her, but the words of Chelsea rang in her ears. What was the truth?

"Please believe me."

"I wish I could. I want the truth."

"I'll obtain the DNA results as fast as I can."

Chapter 22

Matt knew the health of his company depended on his health; not his physical health, but his public relations health. His image determined how the public perceived Harris Properties. This reputation was the reason for the company being able to acquire and develop some of the best properties in the world for such prices.

He had not slept all night. He missed Suzan, and he didn't know how this would play out. It wouldn't be long until the press would hear the story and the gossip pages would be filled with the scandal. While he hated the bad press, he knew Chelsea loved to create such havoc in the world. He needed to make sure he could count on his management team to stand behind him now, more than ever.

"The guys will be here soon." Gail walked over to the edge of the outside patio area where Matt relaxed looking over Manhattan. This special area stood out in the skyline and many of the New Yorkers knew it was his place, which allowed him to have a great location to enjoy his one vice–cigars.

"Thanks. I appreciate all you're doing." Matt smiled at the one woman he knew always had his best interest at heart. She had worked for him for a long time.

"I know it has to be hard to deal with this, but you have great people working for you."

"Yes, I do. I don't want to disappoint them, and I know they're wondering how this latest scandal will affect us." Matt studied the sunlight fading and the office lights glowing to replace them. Soon the city would be consumed with millions of lights. It never changed. The sounds of the city that he ignored most of the time caught his attention. There was no place like New York City, but this is where he grew up. It was so different from his estate in Florida. He relaxed as he allowed his mind to drift back to the first time he had seen Suzan crashing into his compound in Florida. She had a passion, a drive that shocked him at first, and then dominated his curiosity until he had lost his heart. He never regretted it and, in fact, openly welcomed it. He needed to settle down and marry. She was the only woman he ever met who made him want to commit. But now she was gone; maybe not permanently, but gone for now. He had to obtain proof he wasn't the father of Chelsea's baby. He knew Chelsea was pulling a fast one and how she wanted to tear his relationship with Suzan apart. So far, Chelsea was accomplishing her goal.

Matt wondered if Chelsea was really pregnant or faking it. If she was pregnant, who could be the father? She had an eye for men and often got drunk. Could she have been screwing someone else? Anyway, the truth would come out soon.

Matt was still standing and staring out at the city as his management team arrived. He reached for a special box of cigars he had ordered and watched the men smile at their shared tradition. With his Cuban love for cigars, Tony would always show first. Dan walked in next and as always acted like the peacemaker for the team, which suited him fine as being a top notch lawyer. Phil soon followed as he surveyed the area. He always looked for photographers who were onto this place of celebration. Ronald came in last, as usual, and could be heard laughing long before he appeared.

Matt enjoyed watching the interplay between them. He needed them, but had to rise to the occasion and be their leader as he walked over to them. "Men, we have another night of hidden pleasures." He pointed to the cigar box. "I've heard these are the best in all of Cuba."

As usual, Tony moved to the box first. "You know, Matt, this kind of bribing will get you everything."

"I sure hope so." Matt passed out the cigars and watched a hostess bring out trays of champagne for everyone. This tradition that he wished he could do more often reminded him of so many nights before. He glanced at Gail by the doorway and saluted her. He couldn't blame her for not engaging in this one corporate camaraderie. She might be a secretary, but she was so very capable of running his empire if he needed her to.

With a champagne glass in one hand and a cigar in the other, Matt contemplated his toast. "To smokes and friends, may they last forever."

The men lifted their glasses and as always didn't sip but engulfed the glass of champagne as they all wanted to move on to their cigars. The smoke soon swirled around the patio area and drifted over the city. Yes, here they could smoke as they wished and the city *do-gooders* could do nothing to them.

Matt studied the shifting eyes of his team which also held seats on his board of directors. These men were what he had heard many times in the media as his *band of alpha males* or the *alpha male club*. He knew they all could be successful on their own and run their own companies, and which always reminded him of how fortunate he was that they all had agreed to work for him.

Finally, Phil spoke first as the others listened intensely. "I think we've all heard what happened yesterday. This is definitely one scandal I want to stop as fast as I can. By being the daughter of Big John, Chelsea has placed us in an awkward situation and I need some advice."

"Tell me about it." Ronald stepped forward. "As everyone knows we're receiving a major part of the funds for current projects from Big John. I need to do everything I can to make sure he remains happy with us."

Matt raised his hands. "I know I'm causing some problems for us, but for the record, I know I'm not the father!" Matt glanced around at his team to make sure he made his point.

Matt watched the doubting eyes. "I plan to call Big John tomorrow, and then visit Chelsea to see what she's trying to pull."

Dan raised his cigar as he puffed harder than normal. "For anyone else a slander lawsuit would be in order. However, we all know this will be impossible in this case, but just maybe it could be used as leverage to force her to retract the story."

Matt laughed. "For many people lawsuits are scary, but I think Chelsea would love to entertain one. It's just another way for her to keep her name in the public eye. I still have never understood why she likes being involved in scandals like this. You would think she has all of the publicity she could handle."

Tony appeared to be gathering his thoughts. "I have everything cleared to start on the project in Florida. My part is not affected by this, except the uncertainty of the funding. I hope I still have the go ahead on the project."

Ron leaned over to him. "Yes, we can find other partners, but it will be harder. For now, I say keep up the good work."

Matt also nodded his approval to Tony.

Phil blew another monster cloud. "I've one more concern. Suzan's going to her place where she'll be with her mother. It'll only be a matter of time until the press finds her there. We need to provide her with some kind of security.

The situation would be better controlled if we had her at the estate in West Palm Beach."

"She's most definitely welcome to it, but I don't have much control over what she wants to do." Matt pushed one hand in his front pocket and grimaced. "I appreciate everyone wanting to help me. I hope this can be all worked out in time to save the wedding."

Ron patted Phil on the shoulder. "I think we all have one request."

"Which is?"

"I think we all need to make sure Suzan agrees to allow us to keep our cigar nights."

Matt laughed. "I think she would agree to that. That's when we get her back to New York. I don't guess anyone wants to go see Big John for me." The sudden contagious coughs spreading among his friends forced him to laugh. "I didn't think so."

###

This was one time Matt eagerly agreed to meet Big John at his downtown office rather than back at the Harris Property office. He had worked with Big John for a long time, and he had relied on this friendship for years. Since this would test their relationship, Matt knew to proceed carefully as he prepared his responses to what he knew he would be asked.

Rather than taking others on his management team with him as he usually did, Matt knew he had to do this alone. His bodyguard walked inside the building with him, but stayed by the front door. Big John loved being closer to Wall Street than Matt.

After being ushered in to meet with Big John, the two men waited for the other to start. Both expressed the awkward meeting in their eyes. Matt finally broke the silence. "I don't know where to start."

"I guess the obvious question I need to ask is straight forth. Are you the father?"

"No. I'm not going to lie to you. We have been lovers in the past, as I'm sure you know, but we haven't had sex in a long time."

"Of course Chelsea tells me otherwise."

"I haven't talked to her yet. I thought it was best to talk to you first, since the only knowledge I have of this is through Suzan. Chelsea called her."

"Chelsea talked to me briefly, but she acted hysterical. She wasn't too happy with you announcing your plans to marry Suzan, especially with such a short engagement. Most of what I've learned is through her mother, and you know which side she's on."

Matt had met Gloria Townsley, often referred to as the society queen of New York City many times. While Chelsea had learned much of her attitude from Gloria, this was one place he knew to never venture.

"Chelsea's mother is pushing me to ask you these questions. I'm sure you know that without me saying too much." Big John glanced at the door as if hoping no one over heard him.

"I understand, and a simple DNA test will clear this up. I hope you can persuade Chelsea to have one preformed as fast as possible."

Big John squirmed. "I already pushed her and got nowhere."

Matt's stomach churned on him as he worried this might happen. "I see."

"Matt, this has me in a very bad spot. You know I have to support my daughter or my wife will bring fucking hell down on me. Are you absolutely sure you're not the father?"

"Yes, I'm sure. If I have to, I'll be glad to even take a lie detector test."

"You can relax, I think I believe you. You know I hate to be embarrassed in public. Like you, I have an image I have to maintain. I'm sure the press will be all over this soon. What are you doing to contain the news coverage?"

"Phil is working on it full time now. He knows to be careful, but there's one thing I should tell you."

"What?"

"Suzan has left me for now. This has caused her to have second thoughts. Having an undeserved image as an international playboy is hard to live down."

"I hate to hear it. Has the wedding been called off?"

"Not yet, and I have no idea how to handle it. This will be managed by Phil and his mastery of public relations."

"I'm sure our spokesperson will be at it also. I'm sure you understand to take everything with a grain of salt, since you know what to expect from my wife." He leaned forward and whispered to Matt. "I want this to end quickly so we can get on with our project."

Matt offered a wink. "I think we understand each other as I had hoped. We'll get through this my friend, but I do need to try to see Chelsea if I can."

"I know. Good luck with that."

"Thanks." Matt stood to leave as he heard a commotion outside Big John's door.

Without so much as a knock, the door flung open and in walked Gloria, dressed as if she would fly down a runway of a super fashion show. "I see you two are talking. It's about time." She pulled the door closed behind her.

Big John pushed back in his chair. "What are you doing here?"

Looking insulted, but intent on being a part of the

conversation, she walked over and dropped her Gucci purse in the center of his desk. Her attitude shifted as she focused on Matt. "You're the one I wanted to talk to, and I'm so glad we have this chance to do so."

Matt remained still and amused. This would be a chance to find out more about what Chelsea had on her mind. "I haven't talked to Chelsea yet, but I plan to very soon."

"I'm sure you do. I heard the military girl you've been seen with is leaving you."

"No, not really. She has things to take care of back in Florida. Our wedding is still on."

Gloria looked frustrated, but remained pushy. "Chelsea told me you're going to be a father."

"That's what I heard she's saying. However, it's not me."

"Are you calling Chelsea a liar?"

Matt felt the best way to handle her was to return the challenge. "Are you calling me a liar?"

"You wouldn't be the first man to try to dodge his responsibilities."

"I think a simple DNA test will prove things. That's what I need to talk Chelsea into having as quickly as possible."

"Are you suggesting Chelsea sleeps with so many men she doesn't know who the father is?"

Matt glanced at Big John and knew the situation he found himself in. "I think I want to get to the truth as much as everyone else does, and I think that's the responsible thing to do, don't you?"

"Chelsea has been humiliated enough by your sorted affair with another woman. I hear about your engagement at every party I go to lately. I don't know what you have been thinking. Are you really interested in an *Army girl*?"

Matt leaned closer to her to make sure he would not be misunderstood. "She's my fiancée, and I do plan to marry her."

"Well things have a way of changing. I'm sure you'll do the right thing." Gloria turned to Big John. "We need to talk when Matt leaves."

Big John remained speechless, as he observed the heated discussion in silence. Matt felt so sorry for him, but decided to let him fight his own battles. "For the record, I think Chelsea is a remarkable and very beautiful woman. Many men would love to spend time with her."

"Save it. I'm too old to be bull shitted."

"Well it was the truth, but I'll leave you two alone and see if I can get some answers." Matt smiled at Big John and walked passed Gloria. He stopped and turned before leaving. "You don't know where I can find Chelsea, do you?"

Gloria stared directly at him. "I think she doesn't want to talk to you right now, and if I were you, I wouldn't push it."

"With all due respect, I will get answers, and you can fully expect me to, as you said, push it. You can let her know I'm coming to see her as soon as I leave here. I don't wish to embarrass her, but I know and she knows that I'm not the father."

Gloria stared at Big John. "Are you going to let him get away with this?"

"I don't think he wants to get away with anything. I also want to know the truth. This isn't the first time Chelsea has caused us problems."

"Men. I should have known you would stand up for him. Our daughter needs us now. She's your only daughter, and don't you ever forget that."

Matt held his breath. He knew the story of how Gloria lost their second child while on a mission to Africa, and the faulty attempt to save the child's life ended in a miscarriage that also ended the chances of having other children for them. Big John had a big heart, which often explained why he was known as *Big John*. While he had a passion for helping people, he knew Gloria only loved the publicity and fame from doing so. She played a sinister card in bringing it up now.

Matt studied the pain in Big John's face. He needed to leave. "I'm so sorry this has happened, and I'll keep this as quiet as I can. You know that, but I do need to talk to her." Matt turned and walked.

Chapter 23

While sitting in a large patio-style chair on the balcony outside the condo she shared with her mother in Fort Myers, Florida, Suzan switched off her computer as she sipped the last of the coffee. She had discovered nothing on the net about her leaving New York. With all of the parties Matt had scheduled for them, she wondered how Phil had kept it so quiet.

A seagull squalled in the morning air as it passed above her, while the sun shifted into a dazzling display of colors. She didn't sleep well, and her head ached something fierce this morning. Why did life always cause her problems? She only wanted to return to Florida and live on her land, which would now soon be disappearing forever as the development progressed.

Her last eight years in the military had been the only life she knew. Her departure had also left her with a big void. She had no one to talk to. Her mother suffering from early onset of Alzheimer's added to Suzan's problems. She wished she could talk to her mother, but she had her own problems. Suzan felt alone, but she would make it. The Army taught her well on how to survive.

While the work in the Army police unit toughened her, the demands of the CIA perfected her demeanor. They had invested a lot into her, and she knew they wanted to receive more of a return. She should call them, but knew they would contact her when they wanted to.

The last few months in New York added a new layer to her life. Matt introduced her to a world she could not have imagined. He treated her like a princess, and to some extent, like a protective friend. She missed sleeping with him. He had always snuggled so close to her.

While she had a few scattered boyfriends in her lifetime, she never had one like Matt, one who she lived with all day every day. He constantly kept her by his side and wanted to share his life. Why did he have to screw their life up, and why with someone like Chelsea?

Her mother joined her by moving in behind her and massaging a shoulder. It felt good. Somehow her mother must have known the stress she was suffering from. "Mom, how did you sleep last night?"

"Very good. I did wake a few times to see your light on."

"I'm sorry if I kept you awake. I decided to read for a while."

"Your hair's so dark black, and very much like your fathers." Suzan felt her mother running a hand through her hair. "I'm surprised the Army allowed you keep it so long."

"I kept it fashioned in a ponytail most of the time."

"I see. I'll be back in a minute. I want to find a brush."

Suzan smiled, as she remembered her mother combing her hair for hours when she was younger. It would feel good now. "Thanks."

Her dad had died too early. Why didn't her mother notice the signs of his cancer? As far as she knew her mother never talked him into receiving any treatments. Still, Suzan wondered when her mother had drifted into her current state. The early onset of Alzheimer's had shocked her, but she had learned so much about it the last few months. The medication appeared to be helping, but the doctor told her she could relapse at any time. And, even with the medication, her mother had large time periods of not remembering her life.

Her mother returned and ran the brush through her long

black hair. The ends flipped in front of her as she examined them and their needs to be trimmed. She couldn't tell her mother, but she was allowed to grow her hair long in order to complete her missions for the CIA. She needed it to pass as a mid-eastern woman. While not a perfect match for the locals, she managed to pass with a little help from the CIA makeup artist.

"I told you that I saw Uncle Brajesh in India, didn't I?"

"I think you might have mentioned it earlier. I'm sorry I forgot to ask you more about it."

"He looks so much like Dad. He would love to move here, but he's scared to and leave his family. He knows it would be difficult to get them all here."

"I can understand. Your father loved Florida. I'm so glad I could help him."

"Tell me again about how you met."

"I went on one of those around the world tours for a graduation present from my parents. We had a great time. One of the stops was in India. He worked at the university close to where we stayed. We became instant friends, and I managed to help him get a visa to visit me later. We were not supposed to get married, but we did. When it was time for him to go back, I was pregnant with you. This is perhaps the only reason he was allowed to extend his visa, and over time, with many trips back and forth to India, he became an American citizen. He loved it in America."

"So . . . he went back to India?"

"Yes, but only once to extend his visa and change it to a fiancée visa. He was always too scared to return after we married. He didn't want to take the chance they would keep him."

"Now, tell me more on how he purchased the land we lived on."

"Your father always wanted a motel to run. He never realized that dream, but he found this piece of swamp land he could purchase for almost nothing. He hoped to make a lodge or campground out of the land one day."

"He made it sound important to him that I keep it. Do you have any guess why?"

"He always had big dreams for the land. I think he would love to see what's being considered there."

"I hope he approves. Matt's allowing me to have major input on the development." Suzan bit her lip. "Well he was anyway. I don't know how the relationship will be in the future."

"I'm so sorry to hear what happened. What will you do now?"

"I don't know. I need to do some serious thinking. I have to find out if Chelsea is pregnant. Matt said he'll force her into having a DNA test, but I don't know if he can force her to comply or not. I simply don't know."

Suzan felt the stress ease as her mother combed her hair. She knew she could not live here forever; she had to move on with her life. Today might be a good day to do some exploring. She had not had the chance earlier, and she knew much had to have changed over the last eight years.

"Mom, if you'll be okay for a while, I want to drive around and clear my head."

"Sure. I need to get back to my painting."

Suzan smiled at the thoughts of the portrait her mother had painted of her from memory. Matt had purchased and cherished it long before he met her. The story sent new messages circulating in her confused state. Did he really love her like he said, or was he simply leading her on. She needed time, since he moved much too fast for her. She would have thought he would insist on a longer engagement, not a short three month event, but perhaps that's the way he operated.

"Mom, I don't think I ever told you thank you for the portrait you painted of me that Matt purchased."

"Thanks, I forgot about selling the painting. In fact, I think the guy who comes by from the gallery never asked me if he could sell it. He hauled the painting to the gallery with several others."

"I'll be back in a little while."

"Okay."

Suzan walked to the front door and out to the elevator. She wore an old pair of jeans and a rough pull over sweater. However, she didn't plan to get out of her car and see anyone. She wanted to simply drive around for a while. The new Mini Cooper she had purchased only had a few miles on it, and she loved the way the air blew her hair with the top down.

After reaching the bottom level, she smiled at the guard and walked out to the parking lot. Her red Mini Cooper looked great as she hurried toward it. Suddenly, she noticed the first guy rushing at her in a dead run. "Ms. Mercer, can we have a word with you?"

Another guy with a camera followed him as another group hurried from still another direction. The paparazzi had found her. She should've known. She had no makeup on, and wore the worst clothes she owned. No, this is not the life she wanted. She hid her face, but she knew it was too late as the guy stepped right in front of her asking questions. "Is it true? Did you call off the wedding to Matt Harris?"

She tried to walk around him, as he pushed harder with his questions. The camera man reached out to touch her arm, attempting to stop her. He made contact, which was a bad mistake, as she grabbed his arm and forced it behind him.

After the camera crashed to the ground, she leaned over and picked it up, removed the data card and dropped it to the ground, where she stepped on it and pulverized it beneath her foot.

"You can't do that!"

"I just did." She turned to the other photographer. "Are you going to hand me yours, or do I have to chase you down?

He started to resist as the reporter beside him stepped forward with a brassy attitude. "He doesn't have to do that."

Suzan reached out and grabbed his throat. "Without air he can only make it for three minutes, max." She turned to stare at the camera. The photographer complied as she released the reporter. She crushed another data card into the pavement.

The guard stationed inside the complex came running out to meet them. "What's going on here?"

"These men are here to harass me."

"Not on private property they're not." He unsnapped his gun.

"We don't want problems, but the press has a right to do their job."

"They don't have the right to trespass. I think you're all going to jail."

Suzan thought about it quickly. "Leave me alone and you can leave, push your point and the police will be here in a few minutes."

"We'll leave, but we'll report our story."

"Slander is another crime. You shouldn't forget who you're messing with."

The lead journalist snickered. "I'm sure you know this isn't over."

Suzan returned the smile and headed for her car. As she

cranked the motor, she watched them scrambling for their cars, but she knew she would lose them in minutes. After taking the first right, she floored the Mini and never looked back. How long would they stay in Florida? She needed a new place to stay while she worked things out. Surely they wouldn't harass her mother. She smiled, knowing her mother seldom left the condo.

Her mind searched for places she could hide. She had a few options, and with the money she had now from the land sale, she could move anywhere. She never thought she would need to hide behind a gate before. She needed to control her emotions better, knowing that Phil wouldn't like the way she handled the press. He always remained so smooth in his methods.

She flipped open her phone. He had called her many times. She clicked on the messages and listened to the last one again. He acted concerned about her and warned her of this happening. He knew.

When she reached the interstate, she headed north. She still didn't know where, but anywhere would do. She breathed in deep as she turned on to a side exit. Coffee would be great. After pulling in front of a coffee shop, she rested for a minute before she hit the call button.

Phil answered on the second ring. "Suzan, thank you for calling. We've been worried about you."

"I'm sure I've created a public relations nightmare for you. All I can say is, I'm sorry about that."

"I'm doing my best to keep the cover on this story."

"That's good to know, since I just threw gasoline on top of the fire."

The tone of his voice shifted as she expected. "What do you mean?"

"I just left my condo I share with my mom. The

paparazzi were waiting on me."

"Oh crap!"

"Oh yes, I had to fend them off in the parking lot. I think we may need to buy a camera or two."

"You didn't–"

"I didn't hurt them too bad, just their pride."

"I see, and I'll work on it as soon as we hang up. Now, tell me how you're doing."

"I feel terrible, and don't know what to believe. Chelsea sounded convincing. I don't think she made this up."

"I know this is hard on you. I need to know what she told you."

"She said she was pregnant and that Matt was the father. She also made it clear she wasn't planning on giving him up even if he was married. She insisted their relationship wasn't over."

"I'm sure you don't know her well. I need to take some time to explain things to you."

"Oh, I'm sure you do. I know more than you think I do. I know her father is a big friend and business partner of Matt. I also know how you count on his money."

"Yes, it's a complicated arrangement."

"For you and Matt it may be complicated, but for me it's as simple as writing on the wall."

"I think if you allow us some time to talk, you'll see things in a much different light."

"What I need now is time to think, and I know I can't go back to the condo and face wave after wave of reporters stalking me. How did they know I would be visiting my mother?"

"I'm sure they were alerted to it as the news broke. Where are you planning on going?"

"I don't know yet."

"If I can make a suggestion. Why not use the Harris Estate in West Palm Beach? It's heavily guarded, and no one will bother you there."

Suzan enjoyed the place the first time she saw it, but no, it was too big for her. "Why would I want to go to his place?"

"Like I said, security for one, and it will make it look like there are no problems so that the press will back off. I can promise you no one will come to force you into making a decision. We'll give you time to think, as you said you need, while Matt obtains proof for you that he's not the father."

"So, you think he can do that?"

"I know he's working on it as we speak."

Suzan breathed slower. Perhaps she over reacted. Maybe Chelsea was lying. If so, she would owe Matt a major apology, again. "I call you back shortly with an answer. I'm ordering coffee now and I'll think about it." She didn't wait on a response as she ended the call.

Chapter 24

Matt approached the guard in front of the condo where Chelsea lived. "I need to see Chelsea Townsley."

"Is she expecting you?"

Matt knew the guard had been put on notice. "I know and you know she is." Matt stepped forward, pressing his point.

The guard's eyes nervously flashed around. "Let me call her."

"Here let me save you the trouble." Matt retrieved his iPhone and hit her number on his speed dial.

Gloria answered. "I thought you wouldn't waste any time in making it over here."

"I'm downstairs, and I need to talk to her."

"I'm not so sure she wants to talk to you right now."

"That's fine, if you want to play this kind of game. I can call for a press conference on the front steps outside if you prefer."

"You wouldn't."

"I suggest you take a look outside and you tell me." Matt strolled toward the street.

"Choose your words carefully. I don't think you want to enter into a fight with me."

"I'm not looking for a fight, I can promise you. I only want to know the truth."

"If you want to talk to her and work this out–fine. I'm sure you'll understand if I stay to make sure you don't try to pull a fast one."

"I have no problem with you staying."

"Fine, then come on up."

Matt turned to the guard. "She agreed to see me."

In minutes Matt walked into the condo. Gloria looked defiant and positioned like a Samurai warrior. He didn't see Chelsea anywhere. "We need to talk."

"I don't mind talking to you, but I'm here to talk to Chelsea. Where is she?"

"She wasn't expecting company, and she wanted a few minutes to look presentable."

Matt knew she was stalling. "I can wait and stay as long as it takes. I don't plan on leaving until I force her to admit the truth."

"You know you keep calling my daughter a liar."

"And, you keep calling me one. A simple DNA test will confirm the truth. I can live with that."

"That will be up to Chelsea, and I don't think she wants to subject herself or the baby to any test."

"Why are you pushing me to marry your daughter when you know there's no love between us at all?"

"How can you say that? Everyone knows you two have been a couple for a long time."

"We've attended many functions for years for publicity only. I know that, and you know that, so why do we have to beat around the bush at it?"

"Matt, you know better than anyone else we live in a different world, and one where the public expects much more of us than normal people."

"In a way we're so much alike, yes, but down deep we're so different. Why do you think I've waited until I'm forty to marry?"

"Surely you're not planning on marrying the Army girl. Do you think she would ever fit in here?"

"If she doesn't fit in here, then perhaps I shouldn't either."

Gloria laughed. "You're stuck here like everyone else.

Get used to it."

Matt noticed a movement behind Gloria as Chelsea walked in. Her eyes covered in heavy makeup and her face pulled tight in a frown. "I thought you would come by soon."

"Hello, Chelsea. Apparently I should've come by much earlier. Suzan told me what you told her."

"I'm sure that would have been a fascinating conversation. What in the hell do you see in her?"

Matt stopped to slow down his response. "Something we never had. Call it trust, call it friendship or sharing, but I think you can also call it love."

Chelsea acted weak, and as if she had a hard time standing. Matt knew it had to be well rehearsed, but he rushed closer to her to help her stand.

Gloria rushed next to her also. "Here, let us help you find a seat."

Matt walked with her to a nearby couch, where he helped her rest on one end. "If you need a doctor, I'm sure we can have one here in a few minutes."

Matt's choice of words worked, as she immediately started acted better. "No, I'm fine. I still can't get over the shock of you being with someone else."

To Matt this was laughable, as he knew she dated many men, and made no secret of it so many times. "We've never made any commitment to date each other exclusively the entire time we knew each other."

"I'm sorry. I thought we had an understanding."

"No, we didn't, and you know that. Now, I want the truth. Are you pregnant?"

"You don't think I'm telling the truth, do you?"

"Let's say I have my doubts. When is the baby due?"

"I think in about six months."

Matt did a quick glance at her stomach and saw no signs of a bulge. Perhaps it was too soon. How was he to know? He would learn more soon from others. "That would've made it three months ago when you got pregnant. We didn't make love then."

"Yes we did!"

"WE DID NOT." Matt breathed hard. "I'm sorry for yelling. We haven't been together for a long time."

"On your boat we did."

"My boat? You mean the Lady Luck?"

"Yes, during the cruise to Miami after a charity event."

Matt smiled. "I remember that night. You were drunk and I helped you to a cabin to sleep it off."

Gloria stepped forward. "And I think must have taken advantage of her at that time."

"I think I've heard enough." Matt felt the flush of heat in his face. He knew he never touched her. "That's a lie. While you might've had too much to drink, I'll assure you I didn't."

Chelsea started to cry. "I wasn't going to say anything until I heard you were going to marry that girl from the military. I still can't believe you're serious about her."

Matt swallowed and stepped forward. "You know there's a simple way of proving this. They can obtain a DNA sample on the baby before it's born." He watched the raised eyebrows from both women. "I checked on this, and there's no danger to you or to the baby."

"I don't have to prove anything, and I'm not taking any chance on a procedure which might affect the baby in any way or form."

Gloria stepped forward to hug her daughter as she glared at Matt. "I think you know what happened to me while I was off with John in Africa. A doctor ruined me, and it's why we never had any more children. I'm not going to have that happen again and never have any grandchildren."

"That was Africa, and this is America. You can check with your own doctor. It's safe."

"NO!"

"I'm simply asking you to check, and that's all I'm asking."

Gloria moaned with Chelsea, which made Matt feel like a jerk. He wanted answers, but he knew he couldn't persuade them. What was he to do now?

Chelsea glanced at him. "Since you're not going to take any responsibility in this, you leave me no choice but to never allow you to have contact with your baby. I hope that makes you happy."

Gloria arched her back like a cat ready to attack. "Matt, I think I need to ask you to leave."

"I was hoping to have you cooperate in finding the truth, but it also appears you leave me little choose in a decision also. It's only a matter of time before we all know who the father is. And it's not me!" Matt glanced at the ceiling. "Your father's a very good friend of mine. He knows I'll do the right thing. He also trust me to never lie to him."

Gloria stormed forward. "Matt, if there's one thing I do know, you can kiss that relationship good bye."

Matt heard the threat, and he knew that she might be right; after all, Gloria was his wife. He could only hope that she was wrong.

Chapter 25

With the pressure of dealing with the paparazzi circling her place smothering her, Suzan decided to take Phil up on his offer, as her Mini Cooper made great time roaring to Matt's West Palm Beach estate. She knew her disappearance had caused hell for him. Still, if he had impregnated Chelsea, he deserved every bit of it. Phil assured her Matt would not come to see her there. He had, however, reiterated how much Matt wanted to talk to her, and to please consider it. She said she would.

Pulling up to the guard gate, she smiled as she remembered the last time she was there. A new set of guards checked her over as she had anticipated. She knew word of the first trip had circulated. while she now felt apologetic for her actions, she said nothing since there would at a better time later.

After walking in the front door, a housekeeper greeted her. "Ms. Mercer, it's so good to see you. Phil called and said you'll be staying with us. If you'll allow me, I'll be glad to show you to your room and accommodate you any way I can."

"Thanks. It was a long ride, and I'm still not sure how long I'll be here."

"I understand. Matt keeps a full staff available here, and we hope to meet any needs you have."

"Thanks, I would like to be left alone in the room for a while."

"As you wish. We have very few guests here so you should have lots of privacy. You might like to enjoy the pool area later."

"Thanks." Suzan followed her to a master suite, as she tried to imagine who else had used this room. Matt had told her that the company offered it often to members of the management team and important clients they wanted to do business with. She knew that also included Big John, who loved to fish in Florida.

In a way she felt funny using his place, but then again, it made sense until all of the last details could be worked out with the CIA. She wondered what they had planned for her. She needed to stay in shape, and thought the gym here would be perfect.

Suzan turned to the lady showing her to her room. "Thank you, this will do fine. I hope to work out and stay in shape, but don't worry about me, since I don't plan to be much trouble, or stay here too long."

"Please let me know what we can do for you." The woman turned and left as Suzan walked over to the king size bed and fell backward into it. The life of luxury most women would jump at forced her to hesitate and wonder what she was doing. Was she making a major screw up?

She closed her eyes and imagined the last time she made love to Matt. He had focused his attention on her and had acted so attentive to her every need. He had never acted demanding. She would have never thought he acted so nice, yet so hot when he allowed his passions to escape. Thoughts about him excited her as she felt herself getting wet by just fantasizing about their times together. She had to stop this. This was insane.

She opened her eyes and studied the room with the large paintings and intricate art work. She could explore this place for hours and never get bored. She knew Matt loved to shop for items he decorated with, as she wondered how many of these he had personally selected.

She closed her eyes and drifted back to sleep as she played one scenario after another in her mind. Why was it so hard to obtain the truth?

###

Matt waited for Dan to finish a phone call, knowing he had worked on this all morning. While not his general field of responsibility or expertise, Matt knew Dan could get answers for him. He wanted proof that he wasn't the father. He knew he wasn't, but this one time he needed the DNA results to prove to others and especially to Suzan.

Dan hung up the phone. "That was Mike Akron, perhaps the best attorney in New York when it comes to parental lawsuits. He says we can file suit and ask Chelsea to allow for DNA verification. But like he said, by the time we have a hearing and file all motions and counters that would be coming, the baby will probably be born."

"I don't want to wait that long." Matt slapped a fist into an open hand.

"The first step would be sending a certified letter to Chelsea asking her to submit for the procedure. A threat of a lawsuit will have to be suggested in the letter."

"You know, you would think she would want to know who the father is, but for some reason she thinks it's me. I've been thinking about it, and I may understand what she's thinking." Dan crossed his arms and waited. "On the night of the charity cruise, she downed one drink after another. I had to help her to a cabin to sleep it off. I promise I never touched her."

Dan rubbed his chin and grinned. "I understand, and if people watched you leaving together, they would be on her side. This is not good."

"Yes, I could have done whatever I wanted to with her, but I didn't. So much for being a gentleman this time and helping her out."

"I've met Gloria before also, and I know she'll have her lawyers countersuing. She is the type that will not mind having this all over the news. She lives on scandals."

"I think that can be controlled. My main concern is Big John. He has to feel the squeeze coming from her. I need to make sure we keep a good relationship. I think what I need to do is find a way to isolate Chelsea away from her mother so we can talk."

"Good luck with that one." Dan scribbled some notes on a pad.

"Well, work on it and I will also. I think it would be our best shot in getting this taken care of."

As Matt stood, Gail walked in. "I thought I could find you here."

Matt laughed. "I knew we should have gone out for a smoke."

"I've been trying to locate Chelsea for you. She flew out of town earlier this morning."

"Do you know where?"

"I've no clue, but it's obvious she's avoiding you. If her purpose is to create problems between you and Suzan she's doing a good job at it."

"Chelsea's very spoiled and has always gotten what she wanted. It's about time she learned she can't have everything she sees. I'm definitely not going to be pushed into a marriage by her falsely claiming I'm the father of her baby." Matt's voice boomed more than he had intended, but he wanted to make his point.

"I'm sure she'll turn up soon, since she also has a large spotlight on her. Can you imagine the paparazzi after her? A photo of her pregnant would be worth a lot on the market."

Matt closed his eyes. He could only imagine. His next

stop would be to visit with Phil to make sure he was on this. "We need to find her and soon."

###

In the early afternoon Suzan woke and located some workout clothes. The gym offered a perfect way for her to work off some of her frustrations, especially if they had a body bag she could punch. The procedures she learned while in the military police and the CIA were totally different. The military police wanted her to defuse problems and control the situation. The CIA taught her how to kill efficiently.

Most importantly, the CIA taught her how to think, how to focus. She thought she could trust Matt, but it was better she found out now rather than later. However, she had misjudged him before. Could she have made another mistake?

For the next two hours she poured her heart and soul into the work out, as she pushed herself. Whatever the CIA had for her, she needed to be prepared. She felt sure such lavish settings were not in her future, as she remembered the back streets in Afghanistan.

Deciding to take advantage of the opportunity while she could, she went back to her room and looked for a swim suit. A conservative one piece would do, but unfortunately all she found were skimpy little nothings. It was so amazing how he maintained the room, obviously for woman clients, since it was so well stocked. The research she completed on him earlier when she first heard his name resurfaced. He had a large reputation as a playboy, a reputation he so convincingly denied.

After selecting the best, she stripped and glanced at the mirror. While soon to be thirty years old, a major milestone, she looked much younger. However, she knew her looks would change, and she had to face it as she examined a slight drooping in her boobs. The chances of ever marrying now appeared to be disappearing. She knew the CIA would own her life.

As she soon stepped outside, Suzan studied the large waterfall and the cooling mist rising from it. Wow, this had to be the life. As she walked to the far side to pick the perfect spot, she heard yelling behind her.

Sporting a large Florida type hat with long flowing blonde hair which hung to her large breasts, a woman pushed forward with another one of the housekeeper trying to stop her and yelling at her. "Please, no problems. Mr. Harris. He no like!"

The woman marched straight toward Suzan. The hat lifted enough for Suzan to make out a face–Chelsea. "What was she doing here?"

"I should've known Matt would have you hiding out here, but I wouldn't get too used to it. I know Matt well enough to know he'll come around when he sees his baby."

Suzan studied Chelsea's stomach, looking for any signs of her being pregnant. "Phil arranged this for me, and I'm not sure Matt knows anything about it. If I had known they would have invited you here I'd definitely not have come."

"I've known Matt for a long time, and I have use of this estate anytime I want."

"Well enjoy it then. I'm leaving." Suzan wrapped a towel around her.

"You know you can't win. I think you need to go back to your Army world."

Suzan didn't like being talked to as such by this fake little girl. She wasn't ready to defend Matt, but willing to stand her own ground. "I've heard you sleep with guys all over. How can you be sure the baby's Matt's?"

"I know it's him, you bitch."

"Watch it, sister. You don't really want to engage me, do you?" Suzan stepped forward and tightened her hand, looking for any opportunity to strike her. "I understand Matt has been trying to talk you into a DNA test on the baby. Why don't you have it performed so we all know for sure?"

"I don't, because I know. I know, I know. And I don't like everyone questioning my word."

"Well the truth will come out one day, but as for now, you can have him. It's not worth all of this." Suzan walked around Chelsea.

"Oh, you can stay if you want. I'm only going to be here for a few minutes. I think the best way to make Matt pay for this is to never allow him to see his baby. That's unless he changes his mind about who he plans to marry."

A thought struck Suzan. Was it possible she slept with Matt with the sole purpose of getting pregnant? Surely not! If so, she felt sorry for Matt and what life held for him. Still, she could never see him looking at Chelsea like he did at her. While fighting the mixed emotions inside her, she knew there would be moments she would cherish the time she spent with Matt. And other times she would have nightmares caused by the woman in front of her.

Chapter 26

As Suzan pulled out of the gate and headed for Miami, her phone rang. It had to be Matt, but the phone id gave no indication. She held it to her ear and didn't answer.

"Suzan?" An unfamiliar voice waited for an answer.

"Yes."

"We need to talk."

She knew without asking who it was now. "I'm on my way to Miami, but I can make a change if that's what you want me to do."

"No, that sounds good. Be sure to check in somewhere quiet and unnoticed. We'll see you in the morning."

###

Matt couldn't believe the news. Chelsea had surfaced at his estate in West Palm Beach. Yes, he would never have thought of looking for her in Florida. Her mother must have put her up to that. Chelsea and Suzan had confronted each other. He wished he knew exactly what they said, but knew he never would know the truth, and now both had disappeared again.

He tried to call Suzan again, only to receive no answer. Why doesn't she answer her phone?

With no other options, Matt decided to call Big John. The call to his office passed directly to him. "Hi, this is Matt."

"I thought you would be calling soon. I'm catching hell over here!"

"I can only imagine. I'm sorry about everything. I'm not sure you heard or not, but both Chelsea and Suzan showed up at my estate in Florida a little while ago."

"That had to be one hell of a meeting. How did that

happen?"

"Phil had talked Suzan into going there to keep her out of the head beams of the paparazzi, and apparently Chelsea thought it would be a good place to hide. She knows she's always welcomed at the Beach house and how secluded it is."

"Okay, now what?"

"I know they both left soon after. I can't reach either one. I plan to have Phil use people he knows to try to find them, and I wanted to let you know what was going on."

"You mean like private detectives?"

"Kind of, but very discrete ones, if you know what I mean."

"I do. Gloria's giving me hell, and she would kill me if she knew we were talking. I hope you know in public I'll have to support her."

"I know. Thanks buddy. We'll survive this, I promise."

As Matt replaced the phone on the receiver he tightened his fist, wondering what all happened when they met. While he tried hard not to hate Chelsea, he couldn't believe she was costing him a woman he knew without a doubt he loved. But, how was he to convince her?

###

After accepting the complementary newspaper the next morning, Suzan analyzed an attached coupon for a fishing trip with a handwritten note to be sure to take the first boat out. She knew who left it, and how she would have to hurry to make it.

The boat only had a few customers on board, and left as soon as she arrived. No one approached her until they were out at sea. A woman settled in next to her with a large congo style hat, which hid most of her face. She knew to look straight ahead.

"Life can be such a bitch, can't it?" The voice sounded British. "With so many recent developments, we've been working on what might be the best use of your talents and opportunities."

"I understand, and I'm sorry for the problems I may have caused."

"Are you sure you want to do this?"

"Just name it and I'll give it my best effort."

"As the wife of Matt Harris, no one will ever suspect you to be working for us. It'll give you a cover we could have never hoped for. It will be tricky, but over time we'll perfect the way we can utilize it."

"I don't understand. You know the wedding has been called off."

"Postponed is more like it."

"I'm not sure I can do that."

"A few minutes ago you said you would do anything for your country. As such, this is what you need to do."

"What about Matt? This hardly seems fair to him, and I'm not sure he wants to marry me anymore, especially with him fathering a baby by another woman."

"It'll take some time to work out the details, but we think we can. Anyway, you have some time to think about it. We need you on another mission right away. One you have already been trained for."

That was fast. What was up? "Are we talking Afghanistan?"

"Very close. You have an uncle in India, and we assumed you would like to visit him. One of the Afghanistan tribal leaders also has a contact there. We need to establish exactly where and not be detected. Are you interested?"

They wanted her back on the street and doing recon for them. Why not? She needed to disappear for a while as Matt worked on clearing up the issues with Chelsea. "I have time now as you know. Using Matt as an asset is going to be hard."

"We know. The decision will be yours. Think about it. We also know Matt Harris is considering a project in New Delhi. It would provide you with a perfect cover to move about. It'll give us all a chance to see how you can adapt to being a wife and agent at the same time."

"I'm not sure this will be good until after we determine who the father is of Chelsea's baby."

"I understand your reservations. We're not sure yet, but we think the chances are high that it might be another man's baby."

Suzan wondered what information they had uncovered, but the words allowed her to relax. "How long will this mission take?"

"We could get lucky in a week, or it might take many months. We have no way of knowing for sure."

Suzan knew they would not forward much more information than what they had shared. Should she? In the back of her mind she hoped Matt was honest and they could get back together, but Chelsea appeared so certain. "Can I accept this mission and reserve commitment on the rest until it's over?"

"Normally we would say no, but we need you so badly on this one we're willing to bend the rules."

"Good, I'm in."

"We thought so."

Suzan never in her life dreamed she would be asked to marry a man for her country, especially someone like Matt Harris. Her life presented the CIA with a convenient resource to pass her into groups they could never enter. She already knew some of the international operations of Harris

Properties, but she felt sure the CIA had completed much more research than she had.

Properties, but she felt sure the CIA had completed much more research than she had.

Chapter 27

"Gloria called and said she'll be visiting us in the office shortly. She's bringing her husband with her." Gail rolled her eyes as she knew how Big John ruled over many people but only had one ruler, his wife.

"I want Phil and Dan to sit in on this. They have a way of keeping me calm." Matt straightened his tie and rolled his head to relieve a tension in his neck.

"And if Gloria objects?"

"Tough! She's the one who called, or shall I say, demanded this meeting."

"I need to hurry. Gloria may arrive at any time." Gail stood and left.

Matt had to choose his words carefully. He knew Big John agreed with him, but with his wife present, Big John would have to support her, and this time Big John would want answers as well. He didn't like his daughter disappearing without a trace.

Dan and Phil walked in moments before he heard Gloria's loud laughs outside. Big John had to be a patient man. "Men, are you ready for this?"

Dan glanced at the conference table. "I think we need to take a seat before they come in."

They prepared to sit as Gloria and Big John walked in. Matt stood and walked over to them. "Hello, Gloria. It's good to see you."

"Cut the bull. We need to talk." Gloria motioned to the two men at the conference table. "Do you really need them in here?"

"I think I might. I want to make sure what we say here is

presented correctly later, and they might be able to offer some good counsel to us."

Big John walked over to the two men and shook their hands. Gloria started to resist, but like a mother hen looking for a fight, she locked her eyes on Matt. "We cannot find Chelsea. Have you heard from her? You would think you would be concerned about her safety, since she's carrying your baby."

"I've not heard from her, and I want to talk to her. I think you know she's avoiding me."

Gloria held her head high. "I think I know why. She's probably embarrassed with all of the news of you marrying that damn military girl."

"You know that she has a name–it's Suzan."

"Whatever. I think you need to do your part in finding Chelsea."

"Yes, I hope to find her, but for different reasons than you do. I want her to admit I'm not the father."

"I think it's your attitude that has driven her away. How could you?"

Gloria walked closer and looked as if she was prepared to slap Matt when Big John stepped forward. "Gloria, you need to settle down." Big John waved a hand toward the conference table.

"Me, settle down! You're her father. You would think you would want to get answers!"

"I do want answers, and the way you're handling this is not helping."

"Don't you start with me!"

Big John shook his head and walked toward a seat at the conference table. The other two men joined him as they remained quiet.

Matt turned back to Gloria. "If you'll have a seat and

give me a minute, I'll tell you and the others what I've discovered."

Matt watched her fume and glare at Big John, as she strutted over to a seat on the far side of the table and about as far as she could from Big John. "Tell me what you know."

"I learned a few minutes ago that both Suzan and Chelsea turned up at my estate in West Palm Beach."

Matt studied the open mouths and looks of disbelief from around the table as Gail joined them. "Gail's the one who received the call from the security guard at the beach house." Matt looked at Big John, knowing he had kept the news a secret until they arrived.

As all eyes focused on Gail, she turned toward Matt who had put her on the spot. "Yes, I received a call. They didn't know what to do. Both women didn't know the other would be trying to hide out there. They had a few words, and both left."

Gloria huffed. "I would have loved to have seen what happened." Gloria glanced at Phil. "I hope you're able to contain this."

Phil turned toward Gloria. "I don't think this will be a problem, but it needs to come to an end now for everyone's sake, especially before it gets blown out of proportion."

Big John tapped his fingers on the table. "I fully agree. I'm sure Chelsea will call me soon. I have hired several detectives to find her, and this information will be useful for them."

Gloria's face burned red, as the anger inside her appeared to be reaching the boiling point. "Don't you dare make it sound like Chelsea's the one causing the problem here!"

Big John appeared to ignore her rage. "Matt, I hope you keep me up to date on whatever you hear."

"You know I will. Chelsea usually has a way in settling down, and I'm sure she'll be found soon."

"Men! I should have known you would all stick together." Gloria glanced around. "I'll find her on my own, and then we'll decide what's the best way to handle the situation from here on out."

Big John rubbed his hands together, as if he were washing them, but also as if he was controlling the anger inside him by releasing a deeply buried frustration. "Men, and I'm sorry Gail, you'll have to excuse me. I think we all want this behind us, and I hope we can keep the lines of communication open."

Gloria glared at Big John. "We need to talk."

"Gloria, what we need is for you to listen for once."

Gloria's eyes flashed at him. "I'll not be insulted."

"Then I suggest you quit acting like Chelsea and grow up."

Gloria studied the men before she glanced at Gail. "I'm out of here. This is a long way from over."

The men glanced at each other as Gloria left.

Gail spoke as she waited for the door to close. "If you want me to I can try to talk to her later."

Big John raised his hands. "I'm sorry for the outburst, and I hope everyone will be patient with us as we get down to business now. She's my daughter, and I just want her to be safe."

Matt felt the pain of Big John's situation. "I'll do whatever I can. I also have people trying to find both of them. I would think Chelsea might be going to Miami. As far as Suzan, she might be going back to the condo with her Mom."

Big John glanced at the door. "I hope you don't mind if I stay here for a while."

"You're welcome to stay as long as you want, my friend."

Chapter 28

Suzan walked into a small club on Ocean Drive in South Beach. She found a perfect table in a corner, as she remained hidden behind an awkward looking hat. The words of the CIA contact confused her sense of what was right and what was wrong. Her immediate mission was to make contact with Matt and try to defuse the situation. They told her to make it look like a difficult decision for her, but to make sure to keep the door open for later.

She focused on the details they had given her concerning Matt's interest in developing a project in Delhi, which was the town her Uncle Brajesh lived in. Attempting to use Matt as an asset for the CIA seemed so wrong. She realized with time her love for Matt would grow, but who was she kidding? She had lost that battle a long time ago. Current events made it difficult to think clearly. She had to commit to making this work.

A waiter joined her as she refocused on the real world around her. "What can I get you tonight?"

"A large majito, and hopefully some space around me to think."

"Well, it's the middle of the afternoon, so that shouldn't be a problem. And on a day like this most of the customers want to stay outside." He looked Italian, with dark black hair hanging to his shoulders.

She planned what she needed to accomplish before she made the call. Funny, she never felt nervous before. She also knew her phone call would be monitored. While it looked like a normal iPhone, the cell phone she had been given contained many special features she had worked on for the last few hours. She knew her world would never be the same.

The waiter soon returned with her large, make that one very large, majito. "Let me know when you want to order anything else."

"I think this will work for me for a long time."

Suzan wondered how Matt would take it when he learned the truth. She guessed she would have to handle it if he did. While she would do her best to make sure he never did, she also knew she could count on the CIA to do their part. The good benefits in all of this would be a lavish lifestyle for most of the time, and having Matt as a lover would definitely be a plus. With enough thinking about the *what if*, she entered his number and called.

He answered on the third ring. "This is Matt."

"I know you must think I'm crazy, but I need to talk to you."

"Suzan! I was hoping you would call me. I've been trying to find you!"

"I know you have. I went to your estate in West Palm Beach after Phil talked me into it, but it was a bad idea."

"I know. I heard earlier, and I'm so sorry that happened to you."

"In such a case, you know Chelsea was there also." Suzan stopped long enough to enjoy a long cool drink of the majito.

"Her parents left here a few hours ago. They're looking for her, and they have no idea where she is. I don't guess Chelsea told you where she was going?"

"Listen, I know you're like one large family in New York City, and I'm truly sorry for upsetting your world."

"Suzan you're my world now. I'm doing what I told you I was going to do. I want her to take a DNA test to prove once and for all that I'm not the father. You have to believe me on this."

"We had words on this at your beach house. Chelsea's still insisting you're the father. When she left, the last words she said was that you would never see the baby. Apparently, that's her way of getting back at you."

"The truth will come out one day. I can promise you."

"I hope you're right. Until this is over I need some time to think. I think what I'm really saying is . . . I just can't face all of the paparazzi or press right now. This is a life I'm not prepared for."

"Suzan, I can understand where you're coming from. I do."

"Matt, the reason I'm calling you is to let you know where I'm thinking of going for a while."

Suzan waited, enduring a long silence before he responded. "As long as I know you still plan on marrying me, I can extend or reschedule the wedding. I don't want to lose you and I'll not let that happen. Where are you thinking of going?"

"The one place I don't think they'll find me. I want to visit my Uncle Brajesh in India. He lives in New Delhi."

"Even in a place as far away as India you'll not be totally protected. The paparazzi have a vast network they use. I have a project in New Delhi I wanted to consider for a long time. If you'll allow me, I can take you there."

Suzan bit her lip. "I don't know. I still remember the words of Chelsea a few hours ago. She's convinced you're the father."

"I'll be able to prove I'm not one day, and hopefully soon. If it'll make you happy, we can stay in separate rooms. I hope you can still consider me a man of my word. I've never pushed you before to do anything you didn't want to do. I'm . . . not crazy enough to do something stupid and lose you."

"I'll think about it. Can I call you back in a few minutes?"

"Sure. Please let me take care of you and prove to you I'm not the father."

Suzan clicked on the end button. She reached for the majito and downed a large part of the liquid gold. She might need another one of these before the day was over. She needed to call the CIA contact. A special connection was built into her phone, but she knew they had heard the conversation. She had no private life any more.

Her phone rang as she expected. She opened the phone and said nothing. "You completed this part of the mission with flying colors. Keep your iPhone with you, and we'll contact you in India after you and Matt arrive." The line died.

She never agreed to go with Matt, but it appeared she had no say so in it now. Yes, she would need another big majito today. She clicked on Matt's number. "I'm in Miami. Let me know when you can arrange the trip so I can call my uncle."

"Thank you. Suzan, I love you. I'll clear my schedule and leave as soon as I can. I'll call you back when it's all arranged."

"Matt. I love you too."

As tears formed in her eyes the waiter returned. "I'll need another one."

Chapter 29

Arriving in Delhi, Suzan and Matt settled into their suite they would call home for a while. Rooms for the rest of the entourage filled the floor below as Tony, Gail and the two men providing security rounded out the group.

The Gulf Stream owed by Harris Properties made life so easy as compared to flying commercial. Matt's wealth had advantages. Suzan held his hand the entire trip. It felt like he couldn't do enough for her, or take his eyes off of her.

She hoped he could prove he wasn't the father, but if he did, she still needed to find a way back out of the CIA. She had her work cut out for her, and had to concentrate and work out a plan later based on the facts. For now, she was on CIA time and had to play by their rules.

She knew little about her mission. They wanted her to go undercover to help locate a war lord from Afghanistan, or at least the contact he maintained in India. Breaking away from Matt would not be easy, but she assumed her contact had a plan for her. She double checked her phone to make sure it was charged.

As Matt promised, the suite had two bedrooms. She still had not decided if she would sleep with him. Yes, she wanted him, but no, she wanted to wait. The internal conflict mounted the entire trip. She knew he wanted her, but she sensed he would not be pushing her as he promised.

While the daylight ended outside, she felt like it should still be the middle of the day. She walked over to Matt, who was studying a newspaper. "I don't know if we need to eat lunch or dinner."

Matt dropped the newspaper. "Are you hungry? We can

order here or venture out.”

"I think staying inside would be good. I need to call my Uncle Brajesh and make arrangements to see him tomorrow. What are your plans?”

"The real estate market is hot here now, and we have several sites we want to look at. I hope you can go with me to see them.”

Suzan thought about it and would normally love to do so, but knew this would give her the best opportunity to escape from him and work on whatever mission she was summoned for. "I don't know, I think I might be in the way. I'm sure my Uncle Brajesh will want to show me around. I have second cousins I've never met before, and I hope to have enough time here to really explore the city. The last time I came, I only had a few days.”

"I think we'll be here for a while also. We have many people we need to meet with. It'll be fun to explore the city with you.”

"Okay. I hope our schedule will work out so we can.” She still needed more details from her CIA contact. "Let me call my uncle.”

As expected, her uncle had been waiting on her call, and he wanted to see her first thing the next morning. She talked to him for a long time, and she almost didn't notice the incoming call. She glanced around to see if Matt was close enough to hear her. She didn't see him and assumed he was in his bedroom. She walked to her own and shut the door while asking her uncle to hold.

"Can you talk?”

"I'm not completely secure, as you may suspect.”

"Understood. Please listen only then. Matt will be invited to a luncheon tomorrow. There's a small café in the basement level of the building where the meeting will be held. Excuse yourself from the meeting, and you'll receive more information on your mission there. Have a good night."

Suzan glanced around to see if Matt had walked close to her door. He had not. With all clear, she clicked back on her call with her uncle. "I need to get some sleep and I'll see you in the morning so that we can plan my time here better." She discounted the call and went to look for Matt.

With the lights to his room off, she glanced inside. He had fallen asleep. Should she join him? Should she?

Matt snuggled deep in the covers as the warmth enticed him to linger. The daylight invading his room indicated the time raced forward, but the jet lag made his head druggy and he needed the extra minutes. He sank his head deeper in the pillow as he turned to his other side.

Feeling the presence of someone beside him he forced his mind to clear. He recognized the shape, the feel of a woman beside him. He concentrated on any movement or sounds until he heard a light breathing. He wanted to snuggle closer but hesitated. Would any more movement wake her?

Matt fluttered his eyes open. A filtered light coming from a window allowed a limited view of his room. He guessed the sun was starting to rise. He pushed closer to her as he watched for any movement. The smell of her perfume filled his memories as he remembered giving it to her.

She had her back to him as he felt the back of her legs first. He moved closer and rested with his legs enjoying the feel of her silky smooth skin. She didn't move and appeared to be sleeping. He extended his hand to the top of her hip as he inched closer. Her butt rested in front of him and felt as perk as ever. He forced himself to maintain control.

He wanted her more than any woman ever. His dick

ached with the pent up desires he had for her as he fought for control. He was not going to lose her. He came too close to having her disappear out of his life before, and he barely had her in it again. Damn Chelsea, her lies almost cost him the love he wanted. He would have the truth soon. He knew he had not gotten her pregnant. Yes, they had sex at times, but it had been a long time, and the times they had sex he always used a condom.

He pushed memories of Chelsea aside and breathed deeply. A faint image of Suzan's bare shoulder ushered in a new wave of heat which he had to battle. He leaned forward to kiss her naked skin as he pulled the covers higher to keep her warm. He wanted her to rest, but he would also love to have her awaken, and to make love to him with the same passion he had for her.

The time ticked away, ten minutes, then thirty, and after an hour he could not control it much longer. He had maintained an erection the entire time. A thrust in her direction made her shift her weight. While he slept naked, she had worn a simple night shirt. He could easily enter her from behind, but knew to wait until she became fully awake.

She snuggled closer to him as he breathed easier. Was she closer to awakening? He pushed closer, as she turned on her back and yawned. He moved his hand above her head and made room for her to lie on his shoulder. He felt her stretch but not turn further toward him. He did manage to see her face, which looked so peaceful and relaxed. She looked so different when she slept. He knew this was perhaps the only time she allowed her guard down. She could be such a fireball when she wanted to. This side of her he knew she allowed few, if anyone, other than him to see, and he loved it.

Matt heard a low moan. He readily accepted it as a sign

she was waking and help roll her over onto his shoulder. Her leg wrapped over his legs as she melted into his body. Her entire body connected with him as he recognized every part of her. Her soft hair on his shoulder and the smell of her shampoo heightened his awareness.

"Good morning, beautiful." He whispered as low as he could and still be heard. He hoped she would acknowledge him. She did come to his bed on her own. He wished she wanted him as much as he wanted her.

He watched her lips part in a pleasant smile, but her eyes remained closed. Her hand firmly planted on his chest rubbed him softly. Now confident she wanted him, he leaned over and kissed her forehead once. He adjusted to kiss her eyes and nose before shifting to her lip. With a light kiss to gently nudge her awake while adding several more before withdrawing.

"Good morning." She breathed in deeply, filling her lungs, and pressing her breasts in closer to him, as she kissed back.

Matt moved his hand to cup her breast and explore her nipple through her nightshirt. To him, she felt perfect. His lips pressed hard against her as he kissed her deeply with passion. She complied with her mouth open and allowed him to explore her tongue with his own and added a slight sucking sensation that he knew that she knew he loved.

He lowered his hand to her crotch and explored. She felt exactly like he hoped–wet. He rolled over on top of her and lost himself inside her. He knew he could never find anyone like her, and he would do everything he could to keep her. This was love, and this was the woman he wanted forever. She made him happy, and damn it, he would make sure she knew that. He had to prove to her he would never cheat on her. She had to know this. She had to know.

###

Suzan loved how Matt held her after making love. She knew she could perhaps never find a man more understanding of her than him. In fact, considering how he had most of the world catering to his needs, she felt especially happy about being with him. A few weeks ago all seemed so perfect. She looked forward to their wedding, her life and the future.

Chelsea changed all of that. She had convinced her that Matt had sex with her and Matt was the father. Yes, Matt strongly disagreed, but she would expect that from anyone caught with their pants down. And now, the CIA had her in a tough spot. They wanted her to continue her relationship with Matt in order to be able to use him for a cover. She felt love, but confusion as the thought of not being allowed to choose for herself. She would do as asked by her contact in the CIA. It made things complicated and the ability to fully give her love to Matt impossible. However, she would do what she had to do. She felt sure it would come out Matt wasn't the father of Chelsea's baby. How would she get though the events facing her?

She drifted closer to sleep again as she thought about how it could be worse. Matt did offer a great life style and he appeared to act like he loved her. Yes, he also looked very hot, but could she ever trust him as a husband? She had to guard her heart, and pretend all was great. Exactly what the CIA had trained her for–to use people as assets. Now, if she could live with her decision.

Chapter 30

Suzan pulled the white robe around her as she enjoyed the soft luxurious fabric. The smell of spicy food filtered across the table. She felt alert, in spite of her internal clock telling her she should still be asleep. She decided to glance at part of the wall street journal Matt had finished reading.

He looked over at her and grinned. "I know this isn't what you normally read. I can check to see what else they have available."

As Suzan glanced into his eyes, her heart melted again, as he managed to immediately send her into a new trance. He had this gift many people would die for with his ability to penetrate the thoughts of those around him. "No, I'm just waiting on you to finish."

Matt folded the paper and placed it to his side. "I'm so glad you allowed me to go with you."

"Well you made it sound like you wanted to come here anyway."

"Yes, I did. I have had this project on my mind for some time." He reached over and massaged her bare leg above her knee cap. "The investments opportunities here are too good to pass up. I think you'll see what I'm talking about. Listen, I know you're meeting with your uncle today, but I'd love for you to join me at lunch where some people here will be doing a presentation. I think you might find it interesting."

Her CIA contact was correct about being invited. She focused on not giving away that fact as she looked upward before giving an answer. "I'll have to call my uncle. He wanted to meet me this morning."

"I understand. I should have given you more warning, but

I only heard about it a few minutes ago. I received the call while you were taking a shower."

Suzan leaned closer and rubbed his shoulder. "I want to be part of your life. I do. You know this is something I don't know much about."

"I understand. The people I'm meeting with might give you some pointers on what you might want to visit, not to mention VIP treatment in seeing it. And . . . I'm sure your uncle will be invited to go with you."

Suzan wanted to say yes, but she knew to act as if she was only considering it and not jumping at the opportunity. "How long will the meeting be? I know my uncle wants to take me to see other relatives I have here. To tell the truth, I don't know what all he has lined up for me, but I think he wants to show me off here."

"I can understand again. By the way, the meeting will be with members of the Delhi State Industrial Development Corporation. They offer a valuable service to investors like us in the form of market surveys and project evaluations."

"This sounds like a long meeting."

"It will take a while. If you get tired you can leave. However, I thought you might enjoy it." Matt reached up her leg slightly to massage it deeper. It sent an electric like impulse straight to her heart. She had only made love to him a few hours ago, but she wanted him again. She hadn't slipped on any panties yet, and he had a free shot, if he wanted it, all of the way up her leg to her crotch.

Suzan allowed her face to relax as she closed her eyes while imagining making love to him again. "I don't think you're playing fair. Make love to me again, and you'll have me following you like a little kitten."

"The others will be here in a minute, but that's a request I'll never turn down."

Suzan felt him lean closer to her and his arm move under her legs, lifting her from her seat effortlessly. She leaned her head into his chest and never opened her eyes as she felt him walking with her.

In minutes she felt him lower her to the bed which still remained unmade. She glanced up as he untied the front of her robe. His hand felt warm and tender as he reached over and massaged one of her breasts. His eyes focused on her, patiently attending to her needs. "You're a very beautiful woman."

Suzan started to respond with a denial or perhaps something else to lighten his compliment, but hesitated as his eyes drilled home his sincerity. "I think you're the good looking one and I'm the lucky one."

He leaned forward and stopped inches in front of her face. His breath felt hot and tantalizing. He had to know what effect it would have on her. As the direction of his eyes focus drifted lower she knew he was examining her lips. The passion in his kiss never disappointed her. His slow methodical methods drove her crazy, as she leaned forward to make the connection with his lips.

At first he only maintained the contact, but he soon relented and kissed her back, as his firm lips reaffirmed his strength. The kiss intensified as he used his tongue to force her mouth open. His entry into her mouth opened up her world to what she wanted more than anything else–to be loved by a man who also wanted her to be happy.

Suzan reached around him and realized he still had on his clothes. And unlike her, he had already dressed for the day in a starched white cotton shirt and a beautiful golden colored tie she decided to play with, pulling him closer to her.

She felt him lower the passion in his kiss as he slowly

withdrew from her lips, only to add one slight touch as a parting gesture. "I guess I need to undress, or you'll have me looking like a homeless person at the meeting."

"You have my motor running all out, and you did promise me something special."

"I can promise you this; I'll never turn down making love to you."

She opened her eyes to see him stand and remove his tie first, placing it on the side table. Impressive cuff links soon landed beside it. While she hoped he would hurry, the show he put on for her excited a part of her she had never experienced until she met him. He looked fantastic–hot.

His smile acknowledged her thoughts. He appeared to enjoy it. She definitely did. He unbuttoned his shirt slowly, one button at a time, revealing a white undershirt underneath. Good, more clothes he had to remove as she anticipated the strip show he put on for her.

Getting hotter by the second she thought about touching herself while she waited, but didn't know how he might take it. She felt wet and ready but torn between a delightful show and having him inside her pumping away as he had earlier.

"I promise, I'm hurrying." He unbuttoned the last button and removed his shirt. His muscles revealed their character beneath his undershirt, which he quickly slipped over his head. His female personal trainer must have worked on his abs for a long time to get him looking this good. She remembered his personal trainer was a good looking hottie, but she could live with it for these kinds of results. Plus, he knew he had no interest in her but the training. In fact, she now used this same girl and was loving it. Her thoughts were only sidetracked for a minute, as she watched the flexing motion of his abs highlight his hands moving to his belt.

"You know you're driving me crazy, don't you?" Suzan parted her legs slightly to give him a better view so he would be encouraged to move faster. It worked. He unzipped his pants and dropped them to the floor. Leaning over, he untied his shoes and stepped out of them and his pants at the same time.

With only his boxers on she could tell he had a massive erection underneath. He looked ready, and she felt ready. Oh damn was she ready! "Come on, let me see." Her teasing words surprised her, but she managed to follow it up with a wink he appeared to love as he lowered them for her.

His large erection stared at her with its pulsating action appearing to be waving at her, as she rose on her elbows to study it. He moved closer to her and stood still. She reached over and placed a hand around his cock. He felt so strong, stiff and vibrant as it pulsated again for her. She had given him oral before a few times, and this time felt right for her. She leaned closer and stopped inches in front of him.

"You don't have to unless you want to," his voice whispered in a deep hoarse tone.

"I know, but I want to make you happy." She stroked him several times with her hand before kissing him slightly on the tip of his penis. The sound of his groan encouraged her to continue. She opened her mouth but decided to lick him several times. He tasted good. Something she didn't expect. She opened her mouth and allowed him inside her as deep as she could. She couldn't take it all as he grew too big, and she didn't want to gag, but wanted to make sure it felt fantastic as she stroked him with her hand and sucked on him.

She felt his passion peaking quickly. No, she wanted to make him happy, but she wanted him to screw her. She wanted to come with him. They had before, and she was determined to do it again. She stopped sucking on him abruptly and settled back into her pillow, as she felt his hand touch the inside of her legs to spread them, making room for him to slide in between them.

She couldn't stop a groan mounting inside her as she melted beneath his presence. His smell overtook her as his body moved on top of her with a radiating heat she remembered from earlier. His body contained all of the muscles she wanted inside a well toned body. His chest touched her tits and sent them into frenzy as he melted in closer to her.

She couldn't stand the anticipation much longer, as she lifted her legs slightly making it much easier for him to enter her. She knew he knew she was ready, but to make certain there was no doubt she raised her pelvis in his direction and moaned again. "I want you. I want you now."

She felt the tip first being pressed toward her, but being the gentlemen she knew, he stopped briefly and tested her. Yes, she was ready. Satisfied, he thrust inside her and pumped her relentlessly, just as she wanted. The sounds of her groans increased, she couldn't control them. She hoped he could come fast, since she knew she would.

Apparently he knew this, as he continued to wildly attempt to catch up with her impending eruption. He had to as she knew she couldn't contain it for long. Her fingers tore into his back, she knew it had to hurt, but she couldn't control it. A flash of heat blanketed her as she lost all outside connection to the world. She belonged to him now, and she would give him everything he would ever want. After all, he was doing the same.

She couldn't hold it much longer. She would love to come at the same time, but waiting wasn't an option any more as the flood of spasms over took her. She came for a long time, and it felt like forever until she finally collapsed. He, however, never slowed down. Moments later she could feel him peaking. The sensation sent her into a new wave of emporia as she gladly came again and this time with him.

Her body perspired as well as his, melting them into a feeling of oneness, a closeness she knew would bind them together forever. She breathed deeply, she loved him.

Of all moments for this to surface . . . she thought of Chelsea. Surely she didn't experience the same wild sex with him. Surely, she wasn't pregnant with his baby. Surely!

Chapter 31

Matt hurried to the dining room table, where the others on his management team waited for him. Time was disappearing quickly, but this time he knew the reason for being late was worth it. He felt like he had Suzan's trust back. Making love to her felt incredible. He hoped he could contain his late morning pleasure from his team.

Gail glanced at him and then down to her watch.

"I know I'm late. The time change did us in this morning. Suzan will be out in a minute, and she's going with us. I'm not sure how long she'll be staying, but I want her to see what we have in the works. I think our host might be able to line up some sightseeing for her."

Gail handed him a folder. "These are the people who'll be attending this morning. I didn't have much time to research them, but they're key players in handling international investors. They're giving us a royal reception. The economy here is as it is in most of the world."

Matt had a seat and studied the photos and information Gail had handed him. "Since we all know the situations and problems, I hope we can find some opportunities here to exploit. It's good when we both know they need us as much as we need them. They have an upper class here that can afford our properties."

Tony finished a croissant before saying anything. "I'm sure they'll be escorting us all over the city the next few days. However, I think I already know many of the best areas. It will be nice to understand what kind of building codes we might have to contend with, but it's too much to fully analyze on one trip."

"If this works out, you can count on being here often. I would like to see us build something outstanding." After Matt watched Gail glance past him, he turned to study Suzan walking into the room. A beautiful dress made her look so much more enticing than he was prepared for. The long off-white, pastel color of her dress had swirls of intricate designs engrained into it. With a short scarf fitted over the top adding to its flair, she looked fantastic.

"Hi, I'm sorry for running late. I didn't know I would be going until this morning."

Gail leaned back to take in the view. "You look amazing."

"Thanks. This is something I'm getting used to."

Matt walked over to her. "I love it. Now, did you clear everything with your uncle?"

"Yes, I called him. He's disappointed, but he agreed to come pick me up at the meeting later. He has lived here all of his life and knows the city well. You know, he might be a big help to you also."

"Perhaps. What does your Uncle Brajesh do again?"

"He owns a software company with clients all over the world. It's nothing large, but enough to provide him with a comfortable living."

"I see. This city has many people in that industry. I can't wait to meet him while we're here."

"I know he's looking forward to meeting you also."

Gail stepped toward the door. "I think we need to hurry."

###

Suzan enjoyed her meal, but she couldn't name anything on her plate. They were treated as royalty, with many servers busy around their table that included maybe ten people. They promised her special tours to many places, which was exactly what she had hoped for. She didn't know where to start on her mission and hoped to soon hear more details. She had been told to excuse herself after the meal and go to a small shop in the lower corner of the building she was in. The closer the time came, the more anxious she became. Who was it she was trying to locate?

The puzzled look must have shown on her face as Matt leaned over closer to her. "This is part of my life I hope you learn to enjoy. Making contacts with the right people is extremely important."

"I understand. Is it okay if I get some fresh air before we get started?"

"Sure, I'll have one of the guards go with you."

"No, it's fine. I'm just going to go downstairs for a minute. I noticed a small shop there with something in the window I wanted to check out as a gift for my uncle."

"Okay. We'll get started in about thirty minutes, I think." Matt leaned over and kissed her cheek before standing to help her out of her own.

Suzan smiled at everyone and left, leaving the excuses to Matt. Perhaps she should have acted bored to cover her reason for leaving, but in any case she didn't have the guards following her. She wondered about later, and if he would assign one then? That could be a problem.

Within minutes, she walked into the shop and started glancing at the wares. She saw many high quality items and decided it would be good to buy her uncle a present, now wishing she had thought more about it before she had made the trip.

Her phone rang. She retrieved it and glance at the caller ID, no name registered. "Hello."

"We have a tight schedule. Your contact will be part of the tour guide that Matt has lined up for you. He'll give you the target's name and more information. He has a large gold ring on his index finger with an eagle embossed on it. When he suggests a side trip, accept it."

"Anything else?"

"One thing. The clerk will add a magazine to your purchases. Check out page seventeen and memorize the people in the article. Do not go online anywhere to do more research–understood?"

"Yes."

They were baby feeding her with information. Not a bad strategy in one respect. If she was captured she would have limited information on her. Still, she felt intrigued to know more. Who was her target?

Suzan studied a pen with elaborate details on the barrel which she thought would be an ideal present for her uncle. She carried it to the clerk who never looked at her while processing the sale. As expected, he reached over and added a magazine, placing all in a small bag. Without even saying thank you he turned to adjust the racks behind him.

She walked out of the shop and looked for somewhere to sit and read the magazine without being noticed too much. A small table next to a coffee shop appeared as she rounded one corner. She didn't have much time as she knew Matt would be worried about her.

After finding her seat, she opened the magazine and leisurely flipped through it. On page seventeen she read an article about some of the top terrorists being sought by the government. She counted eight names. Which one was her target? She forced her mind to memorize every detail. Realizing she should not continue to carry the magazine with her, she dropped it into a trash can on the way back up the stairs.

As she expected, the large dining room where they had their meal earlier had been converted to a meeting room. A podium had been added with white boards and a screen erected behind it. Each person had folders place in front of them and a glass of water to one side.

Matt turned as she approached him. "You made it in time. We're about to start."

She watched him hold the chair for her as she slipped in next to him. While she loved being close to him, she felt sure he needed his operations manager closer.

A speaker stood and welcomed Matt before beginning the meeting. He soon started a film to give basic information about India, and also explain what his organization could do for Matt. While somewhat interesting, she could tell Matt had his own questions he wanted answers to. The speaker realized this also as charts replaced the visitor video.

This would be the best time to act bored, as she hoped the guy in charge of showing her around would speak up. It worked, and a young slim guy with a full beard walked over to her. "I know this might not be interesting to everyone and actually seeing the sights will be more so. With your permission, I have a tour arranged for your fiancée."

Matt looked over and smiled. She knew he had arranged this in advance. How the CIA intercepted it, she would never know. "Matt, perhaps when I explore the area I might be of help to you. I'll definitely give you my opinion, and I do still need to spend some time with my uncle."

"I thought the same." He leaned over closer to her and kissed her cheek. The smell of his cologne set new waves of desire through her. Yes she wanted him again, and she would absolutely have him again later tonight.

"Good, I guess I'll see you later." Suzan stood and waited for her escort.

Matt edged closer to her. "I want to send one of the security guys with you." He looked determined. This could cause a problem for her later, but she agreed to it for now. Today was a recon that only gave her bearing of where things were. She would become much more familiar with the city over the next week or two.

They soon exited the building located in the center of Connaught place and were greeted by a driver and one of the men on Matt's security team. She didn't need security and Matt knew that, but she didn't resist, since they were trained on how to handle paparazzi if they encountered any.

The guide moved into the back of the limo last. "I'm not too sure how much you know about New Delhi, and I hope this overview will help you see our city in its best light." He handed her a flyer. "We're going to drive by some of the major attractions and show you how the city is laid out today."

"That sounds interesting. I do want to know the city better. What are some of the major attractions you recommend?"

He pointed to a brochure. "Some of the ones I know you'll want to see include the Indian Gate, Rajghat, Jama Masjid, Red Fort, Aksharfham temple, and of course Humayun's Tomb."

"It sounds like you have my day plan. I would like to also see how people get around your city also."

"I'll be glad to explain our transportation system to you. We're very proud of it. I'm sure you'll find much more information inside your brochure." His eyes flashed around to focus on the others in the limo. Then, his stare darted toward the brochure. It must contain much more than simple tourist information. Her fingers explored the brochure, as she realized something was hidden inside one page. She managed a peek and saw an electronic key to what she assumed would be a hotel room. This must be her base she would work out of.

###

Matt answered his cell phone, and felt happy to know Suzan had returned from her sightseeing trip. He hoped this would keep her happy, as he worked all afternoon with the various charts and information he had been presented. The more he saw, the more he liked the opportunities, but he knew that this would only be the beginning. People always offered him the moon to get him interested. Delivering on their promises was always a different story. Still, he had many people to meet while in New Delhi. The more opinions he received and the more contacts he made the better, since it would take a lot of funds to complete a project this size. With funds from Big John now in doubt, he needed new funds more than ever. At the same time, he didn't want to appear overanxious, just cautious. He needed to let them do the selling more than he needed to act like an overeager buyer.

Matt stood to thank his host for the day. "You've definitely given us much to consider."

"As you can imagine, we have many parties and meetings set up for you the next few days." The leader of the group glanced at Gail. "I hope you like what we've put together for you, and if you would like to have others invited, please let me know."

"I can tell you've worked hard on this, and especially with such a short notice." Gail lifted her folder higher to indicate her work was only beginning. "I'll go over this later tonight. We need another day to really get our internal clocks reset."

"We assumed the same. We hope you get some good rest tonight, and we can start some tours for you tomorrow. Will Suzan be going with us?"

Matt glanced over toward Gail. "I'm not sure. I know she wants to spend some time with her uncle here. Living in New Delhi, he knows the area well. I'll let you know in the morning."

Matt's phone rang again. He noticed Phil's name on the caller ID. "Hello, buddy."

"How did the meetings go today?"

"Not bad for a first day." Matt glanced around, trying to determine if he needed to look for a private spot.

"Good, can you talk for a minute?"

As he assumed, Matt knew that meant to find a private corner. He soon noticed a small balcony on the other side of the room. Fresh air would be good. "Men, excuse me for a minute." He walked to the door and opened it to the outside. The weather felt pleasant as the cool afternoon settled in. Traffic noises rose from the street below to cushion his conversation. "Okay, I can talk now."

"Good, I have some news for you on Chelsea."

Matt breathed in deep as he wondered what he had learned. "I hope you have good news."

"I think I know where she is, thanks to Big John. Chelsea and her mother have been seen in Milano attending some small fashion shows."

"That's not surprising. I'd like to be able to talk to her and force her to take a damn DNA test."

"We both know how hard that will be. I need to make sure she's not spreading word to the market in Italy that you're the father."

"Are you planning on going to Milan?"

"I wish I could, but I have too many projects to handle for a while. I thought about sending Ronald to try to make contact with her. She sometimes opens up to him more than others here. And with another project in play there, he needs to make a trip to Milan anyway."

"Perhaps. I do want to build something nice in the Lake Como area. I have for years, and we now have several Italian investors begging us to do so. Since it's their money, and funds may be tight for a while, I think we might be able to take care of several problems at once. Tell him to make plans to go as soon as he can. I'll be with Suzan tonight, and it will be hard for me to talk openly."

"Understood. I'll take care of it and let you know what comes of it."

Matt clicked the phone shut and headed inside. He needed to pluck this one thorn out of his side.

277

Chapter 32

Suzan felt too tired to go out to eat, and she was glad Matt agreed to have a quiet diner in their room instead. She had been rushed around town all day, and it had become confusing for her. She needed to study the map more before tomorrow, and hopefully she would have a chance. She eventually watched Matt usher the last of his team and the guards out of their suite. Finally, they were alone.

"I can't believe how tired I am. This is so unlike me." Suzan flopped in the oversized couch in the living area of the suite.

Matt walked over to her. "I can order us a massage if you think it would help."

Suzan thought about it. "I remember the last time you offered me a massage."

She watched his smile grow as he moved closer. "Yes, I remember it also. However, tonight it does sound good, so what do you think?"

"You know it sounds crazy, but what I think I need to do is work out for a while. We've been sitting in the jet or in a car for most of the last few days. Don't they have a gym here somewhere?"

"I'm sure they do. Let me make a suggestion. I need to make a few calls back to America. Why don't you do your workout and let me catch up with business for about an hour. We can eat dinner here after that."

"I'm not hungry, but that might change after a good workout. I'm not used to being so inactive."

"Good, I'll have one of the men go with you."

Suzan stood. "I don't think that will be necessary. We

both know I can handle myself."

"Still, he'll not interfere with you, and this is why I bring them along."

Suzan grinned and tossed her hip to one side.

"Okay, have it your way." Matt shook his head and smiled.

"Good, let me see what I have to wear."

A few minutes later she walked into the athletic facilities on the second floor where only a few people walked on the treadmills. She decided to join them and warm up a little first. Her fast walk quickly turned into a jog. A TV played in front of her giving the local news, until suddenly the camera focused on the person causing her such hellish nightmares. Chelsea and her mother were walking fast toward a car with a storm of reporters and photographers chasing them, asking questions.

Suzan raced to turn up the volume as Chelsea turned to face the crowd. Her stomach had a small bulge, just slightly enough to confirm she might be pregnant. And of all of the nerve, she leaned backwards to display the fact for the world to see. A reporter jumped in with question about who was the father. Suzan felt her hands forming fist. How could she do this?

"I think we all know who the father is, but I'll not say anything else until he makes the announcement himself. He's an honorable man, and he'll do the right thing soon, I'm sure."

Another reporter moved in closer, but spoke in what sounded like Italian. She had no clue what he asked with the exception of one word–Matt.

Chelsea did not answer, but offered a curtsy smile and turned from the cameras as a large bodyguard type guy stood between her and the reporters. The last thing Suzan saw was Chelsea rushing inside a limo and the door closing.

"That bitch."

The TV station switched to a studio where the attention switched to Matt. A young girl announced that Matt and his fiancée were in India and how rumor has it that he's the father. "That's just great." One of the reasons for going to India was to get away from the press. This would also make her job harder to accomplish. She assumed she would go undercover at some time for the CIA. As quickly as the news story broke, it ended.

Her inner passion for the truth tore at her. Was Matt lying? With the CIA forcing her to act like a couple, she had little choice in confronting him now. Damn it, this wasn't fair.

Suzan discovered a full size punching bag on the other side of the gym. An hour later she was still kicking and punching at it, but the frustration and pain would not go away. There had to be a way out. She knew Matt would want more sex tonight, but she was in no mood for it now. Did he hear about it already? What was Phil doing about it? Surely the news has reached America also.

Suzan punched the bag again and again. It would be a while before she would go back upstairs.

###

Matt checked his watch, knowing that Suzan should be back any minute. He hoped to hear more about the newscast Phil had told him about earlier. While he tried hard not to hate Chelsea, he could only take so much. Phil was working on a statement to be released to the press tomorrow morning, but this time he wanted to read it before it was released. Yes, he trusted Phil and knew this was his area of expertise, but too much was at stake.

As he heard the door open behind him, he covered his

anger with a smile, but she didn't. Thinking about playing innocent would not work. He knew she had heard. She looked hot, sweaty, and angry, but still sexy in a way that caused him to consider his words carefully. "I assume you heard."

"I watched the news story on the TV in the exercise room. She looks pregnant!"

"Phil called me a few minutes ago. I only know what he told me. I promise I didn't get her pregnant."

"She's showing, so someone did."

"What do I have to do to prove it to you? You know I'm pushing for a DNA test."

"Did Phil tell you that the local news here just announced that we're in India together?"

"Is that what you saw on the news downstairs?" Matt contorted his face in a fight to control his anger.

"Yeah, it's all over the news here."

"Perhaps we should leave and come back later."

"No, I want to see my Uncle Brajesh. You can leave if you want to."

"I'll not think of leaving you alone. I've said this many times and I mean it–I love you!"

Suzan breathed in deeply. "I think I believe you, but I hope you understand how it makes me feel."

"I do. It'll be behind us soon, I promise." Matt walked closer to Suzan.

"Please give me some time."

"Okay." He stopped in his tracks.

"I would love to take a long hot bath."

"I think that might be a good idea. I'm trying to get through to Phil and hope he can get this under control. I'll let you know what I find out when you finish."

He watched her stare upwards. "I think I need to be alone

tonight."

The words felt like a knife stabbing in his heart. He didn't want to lose her and since pushing her might do that, he backed off. "I can sleep in the other room if that's what you wish."

"No, I'll take it. If I change my mind I'll let you know. For now, I need to do some thinking." She started to walk past him and stopped. Her eyes looked sad, almost as if she had been crying earlier.

"I love you." He wanted to hold her tight but resisted, knowing it might push her away.

Relenting, she leaned in next to him and offered him a sideways hug. "I believe you." She released him and walked on.

He would have loved to hear the world I love you back, but she said nothing. He would talk to Phil again as soon as she left the room. Damn, he wanted this problem to go away. He had never wanted the love of a woman more than he did Suzan's.

Suzan stopped at the door leading to her room. "I think tomorrow will be a great time for me to visit with my Uncle Brajesh. I need to relax and get this off of my mind."

Matt started to object, but he saw the intent determination on Suzan's face. "I understand. I'll try to get as much as I can completed on this project tomorrow. I do want to spend some time with you and explore New Delhi."

Suzan maintained a frozen stare.

He knew she felt stressed and not to push it any more. "Okay. As you wish. I'll line up a ride for you."

"That will not be necessary, my uncle drives."

"I know, but with the paparazzi here on full alert now, they will find you."

"I think they'll find me if I run around town in a limo.

They'll never expect me to be in a normal car, and my uncle will keep me safe. No one knows me here. I think this is best."

Matt knew he would never win the argument. "I love you, and I just want you to be safe."

"I know you do. Give me some time." She turned and walked away with his heart aching for a return of the words he so freely gave. He wanted to hear her say she loved him, and he would one day, no matter what he had to do.

Chapter 33

Suzan slept surprisingly well during the night. She knew how important the day would be. She hated treating Matt like she did, but she wanted to separate herself from him a little in case Chelsea was telling the truth. It would make leaving Matt easier, but what the hell, the CIA had asked her to stay with him for cover. This might work, but it might not also. She had to keep her options open on that one. She also considered her options of staying with him and faking her commitment. That's what the CIA wanted, but she knew how cold that would make her feel over the years.

The last options was leaving the CIA altogether and being the perfect wife for Matt. If he told the truth and was not the father of Chelsea's baby, she would owe him a major apology. What was it about her that she could not trust him? He had never treated her bad. In fact, he gave her everything she could ever want including himself.

She walked through the lobby with her head slightly covered with a scarf. The selection of clothes she wore helped her to hide her identity. She wanted to walk around freely today. Having her uncle with her might help in many ways. She felt sure the CIA would give her more flexibility and she looked forward to a full briefing soon. She had to find a way to escape to her motel room where she had been given a key. She knew many answers awaited her there.

After stepping outside, she saw her uncle standing by his car. She rushed to him and gave him a large hug, as she heard him laughing out loud. She had told him the story about possible paparazzi, and she felt relieved to see him rushing her inside. In seconds, he slipped behind the wheel and gunned the motor, heading to the other side of town.

A few minutes later, she noticed someone in the back seat, the tour guide Kanan Bala she met the day before. "Hello, Ms. Mercer."

"Hello. I didn't know you would be with us this morning."

"I talked to Matt earlier, and he gave me the number of your Uncle Brajesh. After I called him and told him I can get you some special seats today, your uncle gave in to my persistence. Our government here has much at stake in making sure you have a good time. My job is to ensure that you have no problems seeing whatever you want."

"I understand." What she understood is that this was her contact to the CIA. He had really managed to pull a fast one.

"Brajesh has mentioned a few places he wanted to show you. I have called ahead to make sure you receive VIP treatment."

"Thank you."

The morning rushed ahead as they showed her many parts of the city and always managed to avoid the crowds wanting to see historical places.

After walking back out to the car after seeing one place, Brajesh turned to her and smiled. "I can't wait to introduce you to my friends and family tonight. Some of these are cousins you've never met. Thanks to your escort here, he has offered us the stateroom in the hotel where you're staying. He has also many guests he wants to introduce you to."

As they drove, Brajesh received a call. With his face reflecting a serious expression of concern, he only listened. After he finished the call, he looked at Suzan. "I'm afraid I have some problems at work I need to take care of."

Kanan spoke as if on cue. "I'll be glad to have a car join

us and continue to show Ms. Mercer on the next few stops I have planned. I'll make sure she's ready for the party tonight."

Her uncle acted like he wanted to argue, but changed his mind as he glanced at his watch. "I would appreciate it very much."

"Not a problem." He lifted his phone out of his pocket and made a call.

Suzan studied his appearance, memorizing every detail of his face.

"They will be here in about five minutes. There's a café on the corner. You can leave us there if you wish, and I can order your niece a cup of our tea. I think she might like it."

"Yes, I've been to this café before, it's very good. I'll leave her in your care."

As she walked into the café she noticed another woman who was much the same size and shape as she was, and wearing a dress almost the same as she had on. Kanan moved in close to her. "Stay here for a few minutes until we're gone. Change your scarf and leave by the side door. A hotel is at the end of the block. You have an electronic key to your room. You'll find full instructions on your mission there. Good luck."

She didn't have to turn around to know he was leaving with the decoy. She followed his orders and changed her scarf before leaving the shop. The hotel entrance looked plain, the lobby even more so. No one worked behind the dusty register so she walked to the elevator and entered her floor on the panel.

Her room looked simple until she closed the door and located a small computer that had been programmed for her. She watched a video presentation and forced all of the details into her memory. She knew it would only play one time and be wiped clean. She now had the name of the person the CIA wanted to find. Harmir was a known war lord who she had been briefed on many times before. Some people thought he had been killed, but many also believed he had not. Apparently the CIA had new information saying he was alive.

While she had studied his face before, they gave her new ones to memorize. To blend into the Indian society he would have to appear more civilized than he did while in the rocky nomad land he called home in northern Afghanistan and Pakistan.

According to the information she , they thought Harmir to be in New Delhi looking for money. They didn't know his source, but they thought this money connection might be someone close to a man named Sharif, who owned many commercial properties in India. Now, she understood why the CIA wanted to use Matt.

Arrangements had been made for her to meet him, and it was her job to follow him and learn more about his connections. Someone close to him had to have a strong opinion as to the war, and, in fact, be supportive of the Taliban's fight. It would not be openly displayed but still there. Her job was to try to connect the dots.

Another part of her job was to keep her eyes and ears open and confirm if Harmir was actually alive and in India. She was given strong instructions to not engage him. They would be forwarding more information soon on where he might be holding up in New Delhi, where they also wanted her to check it out as quietly as she could. Her closet contained local clothing she would need. She needed to know which part of the town would be his most likely place to hold up. It should not be too hard. All she had to do was walk the street and listen. Now she knew why they had her running all over town. Where did she hear Afghanistan people talking? With all of the different languages here, she didn't listen as closely as she should have. She should've been told this earlier.

Still, she had four hours until she had to make it back to the hotel. This would a good time to make a dry run around the hotel. The CIA had to have selected it for a reason. She changed and walked out on the street. She would stop at a few shops and become acquainted to the streets around her new base of operation.

Three hours later her phone rang, it was Kanan. "You need to change and head back to the café I dropped you off at, and we'll make the switch again." The connection ended. She walked on, knowing more about what they expected of her for now.

###

Matt hurried to finish his last tour of the day. He pushed for answers and received only partially what he wanted. He had a good team that would come next and analyze what he had found out. In this case he wanted to be here first. Well, really he wanted to be here because of Suzan. She hadn't called him all day. He hoped he was doing the right thing by not calling her and giving her room to think about things. It would be a matter of time until the truth came out, since he knew he had not gotten Chelsea pregnant.

After holding out for as long as he could, he finally called her and felt glad to hear her voice answering. "Hello, Suzan. I wanted to check with you to see how your day went."

"It has been a long one. How about you?"

"The same here. I missed you today."

"Matt, I thought you would be too busy to miss me today."

"I'm never that busy anymore." Matt studied her voice and felt like she was in a good mood. He wanted to enjoy time with her tonight.

"Matt, my Uncle Brajesh wants me to meet some friends of his and some relatives I've never met. The tour escort, Kanan Bala, has set up a dinner party for us tonight. It's in the same hotel. I hope this is okay with you."

"Have you talked to Gail? You know she's the one who makes all of the arrangements. However, I'm sure she can work it out where we can make appearances at both."

"I'm not far from the hotel now. I'll talk to her and then to Kanan again. Thanks for giving me some space."

"You're welcome. You know I just want you to be happy. A party might help you forget about Chelsea. So that you'll know, I'm still working hard on getting her to tell the truth."

"I hope so. I'll see you soon."

Chapter 34

Suzan walked into the lobby of the hotel she shared with Matt and glanced around. No one seemed to notice her as she walked to the elevator. She hoped the paparazzi would not find her and make her job impossible. She glanced at her watch and discovered how little time she had to get ready. She had new electronics she needed to install in her purse to capture any images or sounds she might need to transmit back to the CIA.

Walking into her suite, she found Gail with a stack of papers in her arms. "How are you?"

"I'm fine, but it has been a long day." Suzan knew Gail had been working on the schedule for tonight by the look on her face.

"We don't have a lot of time to plan the events tonight, but I think I can coordinate everything. Matt called me and I also talked to your tour guide, Kanan, who lined up some more people for you to meet. I also understand your Uncle Brajesh has many relatives for you to see. Luckily all three groups will be in this hotel tonight. You're going to be one busy woman."

"How much time do I have?"

"Maybe forty-five minutes at the most. I have descriptions of many of the people here you need to know." Gail handed her a list of guests with a brief overview of who they were along with a photo.

Suzan scanned the list and tried to remember everyone. One the list coming to Matt's party she saw the name of Sharif. His photo matched the one she had seen earlier. "That's a lot of people to remember. Can I take this with me?"

"Yes, this is your copy. Matt knows some of these people, and he'll introduce you to them as well, but he'll be relying on you to introduce your family to him. At the party set up by the tour service, Matt will not stay at it for long. This was mainly set up for you to obtain a glimpse of the elite members of society here. Watch your back with these people."

Suzan flipped to the list of people attending. None of them registered, until she noticed the name of Sharif again. She pointed to the name. "I thought I saw this name attending Matt's party."

"That doesn't surprise me. He's a developer and landlord here with many properties. In fact, he might be one of Matt's largest competitors. Matt might tell you more about him. Be careful what you say to him, since I'm sure Matt does not want to tip his hands on what he has planned. Matt would also like to know more about what he has under consideration. While there's a chance the two might form a partnership, don't hold your breath on it."

"Thank you for obtaining all of this for me. I'm still getting used to all of these parties."

"That's my job. I'll be around all night and will check on you. You also have my phone number if you need my help."

"Thanks again. I better hurry."

###

Matt rushed into the suite, followed by his bodyguards and headed for Gail. "I've been trying to call Suzan. Is she here?"

"Yes, calm down, she's probably taking a quick shower. She looked exhausted."

Matt breathed easier. "I was concerned about her being out in public without a bodyguard with her. I've been thinking about the paparazzi this afternoon, and it's simply a matter of time until they find us here."

"Seeing how many parties you have going tonight, the word will definitely be out there where you are."

Matt turned to his guards. "It might be good to have some extra coverage tonight."

The taller of the two guards spoke in a deep gruff voice. "We have already worked on it. The hotel is providing a large number of extra people tonight, with guards posted at the front door and on the conference floor where the parties will be held. All should be under control."

Content with his response, Matt nodded his approval. "I need to change clothes also."

"Yes, you have very little time. I mentioned to Suzan how important it was to not disclose your intentions here. She appears to be a smart woman, but it might not hurt for you to reiterate what she's not to discuss."

"I plan to." Matt reached for the guest list. "Is there anyone in particular I need to spend time with?"

"Yes, I think you'll recognize one name on the list. But remember the old saying of keeping your friends close and your competitors even closer." Gail winked.

Matt nodded as he recognized the name. "It'll be good to finally meet him face to face. We've talked on the phone before, but that's it. In this market you never know when a competitor could turn into a partner. If we lose Big John's money, we might need to find new money or a partner who knows the turf."

"I've included all of the information I could find quickly on him. If you want, I can do more research in the morning."

"I'll let you know." Matt moved toward his bedroom. "Tell Suzan I'll be ready as fast as I can."

###

Suzan felt uncomfortable in her dress. The fabric restricted her movements and the top was cut too low. She didn't need perverts trying to stare at her boobs. Who needs that kind of attention? She decided to go back to her room and find a scarf she could use to cover up with, but she saw Matt walking in her directions before she made it out of the main living room.

"Wow, you look fantastic tonight." Matt's eyes lit up and his face generated a glow which warmed her heart. His comments did make her feel fantastic, but a little intimidating, as she glanced down toward her breasts. "I think I need something to help cover these a little."

She watched him lower the direction of his stare. "If you wish, but that dress looks beautiful on you. I've always loved you in red."

After finding what she needed, Suzan glanced at the red sequins covering her dress, but making it weigh a ton. However, it was the black four inch heels with only a small platform for her toes to balance on that really caused her problems. "I hate to say it, but I think this all makes me look like a clown."

"I know this isn't what you would want to do, but I do thank you for being such a good sport."

"Thank you for saying so. I would love to wear old jeans and explore the city and hang out in a coffee shop to chill out. Do you know what I mean?"

"Yes, I think so. After we're finished with business here, we can take a small vacation if you want to."

Suzan leaned forward. "To me . . . this was supposed to be a vacation–remember?"

Matt held up his hands in defense. "I do understand. If you want to explore the city during the day and have me attend to business, I have no problems with it at all. I'm so glad you're with me."

Suzan felt herself relax. "To tell the truth, you make me happy and you have always treated me so special. Perhaps I'm over reacting to the news about Chelsea." While she meant it, she also had the thoughts swirling in her head about keeping him happy and allowing her to accomplish her mission. She needed him to introduce her to Sharif. "I'll be back in a minute."

She heard Matt talking to Gail as she walked back toward her room. "We need to start early tomorrow morning so we can line up the next few days. We should have some new information tonight we need to analyze."

"I agree. I'll come to the parties for a little while, but hope to turn in early."

"Very good and thanks."

Suzan liked how thoughtful Matt treated those around him, even when he had so much at risk. She knew she loved him, but there was something she needed to overcome. She couldn't let herself relax, to enjoy what was supposed to be the best time of her life. She soon returned to find Matt waiting on her.

The first stop was to see her Uncle Brajesh. As expected, he had many people at the party wanting to meet her, and she felt extremely happy that Matt and her uncle hit it off so well. Matt quickly asked him to come to the wedding. While she wished he hadn't mentioned the wedding, she also felt a swelling of pride to be associated with Matt.

Brajesh offered to throw another party in honor of the engagement. Suzan had to stop him. She wasn't sure how to do that, but she would work on it. She still needed his help in getting around town and accomplishing her mission. It wouldn't be long until she'd have to take off on her own.

Matt rose first and looked around. "I hate to leave, but we

have many places to be tonight. I hope we can spend some more time together soon."

Minutes later they moved on to the next party, the one he had set up with other business associates and contacts he needed to make. She looked forward to finally meeting Sharif and knew being invited to spend time with him would be a major key in accomplishing her mission. The party had many people walking around as they entered. No one had been seated yet.

Matt held her hand, giving it a small squeeze, as if to say he would take care of her. His years of training in diplomacy and networking always amazed her. He commanded attention with his presence and own unique style, which made everyone want to meet him.

After meeting one business man after another, their names started to run together. The conversation centered on properties in the area and world economics, areas she knew little about. She hoped to hear news on politics, but the subject seemed to be missing entirely, as if it were a plague or something.

A bar attendant came by offering champagne to everyone. She accepted her glass and watched Matt accept one also. He extended his glass forward and leaned closer to her as he whispered, "to the most beautiful woman in the world."

Suzan felt a soothing heat rush to her face. Flattered, she glanced downward to avoid the intensity of his vividly green eyes. "I hardly think I'm the most beautiful woman anywhere. We're going to have to get your eyes checked."

"I think nothing is wrong with my eyes, and it's not my only way of seeing you."

Yes, Matt had the ability to charm. "Okay, I give, and thank you for the compliment." Matt touched her glass again with his. The magical moment almost made her forget her mission for a minute, and then drift off to a world only Matt could provide for her. She couldn't deny it, she loved him. "Matt, I–"

A man tapped Matt on the shoulder. "I'm sorry to interrupt you, but we've heard you have a passion for cigars, and we hoped you would allow us the pleasure of presenting you with something we hope you'll enjoy."

A grin covered Matt's face as he turned to face the guy interrupting her moment of confession. "I see you have discovered my weakness." He turned back to face her with eyes in a begging mode.

"I can see you have a few bad habits I'll have to live with."

His smile grew as he leaned forward. "Thanks, you know I love you very much."

His words evaporated all resistance in her. "I know. I love you too."

"I promise I'll not be gone long. This might be a good way for me to make some contacts, and for you as well."

Being a social butterfly was not what she specialized in, but she had been trained by the CIA on how to recruit assets which she needed here. Outside the protective arms of Matt, she looked around to see who would approach her first. Since she recognized no one, she decided to walk over to a small table to taste some pastries.

A smooth voice startled her as she studied the table. "I think you'll enjoy these."

She turned toward a man in a suit perfectly tailored to his slim but muscular body. His deep, almost black eyes dominated her attention. He could easily have passed for a professional model, even with an appearance of being in his late forties. Her eyes studied the details of his face hoping to match them with one of the photos she had memorized.

"Allow me to introduce myself, my name is Peter Sharif."

Suzan made the connection, but never realized he would have such a smooth complexion with such a sexy masculine appeal. "How are you? I've heard your name being mentioned here. Do you know my fiancé Matt Harris?"

"I know him by reputation, and I think we've talked on the phone a few times. Meeting him is why I agreed to have this party arranged tonight. It appears he has good taste in woman, and I look forward to meeting him. Is he here with you?"

"Yes, he was enticed by someone to enjoy his vice of cigar smoking."

"Oh yes, I heard he loved cigars. I'll see if I can find him outside. I'll talk to you more later I'm sure." He leaned over and reached for her hand, raising it to his lips for a long kiss. Rising, he intensified his eyes on her again.

"I enjoyed meeting you as well, and I hope to see more of you while we're here."

He smiled at her words. "I'm sure that can be arranged. I think we also have another party later tonight where can talk more. I've been asked to introduce you to the more social part of life in New Delhi, as opposed to the business side. I think you'll enjoy being introduced to some of the women here."

"I'm sure it will be interesting to me, and I look forward to it."

He turned to hunt for Matt, as she welcomed her good fortune. She had made contact in a perfect situation. The CIA would be proud of her on this move. She knew her hidden camera had recorded the entire meeting. She looked forward to seeing more of him at the next party.

###

Matt inhaled deeply as he felt the smoke entering his lungs. One day he would have to quit this, but he so much enjoyed it. He heard the teasing about his preference to cigars over the kabatos, the large tanks that feed a pipe. If he had to engage in them to make friends he might try it, but these cigars would be hard to replace.

A man walked toward him with a large smile and pictured exactly as he expected. Peter Sharif carried the same attitude as himself, where he expected the world to accommodate him. His suit fit perfectly over a frame much like his. Considering he could be his biggest competition or his closest ally, Matt stood to meet him, showing him the respect he hoped he would also receive. "Hello, I'm Matt Harris."

Peter extended his hand toward him. "Yes, your reputation precedes you. It's so good to finally meet you in person."

"And likewise. Can I interest you in a cigar?"

"As you might suspect, I prefer the kabatos, but in the spirit of friendship I will, and I hope you join me later on the kabatos."

"Of course." Matt waved to the hostess to indicate he needed one more cigar. "I understand you lined up this party tonight. It was very thoughtful of you."

"I thought the best way to get to know you would be in such a setting. I've invited many people you need to know, and I'll introduce you to them tonight."

"As you know, I would appreciate it very much. India has much to offer."

"Yes, it does. I own many properties in New Delhi, and I'm surprised you waited so long to invest here."

"This has been on my radar for a long time, but we have

so many projects lately that this always ended up on the "to do" list."

"I can tell you the best time is now to invest here. The prices have never been better, and the future looks great."

Matt studied his mannerism, as he wondered what his true motivations were. His obvious intent was to let him know he should be investing here. It could be he had properties to sell. He decided to push further. "We've been going over figures here and they do look impressive. Perhaps we could set up a time to explore opportunities here. We plan to be here for a while."

Peter shifted his eyes to see if anyone was close enough to hear. "I understand you're committed to investing in India. What made you finally decide to come see us?"

"Actually, my fiancée has relatives in New Delhi she wanted to visit, and that is what pushed the scales over."

"Yes, I met her a few minutes ago. You have a beautiful fiancée. You're a lucky man."

Matt glanced sideways as images of her invaded his mind. Yes, he thought she looked beautiful. "It's good to see her taking an interest in my work. She wants to learn more of the culture and plans to explore the city with the help of her uncle."

Peter lit a cigar he was handed and grinned. "I can see where you find such pleasure in these. Are they Cuban?"

"Of course."

"I know Suzan's Uncle Brajesh Mittal. He has some smaller properties here and he's a hard worker. He invited me to another party later tonight he's throwing for Suzan and her relatives. He wanted me to introduce her to some women who are part of our social elite. They should prove to be a large help to her in understanding the culture."

"Thank you. It looks like we'll have many opportunities

to talk. I know Suzan is missing me, so I need to find her again. Please enjoy the cigar." When he turned, a light glistened off Suzan's hair as she walked out to meet him. The bright beautiful smile indicated she was in a great mood, which was exactly as he hoped.

###

Suzan smiled at the two men talking, however, deep inside she worried about using Matt. She had to make sure he never knew about her secret life. She would see to it he never became involved, or that his life was ever placed in danger, a thought she fought with several times lately. At this point she could only second guess her future.

Peter raised his left hand for a minute as his right hand searched the inside of his coat, where he produced an iPhone that he quickly moved to his right ear. She didn't understand what he muttered into the phone, but he pressed the phone next to his chest and raised one finger as if to ask for a private moment. He glanced around and headed for a corner.

Suzan moved an earring designed by the CIA to fit her ear better and activate its range as she listened into his conversation. She hoped no one would notice what she was up to, but this was too important to miss. He acted suspicious as he disappeared.

Luckily, Matt had been sidetracked by one of the men smoking cigars. Peter spoke in an Indian dialect she recognized. With his voice sharp and to the point, he didn't like being disturbed. She heard the name of a restaurant he would meet someone at later. Suddenly, she heard words she didn't expect. It sounded as if he was being blackmailed.

Peter raised his eyes and glanced in her direction for a brief moment. She had to turn away. Did he know she was listening? She moved closer to Matt and hoped for the best.

Matt seamed to love the display of affection and hugged

her openly. "I assume you're ready for me to go back inside."

"Yes, we have many guests we need to greet."

"You're right." Matt handed the cigar to a hostess and extended his arm to escort her back inside. While his charm and attention never disappointed her, it was his smell that drove her wild at times like this.

She decided to push for more information on Peter. "How well do you know this guy, Peter, you introduced me to?"

"I've talked to him on the phone plenty of times, but I've never worked with him on a deal before. He's well connected here in India, and I'm sure we'll talk more soon. I should've already told you a few things. He'll pick you for information, and it would be best for you to act like you know little about my operations. He might be a partner at some time, but he might be our biggest competitor as well."

"Gail has told me the same. I don't know that much about your operation, so I think playing the part of a *dumb blonde* will not be hard."

Matt motioned to her hair. "As black as your hair is, I don't think you'll ever be associated with a blonde."

"Still, you know what I mean. He has been invited to another party we will go to next–the one my Uncle Brajesh has lined up to introduce me to people here."

"Really."

"Yes, I saw it on the list Gail gave me. I thought it was odd he showed up on two different lists."

"I wish I had more time to talk to him, but I'm sure we will before the night is over." Matt directed her to a small room where he could talk easier.

"Is there anyone else I should pay special attention to?"

"We're also looking for people with money and tied to it.

For several reasons we need to know who we can count on for financing, and to help spur sales when the properties are completed. After meeting some of the people here, we'll go over the names and compare notes later. It'll be interesting receiving your take on people."

The host of the meeting soon walked to the front of the room and announced that dinner would be served shortly. The conversation came to a ghostly halt, as the crowd of around fifty people walked toward the main dining room.

As Suzan slid into her seat while Matt held it for her, she looked across to see Peter setting directly across from her, with two beautiful women hung on both arms. Apparently he had the reputation she thought only Matt owned as an international playboy. She had to fight the urge to laugh, but then again, she didn't know the whole story. She waited to be introduced, but none came.

It did give her time to study him closer. He wore several expensive rings covered in diamonds, a large designer watch that she guessed was a Rolex, and had his initials engraved into the sleeve of his white, silky looking shirt. The quality of the suit appeared to be Armani, but she could only guess since she was not totally up on recognizing the names of suits. It did give the impression of being well tailored and fitted to his body.

As her focus drifted higher, she found her stare being matched again. She looked away and snuggled closer to Matt. She had never needed the protection of a man before, but she preferred it to the stares she was receiving. Her thoughts returned to the low cut dress she wore. Was he was checking her out? Surely not, since he had two raving beauties by his side, who appeared to be at his beck and call.

As everyone adjusted in their seat and started on their salad, she glanced around at others close to her and nodded hellos to them, while Matt had engaged into a conversation with a man on his other side. Matt shifted back into his seat so this man and Suzan could make eye contact. "This is the Minister of Labor for India."

Wow, Matt had more contacts than she could ever imagine. They apparently really wanted him to do business here. She leaned forward. "Hello, it's very nice to meet you."

"And you as well. How are you enjoying your visit so far?"

"I really love what I've seen so far. While I've been here before, I want to dig deeper into the city and learn much more this time." The man looked a little surprised, so Suzan knew to explain further. "I have an uncle who lives here. My father was also born in India many years ago."

"I see. I thought I recognized the Indian heritage in you. Where does your father live now?"

"My father had moved to the United States where he met my mother. He died a few years ago." Thoughts of her father's death and the problems caused by the land he had left her returned. He had told her his land would lead her to love. It led her to Matt, and the jury on their future was still in doubt, as she had to force her mind not to think of Chelsea and the pregnancy. She had to complete this mission first. Then, and only then, would she concentrate on Matt. Life was too complicated.

"I'm sorry to hear that. So you were not born in India?"

"No, I was born in Florida."

"Well, I'm sure your father would be glad you're exploring the city. If I can be of any help, please let me know."

Matt turned to wink at her. "I'm glad you talked me into making this trip. It's much more intriguing than I had imagined." He leaned closer. "I also am so glad to see you take an interest in my work."

"You do live a fascinating life." Yes, this could be a rewarding life, and one full of luxuries to boot. She hoped she made the right decision in working for the CIA. She now wished this trip was over and she could put this behind her. Saying good bye to Matt, or to the CIA, would be hard. Combining the two might be even harder.

She still needed to do one more thing tonight. She needed to find a way to place a bug on Peter. This would be a big challenge, but she had several hidden and at her disposal. As the meal came to a close, she watched a small window present itself. The tall vixen on Peter's left motioned to him she wanted to have a smoke. Peter reached inside his coat pocket to retrieve a cigarette case.

"You know, I haven't smoked in a while, but tonight I think I would love to join you for one."

Matt looked surprised, but he pushed his seat backwards and stood to help her out of her own. "Since I enjoy my cigars, I know not to say a word."

Since Suzan had never smoked before, this would be a challenge, but placing a small bug inside his cigarette case would be perfect. She hoped for the best as she followed the girl carrying the case outside. Suzan had the perfect sized bug to place inside.

After walking outside, the girl moved to the far side of the patio and surprised Suzan with her perfect English. "These meetings are so boring."

"I see. Does Peter take you to many of them?"

"He never likes to go anywhere without escorts around him. It's amazing how some guys want this macho manly charisma. Who do they think they're kidding? So, how is it working for Matt?"

"I don't work for him. I'm his fiancée."

"Really!"

"Yes." Suzan started to lift the large diamond ring he had given her, but remembered she wasn't wearing it. "We're supposed to be married in a few months back in New York."

She kept her face skeptical. "He appears to be a nice guy. I hope it works out for you." She opened the cigarette case and retrieved one before handling the case to Suzan.

Suzan slipped the small device the size of a pencil eraser out of her belt and hid it in her palm. She held the case close to examine it, waiting for the girl to light her smoke. With perfect timing she dropped the device into the case. Would it be spotted later–perhaps? Could it be traced? Definitely not.

The cigarette felt strange in her fingers as she held it casually. The woman moved the lighter in front of her face and lit it. Now she needed to fake the inhaling and not disclose her fake wish to smoke. Damn, what she had to do for her country, but compared to life on the streets in Afghanistan, this would be easy. She remembered she had to stay focused. Perhaps she could get more information out of this new asset.

As the woman drawled in deeply, Suzan fought back the first cough. "Since Matt loves cigars, a cigarette here and there might make the smell of them not so bad."

"Peter doesn't mind me puffing on a cigarette occasionally, as long as I puff on his dick from time to time."

"I understand." There was nothing like being open with what the girl was hired to do.

"He has one special woman he lives with, but she never goes out into public with him. She believes in the older ways, and she wants to stay at home and out of sight. He's a generous guy, and this pays my way into a better life."

"You don't have to explain anything to me." Suzan smiled and wondered how much the privileged few got away with such scandalous behavior. Would this make trusting Matt impossible, or simply complicated?

"I heard you say you're one-half Indian. Many men think all Indian women are masters of the Karma Sutra and will bring them untold pleasures. This is especially true for the privileged men who are successful." She stopped and flashed a beautiful smile revealing a softer side of her. "I'm curious. I understand life is so much different in America."

"Yes, it is." This woman needed help and beneath it all, Suzan wanted to help. She had seen so many women in Afghanistan being abused. While it was too big of a problem to be solved by one person, she hoped to make one small contribution. After her mission she would return to help this woman. For now, Suzan needed her help.

"One day I want to move to America, but I know I need money. If you can ever help me, I would be in your debt forever."

"I'll be glad to help if I can." Suzan decided to press. "Besides working for Peter, what else do you do?"

"I speak several languages and work as a translator on occasions."

"That can be helpful in a country like this that's known as the crosswalks of the world."

The woman glanced around. "My name is Sarita Devi." She handed Suzan a small note. "This is my e-mail. Please stay in touch with me, but don't say anything to Peter about us talking about anything personal."

"I will not. I wish you the best in everything."

"Don't worry about me. Peter likes the way I take care of him."

Suzan had thoughts of how she gave Peter head and

squirmed. She could never allow herself to be taken advantage of like that. Closing her eyes for a minute she thought of Matt and how he had always been gentle with her and never demanding. So far, he had been the perfect gentleman. She hoped he would always remain as such. Still, Chelsea was pregnant, but who was the father? She had to know.

"Thank you for the smoke. I needed to get some fresh air." Suzan hoped the woman would not recognize she seldom smoked as she handed the case back to her.

Chapter 35

As quickly as one party ended, another one started a few doors away. Hopefully, this one will be much more relaxed, as it was hosted by Suzan's Uncle Brajesh and it would be purely social. Matt felt glad to have Gail and Tony with them as they walked in.

Suzan rushed to her Uncle Brajesh's arms as he offered her a large hug. She also beamed a smile back toward Matt that rekindled his memoires of why he had fallen in love with her. He never remembered anyone ever having this effect on him–ever. "Matt, I want you meet my uncle. This is Brajesh Mittal."

Matt extended his hand to a tall slim man with distinct dark India features. He wore a black suit and starched white shirt sporting a thin red tie. "Hello. I'm so glad to finally meet you. Suzan has told me much about you. Welcome to our family here."

Over the next hour they were introduced to one relative after another. They all had questions about America, and some had heard about Suzan's work in the military and her award. Matt didn't want this spread too much around town, but knew it would be hard to keep it quiet. He felt proud of her, but knew it would not be good.

Finally, after all of the introductions had come to an end in the outer room, Brajesh opened another door to a larger room where many more people were waiting. These were the friends and people Brajesh thought she would like to meet; so much for a relaxed evening.

One of the first people to walk over to them was Peter. "Hi, it's good to see you again. I know this is a lot to take in so fast so I won't be staying for long, but I do know a few people you'll want to meet. These are the women who are connected to all of the social events here. I'm sure you'll be in great hands with them, and they can introduce you to whatever you want to see."

Matt stepped forward. "Thank you for arranging this for Suzan. I'm sure she would appreciate meeting as many people here as she can. She really wants to take in the Indian culture."

"It's my pleasure. I think a full appreciation of our culture will be helpful in your investment decisions here. While India and the United States have a great working relationship, some of our neighboring states will look at you as an immediate target to attack, especially if you plan to use your name to promote your properties."

"This has been a concern of mine for obvious reasons. My name is one of the major draws to our properties, and it usually adds to the extra value of living there. It would be interesting to hear your opinion on this."

"I thought we might have this discussion while you were here, but first explore the city and do your research. I know you're a man who doesn't make rash decisions."

Matt understood the message Peter was sending, as he assumed Matt needed his help and perhaps his name to protect his investments from attacks and possible losses. "With the amount of money we spend on a project we have to be well informed, which is exactly why we'll be here for a while."

Peter raised an eyebrow and turned his head to one side. "Exactly how long do you plan on staying in New Delhi?"

Matt glanced at Suzan. "I think that depends on many factors. I would assume at least a week, maybe two." He waited for Suzan to add any details, but she didn't. While he knew he would stay as long as she did, he also knew he had many other projects that needed his attention back in New York. If only he could find proof that he was not the father of Chelsea's baby.

Peter slipped his hand inside his pocket and retrieved a golden card holder, which he opened to retrieve one of his cards. "Here's my card with my private numbers on it. I look forward to hearing from you when you're ready."

"Thanks. We're staying here at the hotel and you can reach me here as well." Matt hesitated, but soon followed up with one question. Politics was one subject no one wanted to talk about, at least openly. "I may need the name of someone who can talk frankly with me on repercussions of an American investing here."

"I have many contacts." Peter glanced at the women on his arms. "Perhaps we should have dinner one night soon. I know you love your cigars, but I still hope to entice you into trying the Kabatos."

Matt laughed. "Yes, that would be a cultural activity I might enjoy."

"Good, until then." Peter leaned over and grinned at Suzan before glancing at the other guests. "I do want to introduce your fiancée to some of the women here."

###

"That would be nice of you." Suzan studied Sarita, the woman she had befriended who maintained a steady pleasant smile. If Sarita was on Peter's arm often, she held the keys Suzan needed to complete her missions. Would Sarita know who Sharif was?

Peter caught the stare. "My friend here can also accompany you, if you would like. Sarita has lived here all of her life."

"I would appreciate the help, but I really don't want to be

a bother to anyone. I think exploring the city on my own would be good."

"In this city, a woman needs a man to escort her. This isn't New York City or Florida."

Why do men always think of woman as the weaker sex? However, in this case it might work to her advantage for a while. "Thank you. I'll consider it."

While Sarita tried to maintain a pleasant smile, Suzan felt the desperate cry for help. Sarita's eyes filled with fear, something Suzan recognized instantly from her years in the military. Her training in reading people often focused on the pupils, and Sarita's were large. "I know, perhaps you would like to join me for breakfast tomorrow morning and go over my plans for the week. I would like to receive your input."

As Sarita glanced at Peter without saying a word, he leaned over and kissed her cheek. "I think she would love to help you. Is nine a good hour for you?"

"Perfect."

###

The long hours of standing and greeting people ended as Suzan held onto Matt's arm while he guided her inside their suite. Being such a gentleman made it hard not to fall for him. He had to be one of the most tolerant men she had ever known. She also appreciated that special quality reserved for her. For many people he expected them to take care of his needs. His success came at a price. He knew what his time was worth and packed every minute with work he needed to accomplish.

Gail met them as they walked in. She always maintained a fresh professional look in spite of the long hours she worked. She appeared to be so dedicated to her job and to Matt that there were times she even treated him as if he were a god. "I'm glad to see you also. I know you must be tired and how you talked to many people tonight. If you're too tired tonight to go over your plans we can discuss it tomorrow morning."

Matt hugged Suzan tightly. "That might be a good idea." He reached in his pocket and handed Peter's card to Gail. "I do want to know more about him and his connections."

"I've a complete file on him. With you being so busy, I know you might not have had time to read it."

Matt blinked and rubbed his forehead. "My fault, I'm sure you do. If you can find it again for me and leave it on the dining room table over there, and I'll read it as soon as I can."

"No problem. We'll discuss everything else tomorrow night. I need to get some sleep as well. You do have several calls from back in the States you need to return when you can." She handed him a list.

Matt glanced at Suzan. "I could use a shower first. Will you stay up and wait on me?"

"I'm tired but not sleepy. I think it would be good if I called my mother to check on her while you're busy. I'd love to drink some tea while I'm waiting on you."

Gail spoke as Matt started to loosen his tie. "I'll take care of it for you and hope you have a good night." Gail walked off as Suzan wondered more about her background. But for now, however, this would give her access to those files and more information on Peter.

Minutes later she sat at the table reading fast while Matt showered. Peter was wealthy, and one of the top property owners in New Delhi. She couldn't find any ties to any radical groups, and many parts of his life were masked by his playboy image, which she knew was a farce. While he could have many women throwing themselves at him, he preferred to hire professionals to hide his more private life.

This much she had gained in the brief conversation with Sarita.

She felt her phone vibrate. She retrieved it, but she saw no indication of an incoming call. She knew who wanted to contact her. She activated the hidden button on the bottom and waited.

"Can you talk?"

"Within reason, Matt's in the shower and I'm not sure when he'll return."

"Understood. The photos you submitted were good. Your target is close now. You'll receive more information in the operation room established for you. Try to be there before lunch. How is it going with Matt?"

"Not bad."

"We were hoping it would be great. You might need his help in leaving the country soon, and on a minute notice. This might go down soon." The connection died.

Suzan felt her heart racing. She wished she had more information. She read through the papers in the file faster, looking for any information she might need. She almost didn't notice him moving into the room, as she scrambled to raise the cup of tea to her lips, drinking much of it in one gulp.

Matt's hair was towel dried but not combed. He wore a white robe pulled tight around his middle, and a pair of slippers had replaced his normal black shoes. He had made himself at home in the hotel. Still, he had a raw sexual appeal she loved. While not sure how much his looks, or the fear of being caught, made her heart miss beats, she offered a smile to cover both.

"Were you able to reach your mother?"

Suzan didn't know if he had heard her on the phone or not. "I tried, but I was only able to leave her a message."

"I see. Are you going to stay up for a while or go to bed?" Matt kept a slight inquisitive expression on his face.

She didn't need him to discover her mission. She needed to distract him, and she knew what she needed to do to accomplish that mission. She would allow herself to enjoy tonight. "I noticed a hot tub in your room. Do you mind if I use it?"

Twinkles of happiness danced across his face as he answered without saying a word. While he didn't ask if he could join her, she knew he wanted her to. She thought about teasing him and make him guess her answer but could not. He had never disappointed her in bed before, and this might be exactly what she needed tonight to relax and prepare her for the next few days. She also could not afford to have Matt suspicious of her now.

Matt extended his hand to her. "It will take a few minutes for me to fill it with hot water for you."

"Thank you." She accepted his hand to stand. Her arms wrapped around him as she buried her head into his massive shoulder. The soft white robe cushioned her with warmth she melted into. As far as she could remember, Matt was the only man she ever let her guard down with. She could trust him to take care of her. She could. Damn Chelsea. Why did she have to complicate things? Suzan fought to erase her image broadcasting her pregnancy as she sank deeper into the luxurious fabric.

Matt shifted to the side to lead her to his room. "I think you might be more tired than you want to admit. A horde of people can do this to you. We'll try to pace ourselves for the rest of the week."

She heard Matt close the door behind them as they entered his suite. Standing in front of him, she watched him walk to the massive bathroom and start the water. Since he had seen her naked many times before she didn't feel the least bit apprehensive in undressing in front of him, as she reached behind her to unfasten the dress which dropped immediately to her waist exposing her push up bra which she would never get used to. A quick twist in the front and it dropped also. It felt so good to have her breasts released from the torture, as she rubbed them to get the blood flowing. One nipple hardened as she brushed past the tip.

The allure of the water ushered in as she heard the water filing the large spa sized hot tub Matt attended to. While she was not directly facing him, she assumed he could see her if he wanted to. With her head feeling weary from the long night and perhaps one too many drinks, she imagined the warm if not hot water flowing over her.

She turned her head to find Matt who was patiently waiting on her to enter the tub. His face reflected a strength she loved. While he obviously enjoyed the show, he didn't push her. She kind of liked the attention and pleasure of being made to feel special, even beautiful–sexy. Something she had never thought possible earlier, since she had grown up as a tom boy back in the swamp.

Suzan twisted to lower the zipper lower to allow the dress to fall to the ground. Only skimpy panties designed for looks not function protected the last of her virtue. She leaned forward and lowered them without hesitation, standing perfectly naked in front of him. Now, she felt glad she had taken the time to shave and look civilized.

Still Matt paced, but otherwise patiently waiting for her. She decided to walk toward him as he eagerly greeted her at the door. His eyes that focused on her eyes instead of her naked body made her realized he really had a deep love for her as a person and not a piece of meat. This term she had often heard in the Army, something she knew she would never get fully out of her system.

Matt smelled fresh as she neared him, his scent highlighting her newly found energy. She raised her head to face him and offered him her lips. He eagerly accepted her invitation and pressed hard against them as he pulled her closer. With him sucking on her lower lip, she closed her eyes to disappear inside his world. If only it was this easy to leave her own world. But . . . for now, she openly enjoyed every second of this time with him. Her arms pulled him closer to her as she felt free from all of the restraints caused by her clothes.

Matt eased his mouth to one side and whispered in her ear. "Baby, I love you."

Suzan felt compelled to return the words hoping to convince herself and him that's exactly what she thought. She felt too tired to work on a solution to Chelsea or the CIA. Tonight she simply wanted to make love and be loved. She would deal with her problems later, and she hoped Matt would never learned how she was using him now.

Suzan reached for the tie holding the robe around Matt and gave it a pull. It responded as she thought and revealed his chest, still so well toned that she had to rub him and feel his chest muscles. While many men had a chest full of hair, Matt remained almost baby smooth, which must be undoubtedly a characteristic in his genes. Still, the smooth skin excited her and made her want more, much more. She ran her fingers toward his shoulders and lifted the robe off of them. It fell instantly to the ground revealing the rest of a man who offered her everything she could ever want.

Glancing down she studied boxer shorts hiding the last of what she wanted to see. Yes, she wanted to see him as naked as she was. She bent over and slipped fingers inside the sides as she lowered them. Her eyes slowly became even with his monster dick as she pushed the boxers past his knees before releasing them. With the result exactly as she would have predicted, his dick jumped to attention, pulsating in front of her. Yet, he didn't push himself toward her, waiting for her to make the next move instead. She knew he would love oral, but she decided to make him wait. She wanted him to want her as much as she wanted him.

She stood and pressed her breasts tightly into his chest. He reached around her and grabbed her butt, squeezing it firmly with his fingers. She had no problem with that at all. She also had no problem with her crotch so near to his. She didn't want to be entered while she was standing, but she loved the feel of his manly body wrapping around her.

Still, she knew he would want to enter her if she didn't make a move toward the hot tub. She glanced at it with full attention of diverting him. He helped her over the side to the hot water. She flinched for a minute as the initial wave scorched her butt, but quickly settled back into the hot water.

Matt stepped around her and joined her on a small ledge inside. "Oops, it's hotter than I thought, I'm sorry."

She grabbed his hand, "No, this is fine, but it takes a minute to get used to."

Sitting next to her, Matt used his closest hand to massage her leg. The gentle massage and hot water eased her muscles as she closed her eyes again. The snuggling Matt added to the nape of her neck added to her pleasure, especially his hot frequent kisses. Somehow in the process, Matt had moved his hand to her inner thigh where he continued his massage up and down her leg. On one trip to the top he touched her clit briefly, sending sparks of excitement through her body. If he wanted to make love in the tub, she would not resist.

Instead, he continued to massage her leg and kiss her

neck. Her mind drifted close to the state of unconsciousness for one minute, before back to a world of excitement the next. She felt happy with either, but not both. She breathed deeper as she felt Matt relax beside her and allow his massage to end. Her hand slid down his chest and soon rested next to his dick. It had also lost its vigor, but retained its potential. She allowed herself to drift off to sleep.

Later she woke as the water had cooled. Her body still melted into his, awaiting the next step in what she hoped would be a fantastic night. However, he had fallen asleep next to her. Should she wake him? She inched her fingers lower to check him out. While still large enough, he had lost his stiffness. Yet, he felt so good, so damn good.

Suzan continued to massage him gently, part of her wanted him to wake and another part of her enjoyed the pleasant pleasure of exploring him at her leisure, as she worked her fingers over every inch of his manhood. Moment by moment it grew harder and stiffer. He soon could service her well. Without thinking, she moved her fingers down to her clit and started to massage herself. The combination sent incredible vibes through her body.

She watched him breathe deeply as he adjusted his weight in the water. His dick throbbed harder as he came to life in the water. He raised one hand and extended one finger under her chin to adjust her lips where he planted a firm but gentle kiss. "I fell asleep."

"Yes, we both did. It felt so nice to sleep next to you." She continued the massage working on his dick.

"I can't believe I went to sleep with a hard on."

"You didn't. I hope you don't mind me waking you like this."

Matt slid his hand along her leg until he reached her pussy, spreading it slightly as he returned the favor. His fingers felt so much more invigorating than hers had. She could easily come with him giving her such royal treatment, and it would not take long for her to explode. She had played with herself for awhile already and felt primed, but still, she wanted him inside of her, to complete her needs.

"Maybe we should go to the bed."

"I thought you would never ask." Matt shifted to make his way out of the tub and extended his hand to help her. Two large white towels on a side rack made quick work of the lingering liquid dripping from their naked bodies. A slight shivering coldness replaced the hot tub, but it didn't dent the passion she had building up inside of her. She toweled as best she could as she watched Matt matching her pace.

Suzan turned to walk in front of him as she marched to the bed. She knew he was checking out her butt. She at least hoped so, since she wanted him hot when they slithered under the covers of the king size bed. A large comforter on top added a much needed warmth she needed immediately.

She turned to face him and snuggle closer as he planted another kiss on her lips while massaging her breasts. His fingers found her nipples as he teased her by pinching with just the right about of pressure to make them stiff. He followed that by circling them with a slight brushing stroke, driving her wildly inpatient with any more preliminaries, she wanted him inside and inside now.

Suzan rolled to her back and spread her legs apart. She could not get any more explicit as to what she wanted. As he rolled on top of her, she could feel his manhood on her leg. She quickly reached for his dick to help guide it home. It throbbed in her hand as he adjusted his position. He didn't need to test her to see if she was ready. With one large thrust he entered her completely as she yelled out in ecstasy. She hoped she didn't damage his hearing but would apologize later. "Do it, do it deeper–harder." She bit into his shoulder as he complied. Damn, she thought her mind was going to explode, as the humping sound of the bed rocked the room, and as far as she knew, the entire hotel.

When she finally came several times and collapsed into the arms of man who loved her, she knew somehow she had to work out her situations. He deserved it. He deserved the truth about her past and her current work, but how was she going to make it happen? A small tear formed in her eye as she faced a new fear, a fear of losing him when he discovered that truth.

Chapter 36

Matt woke the next morning and felt more rested than he could imagine. After making love to Suzan he had fallen into a deep sleep. He loved watching her sleep. Her skin looked so well toned and smooth, and it made her appear so different from the fireball she could be when she wanted to be. He knew it was only a matter of time until all of the details could be worked out, and they then would be married back in New York. This reminded him to check with his guy hunting down Chelsea in Milan. He had to put all suspicion of Chelsea carrying his baby behind them.

Ready to take on the day, he rose from the bed and quietly entered the bathroom to shave. He knew Gail had a full day for him. He also wanted to check with her as to what Suzan had planned.

As expected, Gail sat at the breakfast table drinking some coffee. "Matt, I see you finally decided to get up."

Matt glanced at his watch. "Okay, I'm still adjusting to the time change."

Gail gave him one of those amusing smiles which indicate she knew better. Yes, she knew him well, and perhaps too well. As his personal secretary, she knew more about the real Matt than anyone on the planet. A quick memory of their one night together flashed in his mind. He had to look away.

Gail handed him a file. "I think you're going to be busy today. If you need to make any changes, please let me know. I still have some of the people attending last night's whirlwind that I need to find out more about."

"Three parties last night was a bit much." Matt motioned

toward the bedroom. "Suzan is still sleeping. When is her first appointment?"

"I would not call what she has scheduled as appointments, but plans she would like to make. She wants to spend some time with her uncle before visiting some of the historical sites here."

"I know she doesn't like having a bodyguard with her, but do your best to talk her into it."

"Thanks." Gail handed him a list of places Suzan wanted to see. "I think the contacts she made last night might be a big help to her, especially the women who live here."

Matt glanced over his shoulder. "Has Tony been able to make contact with Chelsea yet?"

"He's in Milan, but he hasn't made contact yet. He has a plan that might work. Chelsea will join him for a dinner later tonight."

"Wow, how did he manage to do that?"

"His suits are tailored by a well-known designer in Milano. All he had to do was mention his name and Chelsea was begging for a chance to attend."

"That was smart thinking. Do you know if Gloria will be attending also?"

"She wasn't invited. It'll be hard to know if that will stop her or not."

"Sounds like a plan. Be sure to have him call me later today." Matt looked over his schedule. "After everything last night, I would like a more relaxed dinner tonight. Somewhere special."

As usual, Gail understood his meaning. "I'll take care of it."

Matt rose and walked to the door to his bedroom and peeked inside. His angel was still asleep. After the intense night they shared, he felt content to let her sleep as long as she wanted. However, he needed to go. One quick kiss on her forehead and his morning would be perfect.

###

Suzan pretended to be deep in sleep as Matt kissed her gently. It was best to let him go before she rose. This way he would not ask too many questions. She had work to do today, and she hoped to find many answers in her operations room set up for her before blending in with the locals today.

After waiting until he had left, she hurried to dress in a traveling suit which looked conservative, but would maintain the image Matt would expect from her. She didn't need anyone watching her enter or leave the hotel. She checked the arrangement of scarves in her pocket. These would be perfect.

Gail was waiting on her as she opened the door. "Hello, Suzan. Matt wanted to say goodbye to you this morning, but he was running late."

"I understand. I think we have different agendas today."

"Yes. He has a full day, and I wanted to check with you on yours. Is there anything I can help you with today?" Gail acted like a trusted friend. In time Suzan knew she could rely on her more, but not on this trip, and not with her mission pressing her to act quickly.

"I'll need a ride to the museum this morning. I plan to spend a good part of the day inside."

Gail looked pleased. This would make her job easier. Little did she know she had plans to walk directly out the side door as soon as she changed clothes inside. "We have a limo available and a bodyguard to go with you. I know you don't like that, but he can stay outside and wait on you. Matt's scared the paparazzi will find you."

Thinking about how he'll be cooling his heels while she explored the city, she forced herself not to smile. "You know I don't need a bodyguard, but to make both of you happy, I'll not say a word as long as he stays outside and doesn't bother me."

"Agreed."

Suzan looked above her before returning her stare. "This doesn't mean I want him every day."

"Some things are necessary. I'll make it as easy as I can for you."

"Okay. I'm ready when they are. I'll be back later this afternoon."

"Good. Have a good day."

###

Suzan disappeared minutes after she arrived at the museum and walked as fast as she could to the nearby hotel. She listened to the talk on the street and checked to make sure no one paid her any special attention. For an Indian woman this was not hard. She lost her perfect posture and humped over slightly to make her look much older than she was.

She entered the hotel and climbed the stairways to her room. It looked the same as when she had left it. She opened the computer as she glanced around. She entered her password and waited as the instructions commenced immediately. Harmir had entered the city and had been spotted twice, but his exact current location had evaded everyone. It was imperative he be stopped there, if at all possible. Several assets were in position with several other governmental operatives assisting. His capture would be great, but his death acceptable. Her job was to locate him and set him up if she could. They still expected him to make contact with Peter.

She had been given several new purses. One had a gun with a silencer hidden in a bottom compartment. She also saw a camera and laser targeting device they hoped she might be able to place it in a strategic position on the street. Another purse, which looked identical on the outside, carried an array of explosives.

Still, the message at the end made it clear this was only as a backup. They wanted her to remain the quiet eyes on the street and let their professional hit men take him out. The last part of the message congratulated her for placing the bug on Peter. They suggested that staying close to him might be very fruitful. As the screen darkened, she knew it was being erased.

Suzan located the tracker to the bug she had placed on Peter. He was in a condo complex. She had to check, since it might be where he lived. She needed to change clothes and get on the street to see what she could find out. She had many tea and coffee shops to check out.

###

Matt walked outside a meeting for a minute as Ronald called him from Milano. "How are you?"

"I'm fine, Matt. All is set for tonight."

"Is Chelsea suspicious of you being there?"

"She asked me when we first talked, but since she knows you wanted to explore a development in Lake Como, she accepted that as the reason for my trip. I'm sure she has some reservation, but the chance to meet a fashion designer I know was too much for her to pass up."

"It would be good for everyone if you can talk some sense into her about having a DNA test performed."

"I know how much is riding on this for the company, and for you personally. I also feel for Chelsea. This has to be embarrassing for her as well."

"In any case we need to get to the truth." Matt rubbed his brow to ease his mind. "Let me know what you find out."

###

Suzan had been on the street for several hours when she received a call from her CIA contact. "Peter is on the move. We have located a place he enjoys having lunch. Make it back to the hotel to change before going to the museum. You'll meet someone who will invite you to lunch." The connection ended.

Complying, she hurried as fast as possible, where slipping back into the museum represented no problem at all. As she wandered around, she soon saw a woman she had met the night before. "Hi, it's good to see you again. Have you been enjoying the museum?"

"Yes, it's a remarkable place." Just how many assets did the CIA have working on this project? And if they had so many, why did they need her?

"I was planning on going to lunch. I hope you have time to join me."

"I would love to."

As she exited the building and the bodyguard stepped toward her, the cell phone in her pocket rang. Glancing at it, she noticed Matt's name on the caller ID. "Hello, Matt." Pleasant thoughts of the night before invaded her mind, allowing her to escape the project at hand.

"Hello, love. I haven't heard from you all day, and I was wondering how you were doing and if you had time for lunch."

"I met someone from the night before, and I just accepted an invitation to go to a nearby hotel for lunch."

"I'm sorry. I should've called earlier. In that case, I'll see you back at the hotel later today. We should be finishing early today."

"I have your bodyguard tailing me all day, so don't worry I won't cause you any trouble."

She heard him laugh. "I want you to remain safe. You haven't seen anyone from the news media today, have you?"

"No, all is quiet."

"Good, I'll see you soon."

###

Soon, Suzan and her new contact entered the restaurant on the top of the hotel, where around fifty people were being served. From a quick analysis of the crowd they all appeared to be very well to do. A man in a suit quickly approached them. "Can I help you?"

The woman handed him a small envelope. "I heard the meals were fantastic here."

The man opened the envelope and nodded his approval. "It will be my pleasure to serve you today." He turned and led them to a table. While she remained curious who this woman was and what the note said, she concentrated on the room instead. In minutes she memorized every door and escape route, every person eating at a table and the total number of servers and bus boys.

The one person she hunted for was nowhere to be seen. Her phone vibrated, alerting her to the fact she had an incoming message. Her new friend acted like she didn't notice. Suzan retrieved her phone and checked the text message. "Keep him in play, target is close by."

Suzan's nerves went on high alert. She restudied all of the men in the tables. Had he changed his appearance?

The woman grinned and glanced toward the side door leading to the restrooms. "I think I need to wash my hands before we eat. Shall you join me?"

"Sure, I think it would be good." Suzan followed her across the dining room.

Inside the enclosed woman's room the woman moved

fast. "We're not sure what to expect. Take this." Suzan accepted the Glock 23 inside a small holster which she could strap to her thigh. Having no time to second guess what was happening, she accepted the weapon. Three small throwing knives fit inside the back cover. She had been trained with these extensively.

"I don't think we'll need these, but if we're spotted, all hell might break loose."

"I understand, but I was told to not engage."

"True, but it's always better to be prepared. Peter has been asking many questions about you, and he appears to like you very much. We need to use this to our advantage. It's only a matter of time until Harmir will try to contact him. One quick note–Peter isn't a willing supplier of funds, but is being blackmailed into helping."

"Really!" Suzan acted surprised, but this confirmed what she thought she had heard earlier.

"We plan to make your paths cross many times the next few days."

"I'll do what I can."

"We know. Now act normal when he enters in a few minutes. Hopefully he'll ask to show you some of his properties, etc. Use any excuse to spend some time with him."

Suzan re-entered the dining area and scanned the guests. No one had changed location, but she recognized a change in the staff. The waiters were older. Who were they–one of theirs?

A few minutes later, Peter entered and walked directly by her on the way to an empty table in one corner of the dining room next to a window. His mannerism indicated he had a favorite table. A smile erupted as he recognized her. "Wow, Suzan, I never expected to see you today."

"I went to a museum today not far from here, and they told me this place was highly recommended." She pointed to her new friend. "We bumped into each other in the museum and decided to try it out."

"I can tell you that it's the best in the city. I eat here three or four times a week." As before, he had a girl on each arm. However, he never bothered to introduce them. They seemed to be perfectly happy acting like blonde bimbos, almost to the extent of being drugged. Was that possible? The woman who had acted friendly the day before acted like she had never seen her before.

"In that case, we're looking forward to it."

"Where is your husband today, and why is he not with you?"

"He's busy looking at properties today. You have to remember I'm American and can handle myself without a man around."

"I've heard this about American women."

Bingo, she nailed the attraction. Now, she needed to exploit it. "Don't get me wrong, I'm very happy to be with Matt. However, it would be good to learn more about projects here on my own."

A glint in his eyes indicated he received the intended message. If he wanted to get to Matt, she would be a good vehicle to use. "I'm not sure if Matt and I will ever be partners as such, but the possibility does exist. I wish he had time to visit some of my properties while he was here. If he's too busy I would love for you to see some of them."

"In a way, I would love to see them, but I need to check my schedule with Gail. Matt does keep me busy."

"I understand."

Suzan noticed the stern look coming from the woman across from her, and remembered how impending the connection might be. "I do have some time tomorrow morning, if you're available."

"Absolutely, and some of them are close to here." Peter stopped for a second, as if in deep thought. "However, I do have one matter I need to take care of. It will take about an hour tomorrow morning. I can meet you back in the lobby downstairs then if that's okay with you."

"Sounds like a plan." Suzan knew when he would be making the connection with Harmir. The look in his eyes gave it away. She also knew the entire CIA network knew it.

Chapter 37

Matt walked into his suite and accepted a phone Gail handed him. "It's Ronald."

"Good. Hello, Ronald. Give me some good news."

"I wish I could. She's not giving in on her story, but she has agreed to see you if you want to come here."

Matt squeezed his eyes shut. "That could be complicated. I'm just now getting Suzan settled down, and we have a few more days of meetings set up. She might not be too happy if I go off to Italy to see Chelsea right now."

"If you can get the right answer, Suzan might be very happy. In any case, let me know what you want me to do here. We do have one project you have wanted to check out near Lake Como."

"Yes, and we have solid investors who want us to build one there. Do you think you can set up a meeting with them?"

"I think that will not be a problem."

"I'll give you a call back later. Suzan should be here soon." Matt closed the phone.

Gail waited for him to give her some kind of instructions. "She should be here any minute."

###

Suzan walked in as she forced a smile. All would go down tomorrow morning. She had done her job, but they wanted her for backup coverage, just in case the meet up diverted to different routes. If the operation went wrong, the city could become unstable, with many supportive factions hunting for any Americans.

She needed to have Matt prepared to leave on a short

notice, but not let him know why. Her heart fluttered when she saw him. He deserved better.

"Hello, Baby. How was your day?" His hug felt warm and secure.

"Matt, I'm tired from walking the museum all morning, but I learned a lot about the culture here. In fact, I managed to see many points of interest this afternoon."

"That's good. Do you know how much longer you'll want to stay here?"

Suzan acted much more tired than she really was by rubbing her brow. "I've been thinking that I can't hide here forever. You know, I hope Chelsea would agree to the damn DNA test and we could have that behind us."

"Trust me, I do also. How would you like to make a stop in Italy on the way back home?"

"Do you mean to see Chelsea?"

"That would be one reason. I want to talk some sense into her, but I also have a project I want to look at on Lake Como."

"I'm not sure I want to face her. However, if you want to go and check on your deal tomorrow, I'll stay busy with some of the women I met the other night. They have some kind of party they want me to attend."

"I could fly up tomorrow morning and be back tomorrow night. It will not take long to make the contacts I need to make and view the property. I have one of my vice-presidents in Milan now. Are you sure you don't want to go with me?"

Surprised how easily this worked out, Suzan leaned over and hugged Matt. "You always were a sweet talker. Can I let you know around lunch tomorrow?"

"If I left that late I would have to spend the night and come back the next day."

Suzan forced a puzzled look on her face, in spite of the fact she knew the answer she would give. "I'm working hard on seeing the last of what I came for. This would give me time to do that, and this way I'll not be a draw on your ability to take care of your business."

Matt closed his eyes for a moment before he spoke. "If this will bring you back to New York, I'm all for it."

"I didn't say the wedding was back on yet. I'm still wondering about Chelsea's story, and I don't want to be always known as the woman who stopped a man from marrying a woman who became the mother of his child."

"I promise I'm not the father."

Suzan stopped arguing for a minute, but she had a new thought she had to ask. "Let me ask you one question."

"Which?"

"If it's determined that you are the father, would you marry Chelsea and do the right thing?"

The question appeared to catch Matt off guard as he stopped to think. "I've never thought about it for two reasons. First, I've never thought I was the father, and next because it's impossible to marry one person when you're in love with another."

Suzan pressed her question. "But if I was not around and you were the father. Would you marry her?"

She watched Matt inhale a deep breath. "If I were the father, I would have to consider what was best for the baby, naturally. However, marriage takes more than this. It takes love."

Suzan studied his answer, realizing that he was a man of principals, but smart enough to make good decisions, much as she would expect from an executive of a major international corporation. As she moved closer to him, she felt a strength she could hide inside. She had always been the strong one before, and allowing a man to provide this for her would take some getting used to.

Matt kissed her forehead. "Tonight we do have one party we need to attend, and I think we can leave after that for a private dinner. Perhaps we can forget all of the cares and worries around us and simply enjoy some great food and wine. What do you think?"

The sounds of it made her relax, but she knew she had to concentrate on her mission set for tomorrow morning. "It sounds good, but I want to turn in early tonight."

Matt offered one of his sexy smiles. Yes, she knew what he wanted, but sex with him was always fantastic. Still, she needed rest. She would have to play it by ear later.

Chapter 38

Suzan woke early the next morning and ready to take on her mission. She sneaked out of the bed and hurried to the shower. Matt had a meeting that morning, but he had planned to clear his schedule if she called him by lunch. He appeared eager to go to Milano and explore his future project around Lake Como. In truth, she wished she could join him, but she had to finish this mission first.

Her life would be in danger, but after years of training she looked forward to the adrenalin rush. She had hunted for this guy before, and he was responsible for the deaths of many of the men she knew earlier in Afghanistan. This could provide the perfect closure to her previous life. Now, if she could find a way to end this, and re-enter the perfect life she thought she would have with Matt.

After she finished getting ready and walked out to the main dining room, she saw Gail. Did she ever sleep? Her clothes looked professional, and a warm pleasant smile greeted her. "Hello, Suzan. You're up earlier than I thought."

"Yes, I wanted to make a breakfast meeting this morning with some women I met yesterday."

"Oh, I didn't see it on your schedule for the day."

"I know, sometimes I make my own schedule."

Gail smiled and insisted. "I'll be glad to help you. That's why Matt has me around."

"I know, and you do a great job. I want to be free to move about for a day or two. I hope we can all go back to New York soon."

Gail acted glad to hear the words *New York*. "I take it you and Matt have things worked out and the wedding is back on?"

"Not totally, but I'm trying my best to work through it." Suzan felt best to keep some options open, since she had no idea what the day would hold for her, as well as what surprises Chelsea had left in store for them.

"You know Matt wants you to take one of the bodyguards with you."

"I know, but today I want to feel free. This might be one of the last times I can do this."

"Still, I want to stay in contact with you, and you'll need a driver."

Suzan had prepared for this. "I understand. I hope to be leaving soon, and I'll need a ride to the hotel where the ladies will be meeting."

"Aren't you going to wait and say goodbye to Matt?"

"Yes, I'll say good morning, but only for a few minutes, since they have their breakfast meeting early in the morning." Suzan knew the meeting was set up to allow her to disappear with the help of the new contact she had made the day before. She needed to make it to her hotel command center for new instructions and to change her clothes. She also needed her gear and a weapon, just in case.

"I'll have a car ready for you in a few minutes." Gail lifted her iPhone and clicked on a number.

Suzan looked at the food and helped herself to some of the fruits. She wasn't sure if she would actually be having any breakfast at the woman's group or not. A piece of meat for protein is what she really wanted, as she helped herself to something she wasn't sure what it was other than meat. She noticed Gail watching her, but continued anyway as she stood and motioned toward Matt's room. "I think I'll see if he's up yet."

Suzan creaked open the door where she watched Matt still snuggled under the covers. She leaned over and kissed his cheek, which awoke him instantly. As he opened his eyes, he pulled her on top of him and laughed lightly. "You're up early."

"Yes, I have to get going this morning. I have an early meeting as I told you."

"Are you sure you don't want to go with me today? We would have a great time."

"Matt, I'm sure we will. I'll call you around lunch time and let you know. Okay?"

"I'll agree, since I've no choice in this." He opened his eyes, and the beautiful green color that had captured her heart from the first time they met entranced her again. "I love you, Suzan."

With such sweet romantic words entering her heart, she had no choice but to return them. "I love you too, Matt. I think you know that without me saying a word."

"Yes, but I love to hear them anyway."

Suzan wished she didn't have to leave him and they could simply disappear, but she knew it would never work. She would have to talk with the CIA as soon as this mission was over. "I'll call you soon." She pulled away from him before he could convince her to stay.

###

The command center room in the hotel looked much the same, but she knew others were using it as a base. Someone had slept in the bed the night before. She turned on the computer and entered her password. A new screen offered her an overview of the area she would be working and where others would be stationed. She was to provide the eyes and ears on the back of a building not far from there. They wanted to know if any backup personnel showed up they needed to know about.

She dressed as an older lady under a shawl, which would make her almost invisible on the street. However, she would be packing a Glock 23 under her dress and many mini explosives in her purse. All contingencies had to be covered. They did not want her to engage, and in fact, she could only do so with authorized permission. This placed her life in danger, as she thought about being unable to defend herself properly.

Her cell phone buzzed, she knew who called. "Yes."

"We have all in order. Do you have any questions?"

"Only one. How many other terrorists do you think Harmir has with him?"

"I wish we knew. We think he has a small selection of bodyguards with him. That is, at least, what we're hoping for, since we want to minimize causalities as much as possible. When this is over, we want you to leave the country as quickly as possible and make sure you draw no attention. If you're discovered, say nothing, and we'll come and get you."

"Understood." And she knew they would. The CIA would always take care of their own, no matter how difficult. If you played by their rules and stayed on their reservation, they took care of you. She knew that from before.

"Good, start moving into position, and leave your mic on at all times. We also have built new cameras into your purse. Good luck."

It was show time, so to speak, as she fitted into her clothes and got into character. She picked the oldest shawl she could find and checked the Glock, which was fully loaded. She carried no identification on her. Just as much as it was back in Afghanistan, this was war.

Suzan soon located a small table on the side of the street, where she stopped and started to weave a piece of cloth from her purse. She looked homeless and completely unserious. She directed the camera hidden in her purse toward the back ally, leading to the building she assumed they would be meeting in soon.

She heard a voice in her earplug. "The direction of the camera is perfect. Now turn so you won't be facing the entrance. This will be all over soon."

Suzan complied and worked on the weaving. She wasn't good at it, but who would know? A few others walked the street, and many of them were like her, common people, making their way along the street.

An hour later the intensity of the operation stressed her. She felt like a sitting duck now. What if they suspected her? She had a weapon on her, but she could only use it when ordered to do so. She answered a call. "Get prepared, we have them all together with what we expect is a payoff." A long pause suddenly changed. "There will be an explosion in a few seconds. Find some cover now."

Wow, thanks for the warning. She had nothing close but the table. She quickly flipped it to one side and hid behind it. It drew some immediate attention from some men near the rear entrance, who drew pistols.

"I have men heading in my attention, sir. Requesting permission to engage, sir!"

"Hold until after the explosion, then permission given to protect yourself as deemed necessary. Repeat, permission authorized to engage. You'll have backup in one minute. How many men are there?"

"Two men, sir. And closing."

She heard a shout for her to stand. She hesitated long enough for the explosion to shatter the building behind the men. All hell broke loose after that. She heard several shots hit the table, which luckily stopped them. Oh shit! She knew they were running in her direction from their shouting.

Without any options, she inched over the top and fired three shots at each–two for the chest and one for the head. Both fell, but one recovered, perhaps a bullet proof vest. He hit the side of the table and flipped it toward her. She managed to avoid it, but lost her gun in the process. The blood on his face indicated she had grazed him, but she missed her intended mark.

He lunged for her as she attempted to stand. Both hands went for her throat, while her hand went for a knife. A quick thrush and the knife entered his stomach under his vest. He yelled, but she stabbed again as he pulled away from her. He stumbled, but pulled a different gun and pointed it at her.

She heard a shot and closed her eyes, but she felt nothing. Opening them, she watched him fall. With a quick glance to her side she saw her contact from the woman's club. She fired two more shots at the bodyguard's face, who fell forward. "Hurry, we need to disappear!"

They ran to a corner, where a black suburban picked them up. "Keep your heads down," someone yelled, as they drove quickly through the city, where sirens ricocheted off of the building in all directions. They made a quick turn into an alley before entering a garage. The sudden stillness stopped the world from turning. It was over, she was safe. Now, did they accomplish their mission?

A man spoke over the top of the seat. "I'm sorry. These were extra men we weren't aware of. We have no details on who they were at this time, but we will. You may have completed a major service for your country, but the local authorities here will be looking for you. We need to get you out of the country as fast as possible."

"Were all of the men killed?"

"We're not sure. A few might have escaped. We don't know how many others were near those you stopped. We'll have to analyze the tape your camera captured."

"My purse. I don't have it."

"Damn, that can be a problem. We'll do our best to recover it. The terrorist group does not need to get their hands on it or the local government either. We'll give you a ride back to the hotel, change quickly and head back to the hotel where you and Matt stay. Do not plan any more outings, and act like you're home sick to see your mother who's not feeling well."

"My mother's ill?"

"No, not really, but this will give you an excuse to go visit her."

"I understand."

"We'll have no communications with you for a while. Try to get some rest. It would be best for you and Matt to leave the country quickly. The repercussions on this will be bad."

"He's planning on leaving for Milan today."

"That will be good. I think it will be good for you to go back to America. The least contact with you right now the better."

"You don't think Matt is in any danger, do you?"

"Matt knows how to handle himself, and he does have bodyguards around him all of the time. I'm sure this will make him more alert to the fact he has to be careful. As you know, however, he doesn't fall under our area of protection."

"I see. It's not right to place him in such danger. We need to talk later. Is it okay for me to call him? The sooner I do the better."

"I would agree. Also tell him you've received word your mother is feeling ill. We need to get you back in America now."

"Are you sure I don't need to be with Matt? I think I need to warn him."

"Now is not the time, but I can tell we need to have a serious discussion on your future."

"Agreed." Suzan retrieved her phone and clicked on Matt's number. "Hello, Matt."

"How are you? I heard we had a large explosion in the city and a building was destroyed."

"I heard something about it on the street also. What do you think it was?"

"I'm hearing many reports. I think it would be a good time to leave. Please listen to me and go with me."

"I can't leave until tomorrow morning. I promised my Uncle Brajesh I would spend tomorrow morning with him, but I did receive some news about my mother back in Florida. She's not well, and I probably need to go see her."

"I'm sorry she's not doing well, but I'm glad to hear your thinking of leaving."

Suzan glanced at her contact before continuing. "I have an idea, why don't you go on to Milano today and send the jet back for me so I can go to America tomorrow?"

She waited for a response and hoped he would agree. "Only on one condition. I want to leave one of the bodyguards with you. I think that's the right thing to do. I can pick up another one or two in Milano."

Suzan watched her contact nod his head. "Okay, I'll agree. Have a good trip and I'm sure we'll stay in contact on the phone. Stay safe. I love you."

"I love you too. Call me with any problems you have. I'll leave Gail and Tony here to help you. Ronald is in Milan now to help me."

"Good." She clicked the phone shut. "This is not easy."

"It never is." Suzan heard grunts and groans as answers to whoever called him. Finally the conversation ended.

She heard another call coming in. "One of the men on the back of the building who escaped, we now think was Harmir."

Chapter 39

After drawing one large puff and blowing it out, Matt turned to Ronald. "Thanks for coming to Milano to handle this for me. I know this is asking a lot from you." Matt and Ronald stayed up late into the night discussing the two problems facing him. Chelsea still contended that Matt was the father. She had told Ronald she had not been with another man, but she admitted to getting drunk often and losing control of her memory. If this is what happened to her, Matt felt sorry for her. Who was the real father, and where was he in her time of need?

Ronald added another link to the smoke filtering across the city. "I don't mind. I want to clear this up as much as anyone. I hate losing funding from Big John, but we have investors here who are hungry to do business with us."

Ronald had lined up a trip to Lake Como to look at a possible building site the next morning. Chelsea had also agreed to see him later tomorrow night, but only on certain terms such as her mother would have to be there with her. Matt did not like this idea, and he knew her mother had pushed her into this.

Standing on the roof type balcony outside his room, Matt allowed his imagination to explore the night life below him. He needed time to clear his head and relax. The city of Milano was coming to life with crowds of people making their way from one place to another. He remembered the bars here and how fantastic they looked. He enjoyed the food, and he hoped Suzan would join him there later to explore them.

Ronald shifted his weight from one leg to another. "We

haven't had much time to talk. I heard of a bombing in India about the time you left."

"Yes, I've heard terrorists were involved who hoped to make inroads into India. It's still too soon to have full details, but we both know that if Americans were involved, it will make our project in India much harder to pursue."

"I was wondering about that. I'm surprised you left the others behind."

"They're all leaving tomorrow morning. Suzan has received a call about her mother being sick and wants to visit her."

"I guess it might be just as good. It will give you a clearer head to talk to Chelsea. If she would simply take a DNA test we could move forward. Do you think you can talk her into it?"

"I'm going to do my best. Thank you for being a friend."

Ronald looked out over the city. "I think I'm the one who should be thanking you for giving me such a fantastic job." He tossed his cigar aside. "I think we both need to turn in."

###

After a fruitful day of looking at properties on Lake Como, Matt looked forward to ridding himself of one last obstacle. Chelsea had agreed to see him. There had to be some reason that Ronald had managed to talk her into it. Now, he had to know why she thought he was the father.

Gail had made arrangements by phone from India. He often did not go ahead of her as he did this time, but he wanted Gail to be with Suzan to make sure all was in order for the return back to America. He looked forward to getting the wedding back on track.

The meeting was to be held in his suite over dinner. It sounded civilized to him. Finally, they all get to talk like adults. He had ordered meals he knew they would like best, since he wanted to put an end to any notion he was the father. He also hoped to keep Big John as a friend and investor. It would have been good for him to attend, but he knew Gloria made sure he wasn't around.

The top waiter in the hotel was summoned to take care of their needs, as well as their top chef seduced into cooking exclusively for them. Yes, it was expensive, but it was well worth the attention.

The waiter soon entered with Gloria and her daughter Chelsea beside her. Both were dressed in new designer clothes, which were much too stylish for normal woman, but ones they managed to pull off with a large show of accessories broadcasting their wealth and attitude. Matt almost had to laugh, but he knew to fight the urge.

"Good evening, ladies." The formal greeting had been planned by him to set the tone.

"Hello, Matt. You can drop all of the formalities, since we're the only ones here." Gloria had a sharp biting tongue, which most people hated, but one that she prided herself in.

Matt rubbed his chin and decided not to be pulled into a game of wits with her. So, the game was in play. However, he stood and directed each to the table by holding one chair after another. He had planned a round table on purpose to make it impossible for anyone person to sit directly across from him. This fact Gloria obviously noticed as her flashing eyes focused on him.

Chelsea remained quiet while glancing around. If this was her play at being shy, she had either learned a new trick, or she had been well coached by her mother.

To break the ice, Matt spoke first. "Hello, Chelsea. I've wanted to talk to you again." His eyes suddenly noticed her dress, tailored to make room for her expanding stomach. The small girly figure he remembered was gone. He would've thought Chelsea would want to hide the fact and not accentuate it. Her mother must have pushed this on her.

Chelsea's eye lit up for a moment. "I'm so glad that Suzan's not here. I was scared you might have her with you."

"No, she isn't here, but we're still together and doing fine."

Gloria uttered a small groan as if to break up the conversation. "You don't really think that's going to work, do you?"

"Actually, I do. I love her, and I have no doubt she loves me."

"I'll give you one year, two years on the outside."

"That's one bet I'll take. What is it about Suzan you don't like? Is it because she's not part of the social elite in New York, or is it because she has more smarts and integrity than anyone you've ever met?"

"I know New York and how she'll be received. She doesn't fit in. You need someone like Chelsea who does, and who's carrying your baby for Christ's sake."

Matt motioned for the waiter. "I think we all need a drink before we jump into this. What would you like?"

"I would select champagne, but I'll wait until you admit the truth. I think Scotch is what I need. And for Chelsea, since she is carrying your child, it would be best served to restrict her alcohol to one glass of wine."

Chelsea gave another demure smile, which almost made her look like she was on drugs. Being pregnant, Matt hoped not. Matt thought about it for a minute, and decided it might be good to match the drink of the raging mom and see what happened. "Make that two Scotch." Gloria offered a smile which welcomed the challenge.

While the drinks were being prepared Matt turned to

Chelsea. "It would be good to talk to you in private, but since your mother wants to be here I have no choice but to ask you in front of her. " Matt paused to stare directly into Chelsea eyes. "I have to know one thing. You know we haven't made love for a long time, so what makes you think I'm the father?"

While he felt the rage igniting inside Gloria, he waited for a response from Chelsea.

"Matt. Do you not remember the night we went on a cruise after hosting a charity ball?"

Matt concentrated on the night she mentioned to bring back all of the details. "Yes, I remember the night where we treated a boat load of people to a cruise. The party lasted all night until all the guests left the next day."

"That's a night I'll never forget." Chelsea patted her stomach.

Matt interrupted the message. "We never made love that night. In fact, you were so drunk, I'm surprised you remember anything."

Gloria shouted. "And is exactly the reason she's pregnant today!"

"Are you suggesting I took advantage of Chelsea that night?"

"You were seen helping her to a cabin below."

"Yes, I remember that. I also remember placing her on the bed and leaving her there to sleep it off." Matt turned his attention to Chelsea. "I never touched you that night. That's a promise."

Chelsea cried, the sound muffled, as she appeared to be fighting back the tears. "I knew you wouldn't admit it."

"Chelsea, I only had one glass of champagne all night. I wasn't drunk, or even close to it."

Gloria's mother butted in. "I'm not sure, but this could be

considered rape when you have a partner not given consent. That's something for you to think about, lover boy."

"I think both of you know that a DNA test will prove this once and for all." He turned his face toward Gloria. "As far as I know, slander is also against the law."

Gloria remained defiant. "We all know you were gone for more than a few minutes."

"Yes, I walked around the boat for a while."

"And, of course, no one can substantiate your claim."

"Sorry to disappoint you Gloria, but I was with Suzan the entire time."

Chelsea cried louder. "Why is this happening to me?" She glared at Matt. "I'll never take a DNA test. This will be something you'll have to live with the rest of your life."

Gloria reached for her daughter and lowered her voice. "It's okay, baby, your mother will take care of you." A small tear filled her eyes as she looked a Matt and bit her lip much harder than Matt liked. Yet, her eyes appeared to be pleading with him also.

Matt leaned over to Chelsea. "I'm sorry, and I think I know what you must have been going through. If you thought I was the one who impregnated you all this time, well then it tells me that you're not sure who the father is."

Chelsea sobbed louder as her mother moved beside her.

Matt suddenly had a sickening feeling. Someone else on the boat may have taken advantage of her while she had passed out. Who? Now more than ever he wanted Chelsea to have a DNA test. He wanted to know who the father was, and he owed it to her and to Big John in finding out who it was.

"Matt, this is going to totally ruin all of our lives. Regardless of who the father is, you could do us all a favor."

"I'm so sorry for everything that has happened, but it

doesn't change the fact I'm in love with another woman, and I'm not the father."

Gloria leaned over and reached for her glass of Scotch. "If you're intent of ruining our lives, you can count on the same. This is far from over." She raised the glass and swallowed the entire content.

Matt reached for his and matched her challenge. The liquid poured through his throat like hot melted lead. He knew she meant what she said. It was going to be an all out war.

Chapter 40

Suzan breathed easier as she boarded the company jet bound back to Florida. She knew her mother was not in any danger, but she needed the excuse to go back to America and not stop in Milan where Matt was. She was told to stay as far as she could from him so that he would not be associated with the bombing.

That didn't mean she couldn't call him. She wanted to know how it was going with Chelsea. Was he able to convince her to take a DNA test? As the jet gained altitude, she clicked on his number. She glanced at Gail, who adjusted her seat and prepared to catch a nap. While she normally never looked tired, all of these last minute changes had to have kept her busy.

"Hello, this is Matt."

"Hello, love. How's it going?"

"Oh, much better now. Are you at the airport yet?"

"Better. We're in the air. I hope you don't mind us flying on to Florida. I heard my mother wasn't doing well."

"Not at all. In fact, I'm glad to learn you're out of India. They've posted travel advisories everywhere this morning. There's going to be a large witch hunt for those responsible for the bombing in New Delhi yesterday."

"Yes, that's what I heard. How's it going in Milan?"

"I wish you were here. The Lake Como area is beautiful, and I like it much more than India, which isn't going to be a good prospect now for a long time."

Suzan paused for a minute and hoped he would bring up the big question first, but he didn't. "Also, did you talk to Chelsea?"

She heard him breathing. "I did, and she still will not have a DNA test performed. I think her mother is responsible for that. She's determined to try to ruin my life. I hate to say this, but I don't think she knows who the father is."

Suzan closed her eyes. She still didn't have the answers she needed to make a decision, and she would be meeting with the CIA in Florida for a quick debriefing to another field leader. She wanted to be able to find a way out, but she had no solutions.

"Matt–" She heard the line scramble and die. She had lost communications. She yelled toward a stewardess, who went toward the cockpit. She didn't know if they could help her or not. She assumed she would have to wait until they arrived in Florida.

Gail moved in her seat at the loud yelling and opened her eyes. "What is it?"

"I lost the call to Matt."

"It doesn't surprise me, since we're moving fast and it's hard to lock in on a signal. If it's an emergency the pilot can try to pass you through, but they'll even have a hard time at this point."

"I understand. I'll have to wait. He was telling me about talking to Chelsea and not able to accomplish much. He sounded almost sorry for her, as if she was being a victim of her mother's doing."

"That doesn't surprise me much. Gloria always wants to control everything."

"I know you have known Gloria and Chelsea for a while now. They have to know the truth will come out some time."

"I sure they do, and they have plans for it. Gloria's not happy with you stealing Matt away from her daughter, and she wants to make as much shit as she can while she can."

"Matt's much different than most people understand, but I think you might. In the public view he's considered an international playboy, and one who's ruthless to get what he wants, and when he wants it. You know, the guy who has everything given to him and he never has to work."

"I get the point, and yes I know he's much different. In fact, he's one of the most caring people I know, not to mention extremely hard working. He never takes a break, but he makes sure everyone else does."

"In spite of everything, he'll do his best to make sure Chelsea isn't totally destroyed. I think he has every right to take her to court and to ruin her name for trying to ruin his. He has known Chelsea for a long time, but there really has been no magic with her. Not like what he can offer a woman." Suzan watched the words float off Gail's tongue as she appeared to be reminiscing.

"I think you may know the real Matt more than everyone. You've worked for him for a long time, haven't you?"

"Don't remind me how long."

Suzan kicked back in her seat and prepared to ask one question she had to know and hoped Gail would tell her the truth. "I hope you don't mind me asking you one question so I don't have to ask Matt."

"I wondered when you would. If I answer this question for you, will you promise me to never ask Matt?"

"Yes, I think I can do that. That is, if my question is fully answered, and if he never instigates it. I'll at least promise you not to tell him what you say."

"Fair enough. It was almost twenty years ago. He wasn't anything as successful as he is now and had to struggle with every deal. He had no money, and nothing but a dream and ambition. I personally thought he would live life on the streets based on how bad he ran his company, but he learned from his mistakes and kept improving. He had asked me to join him on one trip to a convention where we obtained many contacts. For one week we found ourselves involved. Like a fool I called it off when we returned to New York. We made a pact to work strictly as business people from then on. Part of me says that was a good decision, another part reminds me I might have made a big mistake. In any case, we've been working together for twenty years, and I'm able to see him every day. Perhaps this relationship will last much longer than it would have if we had gotten married. He has been good to me, and I think I have a fantastic career now."

"What about love, family and the happy ever after?"

"We've evolved the way we are and I've no regrets. I made my decision then, and I have lived with it, which is just like a decision you have to make now. He's not the kind of man you can keep waiting forever. I wish you and Matt all of the happiness in the world. I want him to be happy and I know he is with you. I've never seen him romantically interested in anyone–ever. Hard to believe, but it's true."

Suzan leaned over and gave her a hug. "You're a remarkable person, and now I understand why Matt trusts you so much."

"Thanks, and remember to keep girl talk between us."

"Agreed."

"When we arrive in Florida, will you wait on me as I check on my mother?"

"Sure, if you don't think you'll be staying long."

Suzan shifted in her seat to look out the window at the vast open waters below her. "I don't think I'll be long, but if I am, I'll call you so you can go on."

As Gail drifted off to sleep, Suzan checked in with her

CIA contact by sending a text message. She hoped to hear more about the attack they executed, and also learn how successful it was. She knew the signal would be relayed by satellite and be delivered. Still she waited for a response as she had time to think.

Perhaps she had been thinking about herself when she really should be thinking about Matt. She was so worried about being embarrassed about Matt having an affair while she was engaged she never stopped to worry about what he must be going through. No one knew much about her, but his life was on public display every day. That never stopped him from pursuing her or showing his love for her. He was the one with everything to lose.

Still, the thoughts of the CIA pressing her to marry him, to use him as an asset, rubbed her wrong. That wasn't something she could fake forever. Being a wife was more than a mission. She had placed his life in danger on this mission. How many more times would she be called on to do this?

At the very least, she had ruined his chance of a good investment opportunity in India. This could've been good for both of them, as she would have an excuse to visit there many times in the future. Brajesh had assured her he wasn't in any danger and knew people who could help him. If she had to, she would be prepared to help him and his family to move to America. The CIA owed her this much.

Her phone buzzed. She glanced around to see if she was able to reply. Everyone had their head pushed back into their pillows and asleep. She read the message and blinked her eyes to make sure she read it correctly. The main target had escaped and his whereabouts was unknown. They thought he may have escaped out of the back of the building. She remembered others moving fast when she came under attack. She had picked the wrong ones to shoot.

A thought flashed through her head. They had to know a woman killed some of their men. Could they identify her? She didn't think so, but she wasn't sure. Suddenly, she saw another message. The man who helped her to locate Harmir, the real estate tycoon Sharif, was confirmed dead. She felt sick, mad, knowing he wasn't a willing partner to this crime. She couldn't believe the main person they were after had escaped again. Just to be able to go after him again almost persuaded her to stay with the program and offer herself for another mission. She had come so close this time.

One last message floated across the screen, alerting her to the fact they wanted to interrogate her one more time to make sure they had all of the information she could provide. They would meet her at the airport.

Airport transportation arrived to pick Suzan up as soon as the jet landed. She had no doubt the driver was connected to the CIA. A quick trip across to a hanger and a closed room confirmed her assessment. The questions started almost immediately. The focus of most of the questions however focused on her Uncle Brajesh and Matt, and how much did they know or suspect.

She reassured them they knew nothing. An hour later they acted like they believed her. They gave her little information, but she wanted answers also. She had little to leverage in obtaining any, but she pressed with what she had. "I understand you want me to settle into this life with Matt. Do you really think it's fair to place his life in such danger?"

She received the standard reply she would expect. "We don't have to tell you about making choices concerning the better good, do we?"

"Yes, maybe you should, since you're asking me to do that."

She watched raised eyebrows as she had raised a question and one which struck at their very center of their controversial activities. "In the future we don't plan on you taking such an active role."

"Let me ask a question. What if I want out? What if I don't want to endanger his life?"

"I thought we had made it past this point."

"When I agreed to return to the service, I had no idea you would involve Matt. I'm torn between a life with him, or life without him and with the CIA. I never thought I would have to mix the two."

"This presented us the best of all worlds. It's the perfect cover. It gives us access to many places around the world where we would not be suspected of gathering information. However, it's a decision you have to make. If you decide to leave us and our reservation as we call it, you'll be completely on your own."

Another man stepped forward. "We have another problem now, and while this might the worst time to discuss this, we still must. Harmir escaped the attack we had planned. Apparently, he had walked out the rear of the building shortly before it blew. We're not sure if he was tipped off or not. We also don't know how much information he received, or if he received the funding he was after."

Suzan listened to the information hoping for more. "Do you think he's still hiding in India?"

Several men exchanged glances. "No one knows for sure, but yesterday we obtained photos of several men boarding a plane to Italy. However, it was too late to intercept them. Since their main money source is dead, we think they may be after the next best source."

Suzan couldn't believe it. "You think they may be after Matt."

"It makes sense. If they could capture him and hold him for ransom, they would walk away with a bundle."

"Oh my God! Have you warned him?"

"He has every available agent diverted to his location. We think we have him secure for now, but these people are persistent, and you never know when they will strike. Now, this is where we'll need your help. The best way to hopefully catch Harmir may be during the next few days in Italy. I don't think they know we're on to them."

"You mean you want to use Matt as a decoy!"

"This may be the best way to catch Harmir, and to also protect Matt in the long run. I'm sure you understand that. These people will never stop until we destroy them."

Suzan knew he was right. "I need to be with him."

"In this case we'll have to agree. Hopefully, he'll never know of the threat. We'll do our best to catch him before he gets close. It'll be your job to protect him. We'll discuss your future after all of this is over. You know not to divulge any of this to him. I hope you fully understand what I'm telling you."

"Yes, sir. I do. I need to check with my mother quickly and make plans to return to Italy. We have the company jet here."

Chapter 41

Matt hurried to complete his analysis on the properties he saw in the morning. The thoughts of Suzan joining him in Milano sent his soul soaring as he knew she was close to giving in and becoming his wife. Of all of the goals he had accomplished in his life, this was the most exciting time he could remember.

He had sent one of his bodyguards to be with her. The events in India had unsettled him for the last several days. Being away from New York, where he felt safe with his team of professionals around him, caused him to be more suspicious than usual. The death of Sharif stunned him. Was he mixed up with a terrorist group? The reports he had received offered conflicting opinions.

He heard commotions outside his door, and he knew they were arriving. He stood to welcome them as he watched Suzan sweep across the floor to him. As if he had never hugged her before, he squeezed her tight. "Wow, it's so good to see you."

"Hey, big guy. It hasn't been that long."

"With everything happening in India, it has been too long. I'm not sure you heard or not, but the guy we met a few nights ago, Sharif, has been killed in a bombing of one of his buildings."

He knew this probably added one piece of new information she had not heard before– he owned the building they met in. "I heard he was killed."

Matt leaned closer as he looked into her eyes and the smell of the perfume exhilarated his senses. The soul inside revealed the answers he wanted. She was the woman for him and no one else would ever do. "You know it would be extremely unwise to go back to India for a long time, right?"

"Yes, I'm fully aware of that. It was good that I made the trip when I did, and the main reason I went to India was to escape the paparazzi as you know."

"I'm glad you mentioned that because in Milano they're notorious. We'll have to keep a low profile, especially since Chelsea loves to play into their hands."

Suzan leaned forward and brushed her lips firmly against his before settling on a kiss to his cheek. "I know you've been talking to her. Tell me what she has told you."

"She insists that I got her pregnant the night we went on the cruise, you know the one I offered as a prize for the fundraiser in Florida."

Suzan stepped back from him. "Do you mean the night she became totally drunk."

"Yes, she insists that I helped her to one of the cabins and made love to her before I returned upstairs."

Matt watched Suzan look upward and smile as she let out a large breath of air. "Matt. I have a confession."

Now what? "Yes."

"Do you remember meeting me downstairs that night?"

"Yes, but I'm sure she'll claim this was after I had sex with her."

"Matt, I stood in the hall when you escorted her to that cabin. Out of curiosity, I watched you put her to bed. I know this is wrong, and I felt like a voyeur in watching, but I was kind of stuck in the hallway."

"So, you were watching me?"

"I'll admit I was curious if you would take advantage of the situation, but you acted like a perfect gentleman. Oh God, Matt, I'm so sorry for ever doubting you. Please forgive me."

Matt felt the euphoria exploding inside him. This nightmare would now be over! He felt her squeeze him as he returned the joy. Chelsea had no case anymore. Phil and his public relation department and have a heyday on this."I assume this means the wedding is back on."

"Yes, and I'm so sorry for putting you through this."

"Good, I think we need champagne, and lots of it!"

###

Marrying Matt seemed so right now. She only had one last mission to accomplish. His life was still on the line, and she had to tell him the truth about her past. Neither would be easy. She had agreed to stay in Italy long enough for the CIA's special operation team time to find Harmir. Her job now was simply to keep him out of harm's way.

Suzan drank another glass of champagne as the evening started to engulf the city. While she would have loved to venture out, she knew better. She also knew to keep him inside and off the patio. She had no clue where Harmir or his men were, and she had to give the CIA team time to get in place. They had to be close by.

Matt glanced at the noise coming from outside. "I want to explore this city and take you shopping."

Suzan needed to head this off and knew how to do that. "It has been a long day. Perhaps a good shower would help me to relax before dinner. Is it okay with you if we eat in tonight?" She unfastened the top button to her dress, then another one, allowing him to study the top of her lacy bra underneath, before flashing the most seductive smile she could muster.

He accepted the bait. "I don't mind at all. Is there anything special you would like me to order?"

"No, I trust you." She unbuttoned another to allow a full view of her cleavage, slowly adding to the heat she wanted

him to be aware of. "I think you still owe me a massage."
Turning and walking toward the master bedroom, she knew
he would be following soon and not taking time to go
outside for a smoke. She waited until he joined her before
entering the shower, which gave him no chances of going
outside.

"This will only take a second." He reached for the phone
and dialed downstairs. "We would like to order in tonight
and are looking for something special to celebrate. Yes,
about an hour would be perfect." Matt reached for his tie
and worked it loose.

Suzan walked in front of him, knowing what she had set
in motion and not regretting it at all. All feelings of betrayal
had disappeared. For the first time in a while she knew she
could enjoy sex with him, even if it was only for one hour.
She wished the dinner could be postponed for a while, but
this was fine. She had him now, and she would do what she
had to do to save him. She would not allow him to be in
harm's way for long. She hoped the team was as ready as
she was.

After stopping by the bed, she slipped out of the dress,
unsnapped her bra and lowered her panties in a steady
rhythm. She didn't need preliminaries. She was as ready for
him as she would ever be, but she looked at the shower and
smiled. "Do you care to join me?"

"Absolutely! I can give you a short massage there and
finish here."

Suzan watched him focus on her body. It felt good,
making her feel like a woman he wanted and desired. She
watched him remove his clothes as methodically as she had.
As expected when he lowered his boxers he had an erection.
"I see we're all prepared."

He reached for her hand and pulled her behind him and

into an oversized shower large enough to walk around in and have fun. A couple of seats on the two corners added to the leisurely nature of the shower. Several spouts from overhead quickly squirted water in an array of forms, adding to the moment. The water temperature felt hot, but she soon adjusted to it, knowing her body would become much hotter with Matt near her. His naked body snuggled next to her, which made the world around her vanish. The steam clouded the door and hid any contact with the outside world.

His hand explored her back at first and firmly discovered points he wanted to work on. The power in his hands felt incredible as he started to fulfill his promise of an initial massage in the shower, but the part that felt the most intriguing was his dick touching her stomach, fully erected and waiting for action. Yes, this is what she wanted to massage as she reached for it.

The reaction came immediately as he lowered his hands to her butt and pulled her closer. His height made it impossible to enter her directly, but his strength lifted her off of the ground perfectly. She wanted him here and she knew again on the bed. She had no intentions of stopping him in either.

She opened her eyes to see his eyes drilling directly into her own. She forced her mouth on his and closed her eyes, enjoying the most passionate kiss she could ever remember. She forced her lips harder on his, begging for him to extend his tongue which she sucked on without mercy. If she hurt him she would apologize later. Control was out of the question. She wanted him and wanted him now.

He didn't disappoint her and positioned himself as she wrapped her legs around him, uniting them in a union somewhere north of heaven, as he entered her in one fast thrust. She yelled and then yelled again. Over and over she matched thrusts with him, increasing the pending heat she had stored for years. Tonight she was a woman who had found what she had always wanted and desired. Tonight she knew the full meaning of love.

Chapter 42

Matt enjoyed sleeping late the next morning, which was something he rarely did until he met Suzan. Her naked body thrilled his senses as he wanted to enjoy this forever. Her silky skin held so many promises of times in the future. The thought of having babies crossed his mind. He wasn't getting any younger, and he assumed she would want some. He would discuss this with her soon. Funny, they had never approached this earlier.

Suzan groaned as he rubbed her bare shoulder. As she turned, the sheet dropped lower, revealing one pink nipple which he studied. She was absolutely beautiful, and each detail held his attention. Pleased with her waking, he raised the sheet to cover her but continued to snuggle close, enjoying the last of the morning.

She opened one eye and stared at him. "You know, we're getting lazy."

"I was thinking the same thing. Last night you mentioned you would like to go on a picnic near the Alda River on the way to Lake Como. I think that would be perfect. If we have some time I can show you some property I've been studying."

"Hum, that sounds perfect. How long do I have to get ready?"

"How does an hour sound to you? I think by using a town car instead of a limo we would be much less conspicuous. I do want to take a couple of bodyguards with us after all of the excitement last week."

"Sounds great, but I do need to hurry."

"I'll set it up while you're getting ready." Matt kissed her one last time on the lips, as he crawled out of bed and fastened a white robe around his waist.

###

Suzan selected the best clothes she could find suitable for a trip to the countryside. Still, she felt over dressed. They would be out in the open some today. What kind of trap the CIA had planned escaped her, but she followed her instructions texted to her earlier. With her senses on high alert, she shifted her head often to catch the breathtaking scenery, but studied each encounter along the way. One car had followed them for a while, but had eventually fallen behind. Several bikers peddled along the way.

She loved the way the river flowed along the countryside and understood why so many people around the world loved to live here. The chef at the hotel had quickly prepared a basket of food for them, and now the smell was overpowering her stomach, and reminding her of how hungry she was.

"Do you have a particular place in mind for us to stop?"

"The driver made some inquires earlier this morning, and he's heading there now. I was lucky to find a good bodyguard like him. He came highly recommended."

Suzan could only guess the CIA had planted him. "It's so beautiful here."

"I'm glad you like it, I think we might be spending some time here with a project." She felt his hand engulf hers as the car cornered around the valley.

Soon, the car slowed and edged off the road and down a side road toward the river. She glanced out both windows to study the area. She saw no other cars. Maybe it would be a simple day of leisure after all. She really didn't mind.

After the car stopped, she waited for the bodyguard to open her door. "If you'll give us a few minutes, I'd like to check out the area. The other guard will stay with you."

Matt exited the car and nodded his head. "Sounds like a good idea, but we should be safe since no one knows we're here."

The guard walked off along the river as Suzan and Matt walked closer to watch the flow of the water. The fresh smell of the trees and the grass added to the picnic feeling. As they enjoyed the view, the other guard looked for a place to set up the picnic and motioned to a place even closer to the water.

Matt nodded approval as the guard walked back to the car and opened the trunk. The breeze refreshed his mind as he hoped for some private time with Suzan, knowing what would be upon them when they returned to New York. The sound of the water swirling below him eased his mind as he reached for Suzan's hand.

Walking closer to the water he located a flat place for the blanket. The bodyguard helped in setting up the spot complete with a box containing the food and a bottle of wine. After having a seat on the blanket, he glanced at the guard. "I think we'll be fine here for a while if you want to sit in the car and relax for a while."

"I'll be close by, Mr. Harris."

Matt changed his focus to where the other guard had vanished. "You might want to check on this new guy also."

"I'm sure he'll be back in a minute. He probably wanted to check out the perimeters."

Suzan enjoyed the cheese and wine for a while, but she kept her mind focused on her surrounds. The guard had never returned. "How did you find this new man, the guard who wondered off?"

"I received a recommendation from someone at the hotel before we left. I think Sharif had used them before."

Alarms went off. The assumption of this being a CIA plant disappeared. The possibility of a terrorist implant was much more likely, and now she thought she knew how they knew he had traveled to Italy. She reached inside her purse. "I need to make a call, if you'll give me a minute."

A voice behind her stopped her before she could. "On your feet now."

She turned to see the new guard leveling a pistol at them. Glancing behind him the guard turned slightly in that direction. "Don't worry about him, but he'll have a bad headache when he wakes up."

Suzan waited with Matt, who stepped closer to the guard. "What is it you want?"

"My job's to hold you until the others arrive, but since I've noticed many others with an interest in you, I'll have to make a small change. Our plans for financing ended in India, and we now suspect that you had something to do with it. In such a case you'll have to provide us with what we need."

"Why do you think I'll do that?"

"Because I have the one thing that matters to you." He leveled the gun at Suzan. "You will come with me. I'm sure he'll pay well to get you back."

"And if I refuse?" Suzan stepped closer, ready to charge.

"So be it and you'll die here, and I'll simply take Matt as a hostage. It's your choice."

The sound of a car turning off the road ended the conversation. Was it one of the CIA, or one of his?

From his rapid eye movement, he didn't know either. He kept the gun leveled, but turned to one side to gain a better view. As two men stepped out of the car, he smiled. "It looks like we can receive answers to our questions now. Feel free to have a seat, Mr. Harris."

Suzan crouched down beside Matt, hoping to be able to reach the weapon she had in her purse. She also hoped the CIA was monitoring this and nearby. She needed help now. She knew these men wouldn't waste much time in staying in this area.

As the two new men approached them, one of them pointed toward Suzan. "I think the original plan will work. We'll take the girl." He turned to Matt. "You can have her back when the money is transferred. We'll send you the details soon enough."

Matt began to stand, but the guy turned the gun in his direction. Undaunted, Matt maintained a steady glare at him. "I think we can settle this here. What do you want?"

"Really, more than you might think, but first I want answers. I was almost killed in that explosion. I made some discoveries as I scrambled to stay alive. You've been spending some time with Sharif. Was that the way you helped the Americans locate me, and help them try to assassinate me?"

Matt focused his stare. "I've no clue what you're talking about."

"Are you saying you didn't hear about the bombing the day you left New Delhi?"

"I heard about it, but have no more news about it than anyone else on the street. I did meet this guy Sharif since he's in the same business as I am, but that's about it."

The man turned toward Suzan, who she now recognized as Harmir, the guy she had hunted for in Afghanistan for years. "I did some research on you as well. Who would have ever thought a woman would be hailed as a war hero in America. Someone who has helped slaughter our people like they were dogs. For this you will pay."

Suzan kept her head cool. The CIA had to be close. She had a weapon and only needed a second to get to it.

Harmir pointed toward the blanket. "So convenient." He returned his glare at Matt. "Perhaps when you watch your bride being ravished by my men your memory will improve. And her memory as well. I saw one old woman in the street as the building exploded." He reversed his stare toward Suzan. "That wasn't you, was it?"

Suzan steadied her movement. As soon as they pushed her toward the blanket she would have a chance to retrieve her gun from the purse. "I don't know what you're talking about. I went to India to visit my uncle."

Harmir stepped closer and raised his free hand in an open attempt to fondle her breasts. She allowed him to venture closer, since this would be her best chance to make a move. When he moved closer, she grabbed his hand and twisted, snapping tendons as she yanked as hard as she could.

Another man stepped forward and pressed a gun at her. Matt rushed forward and kicked head high, planting a heel in the man's face with enough force to drive the man's nose back into his skull and maybe his brain as he fell backwards.

Harmir raised the gun, striking Suzan across the face. Her world blackened with the force of the blow. Falling and unable to control it, she hit the ground. She didn't feel like she had passed out long, as she forced her mind to clear. The pain intensified by the second. She felt a warm sticky feeling soaking her hair. She crawled for her purse–her gun.

Over her shoulder she watched Matt spring toward the guard, a man nearly twice his size. The gun held by the guard fired several wild shots. She had no idea where they landed. She continued to crawl for her purse only a few more yards away.

Harmir left her to help the guard. She opened her purse as she saw several vehicles veering off the road toward them. She retrieved her clock. "Stop now or I'll shoot," she yelled, hoping to get him to stop and the guard to release Matt. She had backup now also.

Harmir turned and thrust his gun in her direction, but before he could squeeze off a shot Matt clobbered the back of his head, with a fist driving him closer to her and allowing her time to fire off a shot. Harmir's eyes went wild as he froze. She didn't take a chance, she fired again, striking him in the chest.

She heard a yell behind Matt, and the sound of a bullet tearing through flesh and clothing as the guard dropped. One of the CIA operatives' bullets found its mark. Her vision whirled, as she fought to remain alert. She felt Matt grabbing her as she collapsed.

In the fading moments she watched Harmir rise behind Matt. A bullet proof vest; he must have been wearing one. "Matt!"

She felt the gun pulled from her hand as Matt rolled to one side and fire twice. Two round holes spurted blood from Harmir's forehead as he fell backwards. Her world turned black again.

Chapter 43

Suzan head hurt as she forced her eyes open, and she recognized the hospital setting. A light sheet lay across her body, and the smell of chemicals she associated with a clinic of some kind filled her nostrils. She tried to raise her hand, but felt someone stopping her. She shifted her eyes to the side and saw Matt standing beside her bed.

"Hello, beautiful." His voice was soft and soothing as she felt his hand holding hers.

"I don't feel beautiful. Where are we?"

"We're on a military base, and you're fine. You received a bad blow to the head."

"And the others?

"I think I can answer that one." She noticed another man standing to one side. "We'll talk more later, but your country owes you a very large debt. The man you stopped was one of the highest priorities we have."

"We got Harmir?" Suddenly she remembered the fatal bullets.

"Yes. I know you don't feel fantastic now, but we'll talk again soon"

She couldn't rest without knowing as she forced herself to concentrate. She studied Matt. "I'm so sorry."

The man patted Matt on the shoulder. "We have had a long talk. Matt now knows about the mission. You both need to talk soon, but working as a team you both did a great job."

A team? What the hell was he talking about?

She felt Matt lean over and kiss her forehead. "We'll talk more soon. For now I'll stay with you and let you rest. I'm not leaving you–ever."

Whatever was going on was happening whether she liked it or not. She decided to close her eyes and rest, but held Matt's hand tight as long as she could.

Several hours later she woke again. Matt kissed her cheek as she woke. "How do you feel?"

Suzan glanced around and saw no one else in the room. "Are we alone?"

"Yes, for now."

"I need to know what's going on. Please help me to sit up a little." As she struggled, he pushed a button to lift the head of the bed.

"The CIA has been after an arms dealer by the name of Harmir for a long time. When they thought they had him cornered in New Delhi they wanted to catch him, but an explosion caused in a gun fight set off an explosion which failed to kill him. At first they thought he had died in it, but they soon learned he had not. Harmir thought I was responsible and came after me, especially when he saw a chance to extract additional funds for his operation."

"The CIA told you all of this?" Something wasn't adding up. This wasn't like them to involve a civilian.

"Yes, this and much more. I think I have a little confessing to do before I hear your story. I've been providing information to the CIA for a long time. Nothing dangerous, but simply contacts I make along the way. They, in turn, let me know how to avoid complications that can arise in my business, such as one like this."

So, he was used as an asset and knew it. "What did they tell you about me?"

"Not much, and what I can understand, you'll not be able to add much to it. I now suspect your work in the Army overlapped with theirs."

Yes, she couldn't say a word, but she wanted to know what he knew or was told. "Are you mad at me?"

"No, not mad, but disappointed you didn't confide in me more. As a couple we'll have to learn to trust each other more."

On that part she could agree. "So where does that leave us as a couple?"

Matt started to answer as the CIA contact she saw earlier walked into the room. "I see you're awake and talking. This is not a normal debriefing room, but since information you have is critical to national defense I've no choice but to ask you some questions. In this case it'll be good to do it with both of you present."

Suzan raised the head of her bed higher. "Sir, I'm still at a lost."

"I heard you talking when I came in. As a couple you'll be very helpful to us."

Suzan stopped him. "And if we want out?"

"I understand and that can be arranged, but hear me out first." He moved closer to Matt. "I assume you'll always want to expand your property empire."

"It would be nice to continue to develop."

"Let me fill you in with what's going on. The events that happened yesterday never happened. Suzan slipped on a rock and hit her head on one yesterday, but is expected to make a full recovery. Amazingly, the bodies of several terrorist including Harmir were discovered this morning in a corner of the building that exploded."

Suzan followed the story, knowing the CIA could pull it off and tie off many loose ends this way. "So the mission is completed?"

"Perhaps–perhaps not. We're not sure who else Harmir might have shared the information with. By staying inside our care, we'll do what we can to protect you. If you decide to leave us, you'll be exactly that, on your own."

Suzan glanced at Matt, who was nodding. What would be best for him? What would keep him safe?

Matt decided to speak as he winked at Suzan. "I've had a working relationship for a long time with the CIA. What's wrong with keeping it exactly like what I had?"

"Life complicates things. You both have a history, and I know many couples want to share their life. I need to know that what each of you knows regarding the agency stays a secret. I can't afford to leave any loose ends. I hope you understand."

Suzan decided to speak her mind. "It's one thing to know your enemy wants you dead, and another to know that your own government wants to control you, or even take your life for the better good."

"I wouldn't put it exactly like that."

"I would, which is why I've planned for this day for a long time," Matt said, as he stepped backwards for several steps. He opened his suit and revealed a wire.

"You're taping this?"

"I'll assure you it's secure, and like you said earlier, yesterday or today never happened."

"I take it you both want to say good bye. I don't often extend this offer, but if you should change your mind, you know I can be found easily. Oh, one last question, am I still invited to the wedding?"

Chapter 44

Several days later they allowed Suzan out of the hospital. Matt arranged for a private nurse to care for her as he cleared any plans to see more of Milano. His plans for development here had disappeared as he thought of his new life.

After watching her walk across the room, he realized she might be getting a little cabin fever, and knew the perfect place to take her out to eat. The physician had warned him about flying with her too early, and a few more days there would be highly recommended.

As he approached her with a caring hug which was gentle enough to cause no problems, but strong enough to let her know he was there for her, and not only now but forever, he whispered in her ear. "I want to take you to somewhere special tonight. Are you game?"

With a weary smile, she answered in a responding whisper. "I'll go anywhere to get out of here. I'm not used to having someone do every single thing for me. I'm surprised I'm even allowed to feed myself."

"Good, I still have one dress I purchased for you I want to see you in."

"I still have a lump on my head and bruise. It will take some work to cover them up."

"I'll make the reservation and give you all of the time you need."

The limo stopped in the center of the golden quad where she would have loved to do some shopping, but she knew that would have to be on another trip later. Still, the city lights excited her. The dress Matt had purchased for her he had picked out by himself. He learned what she wanted and further demonstrated why she had fallen in love with him.

"I hope you like this place. I've never eaten here, but I've heard it was the best in Milano." He walked beside her and guided her every step along the way as they entered the elevator to the top. The inside looked to be solid brass. Stopping on the top floor, she studied the windows on every side of the restaurant, thus offering impeccable views from any seat. A charming looking older gentleman walked toward them and seemed to recognize Matt before he said a word. "Mr. Harris, we've been expecting you. Will you follow me?"

Matt wrapped her hand under his elbow and escorted her along to a table in the corner overlooking the city below.

"Matt, what are you doing here?" A woman yelled, as Suzan glanced back at the table they had passed. Chelsea and her mother were glaring at them. "I was hoping to have a good dinner tonight. I should've known you would find a way to change that."

Chelsea pushed back from the table. Suzan felt sure it was to allow her to notice how much she had to show now. Suzan stepped forward. "I think we all know you're pregnant. Matt tells me you think he made love to you on his yacht after the fundraising in Florida a few months ago."

Chelsea passed Matt a sharp rebuke for telling her, but she held her head high. "Well at least now you know."

Suzan stepped forward. "Wrong! What I know is that I was there when he put you to bed. I watched him drop you on the bed, place a blanket on top of you and turn out the light as he left with me. So sorry, that lie will not cut it anymore, sister!"

"What do you mean you were there?"

"Exactly that. I was outside the room watching him put you to bed."

Gloria held her hands to her face. "No, no, this can't be true, look at her, she's pregnant."

Chelsea spoke up. "Mother, drop it! It's time to admit it. I don't know who the father is."

Matt squeezed Suzan's hand. "Chelsea, if you will allow me to help, I would like to help you find the father."

"You would do that for me?"

"Yes."

Chelsea turned to Suzan. "You've every right to hate me." Tears formed in her eyes as she addressed her mother, who kept an astonished look on her face. "Mother, I think it's time for us to go home and face the truth."

"I will not–"

"Mother, shut up!" Chelsea snapped before she turned to them. "I can tell you'll have one of the most beautiful weddings ever in New York."

"Thank you very much, and more importantly, we'll also share one of the most beautiful marriages in New York." Suzan turned to Matt. "I'm so sorry I ever doubted you, and I'll make you the best wife any man could ever hope for."

"In return you'll have a husband who will always love you, and just like I have since I first saw your picture." He reached over and kissed her as she remembered that portrait her mother had painted of her so long ago.

THE END